The Valr Sagas

Volume One

Mimir's Well

Dr. Gregory Pepper

Copyright 2010
Second Edition
All rights reserved — Gregory Pepper

No part of this book may be reproduced or transmitted in any form or by any means, graphic, electronic, or mechanical, including photocopying, recording, taping, or by any information storage retrieval system, without the permission, in writing, from the publisher.

ISBN: 978-1-4457-6296-8

Cover art by Chris Beatrice ©2010
Typography and page composition by J. K. Eckert & Co, Inc.
Published and printed by Lulu.com

17th April 2011

In loving memory of my father
Hubert John Pepper
Wildlife Artist
1928–1985

To John,

I hope these books make for good companions on your trip to Canada!

Best wishes,

Contents

Acknowledgments ix
Chapter 1—What's Up, Doc? 1
Chapter 2—Marcus Samuel Finch 5
Chapter 3—Lights Out 7
Chapter 4—One All 13
Chapter 5—Asgard 15
Chapter 6—Black Beauty 21
Chapter 7—Dr. Neal 25
Chapter 8—Arrival 29
Chapter 9—Duel in the Sun 33
Chapter 10—Saturday 39
Chapter 11—A Friend in Jess 41
Chapter 12—Cole 49
Chapter 13—To Be or Not to Be 53
Chapter 14—Odin's Garden 59
Chapter 15—Evidence 69
Chapter 16—The Devil Wears Prada 75
Chapter 17—Getting to Know You 79
Chapter 18—It's Just a Ride 87
Chapter 19—The Winds of Change 91
Chapter 20—A Day at the Zoo 95
Chapter 21—Hello and Goodbye 99
Chapter 22—Behind Bars 109
Chapter 23—The Wrong Hands 113
Chapter 24—A Surprise for Ruby 121
Chapter 25—Seductions 127
Chapter 26—A Chat with Mickey 133
Chapter 27—Asgard's Wall 137
Chapter 28—Shopping 145
Chapter 29—Giants in Asgard 149

Chapter 30—Officer O'Brien	153
Chapter 31—A Thank You from Ruby	157
Chapter 32—Odin Returns	163
Chapter 33—Two for the Price of One	167
Chapter 34—Chamomile and Lavender	173
Chapter 35—Epiphany	179
Chapter 36—A Close Shave	185
Chapter 37—The Silver Line	197
Chapter 38—Musa Qala	205
Chapter 39—The Mead of Poetry	209
Chapter 40—Forty Commando	217
Chapter 41—Odin's Rings	225
Chapter 42—Black Hawk Down	237
Chapter 43—A Breakfast Date	243
Chapter 44—Frigg	249
Chapter 45—Debriefing	255
Chapter 46—Reprisals	261
Chapter 47—Invisible Thoughts	269
Chapter 48—The Binding of Fenrir—Part One	273
Chapter 49—Hostages	279
Chapter 50—The Binding of Fenrir—Part Two	285
Chapter 51—Afternoon Tea	293
Chapter 52—Behind Enemy Lines	297
Chapter 53—Balder's Dream	303
Chapter 54—Problems with Propaganda	309
Chapter 55—Flight of the Valkyries	317
Chapter 56—A Break for Freedom	329
Chapter 57—The Journey Home	335
Chapter 58—Friendly Fire	341
Chapter 59—No Guns	347
Chapter 60—A Funeral for Friends	353
Chapter 61—Work	363
Chapter 62—Preparations	369
Chapter 63—The Tournament	375
Chapter 64—Consequences	383
Chapter 65—Little Green Men	391
Chapter 66—What's in a Name?	397
Chapter 67—Niflheim	403
Chapter 68—The Chamber of the Valkyries	409
Chapter 69—Idun's Apples	419
The Valkyrie Sagas ~ Glossary of Norse names	423

Acknowledgments

It would be wrong of me not to mention my father first, the late Hubert John Pepper (Wildlife artist 1928-1985). Without his passion and encouragement, I would never have been introduced as a child to the wonderful stories of Norsemen, their Gods, the Vikings and the Anglo-Saxons. The tales he told both thrilled and terrified me. The fighting, the bloodshed, the fierce men and gods all wrapped in a beautiful landscape which completely enveloped my imagination. Beowulf, The Burning of Njal and other books became passions of mine until I left home and went to university. Studies, work, and raising my own family allowed their memories to gently fade until a chance moment recently re-ignited their fire inside me.

It would, of course, be unforgiveable not to mention Snorri Sturluson (The prose Edda), Saxo Grammaticus (Gesta Danorum) and countless other storytellers whose names have long been lost to time. These incredibly talented bards finally put into writing the tales that had been handed down by word of mouth from generation to generation. Their wonderful prose and beautiful style of writing makes my paltry offering pale into insignificance.

This series of books makes no attempt to recount word for word the original sagas. Rather, I have aimed to weave the essence of the characters, places, and stories into a contemporary tale that I hope would be looked on favourably by the forgotten storytellers of old.

Each one adapted his story to their time and audience. Their goals then were the same as mine is now-to inspire, thrill and educate those around them.

Wherever possible, I have tried to keep faithful to their original descriptions of characters and places (where these exist) and build my story as seamlessly as possible around theirs. I apologise profusely to any academics who may take umbrage at the many liberties I have taken in writing this series of books. In my defence, it is better that people get to know of the wonderful Norse Sagas through this book, rather than never knowing them at all.

I would next like to thank my wife, Bina, for her patience, my daughter, Xia, for so many helpful comments and the kind readers of my first appalling drafts. Cecily Frost, Dave Stapleton, Sam Rose, Emma Rose, and Richard Davis spared my blushes and brushed over the many, many typing and spelling errors in these crude, early attempts.

Thank you all so very much for your kind words which continue to encourage me to complete The Valkyrie Sagas.

Finally, I would like to thank my publishers, who have so generously given me this opportunity to share these sagas with the world. They have pushed and prodded and scrubbed and polished and made this book far more beautiful than I could ever have imagined it would be.

Thank you all so very much.

Enough of me.

The Valkyrie Sagas await and "The journey begins . . ."

1
What's Up, Doc?

Kat leaned back and chewed the top of her biro. It was a quarter to six but she was lost in deep thought. Dressed in blue theatre scrubs, she stared at the X-ray on the screen. Her eyebrows furrowed as she gazed, oblivious to the bustle of nurses and orderlies around her.

Something about her patient's chest X-ray just wasn't right.

True, it was an emergency portable image, and the picture was crooked. There were two broken ribs on the left—these were obvious—but something else niggled in her mind. When she'd examined him, his chest had sounded too quiet on the side where the ribs were broken. The lungs behind them also appeared too clear on the X-ray. She couldn't risk it, she finally decided; if it was a collapsed lung she had to do something about it and fast.

If she was right, but didn't do anything, he would be dead within two hours.

"Hi, hon," Suzy slapped her playfully on the back. She tapped her watch. "Ten minutes to go and then—Bingo! We're free for the weekend. You haven't forgotten our little date tonight?" she added hastily, rocking her hand from side to side with an imaginary glass in it. She giggled and winked.

"No, no. Of course I haven't," Kat replied, startled back to reality. "Look, I've just checked in a guy who's fallen off his motor bike. I think he's got a collapsed lung. I can't leave him, not like this." She shrugged in mock resignation.

"Pass it over, pass it over," Suzy chanted with her sing-songy voice. She poked Kat playfully with her fingers as she chanted.

"Hmmm," Kat looked at her watch.

"Look, you all go on ahead. I'll get him prepped and sorted in the next hour, and I'll catch up with you. You'll still be in the Trafalgar Bar, won't you?"

"Just call when you're leaving." Suzy smiled. She backed away, making mobile gestures with her hand. "You always do this you know. You're soooo married to this place!"

Kat turned and checked the X-ray once more.

There was no way she could pass this case over to the oncoming doctor and yes; Suzy was right. Sometimes she did feel married to the hospital. Being a good doctor was tough and came with a price tag.

Nurses didn't understand it; nobody did.

Two hours later Kat emerged from the hospital onto a cold and drizzly New York street. She was tired, more ready for bed than a Friday night on the town.

Shivering in the chill, she paused and turned her collar up. She tried to tuck her damp and tousled hair inside it.

THUMP!

Kat stumbled to the ground, the contents of her shoulder bag scattering around her.

"You've got to be joking," she exclaimed angrily. She knew the street was crowded, but what idiot could be so blind as to walk straight into her? Tonight of all nights; this was the last thing she needed.

Fumbling on the pavement for her things; she smelled, rather than saw, the elegant woman who crouched down beside her.

"I am so frightfully sorry," a perfectly manicured hand picked up her make-up pack and eyeliner. The accent was Irish, and beautiful—just like the fragrant perfume she was wearing.

Kat didn't look up, nor did she answer. She was too furious; hastily fumbling her cheque book, lipstick, mascara, and other items back to where they belonged. As she clawed and grabbed at her possessions, she noticed the expensive black shoes the woman was wearing.

This lady had money, no question about that.

Bag packed, she finally rose and glared at the woman. She hoped desperately to find a sarcastic remark that didn't involve swearing. Trusting to fate, Kat opened her mouth and prepared to vent forth.

She stopped, her mouth gaping in the cold winter air. The intense beauty of the woman had left her speechless.

Long, red hair cascaded about her freckled face, with ice blue eyes that met and held hers.

"I think these," the lady paused still holding her gaze, "are yours."

Their hands touched.

"Oh. Yes, indeed, thank you," Kat blurted pathetically. She dragged her eyes away, meekly accepting the keys she'd been offered.

"I'm so sorry," the lady volunteered again. Their eyes met once more.

"Oh it's nothing, really," Kat tried to unscramble the confusion in her mind. Somehow she knew this woman; she felt certain of it.

She had to say something.

"Look, do I know you?" she enquired hurriedly, blushing at her forwardness. She prayed the lady didn't take it as a pass, because it sure felt as though she was making one.

"No," the woman smiled as their eyes met once more. A warm smile crept across her face.

"But you will," she paused. "Katarina."

This was one of those moments when the world stops. It seemed to last forever. Just Kat, the lady—and those beautiful eyes.

How does she know my name?

Kat stared stupidly, speechless as the seconds stretched into hours.

The throng around them started to swell and the lady began to melt away into the crowd.

"How do you know my name?" Kat cried out—but it was too late. The woman was already out of earshot. As she followed her with her eyes, the lady turned and seemed to mouth something in her direction.

Kat screwed her eyes up.

Was that "Take care," or "Beware"—she wasn't sure. She tried to make it out, but in that instant the woman was gone. Lost from view; drowned by the Manhattan sidewalk.

Shrugging and adjusting her bag, Kat slowly began to walk in the opposite direction. She felt wide awake now, and knew she would be fretting over this incident for the rest of the evening.

Glancing at her watch, she quickened her pace.

2

Marcus Samuel Finch

Marcus Samuel Finch arrived at his fifth floor flat in pretty much the same state every Friday. Tired, stressed, and with a bag of Chinese takeaway. This was a little treat and something to herald the coming weekend.

Unfortunately, this Friday he was also wet.

The cool drizzle of the early evening had given way to more persistent rain, and he had left his coat at the office. Where else would Marcus's coat be but forgotten at the office when it was raining? Snug and bloody dry at the office. It was after all his coat, and a very miserable and very wet Friday.

Time to concentrate, he determined.

Feet planted firmly, files tucked under his left arm, Chinese dangling between his teeth; he squared off to face the front door. This was his Moby Dick. With a deep breath, he inserted the key and began to gently wiggle it in the loose lock.

"Come on, come on," Marcus muttered. Back a bit, wiggle, wiggle, back a bit, wiggle, wiggle. Now just a little further and—twist.

Shit!

He knew he should have changed the lock but mañana, mañana. Busy cops have little time, and even less money. He tried the lock once more, and with one final turn the door opened; but not by his efforts. Anna had heard his fumblings and had opened it from the inside.

Typical, he thought, as he stumbled forward into her embrace.

Bloody typical.

"Good day?" she inquired as she helped him out of his sodden jacket.

"Fucking outrageous," he replied, finally removing the takeaway from his teeth. Saliva drooled from his mouth and he tried to mop this up with his shirt sleeve.

"I wish I was dead," he continued angrily, slamming the sodden paperwork onto the hallway table. He made his way toward the fridge. Anger didn't help, but it sure made him feel better. Sod the sheets of paper as they cascaded from the files. It would take him ages to sort them all out, but at this moment in time, he simply couldn't give a damn.

He was knackered.

"Any cold beers?" he almost pleaded as his eyes darted around the barren contents of the fridge.

"Not unless you put some in last night, darling,"

A knowing half smile crossed Anna's face. *Boy—he'd be cross.*

Marcus raised his head to the sky and clenched his fists.

Of course I didn't. God has truly deserted me tonight, he thought angrily before stopping.

Actually, he was being rather unfair on God. Cautiously he patted the silent beeper attached to his belt. He was on call; it was past nine o'clock, and still no interruptions.

Marcus one—work nil.

He crossed his fingers and touched wood quickly.

Grabbing a warm lager from a kitchen cupboard, some ice, and a tumbler; he sprawled out on the wobbly, brown corduroy settee he'd bought for fifty dollars ten years ago when he was a student. It was still going strong.

Anna spread the feast down on the coffee table and then draped herself beside him. Her fingers teased apart the buttons on his denim shirt, and she slipped her hand inside. His strong, manly chest always made her heart skip that bit quicker. Settling her head gently on his shoulder, she flicked on the TV remote.

Marcus quaffed down as big a gulp of his beer as he could manage and, after taking a deep breath in, he exhaled slowly. His eyes were now shut.

The warmth of the flat was slowly creeping under his skin and his fingers absently twirled with the softness of her hair. Anna smelled good and hey—the weekend was coming.

He prayed for a quiet night.

3
Lights Out

It was ten minutes since her chance encounter and Kat had walked some four blocks. Her feet felt wet and she had left the busy sidewalks some distance behind. She was moving now through less crowded streets, the ones where people tended to walk more briskly and silently. There was little to see, less to do and the shadows around them could hold unwelcome surprises.

She wished now she had gone to the bar earlier with the rest of her friends.

To her left, she passed a dimly lit alley. She glanced briefly in its direction, checking for trouble.

Unfortunately for her, trouble was home and it was hungry tonight.

"Don't fuck with me, bitch." A thug pinned a sobbing, slightly built girl against a concrete wall. "I know you've made more money than this." He jolted her hard against the wall, forcing his face closer to hers.

Broken teeth gleamed in the streetlight.

Kat paused and knew instantly she shouldn't have done so. The drama unfolding down the dirty, litter strewn alley was none of her business. She cursed her nosiness but, knowing the Good Samaritan inside her, she knew she couldn't leave.

"Here, here! Take it," the girl sobbed as she pulled a fistful of bills from her cheap, plastic handbag. "It's been a slow night." She volunteered, keeping her eyes firmly planted on the ground. She prayed Mickey would accept her lame excuse.

Taking the money and stepping backward, he fingered it scornfully.

"My fucking mother could make more than this, you filthy, lazy whore." He struck her hard with the back of his hand, and she dropped slowly to the ground.

She didn't get up; she didn't need any further slaps tonight.

"HEY!"

Kat's shout echoed up the alley, followed by the sound of her footsteps. She felt shit-scared but she forced herself to walk with confidence, hoping that her voice had an air of authority to it.

"Well, well. Looky here. Sexy lady," the thug half turned and eyed her approach. Slowly and scornfully he looked her up and down.

Kat felt his eyes stripping her naked—coat, blouse, knickers, and bra.

"This ain't no business for a dame like you, so why don't you just run along now," he paused and then made a running gesture with his fingers.

"Bitch!"

He spat this word contemptuously in her direction.

Fear can change rapidly. With the right trigger it can become anger and with that offensive word, Mickey had just pushed Kat's button. She hated it with a vengeance. It was so demeaning.

Stopping now a few yards from the man, she tried to control the rage that was welling up inside her. When trouble called, what was the point of a brown belt and five years training in martial arts if you just continued to walk on by?

"Go! Please," the girl looked up and pleaded. Her mascara had run, and her thick red lipstick was now smeared across her cheek. "He'll hurt you real bad."

"Look," Kat tried to hold the gaze of the thug. He was a little taller than her, with greasy, curly brown hair and three days of stubble trying to hide a pock marked face. He was skinny, scruffy, and just one of a thousand cheap, drug pushing pimps that littered the city streets.

"I'm sure you can work this out if you both just calm down," *Christ!* She thought, *I can't believe I just said that mealy-mouthed crap.*

"Oh, yeh, we will, don't worry," he mocked. "Me, little Barbie girl here and my fucking fists. They're gonna do a lot of talking tonight."

He lashed out a short kick and the girl yelped with the pain.

"Come on. Just stop. Please."

I'm talking bollocks. What on earth am I doing trying to appeal to his better nature? He hasn't got one. Can't you see that—you idiot?

The thug kicked the girl once more before grimacing at Kat. "Who's gonna make me, you reckon you can? Hey, bitch?" he snarled menacingly.

Oh no, there was that word again. Kat saw red. Looking him straight in the eye, she slowly slid her bag and coat from her shoulders. These dropped to the floor like a gauntlet being thrown down.

He got her meaning immediately.

"I don't fight with pussies. There ain't no satisfaction. Now if you're lookin' for a fuckin' then that's a different matter," he snorted arrogantly before swaggering forward, reaching out, and pushing at Kat's shoulder.

As he moved forward, the girl on the ground got to her feet and began to hobble away. She was grateful for her chance to escape.

Kat saw his hand coming and she didn't think. It was a reflex. Her left arm swung up in a fist, roughly pushing his sideways.

"K-A-R-A-T-A-A-Y! Nice touch, Bitch," the thug mockingly appreciated the smooth flow of her arm, and the force of her block.

Kat stepped backward.

This was it.

A moment she had dreaded and prayed she would never have to face.

Taking on a man in a one on one fight was madness, but she had no choice. Her fate had been sealed the moment she paused at the entrance to the alley. Ironically, and she chuckled at this, she was quite well dressed for the occasion. Okay the gold strapped stilettos wouldn't have been her first choice but her tight, animal print leggings, chunky black belt and off the shoulder top gave her lots of flexibility. A bit showy perhaps, but thank God she hadn't worn her hobble dress tonight.

The two of them began to slowly circle each other. Eyeball to eyeball, he feigning grabs while she weaved to avoid his touch. He stank of alcohol, cigarettes, and body odour.

Just what the hell am I doing here?

These words screamed inside her head.

Mickey lunged forward and made a grab for her neck. It was a slow and unskilled movement.

Kat pulled backward and caught his arm with a double-fisted block. Her knee jerked upwards and a gold stiletto flashed deep into his groin.

First blood.

"Fuck!"

Mickey staggered backward, legs buckling as a wave of pain slowly spread from his testicles. "You're so goin' to regret that. You fucking bitch!"

There was that word again, big mistake.

Stepping forward, Kat kicked full force to his stomach. The impact of her pointed shoe winded him and he collapsed slowly onto his knees with the rest of his body following suite.

Kat paused. She couldn't believe her eyes. This so-called tough guy woman beater; was writhing, crumpled and prostrate; just inches from her feet. Two kicks and she'd caused so much destruction. A smile of satisfaction curled across her lips.

Saying nothing, Kat turned to go. As she made to walk away, a hand lunged at her ankle. Caught off balance, she staggered to the ground.

"I ain't finished with you yet."

Mickey clawed her toward him, snarling furiously through clenched teeth.

Kat lashed out hard with her free leg. The point of her stiletto thrusting again and again like a dagger as he slowly reeled her in. He pulled himself on top of her and the table turned full circle.

She was the one now fighting for her life.

He grabbed at her hair with one hand and clasped his other tightly around her throat. She choked, and rammed her knee up hard.

His groin again, that's gotta hurt.

Arching her back as she twisted sideways, Kat forced him off her body. Her fist connected once more with his balls and she sunk her teeth into the hand that was trying to cover her mouth. He yelled—and rolled over onto his back.

They were lying together now, side by side and breathing heavily; neither entirely sure what to do next.

It was Kat who moved first.

Rising to her knees, she pulled her fist back and smashed it hard into his face. Her blow struck gold and a shower of blood erupted from his nose. He howled in pain. Pinning a shoulder beneath one knee, she continued to punch him. With each blow of her fists, she was slowly gaining the advantage. He tried to deflect her punches, but enough were connecting to make his defences crumble.

Kat was in control.

Finally, she sat astride his chest. Victory was within her grasp and it felt good. With both shoulders beneath her knees, his defences were gone and her fists could hold court. She struck him hard; first left, then right, and then left again. Blood spattered from his nose and mouth as she pummelled his face with her hands. Spurred on by a sense of fear and the sweetness of victory; she couldn't help herself.

Lost in her moment of triumph, Kat didn't notice the man's hand slide into his pants. He pulled out a small revolver. Running this slowly up her body, he pressed its muzzle against the side of her left breast.

BANG!

The gun exploded and a bullet ripped right through her.

Kat's body went limp; a rag doll falling forward without control. It felt like a gentle thump on her chest, but her sight was failing fast.

She was dead before her head hit the ground.

Her last thought—*those beautiful ice blue eyes. Who was she?*

Mickey heaved her lifeless body off him and staggered drunkenly to his feet.

"Stupid, fuckin,' crazy, fuckin' bitch," he yelled as he tried to stem the flow of blood that was pouring from his face.

No one had responded to the gunshot.

He grabbed her bag, and staggered back down the alley almost bumping into the red headed lady who was turning into it.

Fuck! She would call the police.

He broke into a run.

Jessica didn't. She had only Katarina on her mind as she squatted down beside her body. Gently she brushed the hair back from the lifeless face before closing the open eyes. Then, she pulled a short dagger from her bag.

"Please forgive me," she whispered quietly as she plunged this into Kat's heart.

She paused, and held the blade deep inside the girl's body. A surge of warmth, and a tiny flash of brilliant white light, told her that her job was done.

Returning the dagger to her bag, she fumbled in her coat pocket for a small leather purse. Finding it, she took out a gold coin. Clasping this firmly in her hand, Jess closed her eyes and chanted quietly under her breath.

4

One All

BEEP–BEEP–BEEP!

"Ohhhh," Marcus groaned as he stretched out a hand.

CRASH!

A glass of water tipped sideways from his bedside table in his clumsy attempts to find—and silence—the beeper.

A cursory glance at the bedside clock told Marcus all he needed to know—2 A.M. on a Saturday morning.

Great.

He closed his eyes. The bed was so warm and cosy. Just another five minutes, was that really too much to ask?

RING,RING–RING,RING!

Fifteen minutes had passed, and this time the phone was ringing. There was no escape. Staggering to his feet, he stumbled across the room. Clothes strewn around the floor tried to tackle him as he walked. Finally, he opened the door to the hall. Anna stirred and murmured something inaudible. Two more steps and his hand would silence the unwelcome intruder.

"Hi. Finch here," his clipped voice echoed in the darkness.

The ringing stopped.

Stepping out from their apartment block, Marcus cursed. The cold New York air hit him like a hammer. It was a decent walk to the station and after sinking his hands deeply into his jacket pockets, he tried to break into a run. His tired legs were aching in the cold and he shivered violently.

"Stupid bitch," he muttered irritably as he stumbled on a broken slab. "Getting herself killed on a night like this."

His night, when he could have stayed tucked up warmly in his bed.

"Fucking thoughtless."

5

Asgard

It was late morning on a day in early June. The sun was already showing its summer strength; smiling down warmly on the land below. The sky, clear blue apart from an occasional high wisp of cloud, was filled with birdsong and the humming of busy insects. A tiny breeze sent gentle ripples through the meadows and fields of ripening corn which laced the rolling hills around the town of Asgard.

To the west of the settlement, just visible beyond the plain of Ida, a range of great snow-capped mountains rose majestically into the sky. Here lay the frosty halls of the kingdom of Jotunheim. A large glacier separated these mountains from its foothills, the kingdom of Vanaheim. This was the realm of the Vanir people. Sometimes, in the late evening skies, red, blue, and green lights would dance above these peaks in a wondrous and colourful display.

Away to the south, the fields and sprinklings of huts and farm houses gradually faded into thickening forests. Rich at first with oaks, elms, and beech trees, these gave way in turn to dense thickets of gorse, thorns, and jagged rocky outcrops. This broken scrubland rose steadily in height before ending abruptly in great cliffs, gazing out across Middle Sea. This was a place few dared to cross to reach the Elf Kingdoms beyond. Deep within its waters slept a great serpent called Jormungard. He was its guardian and he, and his kin, disliked sailors and fishermen. They lay in wait, ready to stir up mighty storms to drown the unwary who ventured forth in their boats.

Looking eastward, gentle rolling hills rose, gaining slowly in their size and grandeur. Eventually these merged into a large, almost circular, volcano. This dominated the skyline. Beyond the volcano lay a sweltering desert, carpeted with hot springs and fields of molten lava. At night, these lit up the Eastern sky with an eerie red glow.

Here was the realm of Muspellheim, the kingdom of serpents, ruled by a mighty dragon called Surt.

Finally looking northward and lying immediately beyond Asgard, lay the Great Sea. This stretched to the horizon and far beyond. The Great Sea encircled Asgard, and all the other kingdoms. It was so broad and deep that no mortal had ever sailed across it. So mighty were the waves that crashed upon the shore, some believed it must go on forever.

Today was a beautiful day, and the inhabitants of Asgard were making the most of it. The winding, narrow cobbled streets which ran between crooked, lime-washed cottages were heaving with the bustle of a busy market day. Wisps of smoke rose from chimneys that poked out from their thatched roofs. Women returning home laden with meats and vegetables had already set to work; cooking dinners for their husbands and families.

Despite the seemingly purposeless nature of the meandering streets, they all eventually converged upon a large, central square. On the southern edge of this square lay a great wooden hall. Its roof was thatched and this was laced with silver thread. The name of the hall was Gladsheim and it rose higher than any of the surrounding buildings. Beyond Gladsheim a narrow, stone, hump-backed bridge crossed the river Iving. This separated the town from the fields surrounding it.

To the north of the square, a wide, straight road ran a distance of about three hundred metres up a gentle slope to a castle. This backed onto the Great Sea. Nine arenas were spread on either side of the road and these encircled the flanks of the fortress. Today only the occasional sound of sword on shield, and sword on sword, could be heard coming from them. It was market day, and the Aesir were far too busy shopping and gossiping to be bothered with fighting.

For such a small town, the castle above it was strangely large and noticeably deformed. A ruined wall lay around it, overrun by mosses, weeds, and vines. Its remains stood as a constant reminder of the town's troubled and bloody past. The entrance to the castle was intact, as were the inner towers and ramparts which rose to random and awkward heights around a central courtyard.

What made the castle particularly odd was what stood in the centre of this courtyard. It was a magnificent, spindly citadel, one which rose uncomfortably into the sky, piercing it like a needle. At nearly twice the height of any other tower, it was topped with a chamber and spire of pure silver. This shone brilliantly in the sunlight, making it impossible to look at.

Here was Odin's throne room, and from there he could see everything.

The citadel was unusual in other ways.

Despite its height, there were no windows other than those for the chamber at the top. It had a single narrow door at the bottom, which was made of a mysterious black wood not found anywhere else in the kingdom. The tower was guarded too, both by day and by night, by two large wolves that roamed unchained around its base. Beyond the wolves, the outer defence of the citadel was a slender moat. Its only crossing was by a narrow wooden bridge that looked in urgent need of repair. Two ravens, Muninn and Huginn, circled high above the spire. They belonged to Odin, and their calls blended with those of the other birds of Asgard.

"How much?" Carmel exclaimed as she rolled a large, ripe apple in her hand. "You've got to be joking, right?" she continued, with mock consternation.

Haggling was all part of the fun of market day, and she was going to make the most of it with the excessively handsome street seller standing before her. His sudden appearance irked her. Few good looking men escaped her attention, and something about him seemed oddly familiar.

Loki smiled and stroked his chin absently with his hand. They had been flirting for at least five minutes now and he was warming to his task. Next to trickery and illusion, seduction was his favourite pastime.

Carmel tossed the apple in the air and Loki snatched it; striking like a cobra.

"My," Carmel pouted, and pursed her lips. "Such fast hands for a street trader." Placing her hands on her hips, she thrust them forward provocatively.

Loki whistled appreciatively. The woman looked resplendent, dressed in her fighting tunic.

Knee length, laced boots gave way to powerful tanned thighs which ended in a short leather, pleated skirt. A thick studded belt held a coiled whip, sword and a dagger. Above these her short leather bodice was laced tightly at the front, accentuating her swollen breasts and narrow, muscular waist. A single jewel glittered from her belly button.

She was indeed a fine looking woman; one with few peers in Asgard.

"Fast hands," Loki paused, and bounced the apple to and from the crook of his arm. "Fast tongue," he repeated the trick. "And fast lover." He ended with a flourish. Spinning round on one foot he caught the apple, which he then presented to the woman.

"Bravo, bravo," Carmel applauded with genuine admiration. "Now tell me," she fluttered her eye lids, "what price would you really sell this wondrous fruit to me for?"

Loki pressed forward, his short dark curly locks accentuating his chiselled, olive-skinned face.

"All I ask," he paused, building an air of suspense. "Is the gift of a single kiss from such a noble Valkyrie maid."

Carmel opened her mouth but before she could speak, a ripple of disturbance that had been flowing steadily toward them broke around their shores.

Two beautiful white swans passed close by.

The birds had been meandering slowly down the street, stopping occasionally to preen, whoop noisily, and flap their wings. As they progressed, the crowds quietened and parted. Men took off their hats and nodded, women curtsied and all work stopped until they had passed by. A quiet ripple of respectful "Ma'am" and "Your graces" could be heard.

Carmel smiled and dipped her forehead slightly. It was always good to be respectful, just in case. Out of the corner of her eye she saw Loki make a flamboyant bow and utter "Your majesty" sarcastically and in a voice loud enough for those nearby to hear. His remark roused a loud chorus of whoops and wing flaps from the swans, before they moved on.

Show over, Carmel turned to Loki. Her eyes flashed with poorly suppressed indignation.

"Such behaviour could bring you dire consequences," she scolded. "I could have you flogged." She glared at him, her fingers straying longingly to the butt of her whip.

"I could whip your hide off right now, in the square in front of all these people," she gestured toward the people in the street. "Now that would change your attitude." She added with a sneer. Carmel felt confident that the seller would know of her reputation for giving ferocious floggings.

If indeed he did know about this, he didn't let on. Far from it; rather than showing an expression of fear, the grin on his handsome face grew even broader. His white teeth flashed, and he went back to juggling the apple.

There wasn't a hint of a tremor in his hands.

"You could," he said slowly. "But you won't." His handsome eyes fixed hers with a stare as he continued to juggle.

"And give me just one good reason why I won't?" Carmel was growing weary of his insolence.

With a loud guffaw the man tossed the apple high in the air, span round again, and caught it behind his back. Slamming one foot forward, he presented an outstretched hand.

"Permit me to introduce myself. I'm Loki. Perhaps you've heard of me?"

Carmel lurched backward in shock. Either this was an insane joke or—she glanced at his hand.

There it was on his fourth finger, a ring of dwarf gold encrusted with two gleaming diamonds. She looked into his eyes. For a moment they flashed a brilliant red. She was speechless. His disguise as a trader had deceived her, and her show of self importance had been brought to a humiliating end.

Loki guffawed loudly again, and as a gesture of affection he placed the apple in her hand; wrapping her fingers around the fruit as he did so.

"Here, take it as a present," he chuckled. "Fair Carmel, maid to Gunnr and most beautiful of all the Valkyries."

He stooped and kissed her hand, all the while gazing up into her beautiful, dark brown eyes.

Carmel pulled back abruptly. Blushing furiously, she walked away with all the speed and elegance she could muster. Her face was burning almost as warmly as Loki's words blazed inside her heart.

The great, mischievous Loki desires me!

The thought echoed crazily in her head. She had hungered for his attention for as long as she could remember, and now she knew he desired her, too.

She praised Odin for his generosity today.

Loki drew a long, slow intake of breath as he watched Carmel's swaying hips disappear gracefully into the crowds. He lusted to hold her tightly in his arms—and to feel her body writhing beneath him in his bed.

Shaking his head, he started to return to the stall. The sound of a horn rose high into the air, stopping him dead in his tracks; first one horn, then another and another. Each blew a different note, and each note sounded louder than the last.

Voices began to rise and Loki, shielding his eyes, looked into the sky. A bright rainbow had formed. Quickly he checked the flagpole at the front of Gladsheim. This was just visible over the roofs of the cottages.

A silver flag was being hastily hoisted.

A cheer broke out, then another, and another. Wild clapping, dancing, and excitement erupted on the streets. Loki and Carmel along with the rest of the crowd began to walk, and then trot toward the central square.

As they drew near, a huge, dapple grey stallion broke from the castle and thundered down the road in full battle gallop. He streaked across the square and bridge before charging off in the direction of the rainbow. As Loki stared, he could just make out the shape of the rider.

Without a doubt, the long red locks streaming behind the silver helmet belonged to 'bright battle'—it was the Valkyrie Brynhildr.

6

Black Beauty

Ruby stood on the corner of the street under the shelter of the awning of a convenience store. It was late evening, she was tired, and the drizzle of the early evening had settled into more persistent rain. It was cold too, but then it was December and New York had a habit of being chilly at this time of year.

Across the street, and about one hundred metres from where she was standing, was the dingy motel that was going to be her home. She hoped this would be for the shortest time possible. With a small sigh, she turned and eyed herself wearily in the shop's window. Feeling tired and irritable, she needed to perk herself up. It was vital she made the right impression.

Arriving on the wrong side of town earlier in the day had been a real pain. The dirty, frenetic subway, a day's careful shopping and the large, heavy suitcase she was now pulling hadn't helped either. Still, smoothing out the creases in her dress, Ruby couldn't but help admire herself.

She scrubbed up well.

Turning from side to side, she loved the cut of her figure-hugging, fuschia dress. She had chosen the brightest and shortest frock she could find; knowing her long black legs would turn heads. Finding matching stilettos had been a godsend, too. The black satin bolero jacket she was wearing over the dress was short sleeved and heavily trimmed with black lace. It covered her shoulders, but left her cleavage nicely on display. She loved hats, and the black pillbox with decorative veil she'd chosen sat well on her hair. She had oiled this, and then combed it flat, accentuating her strong Negro features. A heavy gold necklace, chunky ear-rings and bangles completed the outfit. Drivers honked their car horns and men had whistled throughout the day. If this didn't get her noticed, nothing would; and she was determined to be noticed tonight.

Taking a deep breath, and looking left and right, Ruby crossed the road and made for the grubby, splintered doorway to Jack's Motel.

Slouched on his plastic chair, Elijah had been so engrossed in his magazine that at first he hadn't noticed Ruby's arrival. The fuzzy picture on the small black and white TV was blaring, and it masked the sound of the front door opening. It had been a quiet evening with few comings and goings. The chipped veneer reception desk was littered with half-finished paperwork. This would probably stay unfinished for several more weeks to come. The graveyard shift was long and tedious, and Elijah was in no hurry to do anything.

No sir; he was going to chill tonight.

Ruby squeezed slowly through the door and surveyed her new home. What a pile of crap. The overweight bespectacled boy at the reception desk hadn't even bothered to look up, and the air stank of stale coffee, cheap cologne, and cigarettes.

Ruby stepped forward and smiled to herself as Elijah nearly fell off his chair. He righted himself, and then started to furiously wipe his round, gold-rimmed spectacles.

Just the impact she wanted.

Without obviously paying attention, she noted two swarthy thugs sitting in frayed armchairs next to the motel lift. Crumpled shirts, day old stubble, and nicotine-stained fingers suggested these were the sort of men she was hoping to find. Late twenties or early thirties, she hazarded a guess at their ages. They were staring hard at her— subtlety not required. Every sensuous curve of her body was being mentally jotted down for later use.

"Do you have a room?" she asked as Elijah's eyes darted between her and the desk he was frantically trying to tidy. Tipping over the half-finished cup of coffee he had been drinking, he dabbed desperately at it with a cotton hankie. The hankie had his initials in the corner. *A nice motherly touch,* she thought.

"Yes, yes ma'am," Elijah stuttered awkwardly, feeling uncomfortable under her gaze, and wishing he had put on an ironed shirt earlier in the evening. "Room thirty eight has a nice view and hot and cold water. It should be ideal."

Taking the key from a hook behind him, he handed it to her. His hands were sweating and he could feel his face turning red.

"Thank you." Ruby took them with her finger tips and flashed a smile.

"Now do you think you could be a good little boy and find someone who can help me up to my room?"

She loved his fluster. He was like a rabbit caught in a car's headlights; squirming helpless and hopeless.

"I, I, I could help you with them ma'am, if you like, that is," Elijah stammered, trying desperately to get a grip on his senses. He always found talking to women embarrassing at the best of times let alone now; confronted by this goddess in pink.

"Would you? How kind," she flashed another smile. "By the way boy, do you have a name?" She couldn't resist it. Watching his discomfort was making her day.

"Elijah. Elijah Kelly ma'am."

His chubby, moon-shaped face was now a violent shade of puce.

"What a lovely name," she continued as they made their way to the elevator. "Was your mother a religious woman by any chance?"

"Oh yes ma'am, absolutely ma'am," Elijah blurted as he pulled the trolley behind her.

"And tell me, Elijah, was your mother a strict woman?" Ruby emphasised 'strict' as she spoke, but she didn't turn around.

"Oh yes ma'am," he paused, and thought for a moment.

"Very, ma'am."

Elijah pressed the button and prayed the lift would not keep him waiting. He had never felt this uncomfortable in his twenty five years of living—never.

The lift doors opened and as Ruby got in she paused, and looked directly at him.

It was irresistible.

"I guess that's why you find it so hard to talk to pretty ladies then. Isn't it?" She turned on her heel and strutted into the elevator.

As the lift doors closed behind them, Cole's thugs in the armchairs went back to their cigarettes and papers. Cole would definitely be hearing from them later about this new black beauty in town. He would be pleased—and that would earn them favours.

Ruby thanked Elijah for his help and closed the door to her room behind her.

Throwing her head back she laughed long and hard. Oh, she had been wicked but he was so adorable; chubby, shy, and awkward. When had a beautiful woman like her ever made a fuss of him? She guessed never. They would all pass a man like Elijah by, noses held high in the air. Women could be so short-sighted, which in this case was their loss.

Ruby could see Elijah was a gentle, well brought up man with a good heart. His old fashioned manners seemed hopelessly out of place in this new fangled world. She had had her fun, and she swore that for the rest of her stay she would be good to him. Besides—his shyness and politeness brought back memories. Memories she had buried a long time ago.

Ruby studied her room.

Cheap double bed, faded floral wallpaper, veneer furniture—that must have looked vile even when it had been new—and a tiny shower that stank of mould. That was pretty much it. It was the kind of place where you should be paid to stay, and not the other way around. She stretched; and then made her way over to the window and pulled it open.

Resting both hands on its sill, she leaned out.

Sirens blared, cars honked, people shouted and trains rumbled and squealed in the distance; a constant symphony of sound, both by day and by night. Ruby hadn't been in New York for a long time, and the noise battered her senses. The sky line had definitely changed, but she bet that the people hadn't; the pimps, the hookers, and the thugs. They may have new faces now, but the people were the same.

Ruby went to get a cigarette, then paused, and took a leather bound flask from her clutch bag instead. Holding it to her lips, she took a small sip and then carefully replaced it. She must get back into the routine quickly. No accidents this time, she told herself, patting her bag reassuringly as a reminder.

Now where was she?

Ah yes, a cigarette. One of the few things she'd been looking forward to.

Lighting one carefully, Ruby inhaled deeply. She held the smoke in her lungs for as long as she could, letting thin wisps curl delicately around her lips. She sighed lovingly as the nicotine began to work its soothing magic, and continued to stare out at the street life below.

Tomorrow was going to be an interesting day.

7

Dr. Neal

Marcus sat alone in his office in the early hours of a cold Saturday morning. He was bathed in a solitary pool of light, and as he sat, he absent-mindedly twiddled a well-chewed pencil between his fingers. He was flicking slowly through the pages and photos of the file in front of him. He had been doing this now for some time, lost in thought.

He didn't like mysteries, but this case seemed to have a big one.

Okay, as he had half walked, half jogged to the office he admitted he had been angry. A simple open and shut killing of a hooker or druggie on the streets of New York didn't really need him to be woken in the middle of the night. His assistants and officers on the ground could take care of that. He was still angry when, on arrival, he had downed a cup of tepid, black coffee from the hallway machine and barged into the autopsy room startling Tony, their pathologist. Poor Tony, the ever so calm and methodical Tony. He was a man in his early sixties and Marcus, to his mortification, had really laid into him. He had ranted, until Tony's slow explanation of the girl's injuries calmed him down and gradually aroused his interest.

What he needed to do now, was to go over the case in his head carefully once more, and see if he could find something he had overlooked.

There had to be an obvious explanation to his problem.

Firstly, the girl on the slab was no hooker and no druggie. Dr. Neal was a well respected medical officer at the hospital where she worked.

Her identity tag had been found in her coat pocket; a coat that had been taken off before she was killed.

Secondly, the scruffy dead end alley where her body had been found was not the usual type of place you would associate with a woman like her. Fortunately, two eyewitnesses from diners at a cafe opposite the entrance had given a plausible reason for Dr. Neal being there.

Both people had heard a disturbance in the alley, and then seen a woman walk down it. A few minutes later they had noticed a skinny, skimpily clad girl hobbling hastily out of it. Both also agreed that they had later heard a sharp crack—the gun shot—before seeing a second person, a scruffy man, stagger from the alley and break into a run. He appeared to be covered in blood and carrying a woman's bag in one hand. He made off in a hurry.

This had to be the killer, no question about that.

So far, so good.

It looked as though Dr. Neal was the wrong person in the wrong place at the wrong time. She had heard an argument down the alley, gone down to investigate and BAM—she got shot. The skinny girl ran away, and the killer took Dr. Neal's bag when he made off. This all made perfect sense, nice and straight forward. The gun shot wound to her heart, and blood on her body fitted this story nicely—and there was a bonus.

If, as Marcus suspected, the killer was some local low life pimp or drug dealer, then they should find him fairly quickly. New York could be a small place for a man with a record. Finger prints, his gun, her blood on his clothes, the case would be sorted and job done.

Nice and easy, just as all cases should be.

Unfortunately the injuries on her body messed this tidiness up; and messed it up in a way that was puzzling.

Marcus went back over these in the order that Tony had pointed them out to him.

Dr. Neal was about twenty five and pretty; very pretty actually. She had long blond hair, large widely spaced eyes and a strong, square jaw with small dimples in her cheeks. She was an educated, single girl; one from a good background. She had everything to live for, and the sort of girl he would have fancied, but known to be way out of his league.

There had been a lot of blood on her body just as you would expect from a shot to her heart. However, some of the blood belonged to the killer. Tony had pointed out scratches and swellings around her knuckles and the fact that at least two of these were broken. There was bruising to her neck and gouge marks on her face and arms, too. There must have been a struggle and she had put up a fight—one hell of a fight—before she died.

So what about her coat?

At first sight this seemed a bit odd. Lying crumpled, but not blood spattered and some distance from where she was found.

How did that happen?

Marcus felt confident he could explain this if Dr. Neal was not such a helpless victim. Perhaps she had confronted the thug, picked a fight even, and distracted him while allowing the girl to make good her escape? This would explain the fight marks, his blood, and the coat.

When they found the girl, he felt sure she would confirm that this was what had happened.

Okay, still making sense, but this was where things went pear shaped.

After looking at the hands and neck, Tony had drawn Marcus's attention back to the gunshot wound. This was why he had called Marcus in, and this was what made the hair on the back of Marcus's neck stand on end. Approximately five centimetres to the left of the entry wound, there lay a small, neat, three centimetre wide incision.

It was a knife wound.

A wound that had been made AFTER Dr. Neal's death.

The killer had shredded the poor girls' heart with his gun, got up, messed around for a few minutes then decided to have another go at it with a knife. This just didn't make any sense. Why hang around and stick a knife in someone who was already dead? It was madness.

Marcus had to admit he was well and truly stumped by this; but there was a glimmer of hope.

Both witnesses had noticed the killer bump into a lady with distinctive red hair just as he was leaving the alleyway. One of them was certain that she had also gone down the alley. Perhaps the red head could shed some light on the stab wound? She hadn't put in the 911 call to the police but surely she couldn't have missed the blood and the body lying on the ground? If indeed she really had gone down the alley, then she could just be a vital witness.

Marcus sighed, stood up, stretched, and then sat back down again. He pulled a fresh sheet of paper from his drawer and started to make some notes for tomorrow.

They needed to get DNA analysis of the blood and see if they could match it with their database. This should give them the killer and he would certainly lead them to the skinny girl.

With a restaurant opposite the entrance to the alley, hopefully he could pull some CCTV (closed circuit television) footage that might help them identify the distinctive red head. This was a long shot, but worth a punt.

Finally Marcus stretched his hand out for the phone. He needed to make a call.

Picking it up, he paused.

He had been given the details of Dr. Neal's parents and someone had to call them. He could imagine their devastation. She was their only child and they must be so proud of her. Anna and he had been thinking about starting a family and he couldn't imagine what it would be like to lose a son or a daughter.

How could he break this news to them?

How could he tell them that their pride and joy had just been slain?

Their priceless, God-given baby had died alone in a stinking New York backstreet; slaughtered by some low life piece of sleaze.

He put the phone back on its cradle. At least let them sleep in peace tonight; it would surely be their last.

The shocking news about the brutal murder of Katarina could wait until the morning.

8

Arrival

Kat's journey back to consciousness was as slow as it was painful; each sense battling to return—one by one. Like explosions in reverse, shattered shards of reality fighting to reform and come to terms with what had gone before.

A cough came first, forced by the choking sensation of dust and blood in her mouth.

She tried to masticate, but her parched and swollen tongue refused to budge. There was a warm sun overhead and it felt so soothing on her cheek and back. She would have liked to open her eyes, but the lids refused to budge. It was just so much easier to carry on as she was.

Lying still and face down in the dirt.

She could hear—no, she could feel—the sound of a horse approaching. A fast gallop that slowed to a trot, and then a walk, as it drew near. Finally, when she could hear its coarse breath, the horse stopped; and a thud told her that its rider had dismounted.

Footsteps approached and someone was now kneeling close to her head; soft hands were brushing hair from her cheek. It felt good.

Still her eyes wouldn't open.

The same tender hands were now rolling her over and lifting her head into their lap. She could smell leather, worn leather, and a liquid was being forced into her mouth. She spluttered. It tasted sweet and a warmth began to spread throughout her body. She could move again, fingers, toes and then hands and feet.

More liquid followed and this time she swallowed.

"Come on, come on," a voice she knew she ought to recognize was coaxing her. "I'm so pleased to see you again Katarina!" the voice exclaimed.

Reality dawned at last.

Finally, the pieces of her shattered senses fitted into place.

Kat knew that when she opened her eyes she would see those beautiful ice blue eyes again; but what about that terrible blow to her chest? The fight came back into her head and the horror of its climax crashed into her consciousness.

It couldn't be?

She tried to dismiss its recollection. That had to have been a bad dream, but it was worth a reassuring check. Kat's hand came up her chest slowly and felt the hole. It still oozed blood.

She pressed harder.

NO HEARTBEAT!

Shocked into wakefulness, Kat tried to sit up. Eyes wide open, her blurred vision quickly sharpened to reveal a clear blue sky that hung over the dusty, hedge lined track.

This was a bad dream, it had to be, it simply had to be.

Cautiously she dug a fingernail hard into her leg and yelped at the pain.

She wasn't dreaming.

She was alive, no, she was dead. No, she could feel pain so she couldn't be dead.

What the fuck was going on?

The words spun sickeningly in her head.

"Shush, slowly," Jess whispered as she stroked Kat's forehead. She had seen her hand go to the bullet wound and realised what must be going through her mind. "Drink some more. It will help."

Holding her leather bound flask up to her lips, Kat gratefully took a sip.

"Are you an angel?" Kat croaked as she turned to look at the person who was so tenderly caring for her.

Jess laughed; a beautiful melodious sound that any song bird would have been proud to utter. "Oh I should be so lucky."

She laughed again.

"I'm dead, though, aren't I?" Kat enquired nervously. It hurt to talk, but she had to know the answer.

"Errr," Jess had to think. "Not really—but sort of." She cursed her dim wits and her unhelpful reply.

"I've been shot, look." Shakily Kat guided Jess's hand to the bullet wound and pressed it down hard.

"No heart beat."

Jess in turn slowly guided Kat's hand up her chest, and pressed it down firmly.

"Snap!" she cried as she burst into laughter once more.

The merry sound of Jess's giggles gave Kat comfort. Maybe it really was a dream and she still hadn't woken up?

That had to be it.

If she was dead then so was Jess, and there was no way a dead woman could be so cheerful.

"Do you feel strong enough to get up?" Jess enquired rising to a squat.

Kat nodded, and as she began to get up she realised she was naked.

"Here. Grab hold of me," Jess grasped her forearm. "And don't worry," she glanced at Kat's nakedness. "I have my best cloak on my horse for you."

Slowly, painfully, and hanging on to Jess with all her strength, Kat staggered toward the horse. "I never did get to know your name."

Jess laughed again.

"I'm the Valkyrie Brynhildr," she exclaimed. "But my friends call me Jess."

This time it was Kat's turn to laugh. This hurt—but in a good sort of way.

9
Duel in the Sun

Both Balder and Gunnr heard the horns sound out across Asgard and the bright rainbow form where a copse of trees grazed a field of ripening corn. If they had glanced toward the square; they would undoubtedly have also seen the silver flag fluttering above the hall of Gladsheim. However, neither of them chose to join the excited crowds surging toward the square. They were too intent on each other, just as they had been for the last fifteen minutes.

Locked in conflict, they made for an unlikely match.

Balder was the second son of Odin and quite possibly the most handsome man in all of Asgard. He stood just over one eighty five centimetres tall, well muscled and with long, flowing mousy hair streaked blond by his love for the outdoor life. He had a well groomed beard, and twinkling blue eyes that could charm the most chaste of maidens. His chest was bare and this glistened with sweat.

Gunnr, or Silk as she was known to her friends, could hardly have been more different.

Petite and slim, she had jet black, shoulder length hair and the fine features of a woman from mixed oriental bloods. As was her liking, when fighting in her arena, Silk wore a tight fitting, black leotard and black leather boots that reached high above her knees. Around her wrists were thick, leather guards which were studded with metal as was her belt. This was drawn tightly around her waist.

Unlikely as it looked, Silk was more than a match for Balder. Her prowess and love for fighting was legendary. Even her Valkyrie name—Gunnr—meant war. No Valkyrie trained harder or longer than she did, and none could match her skill with the sword. For every blow of Balder's, Silk returned two with equal force. The sound of their conflict echoed around the otherwise silent stadium.

Metal on wood, metal on wood.

Balder was annoyed.

In keeping with tradition, gladatorial bouts began with the throwing of three spears. Balder had strong shoulders and a true eye, but he had only managed to tag Silk slightly on her right arm. This wasn't much help because Silk's sword arm was her left. He hoped that with each blow of his sword, the strength in her wounded shield arm would weaken and eventually give way. She must then surely yield.

Silk concentrated hard.

She could see that Balder was sweating profusely and also breathing heavily. It was a strenuous fight, and with the sun approaching noon the heat was fierce in the windless arena. Pounding at his shield with her sword, she deliberately forced the pace. Ignoring the customary circling and glaring at each other, she had fought him without pause; their tracks criss-crossing the blood soaked arena in straight lines. She was biding her time, waiting for the heat to take its toll on his bigger body. Exhaustion would overwhelm his mind and this would force a fatal error.

She didn't have long to wait.

Feigning tiredness, Silk landed a weak blow with her sword. Balder, sensing victory, lashed out too hastily with his. One last supreme effort and victory would be his.

As his sword sang through the air, Silk darted sideways.

Balder missed.

Caught off balance, he stumbled forward, falling and clutching at the ground with his hands. Sprawled out before of her, Silk stamped her foot down hard. A spiked, metal heel perforated his hand. Howling with the pain, Balder let go of his sword.

"Do you yield?"

Silk stood over him; the blade of his sword now lay trapped beneath her foot.

"Never." Balder hissed angrily. His mind was fumbling, desperately searching for a plan to retrieve his sword—and his dignity.

"Do you yield?" Silk enquired more loudly. Leaning forward, she dug the tip of her blade into his Adam's apple.

She meant business.

Balder looked up into her steely, dark eyes. There was no sign of mercy. This was Gunnr and he could expect no less.

"I yield," Balder sighed as his shoulders sagged in defeat.

"I yield to you but to no other."

Hanging his head, he spread his arms wide in a gesture of surrender.

Silk stepped back slowly, a half smile forming on her lips.

"You see, I win again. I always do." She tapped the tip of her sword lightly on the top of his head and then turned slowly to go; releasing his blade.

Balder watched—one pace, two paces. Silk's narrow hips swaggered as she walked arrogantly away. She was mocking him deliberately with a provocative retreat.

Three paces, four.

Balder grabbed his sword and lunged forward. He had her.

Silk spun around and in a movement that lasted no longer than the blink of an eye, she buried her sword deep into his stomach. She stepped forward, pushing harder and twisting the blade as she did so.

For what seemed an age, Balder hung there. Crumpled and skewered, like a pig on a spit. Then he slowly toppled sideways and fell onto his back. Blood seeped from his split belly.

Silk shook her head scornfully as she pulled her sword from his guts. *The fool!* Carefully she wiped the blood from the blade before returning it to its scabbard. She stood in silence, gazing down at his still body.

The quiet arena suddenly sounded deafening.

She extended an outstretched hand—and waited.

Seconds ticked by.

"Wow, that stung!" Balder reached up suddenly and grasped her outstretched hand, pulling himself to his feet. "I nearly had you this time though, didn't I? Go on, admit it, I did, didn't I?" he teased.

"Not even close," Silk muttered conceitedly as she pulled him up. She could feel the sweat and heat of his body close to hers.

Balder pulled her toward him and offered her a kiss. He ground his hips suggestively as he pressed her against him. Silk pushed him away before stepping back.

"Not here, later. You know my rules; this is my place of war."

Taking his hand from her hip, she walked slowly away. This time there was a happy spring in her step, and the graceful sway of her hips echoed her contentment.

For Silk, Balder was the only man she had taken to her bed. If you asked her if she was in love, she would deny any such notion; adding gruffly that she only cared because, "he was the only man she couldn't kill."

For Balder, second born of Odin, and a man who had bedded many; he would reply that Gunnr was his one true love.

She was the only woman in all of Asgard who had truly captured his heart.

While Balder and Silk fought, Jess, too, was fighting her own peculiar battle. Her's was with Kat and it was an altogether different kind of struggle.

With Kat in her weakened state, getting her to ride behind Jess on her horse was impossible. She could have laid Kat over the rump of her steed, like a pair of misshapen saddlebags, but for Jess, this was far too undignified.

Reluctantly, she took a horn from her saddlebag and slapped her stallion on his flank. He whinnied, before trotting away. He would find his own way back to the castle stables. Jess blew three short loud blasts and then sat down to wait.

In a while, six stout peasant lads came running up the hill carrying a stretcher. Without pausing for rest and with as much decorum as was possible, they picked Kat up and placed her upon it. Lying on a scarlet satin sheet, with her head supported by a gold cushion; she looked serene. Jess's cloak of swans' feathers covered her bloodied and dusty body.

The men huffed and puffed, but some fifteen minutes later the stretcher party arrived in the crowded square. There was much cheering and clapping as the throng pressed forward, eagerly straining to see the face of their new arrival. Men gazed longingly at the fair hair that cascaded around the pillow, while old women reached out furtively to touch the feathered cloak.

It had been many a year since such a fair maid had arrived in Asgard.

After a short while, the procession left the square and made its way up the gentle slope to the castle. The crowd followed at a respectful distance.

Sadly, all the excitement and merry making of her arrival was missed by Kat.

More asleep than awake, her future memory of the journey would be a hazy recollection. The painful jolts of the stretcher featuring more prominently in her mind than the cheering, smiling faces. Eventually, in a palatial room somewhere deep within the castle walls, Kat was gently laid on a large bed. This had been especially prepared with freshly starched sheets.

With a final long draft of the same honeyed liquid she had been given by the roadside, Kat was at last able to sleep.

This was as deep as it was dreamless.

10
Saturday

Saturday morning broke slowly over New York. The dark night sky gave way reluctantly to leaden clouds; threatening yet more rain. A chill wind swirled gently around deserted streets as tired New Yorkers with bleary eyes, woke up and faced the prospect of another gloomy day.

Marcus hadn't slept since his awakening.

After walking home, he had watched a bit of TV and puttered about quietly; trying not to disturb Anna. As dawn broke, he shaved, put on a clean shirt and slipped silently out of their tiny flat. Hailing a cab, he had made his way to the crime scene, now deserted in the early morning air.

Ducking under the yellow and black tape that stretched haphazardly across the entrance, Marcus made his way down the narrow alley.

Shit! What a place to die.

Grimacing as he muttered quietly, Marcus scuffed his feet at the trash that littered the uneven, concrete paving slabs.

Just as he had expected, the alley came to an abrupt end. A wall rising six floors upward blocked his way. Set into the wall was a steel door with a solid lock. Marcus rattled this like he had the others on the street. It echoed eerily in the early morning hush; but it held firm. He looked around at the graffiti scrawled walls and doors.

There really was only one way in or out of the street.

Sure, if you had a mind to, you could scale any of the two or three steel fire escapes. But you would have to pull them down first. Rusty, rattling and resentful; the killer or any witnesses would have been crazy to use them.

No; what came into the alley left the same way.

Marcus turned his attention to the collection of dumpsters and plastic refuse bags that lay all around. A filthy smell wafted from each as he peered into them. He pitied the poor sod who would have to go through them; looking for evidence. A discarded gun perhaps—now that would be helpful.

Finally Marcus reached the place where Dr. Neal had met her death. An irregular, brown stain marked the spot where her life had ebbed away. He squatted down and examined the area carefully. No shattered hole in the concrete.

That was good.

It was likely the slug was still firmly lodged in her spine—this would help the ballistics people.

He stood up, and took one last look around. There was nothing, really. No fresh evidence he could add to her case.

Marcus made his way slowly back to the street. Poor Dr. Neal. She had met such a sad and lonely end in this shit hole. She deserved so much better.

"Don't worry," he murmured angrily.

"I'll get the bastard."

Much later on that same sullen morning Ruby awoke and readied herself for the day.

By coincidence, Jack's Motel was only a few blocks from the alley.

Putting on some lipstick, she headed down to the street and made her way toward *The Candy Girls* night club. This was a down and out bar where dancers well past their prime turned a final few bucks with their fading beauty. A girl like Ruby would blow them away.

Arriving outside the sleazy premises, she paused momentarily before tugging at its grubby brass hand rail.

What a dump.

It was time to audition.

11

A Friend in Jess

Kat eventually awoke feeling far more refreshed than she ought to have been. Peeping out from between sheets that lay largely undisturbed, she could see a shaft of sunlight coming through a long leaded window. By its length and its weakness, she guessed it was late in the afternoon.

Shit! She was still dreaming.

Kat felt her pulse—still no heart beat.

Taking a deep breath in, she tried to rationalize her situation. Shaking nervously, she began a ritual of pinching herself till it hurt, and then moving each of her arms and legs in turn.

This was impossible.

She could breathe, see, touch, smell, and move. Her body felt warm, yet no blood pumped around it. Taking another deep breath in, she realised that far from being dead–as she should be—she was actually feeling rather good.

The aches in her hands and feet had faded, and the wound in her chest had already scabbed over and shrunk in size. To a doctor's mind, one trained to be logical; nothing was making any sense. Looking around her, she added the strange room to this list.

"Got it," she exclaimed loudly, sitting bolt upright in bed.

She must have made it to the bar after all, and somebody had spiked her drink. That had to be it.

This thought was strangely reassuring.

Looking around the large, stonewalled room, it was a relief to know that everything was just some psychedelic, drug fuelled hallucination. That had to be it; she had to be right.

Kat's sudden stirring caught a serf by surprise.

The young woman had been quietly dozing by a hearth that lay on the opposite side of the room. A fire flickered merrily there, its youthful flames growing in strength as they filled the room with warmth for the cool night ahead.

The woman jumped to her feet, opened the door, and frantically started to beat a large gong. The noise echoed alarmingly around the room.

"Whoa!" Kat entreated the girl to stop.

Gingerly she stretched a toe down to the floor and made ready to get up. The bed was high and magnificent. A king-sized four poster, draped with rich embroidered silks and a mattress deep and soft to the touch.

"Whoa!" Kat exclaimed more loudly a second later when she realised she was yet again naked. She remembered her arrival; confused, bloody, and also naked. Hastily she returned between the cosy sheets.

"Did you sleep well?"

Jess's harmonious Irish voice lilted through the door as she entered the room. Her long red locks hung down to her breasts, and she was wearing a beautiful flowing green robe. This was pulled in loosely at the waist by a thick gold belt.

"I'll get you something to wear, Katarina," she announced as she sat on the edge of the bed. "Once we have bathed."

Kat stared at her wonderful dress.

"Wow," She breathed as she stretched out an impertinent hand to touch it.

The sheen was amazing.

"By the way," Kat looked up.

"Please call me Kat. Nobody calls me Katarina." She paused, before adding. "Except my mother, and that's only when she's angry."

"I'm very pleased to meet you then, dear Kat," Jess offered a mock handshake before carrying on to ask once more if she had slept well.

"Excellent. I must have had at least a couple of hours." Kat replied cheerily.

"Hours? My dearest Kat; you've been asleep for a whole day and night! You lay in bed so still I had to keep checking that you were breathing."

Jess patted Kat's leg reassuringly before standing up. "Come on. Let's get you bathed and dressed," she continued. "We'll feast well tonight."

With Kat gaping in astonishment at her extended slumber, Jess threw the cloak of swans' feathers around her shoulders and led her down the corridor.

Bathing was going to be fun.

"Oh my fuck!" Kat exclaimed loudly as they entered the bathroom.

Before them lay an ornate chamber in the centre of which stood a large, sunken, marble pool. It wasn't the size of the pool that had caused Kat's outburst, rather the presence of naked women relaxing in and around the waters.

Her sudden outburst caused a silence in the room.

Jess pulled Kat toward her and whispered quietly in her ear.

"Odin doesn't like profanities, that isn't the Valkyrie way."

Kat suddenly felt dirty.

She had offended all these strangers and now she had upset her new friend; her only friend so far in this crazy, mixed up world. Her eyes welled with tears.

Jess read her distress.

"But dearest Kat how were you to know that?" she gave her a tight squeeze. "Come on, let's get undressed and meet the family."

The silence ended quickly as two girls climbed out of the water and came running over to hug Kat. They did this enthusiastically, excited to meet their new sister. Without asking for an invitation, the girls started to disrobe them; chattering merrily all the while.

Jess snapped her fingers and pointed to somebody kneeling in the corner. The person's face was turned toward the ground. She snapped her fingers again at another, crouching figure.

Oh dear God!

Kat cringed with embarrassment, praying that the floor would swallow her up. The people were men and they were wearing coarse, linen kilts.

"These slaves will clean us first," Jess continued, oblivious to Kat's predicament. "Then we will join Carmel, Emile, and the others in the pool."

Jess turned toward one of them and sighed with pleasure as he poured a jug of warm water over her; wiping her body firmly with a cloth as he did so.

"I'm not sure—" Kat started to blurt.

Jess turned and instantly saw her discomfort.

"Oh," Jess beamed. "Don't worry about them, they've all been castrated." She added this as easily as if she was talking about the weather. It was obviously the customary fate for a slave, and a matter of little consequence to her and the other women present.

Kat gulped and allowed the *thing*—she felt she couldn't really call it a man anymore—to bathe her. Then, after taking hold of Jess's hand, they slipped gently into the warm and perfumed water.

About an hour later, Kat was sitting comfortably in front of a large mirror gently brushing her hair.

She had to admit that once she had got used to communal bathing, it had actually been quite fun. Chatting to Jess, Carmel, Emile, and many others whose names she couldn't remember, had made it a relaxing and pleasurable affair. One she hoped she might repeat, should this madness last long enough.

"Oh Kat," a voice echoed from the doorway. "You look amazing."

It was Jess, admiring the choice she had made in the magnificent, pink gown that Kat was now wearing.

"Let's fix your hair and get downstairs to the hall."

Jess walked across the room and ran her fingers through Kat's silken locks.

"You, young lady, are going to look fabulous tonight."

Hair quickly set, and feeling extremely nervous, Kat followed Jess down the wide open stairway that spiralled into the reception hall below. Torch flames flickered and lit their way as they walked, sending darting shadows dancing amongst the oak beams overhead.

Although the castle was very large and constructed of stone, it felt surprisingly warm and homely. The floors had carpets strewn upon them and the walls were covered with rich tapestries, shields, and armour. Much of the latter was pock marked with the scars of war.

This was a warrior castle and home to the greatest god in Asgard.

Odin.

At the bottom of the staircase and before they entered the feasting hall, Kat paused. She had spotted a much less grand stairwell spiralling down and away to the left.

Her eyes looked inquisitively at Jess.

"Those stairs, my dearest Kat, lead to the Chamber of the Valkyries, the heart of this great castle. Would you like to have a look?" Jess enquired with a cheeky grin on her face.

Kat hesitated.

Was this wise?

Jess's smile was peculiar.

"No, go on, I insist," Jess tugged at her arm. "I swear by Thor's beard that no harm will befall you. Go on, do please take a look."

Kat made to go down.

"Are you going to join me?" she enquired tentatively.

"No, no."

There was that cheeky grin again.

"I would love you to see it for the first time by yourself. Go on; see what you make of it."

Jess motioned with her hand for Kat to go down the steps.

"Okay," Kat leaned forward reluctantly and tried to look as far round the first turn as possible. Straining her ears; she could hear nothing emanating from the gloom below. She took one hesitant step, and then another, and another. *Oh good,* she thought as she reached the point when she lost sight of Jessica. *At least I can see another torch ahead and won't be plunged into darkness.*

She stepped forward. Just one more step—.

"Ha, Ha, Ha!"

Jess was doubled up with laughter.

With her last step, Kat had arrived back where she'd started from.

Grabbing hold of her hands, Jess danced around Kat, delighted with her trickery.

"Of course you can go to the Chamber, but only if you can find the door. Only the warriors know that little secret."

Kat laughed too before slapping Jess's arm playfully.

"Why are you being so good to me?" Kat enquired as her voice suddenly became more earnest.

"You're so kind, and I have done nothing to deserve your friendship." She felt a fraud in this contented place, wherever or whatever it may be.

"My darling," this time it was Jess's turn to be serious.

"You're my guest. If it's Odin's wish and your destiny, then one day you may join me and my sisters as a Valkyrie."

Jess turned and looked Kat squarely in the face. Her blue eyes twinkled beautifully in the torchlight.

"Why on earth would you want that?" Kat returned her gaze. "I've done nothing special."

"On the contrary," Jess took hold of her hand. "You have a good heart and have helped many people. You died courageously at the hands of evil. It will be our honour to have you join us."

Kat's lip quivered.

There was the 'D' word again, just when she'd forgotten it.

"Oh come now," Jess placed her hand across her shoulders. "Please, no tears. Let's enjoy tonight. The feast is in your honour."

Jess whistled loudly, and the doors to the hall flew open. Dragging Kat behind her, the two girls were swiftly engulfed by the festivities within.

The evening passed quickly for Kat. It was a whirlwind of new faces, feasting and dancing. She remembered drinking more of the same wonderful liquid from a large, ornate golden vessel that formed the centre piece of the table. Fish, pheasant, boar, venison—the list of meats and dishes brought to the table seemed endless and each more tasty and satisfying than the last. Many handsome men introduced themselves; Loki, Balder, Tyr, and many others. All had strong white teeth and rippled with muscles. The music was divine, played by Kvasir as she remembered his name. He was a beautiful boy with short black curly locks; and he sang as he played a harp gilded with gold leaf. His voice was sublime; soft and gentle, yet filling the room with its beauty—easing her troubled mind.

Of course, she chuckled self consciously; any soothing could easily have been down to the alcohol, which flowed in abundance.

Tiring before the other guests, Kat asked Jess to take her back to her room. All the merriment and excitement was exhausting and she felt in desperate need for more rest.

Retracing their steps, Jess eventually stood beside Kat in front of the open window to her bedroom. Neither of them spoke as they looked out at the stars above and the lights of the cottages below. These twinkled merrily in the darkness.

Far away to the east, flashes of lightning and rumbles of thunder lit the sky.

"That will be Thor," Jess murmured. "Crushing dragons."

She pulled Kat close to her, and felt her warm body next to hers. It felt good, their friendship and warmth against the chill of the night.

Suddenly, like an express train, the truth hit Kat.

Its impact was violent, shocking, and without warning.

Collapsing onto Jess's shoulder, she started to cry; gentle moans that gave way swiftly to much deeper sobs. With tears streamed down her cheeks, Kat's shoulders heaved as her heart ached—and then burst.

She was dead.

She knew that now beyond any shadow of a doubt.

This wasn't a dream; nor was it a hallucination.

Her world of cars and planes, and her life of patients and medicine was gone. If heaven or hell existed, then this was it. This was eternity. New York was her past. Here, wherever that was, lay her future; and it would be hers for evermore.

Kat wept for her friends; those who she would never laugh with again.

Kat wept for her parents; who would never hold her in their arms.

Finally, Kat sobbed for her family; the unborn babies; sons and daughters she would never know.

Jess held her close as tears welled in her eyes, too.

Poor Kat.

Death was such a bitch.

Kat's pain broke her heart and as she comforted her, Jess vowed a vow she wouldn't break.

She would ask Freyja for a favour, a really, really big favour.

Jess swore this grimly—and upon Odin's blood.

12

Cole

"Sweet."

Cole murmured this word as his head nodded up and down, but not in time, to a heavy bass. This was pounding at the walls of *The Candy Girls* late this Saturday evening.

The club was half full and a disco ball flashed a rotating kaleidoscope of colours around the small room. Cole was sitting in his usual place; a semi-circular alcove with a faded red, velvet sofa wrapped around a central table. If the lights had been fully on, the cigarette burns, worn fabric, and suspicious stains on the seats would have exposed the club for what it was—a sleazy knocking shop in down town New York.

This was a place for prostitution, drug dealing, and crime.

"Sweet."

Cole murmured and nodded again, his eyes firmly fixed on the body of a girl on the small wooden stage. He flicked his hand toward an empty tumbler on the table and in an instant, a waiter reverently replaced the empty with another; a glass that rattled with ice cubes and the strength of Jack D.

It was good to be the boss, Cole mused without acknowledging or thanking the waiter. He didn't actually own the place, not the bricks and mortar nor the tables and chairs. No; what Cole owned was the people; everybody and every deal that took place behind its sleazy doors.

For every dollar spent on a drink, a line of coke, a trick—he took thirty percent.

Pretty reasonable, he thought, *by others' standards.* Takings weren't great, but that didn't really matter. Cole's kingdom covered four blocks, five if you counted the pushers in the square; and he made enough money to lead a good life.

He had worked hard to get where he was today, he reminisced, as his mind wandered back to his youth. He could hardly remember a time when he wasn't selling coke, beating up bigger guys, or being banged up. He had killed his first victim when he was still a minor. Not some easy gun crime, a distant shoot-and-run kill; but an up close and bloody murder; one done with a knife. He had no regrets. This slaying had earned him respect, and given him access to a gang where he quickly rose to become the leader.

He was hard, he was violent, and his reputation spread far wider than his fiefdom.

Sure, everybody resented paying him for protection and taking a cut in their deals, but what they got, thanks to him; was stability. His fearsome reputation stopped other drug lords muscling in on his turf and that was a good thing—no divided loyalties, no duplicity. If people paid up and didn't do anything silly they lived well; and Cole's protection meant protection. Any funny business and he sorted it.

Justice was fast, simple, and permanent.

That was Cole's way.

"Sweet."

Cole muttered as his attention returned once more to the black beauty on the stage.

Long, long legs beneath a pert, juicy ass, gyrating provocatively around the dance pole. The girl had fine breasts, Cole noted appreciatively with a grunt. These weren't the usual inflated silicon ones, but smaller, firmer, more natural ones. The kind men begged to get their teeth into. Her stomach was toned too, showing definition that came from hours of physical exercise.

She was a beauty; a hot, black, sassy beauty.

What ultimately sealed the deal was her face. Pure African Cole wagered. Her eyes were big and almond-shaped, and she had high cheek bones that accentuated a proud and angular jaw. Her mouth was broad with full Negro lips; large white teeth fluoresced vividly in the harsh, ultra-violet light.

Oh yes, Cole mused conceitedly, he was going to fuck this leggy ho'; but not tonight.

Motioning with a finger, the chubby man sitting next to him leaned forward. Cole whispered in his ear for some minutes and the man nodded, repeatedly. When he had finished, the man left; slipping out through a back door.

Cole needed the low down on this fine piece of ass.

He was old enough, and wise enough not to screw new blood without asking questions first. He was wanted by the police, by the mafia, and practically every other two bit gangster who hoped to get a piece of his action. It wouldn't be the first time someone in Cole's position had fallen for a honey trap. No, Cole would play it cool for now.

He wanted to know everything about this bitch and he wanted to know it fast.

As Ruby posed and strutted her way around the stage she noticed the cool black dude, eyes firmly fixed on her body. She had recognised the two thugs from the hotel sitting next to him, too.

Oh yes, Ruby thought with satisfaction, she had gotten what she had come for.

She had gotten Cole's attention.

13

To Be or Not to Be

Sunday morning dawned bright and clear over Asgard. In the castle and town there was an air of excitement that had started long before dawn, even before the crowing of cockerels. The square had been diligently swept and washed, bunting had been hung up, and the silver flag above Gladsheim had been taken down, cleaned, and then raised once more.

At approximately nine o'clock, and to a loud flourish of horns, the hall's mighty doors swung open.

A scrum mage erupted briefly as townsfolk fought to find a coveted place inside the hall. It was mainly good natured, but an occasion fist flew in the melee; which was by no means unusual amongst the Aesir. As the final seating disputes came to an amicable end, the fortunate few sat smugly in the hall whilst those less fortunate lined the square.

As the minutes ticked by, excitement mounted steadily.

In the castle there was a state of orchestrated chaos.

Serfs and slaves rushed around madly, tending to the whims of the gods, warriors, and maids. Throughout the commotion, Jess chose with great precision exactly how she wanted Kat to be presented. A beautiful, white satin dress had been brought, and this was fastened by two large silver clasps, one over each shoulder. Both the front and the back of the gown plunged from these clasps, crossing over her breasts before being gathered tightly at her waist. Here it was held in place by a heavy silver chain with a central clasp of swan's wings. This matched the ones on her shoulders. Below the belt, the dress cascaded in pleats to the ground which swished as she walked. Kat had always felt herself to be flat-chested, but as she admired her reflection in a mirror, she had to agree that even her cleavage would turn heads.

A great deal of fuss had been made over her hair, too.

Jess had combed a parting in the middle before fashioning two plaits from the hair at the front of her head. These had then been pulled backward and fastened behind her head with a silver clip. Jess hung a beautiful jewelled pendant along the centre parting. This sparkled high up on her forehead.

To complete her ensemble, and after some negotiation; a magnificent silver neckpiece had been borrowed from Freyja. Kat gasped at its elegance and finery. Fashioned from finest silver, three delicate stems entwined and wove their way around her neck; each ending in flourishes of silver oak leaves studded with clusters of diamonds. These represented acorns.

Kat looked fabulous, and every inch the Valkyrie maid that Jess hoped she would become.

With so much activity going on, they had had little time to talk. Kat could sense a tension growing in Jess. Her smile appeared more nervous and less radiant than the day before. On questioning, Jess explained that although she had chosen Kat to become a Valkyrie, the final decision would rest with Odin. What she hadn't explained, and this perturbed Kat, was what would happen if he said "No."

Flashing a smile, Jess reassured her that no harm would come her way; even if this was so. She vowed this not only by 'Thor's beard' but also upon 'his hammer'—her oaths causing great hoots of laughter from those around them.

Kat felt a little reassured; but not much.

Odin and his small retinue arrived early at Gladsheim and, after the customary bowing and exchanging of pleasantries with the townsfolk, he had taken his place on one of the two thrones that stood toward the back of the hall. Lounging across one of these, Odin was deep in conversation with Balder and Hod, two of his three sons by Frigg. She, unfortunately, was not there today because of personal reasons. She hadn't elaborated upon these, but he felt sure he knew them only too well.

At his feet lay Freki, one of the wolves that kept guard over his citadel; and on his shoulder perched his raven Huginn, who from time to time nibbled at his ear. On one hand, which rested casually on the armrest, a ring gleamed from his fourth finger. This ring was encrusted with a cluster of nine small diamonds.

These sparkled without any obvious need for light.

Odin's scruffy blue cloak, spear and battered, wide brimmed hat adorned the back of his throne. Sprawled as he was, casually and without ceremony, there was little to show that here sat the most powerful god in all of Asgard.

At eleven o'clock, two loud horns blew from the castle, and an expectant hush fell upon the gathered crowds. Slowly the drawbridge rumbled down and the townsfolk caught their first glimpse of the royal procession.

First across the drawbridge came six beautiful dappled grey stallions. Snorting and trotting expectantly, they could barely keep their excitement under control. They were large, powerful horses bred especially for war. The weight of their riders, and the noise of the crowd, made them expectant for a battle cry and to break forth into a thunderous charge.

Upon their backs rode six Valkyrie warriors, who rode in pairs. As Jess had explained to Kat, there were in fact nine warriors but only six were present at the castle today. Each woman was wearing a resplendent leather tunic and upon their heads were helmets made of dwarf gold. This was a strong and light metal that was extremely rare outside the castle. The helmets shone brilliantly in the sunshine and each was richly carved with effigies of swans' wings. Each warrior carried a spear and a brightly coloured shield, the pattern of each being different to the others. Thus the crowd could see that the Valkyries Brynhildr, Gunnr, Hlokk, Goll, Mist, and Herja were present today. Each warrior wore a cloak of swans' feathers, and these draped over the haunches of their steeds.

Behind the Valkyries and riding on a jet black stallion was their Queen.

Her name was Freyja.

Next to Odin, she was the most important person in the realm, a priestess and a sorceress, the supreme leader of the Valkyries.

Kat had been presented to her just before the start of the procession. Such was Freyja's presence that, without even thinking,

Kat had dropped into a clumsy courtesy in front of her. To have done anything less would have felt unnatural. Freyja was older than her warriors, early forties if Kat had to hazard a guess. Her jet black hair was straight and cut in a short bob that angled up sharply to the back of her head. This complimented her pale cheekbones, long straight nose and deep set blue eyes.

Their meeting had been brief.

She flashed Kat a weak smile from her reedy lips, complimented Jess on her choice in the necklace, and, after nodding politely; she had turned and mounted her horse. She now rode upon him imperiously. Her legs covered by tight black leggings, gripped his flanks strongly; and her loose fitting black top festooned with gold and precious gems sparkled brightly in the sunshine. Over her shoulders she also wore a feathered cloak; but these feathers weren't from a swan. Kat later learned that her cloak was made from falcon feathers, and this complimented her fine helmet which rose in the front to a figurehead of a bird of prey.

Behind Freyja, who rode alone, came four pole bearers carrying a casket. This was also made from dwarf gold and was richly decorated with effigies of birds and oak leaves wrought from silver and gold.

After the casket and riding on lesser horses were the Valkyrie maids. There was one maid for each warrior and they would succeed them if they fell. Amongst these girls was Carmel, whom Kat remembered from the night before.

Behind them all, and standing alone in a small chariot drawn by a single chestnut mare—stood Kat.

The crowd cheered as the procession rode by, horns blew and drums were beaten at a frenetic pace. As they neared the hall of Gladsheim and made ready to dismount, the crowd began to stamp their feet and chant in unison, "Freyja, Freyja." This gained in intensity as they entered the wooden building.

"FREYJA! FREYJA!"

Odin rose as the Valkyries came into the hall.

They fanned out to the left and right of the aisle which led from the door to the rough hewn, stone alter that stood before the two thrones. Freyja entered the hall, and walked until she was in front of the altar. The pole bearers followed immediately after; carefully placing the casket before her before retiring to the back of the hall.

Finally, Kat made her way up the aisle. Her knees were trembling and she prayed her legs wouldn't collapse as she took her place beside Freyja.

"FREYJA! FREYJA!"

Odin, Freyja, and the Valkyries raised their spears as the chanting, drumming and foot stamping reached a crescendo in noise.

THUMP!

Suddenly and without a signal, they brought these down to the floor with an almighty thud.

A deafening silence fell upon the hall, such that Kat could hear her ears ringing. Without realising it, she had bowed her head along with the rest of those assembled. The Aesir, too, had bowed their heads; but they had also fallen to their knees and were now gazing silently at the wooden floor.

After what seemed an age, Kat looked up, slowly and hesitantly, not knowing what to expect.

Odin stood before her.

He was slim and shorter in stature than she had expected. His mouse coloured hair was cropped short and beginning to recede from his forehead. Grey hairs were in abundance, prominent around the nape of his neck, sideburns, and his well manicured goatee beard. Interestingly one eye was covered by a patch but the other was brown and clear. Kat pondered briefly what story might lie behind his missing eye.

Odin's face was kind and disarming. He wasn't excessively handsome, yet he had the sort of face that you could trust and that you knew you would grow to love.

"Greetings dearest Freyja and my Valkyries."

Odin spoke softly, so softly in fact that Kat found herself straining to catch his words. It seemed incongruous for so great a god to talk so quietly. She looked around and could see that everybody else was concentrating and listening intently.

You could have heard a pin drop.

The quietness of Odin's voice commanded more attention than any amount of bellowing or raging.

After kissing Freyja's hand, and nodding to each warrior in turn, Odin spoke once more.

"Please step forward Katarina."

This was it. Kat gulped, and stepped forward nervously.

Odin circled her slowly and in silence. He looked her up and down and as he passed her shoulder, he ran a hand through her tresses. Finally he stood in front of her once more; his deep brown eye piercing her soul.

"Greetings my dear Kat."

Odin's face broke into a warm smile and he raised her hand and kissed it softly. "You have chosen well Brunhildr, very well indeed," he added, smiling at Jess.

Kat felt like crying.

All the fear and tension in her heart melted with his use of her name. A smile lit up her face too, one that was broader than any she had yet made in Asgard.

"Come quickly, the runes."

Odin clapped his hands excitedly.

Freyja opened the cask on the table before them. Carefully she withdrew nine flattened, tear-shaped, metal tablets and placed them in Kat's outstretched hands.

"Now," said Odin as he indicated to the stone slab. "Throw the runes onto the altar. Don't be afraid, they will tell us much."

Kat obliged, letting the tablets slip between her fingers and these clattered to the stone below. They looked heavy yet felt strangely light. The same dwarf gold as the cask she noted.

With the runes cast, both Odin and Freyja studied them intently, glancing at each in turn and nodding as they went.

Finally Freyja stood up and delivered her verdict in a loud and clear voice.

"THE RUNES ARE GOOD!"

Frenzied cheering and clapping erupted both in the hall and outside. This was the news everybody had wanted to hear. These were the words that told them Kat would become a Valkyrie.

"Congratulations, dear Kat," Odin smiled once more, shaking her hand with warmth and obvious affection.

"I'm sure there are many questions you would like to ask, but perhaps we should go somewhere a little more peaceful to talk?" he suggested.

Holding onto Kat's hand, he drew his other across his diamond encrusted ring.

14

Odin's Garden

It wasn't for the first time that Kat had stood dumbstruck.

Where once had been a bustling, noisy hall there now stood a tranquil garden, one filled with birdsong and insects humming. Just when she thought she was making progress with her strange new world—wham! Another surprise crept up and slapped her hard across the face.

She felt completely stupefied.

Where was she now?

Odin glanced over and saw the look on her face. He stood quietly, allowing her to adjust.

Slowly Kat took stock of her new surroundings.

They were indeed in a garden, festooned with fragrant and colourful flowers that blossomed all around. Directly ahead and standing upon a small rise in the ground was a huge ash tree. This rose from three giant roots into a lush and green canopy. This extended so high that in the harsh, sunlit sky she couldn't see its top, even when she shielded her eyes with her hand.

Looking down, a small spring rose close to one of its roots. Its waters bubbled merrily as they wound their way toward them. Rabbits and deer nibbled around the tree, and a red squirrel called Ratatosk, scurried up and down its enormous trunk. He hardly paused for rest at either end of his journey.

"Ah, this is better." Odin sighed deeply as he extended his hand toward Kat.

"Come, let's sit beneath Yggdrasill and talk."

Kat would learn more about Yggdrasill, the garden, and its inhabitants at a later date. For now though their mysteries were overshadowed by far more pressing matters. A volcano of questions was threatening to burst inside her head.

Meekly, she took his hand and they made their way toward the shade of the tree.

"Would you like to meet the Norn? They look after my garden."

Odin waved a hand toward the trunk of the tree. Kat noticed, to her surprise, that three maids had been tending quietly to the garden around the massive roots. The girls were extremely fair, almost albino, and each had long, blond hair that cascaded down their backs to their waists.

"Urd, Skuld, and Verdandi." Odin introduced each girl in turn and they curtsied politely. "Or perhaps I should call them Fate, Being, and Necessity. You might find these names easier on the tongue." He could see that Kat was struggling with their Asgard names.

Introductions over, they continued to walk and the Norn went back to their gardening. This time they sang to themselves. Kat heard their voices, and felt overcome with a desire to kiss Odin.

Actually, the sensation was much more than a desire. It was a hunger, a lust to rip his clothes off and have him make passionate love to her right there and right now.

Losing control, she placed an arm around his waist and pulled him toward her. Her lips began to caress his neck. She was burning with passion and need.

"Oh," Odin exclaimed, looking surprised.

"Oh!" He exclaimed more loudly when he realised what was happening. Clapping his hands with some urgency, he beckoned for the Norn to stop their song, which they did.

As the singing ended, the feelings of desire, which had welled so quickly inside her, subsided with equal swiftness.

"I'm so sorry," Kat stuttered apologetically. "I don't know what came over me." Awkwardly, she smoothed imaginary creases from her dress. Kat couldn't look him in the eye anymore.

"No need to apologise," Odin chuckled. "The song of the Norn can have that effect on women. Most do get resistant to it with time. Come, let's sit over here in the shade."

They both sat down on the grass, and Odin took an apple from a wicker basket that lay next to him.

"Would you like one?" he enquired casually.

Kat nodded, grateful that her lewd behaviour had been dismissed so inconsequentially. Casting her gaze over the apples, she couldn't help but notice the shimmering of their skin. They appeared almost golden in colour.

"They really are very good," Odin continued. "Idun picks them from her apple tree and leaves them here for us."

Kat took one and they both sat and ate in silence for a while.

"I love this place," Odin spoke at last. "When I need a bit of peace, a time to think, or a private chat; this is where I like to come. In fact," he continued. "I think this is my favourite place."

He looked around him with an expression of contentment on his face.

"Odin," Kat began hesitantly.

"I know," Odin interrupted her. "So many questions and here we are, munching apples and making small talk. Perhaps I should begin with some answers, hey?"

Sitting up a little straighter, he turned and looked at her.

"If I was to tell you that I am God, and that I have brought your soul over a flaming rainbow bridge to heaven would that help?" he gazed at her quizzically, and continued to munch on his apple.

Slowly, and without really thinking, Kat found herself shaking her head.

"No," she said at last.

"I'm sorry, but no."

"I didn't think so," Odin replied. He had expected that answer.

He stopped eating.

"If instead I told you that I was a being from another universe, one parallel to yours, that your mortal body was dead and I have rescued your consciousness and given it physical form here, in my world; would that help? If I also told you that the bright rainbow when you arrived was in fact the opening of a wormhole between my universe and yours—" he paused, staring intently at her face.

He wanted to read her reaction.

Kat looked up, and met his gaze. She could see him searching for her response.

The many wonders of her strange new world, and her presence there, it could possibly now make some sense. Like tiny pieces of a very large jigsaw puzzle, it was all slowly coming together.

Odin watched as the veil of Kat's confusion lifting slowly from her face. He felt a deep sorrow. He could see in her eyes that the people of Midgard were losing their naivety, and this saddened him greatly.

"Are you God?" Kat asked cautiously. She didn't really know where the question came from, but it felt kind of right.

There was a long pause.

"In the beginning…"

Odin began slowly, a smile growing once more. He couldn't resist the impulse to quote from Genesis, the first chapter of the bible and a book hugely popular in Midgard.

He paused yet again, but this time only briefly.

"I don't really know," he continued abruptly. "If by that you mean am I the Christian God, or the God of the Jews, or Mohammed or Krishna then I don't know. If, however, what you are asking is am I a creator of worlds then yes, yes I am. I created this world, this universe, and everything you see around you." He waved his hand nonchalantly to emphasis the point.

"But that's impossible," Kat exclaimed, shaking her head as she rejected this ridiculous notion.

"Is it now?" Odin decided to test her. "You have heard of the big bang theory haven't you? You people of Midgard, or earth, as you like to call it. You now know that everything around you began as a huge explosion of energy. You accept that as a fact, don't you?"

She nodded her agreement.

"And people on your world. They have built a machine that will produce a collision with so much power and energy that it might create a black hole?" he paused, leaving the question hanging expectantly in the air.

Kat nodded again. He was talking of course about the Large Hadron Collider, a huge particle accelerator that spans the frontiers of France and Switzerland.

"Well then, is it really so inconceivable that a civilisation far more advanced than yours could build a machine even more powerful? One that is so enormous that it can create new universes, starting each with its own big bang?" he asked.

Kat nodded once more. What he said really did make good sense. Just as people had once believed the earth and the sun were unique, scientists now believed that the universe was but one of many. She had always enjoyed astronomy and although she was no expert in these matters; she was aware of current theories.

"Okay," she finally spoke. "I agree that it's possible, and if indeed you have rescued my consciousness from death then thank you, thank you very much. But what I now don't understand," And this time it was her turn to pause. "Is what all this has to do with me? I must mean nothing to you, absolutely nothing; an insect or less. So why rescue me?"

She emphasised her last words, pressing her hand on her chest as she spoke.

"Oh Kat, dear, fair Kat," Odin sighed and lay back closing his eyes. "You, Brunhildr, Gunnr, Hlokk, and my other Valkyries; you cannot begin to imagine how close you are to my heart; nor how very important you are to me."

Kat didn't reply. She could sense that Odin was about to explain some of the mysteries of Asgard, and she listened intently as he did just that.

Like earth, or Midgard as he called it, Asgard had started in a ball of fire. There had been several ice ages and gradually as the world took shape, he and others of his race, twenty six gods and goddesses in total, had settled there and raised their families. It was a world of plenty and times were good. He likened it to a golden age, and his eyes misted over with the countless happy memories that flooded back.

Unfortunately, like all people, the gods and goddesses began to quarrel, splitting them into two groups. The Aesir, who loved to hunt and fight; and the Vanir, who enjoyed peace and farming. Trivial squabbles became arguments and these eventually turned into a long and bloody war. This, he explained, was how the wall around the castle had been destroyed. Finally, realising that neither side could win, they had agreed a truce by way of an exchange. Freyja and Klavsir came from the Vanir and joined him in Asgard, while Honir and his best friend Mimir joined the Vanir in the realm of Vanaheim.

Odin's voice now changed tone.

With a mixture of sorrow and anger, he recounted how the Vanir had abused Mimir, and left him in a very sorry state. It was a state he wouldn't elaborate on. What he did say, and Kat pricked up her ears at this, was that Mimir knew everything. All that had happened on Asgard, and all that would happen. Much of Odin's distress at the loss of his friend was because of this loss of knowledge. This seemed very important so she asked him why.

"This, dear Kat is where you come in," Odin continued, looking more seriously at her.

"Mimir had foretold that our worlds would become ever more troublesome. Other peoples and creatures seeing our fighting would rise up and make mischief. Order would turn to chaos, and eventually a great war would overcome us all. Not only here in Asgard but possibly in Midgard as well." He spoke solemnly and squeezed her hand hard.

"But you can stop that," Kat exclaimed loudly. "You're God and this is your world. Change it. You don't need me, surely?"

"If only it were that simple," Odin signed deeply. "When the universe begins, in the moment of the huge explosion it grows to its full size—instantly."

"Inflation," Kat interrupted; eager to demonstrate that she understood and could match his intelligence. "Inflation, that's what we call it on earth."

"Exactly, inflation; but what does that actually mean?" at this point he gazed intently at her.

Kat didn't reply because she didn't really know the answer.

"What it means is that in that very instant, not only does space expand to its full size, but time does as well. This runs its full course, from its start to its end. Everything that can happen and will happen does so in that instant. We are all now merely passengers travelling our destinies through history, discovering a future that has already been ordained. We cannot change our fates, even I can't do that. That lies beyond my power."

Odin paused to allow Kat to take in the significance of what he had just said.

Kat gulped. She sort of understood what he was getting at.

"As I was saying," he continued. "We have known for some time that there will be a great war, but we don't know the outcome of this war. For a long time my Valkyries have searched Midgard, choosing the greatest warriors to come and join me in a great army. This was their only purpose, to help me create a mighty force, one that may save both our worlds."

His voice now darkened.

"But what has also come to light is a second part to Mimir's prophecy. A great evil will arise in Midgard and this will bring about the start of the war. My Valkyrie warriors now search for that evil, stopping those who could be responsible and bringing them here for justice. This may prevent the war from ever beginning, if that's possible. That is why I need you."

Odin finished his speech and stared intently at Kat.

She looked into his eyes.

This was it.

"If you choose to become a Valkyrie then I can offer you many things. You will not age, you will not get ill, and you will be able to return to Midgard; helping me to rid that world of evil and bringing its greatest warriors to join my army." Odin spoke confidently, hoping she would see this as a good deal.

"And if I refuse?"

Kat prayed she wouldn't regret this question. She suddenly felt afraid once more.

"Then I will release your consciousness and you may go to whatever heaven you believe in." Odin patted her hand reassuringly. "You have my blessing and my word on this, I promise."

For a while Kat pondered in silence.

She trusted him.

If she wanted to, she could choose to die now, and leave this strange place behind. Surprisingly, she felt she would already miss it, even after so short a stay. And what about returning to earth? Surely that was an opportunity too good to miss?

"If I do choose to become a Valkyrie," she started hesitantly. "What about the downside? There has to be one doesn't there?"

"Absolutely," he nodded.

Damn! She so wished he hadn't said that.

"You will have to be brave and fight both in Asgard and in Midgard. You will feel pain and suffer injuries. You can never bear children and," he paused to emphasis one last important point. "With each passing year you will yearn for Valhalla. This craving will grow ever stronger until eventually it will consume you."

"Valhalla?" Kat interrupted him with a question. This wasn't a name she recognised.

"The feasting halls for my Einherjar, my heroes, my heaven for the brave, the place where my final, magnificent army is being assembled." Odin continued proudly. "You'll not regret going to Valhalla when it is your time to do so, dear Kat. It is a wondrous place; that's why all my warriors crave it so."

With his explanation complete, a silence fell between them. It was a silence that stretched almost into awkwardness.

"Will you join me, fair Kat?"

Odin broke the stillness; but this time his voice was almost a whisper; hesitant and unsure.

"Yes."

Kat said this slowly but with confidence.

Her mind was made up; she would not turn back now.

After taking her hand in his, Odin drew his hand over the ring.

Odin and Kat returned to Gladsheim at exactly the same moment they departed. Everybody was still clapping wildly. Their talk, which seemed to have lasted for hours, had taken place in an instant—a single twinkle of a star. Odin raised both hands in the air, and tried in vain to quieten the ecstatic crowd. He had an important announcement to make. Slowly the sound fell from a deafening roar to a gentle hubbub.

Eventually, a silence fell upon the hall.

PRAAAPPP!

From the back of the hall a wizen old man clutching a walking stick broke wind, loudly and with great gusto. The throng turned as one.

"What? What?" he cried, waving his hands and staff in the air in mock exasperation. He was trying desperately to stifle a laugh.

"LOKI, LOKI, LOKI!"

First one, then another, and then another began to chant this name. They pointed accusatively in the old man's direction.

Throwing his head back with a howl of laughter, the man stretched up to his full height. Before their eyes, the wizened face and body slowly transformed into a handsome and athletic figure.

It was Loki.

Odin shook his head in despair. Trust him to lower the tone.

Sniggering, and with eyes flashing yellow and green, Loki left Gladsheim feeling very pleased with himself; very pleased indeed. He had embarrassed Odin and in public too. He rubbed his hands gleefully.

Back in the hall, Odin tried once more to calm the crowd. This time, no one would dare repeat Loki's rudeness.

"All hail the new Valkyrie Katarina," Odin cried, thumping his spear down dramatically.

"HAIL WAR!" The people cheered.

"HAIL VALOUR!" The people cheered.

"HAIL ODIN!"

The hall erupted for a third and final time as they roared their salute for Odin's newest maid.

As the crowd chanted and cheered, Loki slipped silently away. He threw a saddle over his horse before galloping off across the bridge.

He was headed in the direction of the white-capped mountains and his departure would have gone unnoticed were it not for Carmel.

She had followed his every move out of the corner of her eye.

Where was he going?

She hoped with all her heart that he would come back soon.

Much later that same day, Odin sat once more in his enchanted garden. Although the sun had long ago set in Asgard, it remained high in the sky here.

Odin's garden was a place outside of space and time; and its sun never stirred in the sky.

Freyja lay beside him, and they talked as they munched the golden apples. They discussed Kat, Odin's wife, Loki, and many other things both past and present. As they chatted they drew closer, and their conversation turned slowly to kisses and to caresses.

While the Norn went about their duties, singing as they tended his garden; Odin and Freyja made love.

They had done this many times before, lying in the shade of Yggdrasill; tenderly wrapped in each other's arms.

15
Evidence

Several days had passed since Dr. Neal met her lonely death in a darkened alleyway. A ridge of high pressure had caused a veil of cold air to hang obstinately over New York. Temperatures were falling and the first snows of winter had arrived. Lacey flakes scurried up 5th Avenue, whipped into flurries by a biting, northern wind.

The days were drawing shorter, fraying tempers with their gloom.

Marcus sat at his desk.

He wasn't a happy man.

To help reduce the size of his in-tray, every Thursday afternoon he would have a clear out; methodically going through the files that lay piled high on his desk. Each week he hoped to close more cases than he opened, but each week he felt a failure. Closing one case while a dozen more opened.

It was a doomed battle.

Like King Canute, he would eventually be drowned by a tide of rising paperwork.

Marcus sighed as he flicked through the files. Two muggings, what looked like a gangland shooting, and a crazy old lady who swore that a neighbour had first kidnapped and then killed her pet cat. Oh yes; this was just another regular week in New York. A sprawling metropolis in the land of the free and home to every loon and two bit criminal who cared to drop in and stay a while. These thoughts cheered him as he scratched at his head; trying to off load files to his assistants.

There was, of course, Dr. Neal's case.

Her file was waiting impatiently near the bottom of his pile. Reaching it at last, he sank back into his chair; tapping a pencil lightly on his desk.

At least here, there had been progress.

As he had suspected, the bullet was lodged in her spine and ballistics had given it a good going over. All they needed now was the gun that fired it. Some poor sod had indeed been through all the dumpsters and trash cans of the street and surrounding areas, but no discarded murder weapon had been found; neither the gun nor the knife. It must have been a thankless task, but every junior had to start somewhere.

The pathologist, Tony, had done a good job in writing up the autopsy report. Cause of death: a single gunshot wound to the heart. He could have considered leaving the single knife wound out, but being the true professional that he was, he had mentioned its presence on the chest without commenting further. He certainly hadn't mentioned the timing of the stab wound; he just left it nice and vague. Part of his routine documentation of other injuries sustained.

DNA from the copious blood stains had come up trumps.

They had a name.

Michael Xavier Warren, or 'Mickey' to his friends—if he had any. About as low a scumbag as you could possible find. A long list of petty convictions and prison stretches going back almost to kindergarten. Marcus held his mug shot in his hand and chuckled to himself.

Xavier? What was his mother thinking?

Middle names never ceased to amaze him. It was the time a mother or father could let rip after the compulsory grandparent's first name, and boy, did some of them do this in style.

Xavier! More like fucking crazier.

Marcus chuckled again.

He had a warrant out for Mickey's arrest, and he knew he would be found soon. Like a bad penny, Mickey would need a score or do something stupid; you could rely on scum like him to turn up. He wouldn't have the money to skip town, and certainly didn't have the sense to lie low.

CCTV footage from the restaurant had been one major disappointment in the case so far. It was poor quality and black and white only. With careful scrutiny both Dr. Neal's and the redhead's entrance to the alley could be seen. They were at the top of the camera's field of view and very blurry. Even with the best possible digital enhancement, there was no way to get a decent image of either from the footage.

One other minor problem in the video recording had been pointed out to him by his assistant. Although you could see the red head entering the alley, there was no footage of her leaving.

This puzzled Marcus.

He had checked the tape and run it forward over two hours after the incident.

There was absolutely no sign of her departure.

He himself had checked the locked steel doors and inhospitable fire escape ladders. There was no other practical exit from the alleyway. The time code on the footage was continuous, so no gaps where they could have missed her. The view of the alleyway too was complete, so no sneaking out either.

He had to confess it was yet another little mystery in Dr. Neal's file that irked him, but as it didn't materially affect the case, he wasn't going to follow it up. He guessed a passing lorry or someone leaving the restaurant could have masked her leaving. That would have been easy to do.

What about the skinny blond girl?

No progress there, but once they got Mickey he would surely rat her up. A shit like him would sell his own grandmother if he thought it would make him money—or cut his stretch behind bars.

Poor Dr. Neal, Marcus sighed; what a crap way to die.

RING-RING, RING-RING!

Shit! More work.

Marcus put the file down and picked up the phone on his desk. The receptionist promptly put him through to an FBI agent by the name of Woods.

"Hello, Finch here," Marcus began, hoping it wasn't going to be another case.

"Good afternoon. Agent Woods here. I understand you are the detective in charge of an incident that occurred last Friday the tenth of December. It was the murder of a young doctor, a lady by the name of Katarina Neal. Would this be correct?"

"Yep," Marcus replied curtly. Nobody liked the FBI snooping around. What were they doing, poking their noses into this particular case? Nothing remarkable about it, unless, that is, Dr. Neal or Mickey were some deep undercover agent or terrorist.

He smiled at this crazy thought.

"How's the case going?" Woods enquired casually.

"Good," replied Marcus. "We have the name of the only suspect and a warrant out for his arrest." He continued; better humour him.

"Ah yes, Michael Xavier Warren. Tell me; how did she die?"

"A single gunshot wound to the heart." Marcus confirmed what Agent Woods already knew.

What did he want?

Fretfully, Marcus screwed his face up as he tried to second guess where Woods was going with his questions.

"I understand there was also a stab wound to the chest. Can you tell me more about this?" Woods continued with his interrogation, politely and calmly, without emotion or a hint as to the reasons behind his questions.

"Yes," Marcus replied, still puzzled. "It was on the left hand side in the region of the heart. It was a clean incision, about three centimetres wide."

"Have you found the knife?"

"No. Nor have we found the gun, but we suspect they will turn up when we detain the suspect." Marcus replied defensively.

Was Woods checking up on his detective work? Was someone trying to accuse him of sloppy practice? Marcus felt his hackles rising.

Just try my job, arsehole; see how you like it.

"I'm sure they will, Detective Finch. Tell me did the pathologist comment on when he thought the stab wound might have been made? Specifically, did he say if it had been made before, or after, Dr. Neal died?" Woods continued without a change in his voice.

"Afterwards," Marcus felt a sinking feeling. Shit, someone WAS checking up on his competence.

"And tell me, Detective Finch, did the pathologist comment on whether the knife had penetrated the heart?"

Oh dear God; he hadn't thought of that!

This was what their conversation was all about. He had been so convinced that a bullet had killed Dr. Neal, he hadn't even considered if the knife might have done so.

Suddenly he felt about two feet small and shrinking fast.

"No he didn't. I'll ask him if you like, and call you straight back." Marcus offered, hoping his voice didn't betray his wilting ego.

"I'll hold, if you don't mind." Agent Woods was polite—but insistent.

Thankfully, a flurry of phone calls quickly tracked Tony down and Marcus put the question to him. To his immense relief, Tony was able to confirm that the knife had penetrated the heart, the left ventricle to be precise. He also kindly re-iterated his presumption that it was the gunshot that had been the cause of death.

Marcus returned to Agent Woods.

"The pathologist has confirmed that the knife did penetrate the heart," Marcus paused, and then added for his own benefit. "He also confirmed that the cause of death was the gunshot wound and not the knife wound." *So "F.U." Mr. high and mighty Agent Woods.* He mouthed this last part silently at the phone.

"Thank you. I agree with you about the cause of death. May I ask where Dr. Neal's body is now?"

"Still in the morgue." Marcus answered this question without really caring. Knowing that his competence was no longer in question, he suddenly felt relieved and exhausted.

"Good. An agent will be down later to collect it. Thank you for your help Detective Finch. Goodbye."

Woods hung up.

Sighing deeply, Marcus returned the phone to its hook before sinking back into his chair.

What the hell was all that about?

16
The Devil Wears Prada

Where was Cole?

As she walked home from the club, this question kept repeating in Ruby's head. It was becoming a mantra. Almost a week had passed since their first meeting, and she hadn't seen or heard from him since. She felt frustrated, and time was short. Dancing night after night before an audience only interested in the size of a woman's tits was not her first choice in careers.

Where was he?

She picked up her pace, walking as fast as her scarlet stilettos would let her. It was a short-ish walk from *The Candy Girls* night club to Jack's Motel, but the weather had turned bitterly cold and a few tired-looking snowflakes were fluttering lazily from the sky above. Ruby had bought a warmer coat and a beret, but they seemed to add little warmth over the skimpy red dress and black belt she was wearing. She knew that Cole would reappear, and she had a hunch that he was checking her out; making sure she had no connections with the police or other criminal gangs. Reassured by this thought, Ruby looked both ways before crossing the road.

Although she didn't want to admit it, she also felt disappointed that Elijah had vanished as well. She hadn't seen him since her first night and she hoped her quip hadn't scared him away. He was a sweet kid, and she meant to keep her word. There would be no more jokes or smart Alec comments at his shyness and old-fashioned politeness.

Finally, she reached the motel.

One good push on the door and she'd be inside.

"Why hello Elijah, how lovely to see you."

Ruby's face lit up as she spied his chubby face behind the desk. It really was a nice surprise and she immediately forgot about Cole.

"Hello, um, I mean, good evening, ma'am." Elijah half bowed, half stood up in a floundering attempt to offer a polite and suitable response.

Ruby looked around. Good, the reception area was free of Cole's goons tonight. Taking a moment, she gave him a cursory inspection.

He had put on a clean shirt and dispensed with that dreadful centre parting he had sported the other evening. She could almost convince herself that he had lost a couple of pounds, too. Yes, she mused, an altogether much smarter turn out tonight.

"Elijah."

"Yes ma'am."

"Would you care to join me for a cup of coffee?"

Ruby genuinely felt she would enjoy a bit of company tonight. Entertainment that was altogether different from the leering, boob pawing, and arse grabbing inhabitants of the club.

"Thank you kindly ma'am, but I can't. I'm on duty."

Ruby was a little taken aback by his rejection.

Perhaps he needed some encouragement?

Slowly, she took off her coat in front of him. It wasn't exactly a strip tease, but she made sure there was enough showmanship to spark his imagination.

She had another idea.

"Would you be kind enough to come up to my room and sort out my shower for me. The hot tap is stiff and I can't turn it on fully."

Ruby looked him squarely in the eye.

"I, I—" Elijah hesitated. This was intimidating. He really shouldn't desert his desk, not when he was alone and so late in the evening.

"Come along," Ruby snapped her fingers in his direction as she walked slowly away toward the lift. Swaying her bottom provocatively, she could sense Elijah's eyes as they followed her every footstep.

"You wouldn't want me to call your manager now, would you?"

Elijah got up hastily and scurried across the hall to join Ruby. He stood close to her, pleading for God's help in keeping his eyes from her shapely waist and peach-like behind.

"Satan's temptress."

His mother's words echoed harshly; and he tried to focus on these as they made their way up to her room.

"It's in there."

Ruby waved her hand in the general direction of the shower when they arrived. Kicking off her Prada stilettos and throwing her coat onto the solitary chair, she lay down on the bed and clasped her hands behind her head. Through half-closed eyes, she watched Elijah as he fiddled with the taps.

"I think it's sorted now, ma'am," Elijah dried his hands and made his way across the room to the door. "Will that be all, ma'am?" he added politely, hand poised over the doorknob. He was in reach of safety; almost free from the temptress—and his own carnal desire.

"Hmmm," Ruby paused, rubbing her right foot provocatively up and down her left shin. "Could you be a real angel and give me a foot massage, please?"

She looked up, grinning cheekily as she pouted coquettishly.

Elijah sighed as he reluctantly inched himself onto the corner of the bed. It was pointless to say no. He knew she would get her way, and he had to end his agony quickly. He fumbled to find a foot, looking away as best he could.

Dear God!

Her breasts were gorgeous.

"Mmmm," Ruby let out a deep gasp of contentment and relaxed backward, shutting her eyes.

Where had he learned to do that?

Elijah had large, soft hands and his massage was both firm and gentle in equal measure. It was, and Ruby felt shocked to admit it, quite possibly the best foot massage she had ever had. It was paradise.

Elijah massaged both of Ruby's feet with all the skill and care he could muster.

Gradually, as the minutes ticked by, they began to relax and to talk about themselves. Ruby was amazed to learn that not only did Elijah have plans to become a doctor, but that he had already got a place at a medical school. He was only working part time to earn the money to pay for his tuition.

He was a nice kid, a really, really nice kid.

For his part, Elijah learnt that Ruby had nothing to do with Satan; far from it. She had a charming personality, one that rivalled her good looks. As he turned to leave the room, he wished her a good night.

For the first time he neither blushed nor felt embarrassed.

The following evening held two pleasant surprises for Ruby.

The first was waiting at the club. It was an exquisite bouquet of twenty-four red roses bound by a large white ribbon. There was a simple message attached: See you soon, sweet cheeks. C—she left the roses on her dressing table.

The second surprise was waiting at the hotel. Elijah hadn't been on duty that evening but lying on the floor outside her room was a very small bunch of pink and white carnations with the message: Thank you, Elijah xx.

Carefully, she arranged these in a vase by her bed and, just before she turned out her light, she wished them a silent goodnight before blowing them a tender kiss.

Elijah was getting under her skin.

17

Getting to Know You

Kat's first week in Asgard passed quickly and peacefully.

In many ways it was her golden era.

At first she dreaded the thought of no mobile phone, no Internet, and no television; but as the days rolled by she didn't think of them or miss them at all. The Valkyries and the other folk at the castle made excellent company and for Kat, it was a pleasure to join such a happy fellowship.

Growing accustomed to castle life, she found that each day followed a similar pattern.

Breakfast would be a leisurely affair with people arriving in dribs and drabs from dawn to mid morning. Porridge was served, made from coarse but freshly milled oats and fortified with wild nuts and berries which tasted delicious. Hunks of rye bread followed. These could be dipped in honey or jam or lightly toasted and then covered with salty, full cream butter. It was a time of light conversation and chat about the day ahead. They all ate heartily as they wouldn't dine again until supper time.

Kat quickly discovered how skilled the Aesir womenfolk were as seamstresses.

New dresses, shoes, and outfits arrived daily and they all fitted perfectly. She was able to make suggestions about the style of clothes she wanted to wear, and diligently the ladies would bring life to her creations. No colour or design seemed beyond their dexterity. When they were within the castle grounds, or practicing in the arenas, the warriors and their maids would often dress casually. However, when they ventured into the town or further afield they dressed more formally in their leather tunics.

As the week went by, Kat learnt more about the code of the Valkyries and she came to accept its value and its worth.

A Valkyrie's first loyalty was to Odin and Freyja, then to each other, and finally to their maids and the Aesir. The Valkyries didn't curse, didn't betray their secrets, and they tended to limit their socialising to the people at the castle. When relaxing and chatting amongst themselves, they used their Midgard names, but when out and about, or talking about each other, they always referred to one other by their formal names. Gradually Kat learned to connect Brynhildr with Jess, Gunnr with Silk, Hlokk with Emile, Herja with Jameela, Goll with Mika and Mist with Eve.

The other three Valkyries remained absent from the castle.

This intrigued Kat, particularly as Jess was vague about their whereabouts. "They were away on important missions," and that was all she would say.

Kat also learned that each warrior only had a single maid. To her immense relief she had become Jess's, and this pleased her greatly. Jess was kind and thoughtful, helping her to adjust slowly to her role, and shielded her from more unpleasant duties that would lie ahead. Their friendship grew ever stronger, and most evenings would end with them chatting by hers, or Jess's, window. When they were alone they would laugh a lot and hold hands like a couple of excited school girls.

It felt good, and they both drew joy from their companionship.

As part of the code, at any one time there could only be nine Valkyrie warriors. When one of them was slain or departed to Valhalla her successor would be chosen from the maids in a tournament. The victorious maid would then be initiated as a warrior in a secret ceremony. It would be during this ceremony that her Valkyrie name would be chosen, and this would stay with her for the rest of her life. Kat found much to admire in the Valkyrie code and its values, and she prayed that she would live up to their high expectations and traditions.

Much of each day was spent training in the arenas, learning the skills needed for war.

Kat was amazed by their fighting prowess and their passion for horses. The Valkyries could ride bareback as well as they could with a saddle and bridle. She loved watching them as they leapt onto their steeds and charged around the arena performing tricks such as hanging from the sides of their horses and twirling around their horses' necks. The most skilled horseman was Balder, and he became her trainer for this discipline.

If ever there was such a thing as the perfect man, it was he; chiselled, hunky, and with endless patience. Kat particularly appreciated this last attribute as her early attempts at riding were pitiful. Oh how she wished he wasn't so totally in love with Silk.

During the day Odin would often wander into Jess's arena and 'borrow' Kat; whisking her away with his ring for an hour or two. Taking her to his garden, he would discuss at length current affairs in Midgard.

Kat quickly became accustomed to using this name for earth.

At first, she was surprised by his detailed knowledge of technology and history. He had a passion for weapons and war, and had an intimate knowledge of these both from times past and times present. She could just imagine him and the Valkyries, stalking the battlefields as war raged all around.

Kat also learned more about Asgard and the mighty ash tree Yggdrasill.

She learned that it embodied the spirit of the realm, and that each of its three great roots ended up in a different kingdom. One ended in the frozen mountains of Jotunheim, another in the volcanic lands of Muspellheim, and the third in Asgard itself. The castle had been built on top of the spring that flowed from this root, and this spring had in turn been made into a well. Odin had named this after his friend, Mimir.

The animals that nibbled around the base of Yggdrasill represented the wildlife of Asgard and the canopy of the tree was its fields and woodlands. As Odin demonstrated, the constant damage due to the roots being frozen in the mountains and boiled in the lava was causing many leaves to wither and die. This was getting worse, and he believed it was evidence that the final battle was drawing near.

Odin knew the name of this battle but he wouldn't speak it.

No-one would.

The battle was cursed, and to utter its name would bring death and destruction to them all.

During their chats, Odin would munch on the golden apples, as would other gods who wandered into the garden. In her naiveté, Kat thought they might get bored of these so on one occasion she presented him, Balder, and Freyja with a napkin of freshly picked strawberries. How they hooted with laughter. They ate the fruit and after thanking her kindly for her consideration, they went back to their apples.

They never did explain why they found this so amusing.

Kat also learned to recognise who in Asgard was actually a god. Each wore a ring made of dwarf gold and their rings were encrusted with diamonds. This important fact helped her, because in all other ways the gods appeared just like everybody else. She also discovered that the more senior in rank the god was, the more diamonds he or she had on their ring.

Evening was her favourite part of day.

After the initial shock, Kat came to love bath time. This was a time when the Valkyries relaxed together and behaved like girls again, leaving their warrior customs behind. Bathing usually lasted about an hour, and afterward they would all dress up for the night's feasting. This was the happiest time, as they swapped outfits, shoes, and jewellery; and spent time helping each other with makeup and hairdos.

Each evening after bathing, a feast would be held in the castle hall. This would be heralded by a loud fanfare of horn blowing and drum beating. Odin or Freyja would start the feast by bringing in a large gold vessel overflowing with the delicious red liquid she had first tasted on her arrival. She soon learnt that the name of this liquid was mead; a potent beverage made from water, fermented honey, and the juices of berries.

The mead in the vessel was particularly special—it came from Valhalla.

Only the warriors and maids were allowed to drink it and the mead never left the castle, other than in the leather flasks the Valkyries carried. It had a miraculous power of healing, and they were encouraged to drink as much of it as they wanted everyday. Kat certainly needed to as she was constantly injuring herself.

Although the company changed from day to day, many faces soon became familiar.

Kvasir was the young, talented harp player who sang so beautifully. Kat soon found he had a wit like a rapier and could compose songs on the hoof. He reduced the hall to tears of laughter one evening with a ditty he made up about her attempts to ride a horse. He was a fun companion and would compliment the Valkyries on their dresses and apparel. Kvasir could pick up and play any instrument. The lute, drums, and the flute all sounded divine in his hands or on his lips.

Hod was also a regular in the evenings. He was the youngest son of Odin and Frigg, and the antithesis of Kvasir. Where Kvasir was outgoing and lively, Hod was quiet and introspective. He was tall and slim to the point of being skinny, and had rounded shoulders and a prominent Adam's apple. In the tradition of Aesir men he was trying to grow a beard. Unlike those of Tyr and Balder which were full and manly, his was merely fluffy and wisp like. In the middle of his upper lip was a small scar from an accident he had suffered as a child. Despite these short comings, Hod was neither ugly nor bad company; he just seemed a little geeky and creepy to Kat—particularly when she compared him to the other more rugged stereotypes.

Considering his unmanly physique, Hod was a surprisingly good hunter and archer, and he was given the task of teaching these skills to Kat. She enjoyed her time with him at first, but quickly realised he was becoming attracted to her. It was the way he held her too close when drawing her bow and how his hands lingered on her bottom when helping her onto a horse. He was always hanging around, and she often caught him staring at her.

Blushes betrayed his desire.

After a few days, Jess banned him from the arena, and Kat was secretly pleased that she had done so. Had Hod not been so young or the son of Odin, Kat would have put him in his place. Patiently, she put up with his infatuation, dismissing his interest as a crush he would quickly grow out of.

Another Valkyrie maid, Carmel, grew on her during the week.

She was buxom, brash, and full of herself, but was always fun to be around. Carmel's skill was in the wielding of the whip, and in time she would teach Kat how to use it. On one memorable day, Carmel put on a stunning display. Throwing the whip from hand to hand she cracked it this way and that, snapping it with equal accuracy and ferocity from each hand. She flicked goblets from posts, snapped small branches from bushes, and tore weapons from hands. On one occasion she cracked her whip in front of Kat's face, a frightening experience she would never forget. Even Jess had to admit that Carmel had nearly as much talent with the whip as the great Prudr herself.

In the evenings, Carmel loved to dance and drink, and she did both with more enthusiasm than skill. As Loki was absent from the hall, Carmel amused herself with seductive displays over the laps of the other men. Fortunately, no one took advantage of these drunken flirtations.

Curiously, Carmel never danced for Hod. She ignored him and never looked at him.

Kat shrewdly guessed that they must have some history together. Certainly, when Hod was not looking at her, he cast longing eyes in Carmel's direction.

Tyr was another god who regularly attended the evenings of feasting. He was strong and brave, and a gifted teller of jokes. Each night he, Balder and many others would tell stories that would have them laughing and crying in equal measures. Some would be true and some complete rubbish, although it was often anybody's guess as to which would be which.

Kat also grew attached to Emile, the Valkyrie Hlokk. She was French by birth, and retained her wonderful accent. Emile was short with long, wavy, mousy hair and a cherubic face. Her nose was pert and upturned and she had dimples on both cheeks.

Emile was the female equivalent of Loki.

Loud and bubbly, she was always the first to play a practical joke or start a fight. Kat felt she lived up well to her Valkyrie name, which meant 'the noise of battle.' She was the finest warrior with a spear, and Kat soon discovered that she too had a natural talent with this weapon. Perhaps it was because she had excelled at athletics at school, or because of her strong arms from marshal arts. Either way, this was the weapon she was most comfortable with.

These idyllic days rolled by all too quickly, and it was not long before a week had passed. It was then that a gentle wind of change passed through the castle.

It started with Kat being awoken by a fearful noise. A constant barrage of clanging and banging that was coming from somewhere around the castle, making the room shake with its ferocity.

Following the trail of the hammering, Kat found herself in the small foundry next to the stables. Standing in front of the furnace, and bashing away at a piece of metal on his anvil, was the silhouette of a short, squat man. His head appeared almost shaven, and his face sported a long and unkempt ginger beard. There was only one person in all of Asgard who could match the description of this new arrival at the castle.

Thor.

Kat stepped forward hesitantly and called out "Hello."

There was no reply.

She stepped closer and called again—still no reply. Finally when she was about an arm span away from him she bellowed "Hello!"

The hammering stopped and Thor turned round.

"Do you like eating?" he asked, looking her slowly up and down.

"Yes, Yes, I suppose I do," she replied cautiously.

"Do you like drinking?" he asked again, spitting a spittoon of herbal leaves crudely onto the straw below.

"Yes, of course," she replied more assertively. Just why he asked these questions she didn't know.

"Hmmm," he paused as he rubbed his beard. "Then I suppose we'll get along."

And with that, he went back to his hammering.

Kat watched and waited politely as he continued with his work. She had never seen a man built more squarely than Thor. He seemed as wide as he was tall, and had the largest muscles on his arms and chest that she had ever seen. His neck was short and bull like and he never wore a shirt. He had a rugged but kindly face with sharp blue eyes. Thor's breeches were stained and dirty from his travels, and they were held up by a mighty leather belt into which were tucked his chain metal gloves and hammer. The hammer seemed quite small and had an unusually short handle.

After some minutes of waiting, Kat deemed that their conversation must be over. As she turned to go, Thor suddenly stopped what he was doing and turned to face her.

This time he had a smile on his lips and a hunk of white hot metal in his tongs.

"Now tell me fair Kat, how long would you like your sword?"

18

It's Just a Ride

Cole straightened his tie carefully, turning from side to side as he admired his reflection in the limousine's small mirror. He checked the time on his large jewel encrusted watch, and then casually played with the neck of a bottle of champagne that lay in the cooler beside him. Sitting back in his chair, he took a small sip from a glass of Jack D that was close at hand.

Cole was a sharp dresser and tonight was no exception.

Charcoal grey pin stripe suite—tailor made of course—crisp white linen shirt and an exquisite pink and blue striped Italian silk tie. His black leather shoes were made by hand, and they had been buffed to a shine that was almost luminous. He liked to look good, and for Cole these days that look was expensive.

There was a tap on the window and the door to the limo opened. A white stiletto shoe presented itself followed by a long, long black leg—Ruby at last.

It was the day after the bouquet of flowers and Ruby had anticipated Cole would show tonight. She had paid extra special attention to what she was wearing before leaving for the club. Choosing a short, strapless, white satin dress that hugged her body like a glove, she had accessorised with matching white stilettos, jacket, and, of course, fish net stockings. These were always good for a man's imagination. She had pulled her hair back tightly, its sleekness accentuating her high cheekbones and large eyes.

Ruby had expected him to come and watch her in the club, and had been caught out when the floor manager curtly pulled her early from the show and told her to get out back where she was wanted. As she stepped into the limousine she felt quietly satisfied. At least Cole turned up with a touch of class and theatre. This would help make the evening easier and pass much more quickly.

A brief greeting over, Ruby sank back into a sumptuous leather seat. She finally had the time to study Cole properly, and she did so as the limo sped deeper into the city lights.

Cole was a handsome man, dashing and immaculately groomed. 'Vain' would be the one word she would have used to describe him, if she could choose only one word. He was a big man, in all departments, as the other girls at the club had delighted in telling her. He was well muscled and had a clean-shaven head, apart from a thin sliver of groomed stubble. This traced a line from the front of his ears, around the angle of his jaw and ended just before his chin. He was wearing black sun glasses, as he usually did, and the skin around his neck and sunken cheeks bore pock marked scars from acne when he was a teenager. There was a long, jagged scar that ran down the middle of his left cheek. This scar was heavily pigmented and raised, Keloid in nature. Far from making Cole look ugly, these markings enhanced his rugged looks.

If it weren't for his past, he would have made a fine catch for any upwardly mobile woman.

Cole had arranged to take Ruby to a smart up town restaurant close to Broadway. He hadn't decided if he wanted to watch a show with her or not. If he chose to, the best tickets in any house were only ever a phone call away. It was a perk of his particular line of business.

The limo wove slowly through the late night traffic and Cole and Ruby sat side by side; mostly in silence. Cole was a man of few words, and Ruby found conversation with him awkward and painful—a bit like pulling teeth. In many ways she was grateful for the silence, she had little she wanted to say and less she wanted to hear. The lull in conversation continued throughout the meal, which was at an intimate VIP table in a restaurant steeped in classical grandeur. A string quartet played music in the background, large bouquets of fresh flowers festooned rich mahogany tables and the waiters wore dinner jackets and bow ties. It was the sort of place where rich people with generations of pedigree dined, and where the nouveau riche ate with hopes of joining their elite, but knew they never could.

The snobbery didn't seem to affect Cole.

There were frequent interruptions to their meal as he fielded calls on his mobile phone. He spoke quietly in clipped sentences, and on one occasion he got up and moved somewhere where he could talk out of earshot. Ruby wasn't going to be invited into his inner sanctum of trusted friends any time soon. Ruby relaxed and enjoyed the excellent food, the best she had tasted since her arrival in New York. Conversation with Cole was unimportant, as was the limo, and the meal. It was all just meaningless foreplay; a peacock's display laid on to impress her and let her know that he was a man of substance and breeding.

She had read this book before, and bought the T-shirt, too.

Meal out of the way, they returned to the limousine. As they stretched out in the back, Ruby thanked Cole for a lovely evening.

"So, where to Legs?"

Cole turned toward her and flashed a smile. This gleamed with perfect white teeth, all beautifully crafted by dentists in hours of costly and painstaking work.

It was the million dollar question—and bang on cue.

Ruby reached forward slowly and tapped on the smoked glass screen that separated them from the chauffer. This glided down silently.

"Cole's place," she requested calmly, and the screen glided effortlessly back up.

Ruby returned to her seat and without looking at Cole she lit a cigarette, inhaling deeply. She liked her nickname "Legs." *Rather appropriate,* she thought.

Exhaling slowly, she watched the smoke as it curled from the corners of her nose and mouth.

Now it was her turn to put on a show, let him feel the pedigree of her breeding.

"Sweet," Cole murmured appreciatively as he took another sip of Jack D.

19

The Winds of Change

On the same day that Thor arrived at the castle, Odin departed. He left suddenly and without fanfare. Had Kat not been awake so early she would never have seen him go. Blue cloak blowing in an early morning breeze and hat pulled down over his eyes; his horse trotted slowly down the hill and across the river Iving before breaking into a slight canter and disappearing amongst a thicket of trees. Apparently, this was not at all unusual as Jess explained later at breakfast. Odin loved to travel, and when he and Thor were together there were usually arguments. For the sake of everyone at the castle, it was probably better this way.

Kat felt she would miss him; she had enjoyed their little chats.

Breakfast over, they both went upstairs to their rooms and got ready for the day. Kat had finally received her fighting tunic and she was itching to try it on. The short pleated skirt was made of heavy leather and had been reinforced with metal studs to add weight and a menacing look. She put on the broad belt, which had a loop ready for her sword. The thought of this sent a tingle down her spine. Thor himself was making this for her and she could hardly wait to hold the finished blade in her hands.

Lacing her leather bodice tightly at the front, she traced her fingers round the etchings of swans, falcons, and horses. These had been intricated carved. Finally, she could pass as a Valkyrie.

Already hours of strenuous training were beginning to show.

Gone were her soft arms and the ripple of puppy fat round her belly. These had been replaced by a tautness and muscle definition which would have been the envy of her friends. For the first time, she paused and reflected on what they might all be doing now. Her life as a doctor in New York seemed such a long time ago, and surprisingly, it no longer seemed to matter. It was as though a veil was being slowly drawn between then and now, the memories fading faster than a winter's sun.

Sighing at her brief moment of nostalgia, she turned and headed off toward the arena. She walked proudly, appreciating the nods of approval from townsfolk she passed on the way.

At last, I look like a Valkyrie, she thought smugly.

In the absence of a sword, Jess had decided to start teaching Kat in the art of knife fighting. This was her speciality, and a skill admired by the other Valkyries. Jess could throw knives faster and more accurately than anyone else. She enjoyed winning bets by stabbing her knife repeatedly between the outstretched fingers of terrified volunteers whilst she was wearing a blindfold. It was showy, it was fun, and no one had lost a finger yet.

Just as they were about to start training, a drum started to pound a dull beat. The sound came from Gladsheim and it echoed with a slow, pulseless rhythm; which was both melancholy and foreboding. Kat noted a black flag had been hoisted and the presence of a bright rainbow in the sky.

She turned to Jess expectantly.

"A new prisoner from Midgard," Jess began grimly, clearly not wanting to discuss this with Kat. "I might have to go…" her voice trailed off as the sound of horses' hooves clattering on cobbles passed by. It was Freyja, with Silk and Carmel close behind.

As they passed, Carmel waved from her horse before flashing a wicked smile and making a gesture of a knife being drawn slowly across her throat.

Kat shuddered.

This was the dark side of being a Valkyrie and Carmel seemed to relish it. Kat knew that part of their role was to deal with villains, but it was harsh and distasteful work and she was dreading the moment when she too would get involved.

Carmel's cavalier attitude alarmed her.

Jess turned back to Kat and smiled. There was a visible air of relief about her face, knowing that Silk would assist Freyja in judgement today. It was important that Kat's training became more intense and much more focused. Kat was now a maid and yet had only the fighting skills of an average Aesir teenager.

Things had to improve and fast.

Jess was about to say something when a dreadful bellowing erupted from below her arena.

"Oh botheration; what now?" she exclaimed irritably as she excused herself; disappearing down some steps that lead to a heavily bolted iron gate.

Kat knew there were cells beneath each of the nine arenas, and both prisoners and wild beasts were chained there. She also knew that the steps lead down to these cells. The prisoners were Jess's responsibility and they were used for live training. Fortunately, Kat hadn't taken part in any of that yet. As she listened, she realised it was the first time she had heard noises from below. She guessed that the sound of the drum had aroused them. The noises continued, until there was a dull thud. Shortly afterwards, Jess reappeared.

Blood was on her hands.

Neither of them spoke further about this.

Jess worked Kat hard that day, hoping that the physical strain on her body would stop her thinking about the morning's events. It was important that Kat accepted the life of a Valkyrie at her own pace, and didn't worry about duties that would come naturally with time. When they finally finished they found Hod, as usual, waiting outside the arena.

Since Jess had banned him from coming in, he had taken to hanging around outside, waiting to walk back to the castle with Kat. This afternoon he complimented her enthusiastically on her new clothes, using it as an excuse to toy with the detail in the pleats of her skirt and bodice. Kat could feel his hands pawing lecherously at her, and she counted slowly to ten. She didn't want to hurt his feelings, but she found his clumsy attempts at flirtation annoying. If he was really interested in her, then why didn't he just go ahead and ask her out? She might even say yes, you never knew. *Oh, but all this adolescent dithering!* She shook her head irritably as they continued on their way to the castle; where they were greeted with a flurry of activity.

For the first time since her arrival, bathing was a brief affair.

The warriors talked in hushed tones amongst themselves, and no one would enlighten Kat. They dressed quickly, and put on their cloaks of feathers and helmets. Bearing their spears and swords, they hastened down the stairs to be met at the bottom by Freyja. With barely a word spoken, they formed up in pairs and marched down the final spiral until they were out of view.

They had gone to the Chamber of the Valkyries.

Time passed slowly for Kat as she waited patiently for Jess in the hall.

At one point, the castle seemed to shake slightly. It was as though an underground train was passing beneath it. The vibrations didn't last long, but they struck her as unusual. Too small for an earthquake, yet too large to be man made. After what seemed an age, but was probably no more than an hour, the warriors finally re-emerged.

Six Valkyrie had gone down, but only five came up.

To her immense relief Jess was amongst them.

The Valkyrie who was missing was Herja—the 'devastator.'

Kat knew her as Jameela.

20

A Day at the Zoo

*I*t was just sex.

Ruby reminisced over last night's encounter with Cole as she waited by the lift in her motel. Good sex it may well have been, but that was all it was—meaningless, emotionless, pass-the-time sex.

The night had ended in his penthouse in a totally predicable fashion.

She had put on a show, and his eyes had greedily followed her. They had enjoyed a brief cocktail before subduing the lights and slithering seductively into bed; writhing and heaving between black, satin sheets to the strains of *Tangerine Dream*.

Cole had fucked her hard, eager to prove that he was the boss and that size, in his case, really did matter. For her part, Ruby had reciprocated with gusto. She rode him ferociously as if she were on a rodeo steer; nails and heels digging into his body until they drew blood. They jousted like sexual gladiators between the sheets, first one on top and then the other, each determined to fuck the bigger climax from each other. In the end, it was probably a draw. Ruby suspected that Cole had met his first sexual equal in bed.

She was hooking him hard, and she needed to for what she had in mind.

Ruby hadn't stayed the night, preferring to hail a cab and return to the motel in the small hours. Today was her day off, and she had happy plans which she wanted to enjoy to the full. She left her thoughts of Cole behind her as she got into the lift and went downstairs.

Elijah was waiting patiently in the cold outside. It was ten thirty, and a watery sun was trying to peep through the cold December sky. *It is so lovely,* Ruby thought as she stepped out onto the sidewalk, *not to have to dress up today.*

She had thrown on some tight denim jeans, boots, and a loose but warm sweater. She wore minimal make-up and had barely combed her hair. It didn't matter. To Elijah she would be a goddess even if she'd turned up in a bin liner. She kissed him warmly on the cheek, and they headed off toward the subway.

Since the evening of the foot massage they had struck up a friendship.

Elijah remained shy and polite while Ruby did the courting. It was fun, gently encouraging him to come out for a walk or a coffee, watching his blushes fade and his confidence grow with each encounter. After a whole week of flirting, she had finally persuaded him that he really did want to take her out and show her the sights of New York.

The day passed quickly.

They window shopped, ate lunch in a sandwich bar, and then enjoyed a visit to central park zoo. Ruby loved animals, and enjoyed the rich variety they found there. She loved the ruffed lemurs, parrots, and tamarins in the tropical zone. Creatures she had never seen before.

Unfortunately Ruby's delight in seeing the animals was not always reciprocated. To Elijah's alarm, the polar bears roared and paced, and the snow leopards snarled and pulled back their ears. The animals' sixth sense told them that Ruby was different, something to be feared, and that her presence was unwelcomed in their safe and cozy zoo.

Afternoon tea and cakes followed at the zoo's restaurant, and despite the freezing winter weather, they licked ice-creams as they walked across Central Park. The setting winter's sun glowed weakly in the sky and Elijah didn't notice the pet lovers who straining at their leashes as their dogs barked and snarled fearfully at them.

Catching a bus back, it was well after sundown when they finally arrived at the motel.

"Would you like to come up for a coffee?"

Ruby held both Elijah's hands in hers. She already knew the answer, but she wanted to invite him anyway.

Elijah hesitated and flicked a glance at his watch.

"I can't I'm sorry. My Mom will be worried and I have to get her tea ready."

Ruby already knew that his mother, Rosemary, was crippled with multiple sclerosis and confined to a wheelchair. She depended on him.

"I understand."

Ruby felt sad, really sad. The day had been so relaxed and such easy going. There had been no pressure, no pretension—just two friends enjoying each other's company. She wanted the day to continue, feeling safe and secure with Elijah—confident in his honourable intentions. Squeezing his hand, she leaned forward and planted a kiss on his lips. She lingered for a minute, letting him know it was more than just the kiss of a friend.

Elijah recoiled, heart pounding and blushing once more. He tried to speak, but he couldn't find the words. Beaming broadly, he stuttered good night and sped off down the street. Ruby followed him with her eyes until he turned the corner and disappeared from view. He was such a sweet boy, so like the one true love she had had long ago.

Turning, she pushed her way through the heavy motel door. Neither she nor Elijah had spotted a man sitting in a car on the opposite side of the street.

He was known as "Slim," and he was one of Cole's men.

Unfortunately, Slim had noticed them.

21

Hello and Goodbye

The day after Thor's arrival seemed to start well. During the night a rumble beneath the castle heralded the return of the Valkyrie Skogul. This news cheered everybody at the breakfast table. Despite the general air of jocularity, Kat could see that Jess was pensive and preoccupied. When she asked why, Jess put this down to planning what they would be doing for the day. However, just before they set off for the arena, Freyja called Jess for a private talk in her chambers. These lasted over an hour. When Jess finally emerged, she was even less chatty and more withdrawn.

Something was going on, and this made Kat uneasy.

The two girls walked in silence to the arena, which was in marked contrast to the excited atmosphere that buzzed around them. Today there was going to be a public flogging, the prisoner who had been sentenced from yesterday, and the Aesir were already fighting for the best seats.

Unfortunately for Kat, this would take place in Skogul's arena, which lay next to theirs. Any hope of serious training was immediately dashed by an endless procession of townsfolk, skipping merrily across their sandy arena.

The mirth and happiness of the Aesir was in marked contrast to that of the prisoner, who Kat could just make out through the entrance to Goll's arena. Stretched and spread eagled between two tall posts, he hung there naked; his head hanging limply forward. Stripped of his clothes and his dignity, Kat felt a wave of pity for the man. This punishment seemed ghoulish and barbaric, and to her horror she noted there were similar posts in Jess's arena. She knew she could never get used to this sort of cruelty, no matter how long her stay in Asgard.

She could never whip someone, ever.

As the seats gradually filled up, the stream of passing Aesir settled to a more manageable trickle. They could finally get to work.

"HEY!"

Jess erupted suddenly, in a loud and ecstatic greeting. She held her arms triumphantly above her head.

Kat turned, and saw the figure of Skogul walking slowly across the arena. She embraced Jess warmly before Kat was presented to her.

"Lovely to meet you fair Kat," Skogul extended a firm handshake, and then added. "Please call me Zara, it sounds so much friendlier."

Kat smiled and nodded.

Besides being the tallest of the Valkyries, hence her name Skogul, she had noted Zara was limping as she walked. Now being up close, she could see a large bruise on her right cheek and a deep gash across her shoulder. The mission must have been tough, although her injuries did little to spoil her beauty. She had short platinum blond hair and an angular face that lit up when she smiled.

"Is he one of yours?" Jess nodded her head in the direction of the prisoner.

"Yep, He's a real bad piece of work. Drugs, murder, rape. The usual rubbish you get in Midgard." Zara spat on the floor and then winced. Flecks of blood stained her spittle and moving her jaw caused obvious pain.

"Did you have much trouble?" Kat enquired.

"Some, but nothing I couldn't handle," Zara replied dismissively. Her injuries were trivial and of little consequence.

"Are you giving the flogging?"

"Gracious no," Zara exclaimed. "It needs someone with much more zip in their arms. I've asked Gunnr if she would permit fair Carmel to do it. She's the best, in the absence of Prudr, of course."

Kat was still getting used to the way the Valkyries spoke about each other. She found it quaint when they referred to their maids as fair this and fair that. As far as she could see, other than in her face, Carmel was anything but fair.

"How many lashes?" Jess asked as casually if she was asking how many lumps of sugar Zara would like in a cup of tea.

Zara shrugged her shoulders as a loud voice answered suddenly from behind.

"Fifty!"

It was Silk, closely followed by Carmel, who was relishing the prospect of being centre stage in the morning's show.

The five of them formed a small group; Silk had her hands on her hips while Carmel's twitched eagerly at the butt of her whip.

This dangled menacingly from her belt.

"Would you like to come and see a real demonstration of whipping, hey, Kat? You can have a ringside seat," Carmel sneered, her face transforming into a wicked contortion as she spoke about the horror she was about to inflict.

Kat felt her blood run cold.

Words couldn't describe how much she didn't want to join the spectacle, but how could she say no?

"Come on Kitty Kat," this time it was Silk's turn to goad her. "You're far too soft on her, Brynhildr. This will make her tough, like my Carmel here."

With obvious pride, Silk patted Carmel affectionately on her bottom.

"Yeh, I might even let you have a go."

Carmel was taunting her, too. She could see Kat's discomfort and was revelling in it.

"I, I, I..." Kat stuttered. It seemed her only hope of escape was for the ground to swallow her whole.

"Sorry Silk, she can't," Jess mercifully came to her rescue. Pulling her knife from her belt, she twirled it casually in her hand.

"You see, I've already made plans to emasculate a couple of prisoners this morning," she toyed provocatively with her knife. "Kind of thought she might enjoy it, get to taste some REAL action." She added, staring deliberately at Carmel.

"Okay, okay, you and Kitty Kat, you go and have some fun."

Silk sidled away, taking Zara in tow.

"Yeh, Kitty Kat, have fun. Meow!" Carmel added mockingly as she swaggered after them. She accentuated her usual strut as she walked, hoping this would add insult to injury.

"We aren't really going to—" Kat faltered, alarm rising in her voice. "You know?"

"Of course not," Jess hugged her reassuringly. "Just couldn't let Gunnr get one over me, that's all."

Kat giggled, a wave of relief flooded her body.

Thank goodness for rivalry between the Valkyries.

"Come on, let's get out of here and go fishing," Jess took her by the arm and they headed off toward the river Iving. They had to travel a long way before they could no longer hear the crack of Carmel's whip, the screams of the prisoner, and the excited roaring of the crowd.

Late that afternoon, Jess and Kat returned empty handed from their trip. Despite not catching anything, both were in good spirits and Jess's melancholy seemed to have lifted. They knew that bath time tonight was going to be riotous, and it didn't disappoint. In the thick of it was Carmel, gleefully holding court and accepting praise and lavish compliments for her prowess and ferocity that morning. Kat tried to ignore her, choosing instead to reflect upon Jameela who was now absent from their fellowship.

Jameela was an Indian girl and like the other Valkyries, she was reluctant to talk about her life on Midgard, or how and why she had come to Asgard. She was a quiet girl, in her early twenties, who tended to keep herself to herself. She had bold features, a heavy jowl and full, pouting lips. Her eyes were her finest attribute. Large, brown and almond-shaped, she accentuated them with kohl so that they flashed and smouldered in a manner that made her the scariest looking of the warriors. It had come therefore as something of a surprise when, as Kat got to know her, she turned out to be both charming and gentle. She was an excellent classical Indian dancer, she sang beautifully, and she enjoyed reading. Her gentleness seemed in stark contrast to her ruthless proficiency with the Chack ram. This was a sharp, disk-shaped weapon once used by Sikh's in Midgard. This weapon was unique to her, and Kat was relieved she didn't have to master it.

"So Kitty Kat, what did you think of Carmel today?"

It was Emile, splashing her with water, who drew her back into the conversation.

"Oh, I'm sure she was excellent. Sorry, I was miles away," Kat splashed Emile back. Obviously Kitty Kat was going to be her new nick name, and it sounded warm and friendly coming from her lips.

It was a good sign, and one that proved she was beginning to fit in.

"What were you thinking about?" Zara joined in their conversation. She too, was getting a little bored with Carmel's one tracked ego ride.

"I don't know what to do about Hod." Kat thought fast and then deliberately lied. She knew if she spoke about Jameela the conversation would quickly dry up.

"He's always hanging around and it's getting annoying. I would like to do something, but he's the son of Odin. I don't know how to shake him off without offending him, or Odin, for that matter."

"Oh that's so easy," Carmel butted in to howls of raucous laughter as the other girls splashed Kat.

"How?" Kat coughed and spluttered, half drowned by their onslaught.

"Well let me see, how did Jess and I get rid of him when he had crushes on us?" Carmel teased.

"Jess?"

Kat turned to her. She was surprised by this revelation.

"I just offered to emasculate him," Jess made a slicing motion in the air with an imaginary knife. "And that was that, he lost interest immediately. What a shame." She smiled slyly as she faked wiping a tear from her eye.

Kat had already learnt from the other girls of Jess's fascination with castration. She loved its effects on men; calming them down and making them more docile. "Asgard is a safer place without testicles," was her favourite phrase, and she frequently put her words into deeds.

"I think I'll pass on that one if you don't mind. What about you Carmel?"

Kat turned to her hopefully.

This innocent question caused a further uproar in laughter around the room. Clearly whatever she had done had created quite a stir.

"I arm-wrestled him, and won," Carmel finally declared when the merriment died down; slapping the water hard as she did so with a theatrical flourish.

"I beat him in the great hall in front of everybody. He was so embarrassed; we all nearly died with laughter."

The girls collapsed once more and Kat waited calmly for their laughing to subside. They were in high spirits tonight.

"Are there any sensible suggestions?" Kat asked more hopefully than expectantly. No one seemed to be taking her situation at all seriously.

"What you need," this time it was Silk's turn to chime in. "Is to take a lover. That will get him off your back." She spoke in her characteristic flat and expressionless voice.

The girls all smirked at one another, behaving as if they were about to let Kat into one of Asgard's biggest secret.

"Shall I tell her who we have in mind?" Carmel enquired.

After giggling loudly, they shouted together in a chorus of appreciation.

"FREYJA'S BROTHER!"

The tub erupted once more into a water fight and fits of laughter.

Whoever this person was, his ears must surely be burning.

"Hey Kat, come over here, come quickly," Jess called excitedly to her to come over to the window. Something unusual was visible in the sky, and it would help distract Kat before she gave her the bad news.

Both girls had come up early from the supper feasting tonight, bored with the umpteenth retelling of Carmel's exploits. She was still going strong, milking every last drop of praise from their friends.

Kat came over to the window and looked out. The sun had set less than half an hour ago, and in the sky above the snow-peaked mountains, veils of coloured lights weaved and danced in the gathering darkness.

"Wow!" Kat breathed, awestruck by the magical display.

She drew closer to Jess.

"It's the dwarves making gold," Jess whispered, hoping to hold Kat's happiness and attention for just a little while longer.

"Mmmm," Kat murmured jokingly. "Seems more like the Northern Lights in Midgard."

She laughed, and Jess joined in.

There were many instances where the beliefs of the Aesir could be explained by natural phenomena.

Kat had learned a bit about Jess's past since they met.

Jess had been brought up in Ireland in the 1960's and 1970's and had died in some undercover military operation there. Because of this, she could discuss issues like the Aurora Borealis without risking offence. Some of the more senior Valkyries, and Prudr was the most senior, had lived in times far more distant and sheltered. They fully accepted the Aesir's superstitious folklore. Kat had to be careful with whom she shared her opinions, and how far she took them. At least with Jess, she felt she could discuss anything. It surprised her, however, how little interest Jess and others had in their former lives.

Maybe they didn't want to be reminded of the pain they'd suffered? She hoped she would always keep an interest, although she could already feel this gently slipping away.

"Did you hear that?" Kat enquired anxiously, putting her arm around Jess and squeezing her close. A dreadful howling and baying was coming from the direction of the mountains.

"Shush," Jess was listening intently. "They're Fenrir's wolves. Listen, can you hear that one?"

Kat nodded. A howl rose louder and higher than all the others.

She shivered at its eerie sound.

"That one's Fenrir. He's Loki's wolf. He's the leader of the pack." She looked at Kat and could see her shaking.

"Don't worry, dearest Kat, they're many miles away in the mountains, in the kingdom of Jotunheim. There's no need to be afraid."

Stroked her hair lovingly, Jess wrapped her arms around Kat, rocking her gently from side to side. She hummed a lullaby softly in her ear as she did so.

Kat loved feeling Jess so close to her. She was always so calm and so strong.

They cuddled like this for a long time, listening to the wolves fading into the distance and watching the lights flickering across the sky. Finally, when Kat seemed calmer, Jess pulled away. Taking both of Kat's hands in hers, she turned and faced her.

"I have to tell you something," she began.

They stared at each other.

It was hard to say who was going to feel the more pain with what was about to be said.

"I'm going away soon on a mission."

"How soon?" Kat interrupted anxiously.

"Very soon—tomorrow."

Jess looked down at her feet; she couldn't bear to see the pain in Kat's eyes.

Somehow Kat had guessed this was coming. It was a woman's sixth sense, or something like it, but it didn't make the news any easier. The bottom was falling out of her world. Her one true friend was leaving and she would be alone once more in this strange and scary realm.

Emotions welled swiftly.

What if she were never to see Jess again? Never hold her hands or see those beautiful, pale blue eyes? Her wonderful smile and her laugh like the sweetest of birdsongs?

Without thinking, Kat pressed herself close to Jess. Clasping both her cheeks in her hands, she kissed her lips hard.

"I love you so much," Kat whispered tenderly when at last their mouths parted.

It was all too much.

She was losing her best friend, and now the stupid 'L' word meant Jess would be lost forever. Kat hurried across the room to the door, tears welling in her eyes. She had to get away before humiliating herself further. She cursed her sudden rashness, what on earth had made her act so stupidly?

This just wasn't her, feeling so intense and behaving so emotionally.

"Please Kat, wait."

In one quick bound Jess leapt across the room and forced the door shut. She wasn't going to let her leave, not like this. Turning Kat around, she pressed her roughly against the door; crushing her body firmly against Kat's.

Kat was breathing rapidly, gripped by the wildest feelings of fear, excitement, anxiety, and passion.

"Thank you, my dearest darling."

Jess returned the kiss, but this time her lips parted and their tongues entwined, furtively tasting each other's desire.

Kat felt Jess's hands caress her body, and she knew that Jess wanted her.

In a frenzy of crazed emotion, they twirled toward the bed; tearing excitedly at each other's clothes. Falling in a heap, Kat landed on top. She straddled Jess's hips and held them firmly between hers. Embracing once more, she thrust her tongue deep into Jess's mouth, hoping she would understand her intent, and know her desire.

Jess did.

In one swift move she flipped Kat over and forced herself on top. Sliding her hand up between Kat's legs—she parted these hungrily.

Kat begged to have Jess inside her.

Jess's lips were moving swiftly now, nibbling and caressing first her neck, then her breasts, and her stomach. Kat gasped, and clenched Jess's hair between her fingers. She could feel the warmth of Jess's hand, soft fingers gently probing at her sweetness. Kat's breath now came in short gasps, as waves of pleasure wracked her body. It felt so good, so pure…so right.

Closing her eyes, Kat gave herself to Jess.

Kat stayed the night, safe and secure in Jess's bed. In the early hours of the morning they made love once more. This time it was less frenzied as they tenderly explored each other's bodies.

Dawn broke at last, and while Kat carried on sleeping, Jess got up, changed quietly, and then went about waking the other warriors.

By the time Kat finally awoke; Jess was gone.

22

Behind Bars

Marcus had a satisfied smile on his face. It was one of those rare days when just occasionally you get things right. He hadn't had one of these for a long time, so he took his time and savoured the moment.

He was standing behind the one way glass looking into the interrogation room. Sitting and fidgeting nervously before him was Michael Xavier Warren. If ever there was a contender for failure of a lifetime, Marcus knew he was looking at it.

Drug dealer, user, pimp, thief, thug, the list went on and on. Now, at last, Mickey had joined the big boys' league—murder, first degree. Congratulations, he smiled ruefully; you've graduated.

As he had predicted, Mickey didn't skip town and hadn't had the sense to lie low. No, his friend Mickey got into an altercation at the local corner store whilst he was holding it up. Presumably he had run low on cash and was looking for money for his next score.

Mickey looked in a bad way.

Nervous, agitated, sweating; with those horrible little muscle spasms you see when someone is about to go cold turkey. He didn't look well, not well at all.

For some inexplicable reason, Mickey hadn't got his gun on him when he was arrested. However, the pistol had turned up in a cursory search of his flat. Ballistics confirmed that it had fired the bullet which killed Dr. Neal. Mickey's fingerprints were all over the gun, too.

They had the gun, the bullet, and his blood at the crime scene.

"Jesus Christ," Marcus guffawed as he spoke out loud. "All we need now is a bleeding T-shirt and video of him pulling the trigger."

He pitied the poor state attorney who would have to defend him. There was no way out of this rap, no sir.

Mickey was going down—and for a long time, too.

Marcus picked up Dr. Neal's file and went to open the door to the room.

Must remember to ask Mickey why he stabbed Dr. Neal.

Marcus decided to make a mental note of this. After all, that was about the only interesting thing left in this case. He still couldn't get his head round it, why stab her after he'd shot her?

He was looking forward to hearing Mickey's reply.

"Good afternoon."

Marcus sat down on the plastic fold up chair across the table. Mickey didn't look up; and he didn't reply.

"Can you confirm that you are Michael Xavier Warren?" he asked.

Mickey sort of grunted and nodded a reply. He still didn't look up.

Marcus would take that as a "Yes" then.

"Can you tell me where you were on Friday the tenth of December from about eight in the evening?" he decided to press on with his questioning.

"Dunno," came an unhelpful mutter.

Marcus wondered why he had bothered asking the question.

"Do you recognise this person?" he pushed some photographs of Dr. Neal across the table. Mickey didn't pick them up.

"Nah," he continued to stare at the floor, nervously chewing at his fingernails.

Marcus drummed his fingers on the table. He was getting pissed off. This was not what he needed this afternoon. Signalling to the police officer, the tape recorder was switched off.

"Look, you worthless piece of shit! I know you killed this woman. I've got your gun, your finger prints, your bullet, and your fuckin' blood at the crime scene. Now, stop jerking me around and start talking!"

Mickey looked up.

Finally, Marcus had his attention.

Looking at Mickey's face, he could see, with some satisfaction, cuts and fading bruises from his encounter with Dr. Neal. His nose was swollen and crooked too; definitely broken. He had been right, Dr. Neal had given this loser a good beating before the coward had shot her dead.

Mickey picked up the pictures and held them close to his face. Screwing up his eyes, he studied them intently.

"That fuckin' bitch!" He suddenly cried. "She fuckin' attacked me! She was crazy, like some fuckin' animal, totally whacked out on speed or something. I'm the fuckin' victim here, not 'er. I had to shoot 'er. Get 'er off me, it was fuckin' self-defence."

Mickey was shouting and swearing hysterically.

"All right, all right, calm down, calm down," slowly Marcus got him to stop ranting and raving. "Do you have any witnesses who can support this claim?" Feeling relieved that at last Mickey was talking, he signalled to the officer to switch the tape recorder back on.

Mickey paused, and thought hard.

"Nah."

"What about your girlfriend? We've got a witness who says he saw someone with you. Can you give me her name and address?"

"Nah, She's no good, we ain't seein' each 'uva no more," he mumbled this before returning his gaze to the floor.

"Look, Mickey," Marcus tried to be helpful. "I need a name. If what you say is true, then maybe we can get the charges reduced, perhaps to accidental manslaughter or something like that?"

There was a long pause as Mickey digested the possibility of a lifetime that wasn't going to be spent behind bars.

"Rose. Her name's Rose. I dunno her address but I've got her phone number."

Marcus breathed a sigh of relief. Progress at last.

"That's good. If you can give the details to the officer here we can pull her in," Marcus got up to leave—and then stopped.

He looked at Mickey.

"By the way, why did you stick a knife in her after you shot her?"

Mickey looked up in amazement.

"What?"

His expression said more than any words.

There was absolutely no way Mickey had stabbed Dr. Neal, Marcus would stake his reputation on it.

"Okay, okay. Relax, don't worry," Marcus tried to calm Mickey down again. This last question, or his withdrawal from drugs, had clearly set him off again.

"Thanks officer." Marcus nodded to the police officer before letting himself out of the room. As he made his way slowly down the corridor he pulled at his lip. The case was all but closed. Mickey had confessed, of sorts, and he felt sure that Rose wouldn't support his self defence story, no matter what Mickey might think.

So what about the knife wound?

He didn't really have to pursue this, but the mystery bugged him. He knew he wouldn't be able to let it go, that just wasn't his style. "Too obsessive," as Anna would say. He chuckled at this thought. What he needed to do was to get hold of that redhead. Somehow he felt she could clear this problem up. To do that, however, he would have to get hold of the CCTV tapes again. Agent Woods had requested these too, shortly after he had taken Dr. Neal's body from the morgue. Getting them back from him would be a pain, so was it really worth the hassle?

Still debating this in his mind, Marcus barged through the station's entrance.

"Oh!" a voice exclaimed loudly.

He had nearly knocked over a police officer coming through the doors the other way. The officer was a woman.

"I'm so sorry," Marcus stepped back and held the door open for her. He had been miles away, lost deep in his thoughts.

"That's all right, no harm done."

The officer smiled sweetly at him, and after thanking him for holding the door open, she walked elegantly into the station.

Was it really worth it, trying to track the red head down?

Marcus continued to mull this over as he walked slowly away down the street.

"Good afternoon," the woman, whom Marcus had so nearly knocked over a moment ago, was now standing at the reception desk, and seeking help.

"I'm Officer Jessica O'Brien. Can you please tell me where a Mr. Michael Warren is being held?"

She took off her hat as she spoke and shook her head.

Bright locks of beautiful, red hair cascaded down around her shoulders.

23

The Wrong Hands

It was nice to feel at peace again; and nicer still to have a purpose once more.

Kat was walking cheerily down the cobbled road that lead gently down the slope from the castle to the arenas. The mid morning sun was shining warmly and it felt like it was going to be a beautiful day.

The friendship, the love, which she and Jess shared last night, marked a change for Kat. Even though Jess was gone, she no longer felt alone. Freyja had called her to her chambers during breakfast, and for the first time they had had a proper conversation. Kat was taken by the serenity of their Queen, and her wisdom. Her parting words had also struck a chord in her heart.

"Don't mourn Brynhildr, honour her. That's the Valkyrie way."

Freyja was right; Kat was a Valkyrie now. There could be no room in her life for tears and regrets.

As she walked, she hummed the lullaby that Jess had hummed last night. She thought of Jess' smile, and wandered where she was now.

What did go on in the Chamber of the Valkyries?

Odin had told her that the castle was founded on top of a spring, or was it a well? That was it; the castle was built on top of Mimir's Well.

Kat pondered whether somehow this was linked to the Chamber, perhaps a secret tunnel by which the warriors could come and go from the castle without being noticed? And what about the strange rumblings every time a warrior disappeared on a mission? Was that also linked to the Chamber too? Maybe Jess had gone back to Midgard?

Kat had so many questions—but so few answers.

Passing the arenas by, she headed toward Gladsheim. Thor was waiting for her there and she knew what it was about. Her sword was ready at last. She skipped with excitement when she thought of this. The great Thor himself had made her sword! People in the streets were watching her now, but she didn't care if they witnessed her joy. Kat smiled and waved enthusiastically at a family that was watching her; a small boy, his mother, a few geese, and an obedient cow with a large bell tied around its neck. The boy smiled and waved back, but the mother blushed and looked away, overcome at being noticed by her. The awe that the serfs held the inhabitants of the castle in still felt awkward to Kat. It was just another piece of her life that would take some getting used to.

Arriving at Gladsheim, she went in.

"Greetings, fair Kat!"

Thor's voice boomed from across the room as he rose from the throne to greet her. Kat swore that he was still wearing the same breeches from the first time they had met.

"Come over here," He beckoned to her excitedly as she hurried over.

After the rather stand offish start to their relationship, Kat had really come to like Thor. He was loud and crude by the other gods' standards, but he had a good sense of humour and was very chivalrous. Where Odin was aloof and studious, Thor was common and physical. He loved to work up a sweat, to eat and drink, and to chat with the local farmers and townsfolk. This latter was something she had never seen Odin do. Thor was definitely a people's champion, and she respected him for that. Odin and Thor were like chalk and cheese, and she could see why Odin didn't get along with his first born son.

They were two sides of the same coin; both great men but looking in opposite directions.

"Well now, fair Kat, what do you think of this?"

Slowly, Thor unwrapped her sword.

Holding it in his hands, sunlight flashed from its blade sending glittering reflections dancing around the hall. Gasps of admiration arose from the Aesir surrounding them. Gladsheim was a public meeting place, and when it was not being used for ceremonies, people gathered there to chat and to barter for goods.

"Wow!"

Kat was speechless again. The sword was truly beautiful.

Thor held the blade carefully in his hands before offering her its hilt.

"Take it. Feel its weight."

Kat wrapped her hand around the handle and prepared to take its mighty weight. To her surprise, as Thor released the sword, it felt as light as a feather. Certainly it was no heavier than a tennis racket or golf club in Midgard.

Carefully, she studied its finery, drinking in every detail.

It was obvious to Kat that the sword was special, and identical to those of the other Valkyries. She had held training swords at the arena and they were much heavier and made of iron. This was so much lighter and made of the same white metal as the warrior's helmets and Freyja's cask. They called it dwarf gold but no way could this metal be gold. Its light weight and strength meant it had to be titanium, or an alloy of some sort. No wonder it was in such short supply and impossible to find outside the castle.

She gazed in wonder at the lustre on the weapon.

It was a double-edged blade, about sixty centimetres long with a large central fuller (blood groove) that ran down its shaft. This in turn was welded to the hilt and handle which were both made of bronze with silver tracery. These parts were shaped in the form of a swan. The handle formed the head and arched neck of the swan; and its body was the pommel (the pommel being the part of the sword where the handle meets the shaft). The quill ions that would protect her hand in combat, lay on either side of the pommel, and were fashioned into a pair of outstretched swan's wings.

"Thank you."

Looking up at Thor, Kat almost whispered these words. They seemed so inadequate.

"You must name your sword, fair Kat," Thor's voice echoed loudly around the hall. He was pleased with her obvious admiration of his handiwork. "And when you have done so, we will drink a toast."

The Aesir around them broke into a spontaneous round of cheering and clapping. They huddled around Kat, eager to get a closer look.

"Come now, come now," Thor bellowed again in a humorous manner. "Give the fair maiden room. Let her pass, she has work to do."

Carefully he cleared a pathway for her.

Kat stepped out of the hall and back into the sunshine. She screwed her eyes up at its brightness and picked up the shield which she had laid outside. Its scarlet painted hide decorated with white dagger motifs felt more natural in her hands, now that she had her Valkyrie sword.

Thor was right; there was much work to be done.

Kat felt more determined than ever as she headed off toward the arenas.

She would honour the scarlet and white colours of Brynhildr and prove her true worth.

The rest of the morning and afternoon passed quickly and strenuously for Kat.

In the absence of Jess, she had chosen to join the arena of Zara and her maid Vicki. She felt an immediate warmth toward the warrior; and it helped that prior to Kat's arrival she had been Jess's best friend. At breakfast Carmel had invited Kat to join her and Silk, but after yesterday's display this was a choice she dreaded.

Carmel's attitude was part of the reason for Kat's new found determination.

During the time she had spent with Odin, she had understood his need to give the Valkyrie warriors another direction. If he could prevent the terrible battle that was coming, then he was right to hunt down evil in Midgard. However, she couldn't help feel that letting the Valkyries become judge, jury, and executioners of his brand of justice was a dangerous thing to do.

"Absolute power corrupts absolutely."

Kat paraphrased a quote which she had once learned. She had a feeling that Carmel would not be able to cope with such responsibility. She seemed such a sadist, enjoying inflicting pain. In her hands, such power could unleash a torrent of gratuitous violence. If one of the warriors died or decided to join the heroes in Valhalla; Carmel was the most likely maid to win the next tournament. Kat needed to prevent this—hence the urgency to improve her fighting skills.

Under the hot midday sun, Kat toiled hard with Zara, who was an expert in the use of the battle axe. Blow after blow they pounded at each other, until sweat flowed like water and blood poured from their hands.

"Bravo, bravo, my excellent warrior Kat."

These were Zara's final words as the exhausted girls laid down their weapons, too tired to carry on. She had obviously impressed with her stamina and strength.

Kat was still drenched in sweat when Hod decided to walk with her as she returned to the castle. With Jess out of the way, he too seemed enthused with a new determination. Placing his arm around her waist, he tried to steal a kiss—before she nudged him gently away.

Hod was also on her 'to do' list.

Kat no longer cared if he was the son of Odin. If an opportunity arose this evening, she would have words with him. His continuing affections were a distraction she neither wanted nor needed.

He was a fine friend, but he wasn't welcome as a lover.

"Greetings, greetings everyone!"

The doors to the feasting hall flung open and with a flamboyant flourish, Loki bowed as he entered and greeted the assembled crowd. He was grinning from ear to ear, delighted to be back once more from his travels.

"LOKI!"

A voice roared above the clapping and cheering. It was Thor, who leapt across his table and hugged his dear friend and drinking partner enthusiastically.

"Fetch us two horns of mead," he exclaimed. "And make them the largest you have." He continued, embracing Loki as he dragged him back to his table.

"Come my friend, we have much to talk about."

Sitting down together, Loki gazed furtively around him, hoping to spy the shapely Carmel.

"You know everybody here? Have you met the fair Kat?" Thor enquired, pointing in her direction.

Loki nodded as he opened his mouth to reply.

"Come now quickly, where's our mead?" Thor was in full flow and gave Loki no chance to speak.

Two horns of mead arrived, and to a chorus of cheering and foot stamping, the pair drained them in one long draught.

The horns were refilled immediately.

Tonight was indeed a night for celebration. For now, all thoughts of Carmel had to be put on hold as Loki became absorbed in a deep conversation with Thor; one punctuated with frequent outbursts of cheering and laughter.

From her table Kat could make out snippets of what they were talking about.

Apparently Loki had been travelling in the mountains of Jotunheim, and had brought back a fine horse for Odin. It was a gift from the ruler of that realm. The stallion was called Sleipnir and considered to be the fastest in the land. This caused a fierce and prolonged debate which many others joined in. Loki also mentioned that he had arranged for a visitor to come with an interesting offer for Thor. Thor begged him to say more, but Loki held his tongue; merely adding that he would be arriving in a day or so.

Food followed mead and mead followed food such that the evening passed swiftly and with good humour. As Kat bade her farewells and made to leave the hall, Hod stopped her at the door.

"Why are you leaving?" He challenged with an unusually assertive tone to his voice.

"I'm tired, and it's been a busy day. Why don't you go and join your brother and Loki? They're having so much fun and the night is still young."

Kat indicated with her eyes to the table where Thor and Loki were now playfully arm wrestling.

"I thought you and I could spend some time together, now that Brynhildr is away. I thought you might, you know, need someone." Hod toyed hopefully with her fingers, then putting his arm around her waist, he pulled her close.

He needed to give Kat a message.

She had to understand that saying "No" tonight was not an option. He was the son of a god—while she was merely a maid. It was time to make his move, it was time to take control—it was time to be a man.

Kat sighed; this was a headache she could have done without tonight. Still, his increasing boldness and constant pawing had to end. If she didn't sort this out now, it would only get worse for both of them.

"Come on, we need to talk."

Taking his hand reluctantly, she led him swiftly upstairs to her room. She prayed no one had seen them leave.

"Look," Kat started, as she closed the door behind her and ushered him over to the window. There was a full moon and the town looked beautiful bathed in its silvery light.

"You are a good man Hod, a fine man, and I really do enjoy your friendship, but you need to understand something."

Kat took his hand and hoped it would ease the words that were to follow. To her surprise, Hod picked up her other one and squeezed them both tightly in his.

"I know what you're going to say and don't worry, I've felt it, too."

Hod's response and gesture was not what she'd been expecting. A nasty thought crept slowly into her head.

Maybe the invitation to her room had sent the wrong signal?

"Look, let's go somewhere where we can be properly alone." Hod suggested excitedly as he ran one hand over the other.

He was taking Kat to Odin's garden.

24
A Surprise for Ruby

"**N**ot tonight, love." The bouncer barred Ruby's way into the changing room at club. "The boss wants you out back."

He nodded his head curtly backwards to emphasis his instructions. Ruby was pleased.

It was two days now since her night with Cole, and her first night back at the club. He was obviously eager to see her and her plans seemed to be taking shape. She patted the leather flask in her jacket pocket. It still felt half full. Good, she had plenty of time. Stepping back outside, she whistling cheerfully as she nodded to the chauffer before climbing inside the limousine.

"Hey, Legs," Cole nodded and waved a hand for her to sit down beside him.

"Hey babe, what's up?" Ruby smiled as she kissed him lightly on the cheek.

"Lookin' fine girl, real fine," Cole nodded as he leisurely eyed her up and down, appreciating the shortness of the bright yellow dress that was visible beneath her black leather coat. "Sweet," he murmured and nodded once more, before taking a sip of Jack D from his glass.

"Looking sharp yourself." Ruby replied as she fussed with his tie and ran her nails provocatively down the front of his shirt. Pleasantries aside, Cole seemed a little pre-occupied, or was that just her imagination?

"Are you my woman?" Cole took off his shades and looked her straight in the eye.

"Course I am, babe. If you want me to, course I am."

Ruby stroked his head. This was a bit weird; she hadn't seen that question coming.

"Are you sure, Legs?" he repeated, just to be certain.

"Positive, Sugar. You're the man, you're my man."

What was wrong with him tonight?

Ruby laid her head against his shoulder and pushed her hand inside his shirt. She stroked his chest. This wasn't making sense.

"Good, good," Cole paused. "I've got a surprise for you," he added, but didn't look in her direction.

"Oh babe I do love surprises." This was better, maybe a gift of some sort.

Settling back into her seat, Ruby gazed out of the window as the city lights drifted slowly by.

About half an hour later, the limousine pulled up outside a darkened warehouse. Ruby had noticed that the car was heading out of town, and although she thought it a little strange; she hadn't felt any alarm.

Now she did.

The warehouse stood alone on a deserted industrial estate. This was definitely not the sort of place for a romantic evening.

After getting out of the car, the chauffer tapped three times on a metal door in front of them. It opened, and they stepped through into darkness.

Ruby focused her mind quickly.

If this was a drug deal, or Cole was planning a show down, then that was okay. It would cut her trip short and that suited her fine. If he was looking for trouble, she would be happy to oblige. All things considered, she felt prepared for almost anything.

Unfortunately, nothing could have prepared her for what was to follow.

Cole snapped his fingers and bright neon lights flickered slowly on. One by one, the darkness in front of them rolled back to reveal the true horror inside the room.

There, taped to a chair with his head slumped on his chest; was a man. Battered and bleeding.

"I've got someone, Legs, that I want you to meet."

Cole motioned for her to follow him closer to the chair.

Oh no. Please, oh Odin no, no. NO!
Ruby felt a wave of nausea and her legs felt like jelly.
Sweet Freyja please don't let it be, IT CAN'T BE!
Her head was swimming as she prayed to the gods with all her might.

The man in the chair was bleeding heavily. His nose was broken, his cheek was deeply gashed and his lips were split. His eyelids were so badly swollen he could barely see out. Despite these terrible injuries, she knew she would always recognise him.

The battered mess was Elijah.

Shocked and bewildered, Ruby quickly made a note of the two thugs standing over him. They were Cole's men. The man with the knuckleduster was Slim. He was smirking and had clearly enjoyed his afternoon's work.

"Do you recognise this man?" Cole enquired gruffly.

Ruby nodded, fighting desperately to keep her emotions in check. There was no point in denying it.

"He's the porter at my motel. Why?"

"Well babe," Cole walked slowly around the chair, choosing his words very deliberately. "If you're my woman, then what were you doing kissing this piece of trash?"

He stopped—and eyeballed her.

Ruby had to think fast.

She had to save Elijah.

"Oh sugar," She purred, hoping she could mask the quiver that was threatening her voice. "It was just a friendly good night kiss, it meant nothing. You can't be jealous of that now, surely, honey?"

"Hmmm," Cole paused, and then continued his walk around the chair.

Her answer hadn't satisfied him.

"If that's so, then why'd ya spend the whole day with him?"

By Odin's beard, he had had her followed!

The window shopping, the zoo, ice-creams in the park, and that stupid unnecessary kiss on the steps. His goons had seen it all. Things were looking really bad, not only for Elijah but also for her. Not that she cared two hoots about herself. She just couldn't let Elijah die. Not because of her, she just couldn't.

Ruby paused.

What she said next would seal Elijah's fate and probably her own. She had to get a grip on herself. She was here to kill Cole, that was her mission. She had to stay focused. She couldn't confess to having feelings for Elijah as they would murder him there and then. Somehow she had to get out of this, keep close to Cole, and with Odin's luck, save Elijah's life.

"Honey, I know this man's family. He's a simpleton and his mom asked me to look after him for the day. He didn't mean no offence by a kiss; he just got a little over excited, too much ice-cream." She added hopefully.

"You are my woman," he paused. "Right?"

"Yes Cole, yes. This poor simpleton, he ain't nothing to me honey, you must know that surely?"

Ruby was pleading, begging him to believe her.

"Hmmm."

Cole started a second slow circuit of the chair before stopping behind Elijah.

"Look at her you fucking worthless piece of shit. Look at my fine piece of ass! What the fuck were you doing, FUCKING WITH MY WOMAN?"

Cole screamed at Elijah, saliva spattering against the back of his head.

"Apologise to her now, you mother fucker. Apologise for kissing her with your filthy, bastard lips!"

Cole was on fire, ignited by a fury that some cheap arsed punk had dared to fuck with his bitch. He owned Ruby, just as he owned everything else that landed on his turf. No mother fucker messed with his shit—ever.

From somewhere in the broken and bleeding mess that had once been Elijah's face, a mumble emerged.

"I can't hear you," Cole motioned to Slim who, with a sickening thud, smashed his knuckle duster into Elijah's face.

Blood and teeth spattered from his mouth.

"I'M SORRY!"

Elijah looked up briefly as he screamed these words, then his head lolled pathetically forward once more.

Cole stood back contentedly. A smile twitched across his lips.

Ruby clenched her fists as every muscle in her body strained to be unleashed.

Hit him Cole, hit him you bastard!

She wanted to scream these words out loud; curse Odin and his stupid law that forbade her from taking an evil soul without witnessing evil first.

Hit him and let me rain down my vengeance upon you!

Silently she pleaded for the right to take his life.

"What's wrong, Legs?" Cole could see the rage in her eyes.

This wasn't good; she had to calm down.

"Nothing, babe," Ruby tried desperately to compose herself; she had to keep up her act. "Now you put it that way, I can see why you're so cross."

"Good Legs, good."

At last Cole seemed to relax. He walked round the chair and stood in front of Elijah. Pulling Ruby toward him, he kissed her roughly—and deliberately—on her lips.

"See," He flashed evil eyes toward Elijah. "You ain't got nothing; you ain't worthy to kiss the feet of a fine woman like this."

He squeezed Ruby's bottom tightly. She felt like vomiting.

"Yeh, see," Ruby returned Cole's embrace as she pulled him closer to her, grinding her hips suggestively against his. She prayed that her scorn and show of affection would allow him release Elijah.

Things might finally be looking better for both of them.

"Sweet," Cole kissed her once more, and then nodded to Slim.

Without saying a word, Slim stepped behind Elijah and drew a knife. In one swift move he jerked his head backward, and slit his throat. Elijah slumped forward, gurgling and convulsing. His blood formed a crimson pool around the chair which swiftly widened.

"WHAT?"

Ruby couldn't control her anguished scream.

"Why Cole, why? He was a simpleton, why'd you have to kill him, why?"

Tears were welling in her eyes, not just for Elijah but tears for another time buried deep in her past. Joe had died the same way, and it had been her fault then, too.

Cole shrugged nonchalantly.

"Hey babe, bad for business if I let him go."

The thugs around him nodded and smirked. They were loving this spectacle.

"You are my girl. Right?"

Cole stared hard at her once more.

If she faltered, it would be her turn to die.

Ruby knew it was over.

Because of her stupidity an innocent like Elijah had been killed. She couldn't even take his soul to Valhalla, because he wasn't a hero. All she could do now was watch as he slowly died; a humiliating and painful death before her grief-striken eyes.

He was beyond her love and help.

"Calm before anger, reason before rage—calm before anger, reason before rage."

Freyja's words kept repeating in her head, over and over again, bringing peace and reminding her that she was a Valkyrie; that she was Prudr; and that she was 'the powerful one.'

Icily she looked Cole in the eye.

Eyeball to eyeball, no blinking.

She could kill him now and take his soul, but that wouldn't bring Elijah back. No, that was no longer her plan. Elijah's death screamed for justice, and justice would be done—her way.

"Course I'm your girl, Sugar," she purred at him once more.

Cole motioned for them to go, but before they left, she turned and caught Slim's eye.

"What's your name, honey?" she asked in a voice that betrayed no emotion.

"Slim, ma'am, everybody calls me Slim." He replied with a hateful smile still glued to his face.

"Remind me, Slim," Ruby paused.

"To thank you properly for this."

25

Seductions

The moment Kat saw Yggdrasill swaying gently in the bright sunshine she knew she was in trouble.

She also knew she had very little time.

"Hod, this isn't a good idea, this isn't what I want." Kat pulled her hand away from his and tried to reason with him.

"No Kat, this is what we both want, that's why you invited me to your room, remember?" Hod clapped his hands and the Norn stood up. Each bobbed a quick curtsy.

"Please, Hod, no, don't make them sing."

Kat's eyes pleaded with his. She could see a boyish smile spreading across his face.

"So you know about the Norn do you. I wonder how?" Hod was genuinely surprised by this, but it altered nothing. "Come fair maidens, sing for us." He gestured to the Norn and they began their song.

Kat felt their effects immediately. It was not quite as strong as when she'd been there with Odin, but her emotions were rising fast. She was grabbing hold of Hod's hand.

"Please Hod, make them stop, this isn't fair," she pleaded.

Hod laughed as he pulled her toward him.

"Come fair Kat, you know you want me; I've seen the way you look at me."

He stroked her hair clumsily.

Kat's knees were turning to mush and she had her arms around his waist.

"Hod, it isn't like that."

His hand in her hair felt wonderful, so tender, so kind. She had to snap out of it.

Focus Kat, stay focused.

"This is the perfect place for us. Look around you, it's paradise."

Hod waved his hand as he lay on the floor, pulling Kat down awkwardly on top of him. His hands were squeezing her firm bottom into his groin, and she could feel the warmth of his body beneath her.

"Hod, stop, please."

The situation was getting desperate. She could feel his manhood swelling, rising now against her stomach. She wanted him inside her more than anything. Her resistance was failing, the Norn were overwhelming her.

"Sweet, fair, Kat."

Hesitantly, Hod tried to kiss her neck as a fumbling hand slid up the side of her body toward her breasts.

"Hod, please," this was her last chance, and Kat knew it. "I like you but please, let things happen naturally. You don't need the Norn to seduce me. You don't need to do this, let me grow—*to love you!*"

She gasped as she uttered the last words, he just felt too good under her. The Norn had almost done their job. If he didn't stop now, she would be seducing him—rather than the other way around.

Hod froze, and then stopped abruptly.

He didn't know why.

Kat was there for the taking, he could feel her lustful body grinding against his. However, something in what she had said made sense. She loved him; he had definitely heard her say that.

Maybe he didn't need the Norn after all?

Hod moved his hand toward his ring, hesitated, and then reluctantly waved it over the diamonds. In the blink of an eye they were back in Kat's room; lying together on the floor, Kat on top of him.

Kat got up slowly.

She was aching, her head hurt, and her mind was spinning with a kaleidoscope of emotions—lust, anger, relief, sorry, rage, joy. She had to make sense of these and what had just happened. She felt so confused and so angry.

Hod was now getting up, too. He rose hesitantly and stood opposite her; blushing furiously. They looked at each other, both breathing hard, wondering who would make the first move, and what that would be.

"Hod, you idiot! What were you thinking of?" Kat began angrily.

"I, I—" Hod faltered, his 'manly' assertiveness collapsing faster than a punctured balloon.

"I thought you loved me," he stammered lamely.

"Hod, I like you but that was, that was..." She was struggling for words as an extraordinary rage rose inside her. It felt impossible to control.

"...Was that your crazy idea of seducing me?" she hissed in bewilderment as she tried to get a grip on herself.

"You said you loved, me, I heard you say it," Hod repeated himself and moved closer to Kat. He stretched his hand out to pull her close once more.

SLAP!

Kat snapped and lashed out.

She slapped him as hard as she could and he span dizzily across the room. *Wow!* She never knew she could hit so hard. It felt good, so powerful—and so satisfying.

"Get out Hod, Just get out now."

Kat snarled as she bared her teeth. If he didn't leave this instant, she knew she would kill him. Her fury was so strong.

What was happening to her?

Hod got up slowly, mumbled an almost inaudible "Sorry" before heading for the door. Just as he was about to go, Kat spoke again.

"Why can't we just be friends Hod? Why do you have to go and spoil things?"

She saw red, but luckily Hod saw this, too. As she prowled menacingly toward him, he turned tail and beat a hasty retreat. He wasn't going to chance another powerful blow from her hands.

Kat pushed the door shut behind him and her body slumped against it. She took a few deep breaths in. She was furious with Hod but equally furious with herself. His clueless attempt at seduction was just that, boyish and ridiculous. She was right to be angry but the fury she had felt was far too extreme. It was distorted, a purity of emotion that she had never experienced before. Its intensity was frightening and yet it thrilled her even more.

Gripped in its embrace, she had been so powerful and in control.

As she walked slowly back to her bed, Kat knew she had to make a decision. Perhaps Silk's suggestion was right. Perhaps she should take a lover?

Maybe that would bring Hod to his senses before she did him real harm.

After Hod left the room, he rushed along the corridor and headed downstairs. He wanted to get out of there, to run away from his humiliation. His face hurt like stink and he was sore as hell.

This was the third time he had messed things up with a maid, and he had had enough. He heard her say she loved him, she couldn't deny that.

Fair Kat would be his; he knew that in his heart. He shouldn't have stopped her passion in the garden, *what had he been thinking of?*

In his anger and frustration he didn't even see Carmel, who was coming up the stairs toward him.

Carmel left the feast downstairs soon after Kat did. She was bored and frustrated. Last night the attention had been on her, but tonight it was all Loki. Loki this, Loki that. She was sick of hearing his name—and sick of him.

As she walked slowly up the stairs, dragging her feet one step at a time, Carmel finally admitted the truth.

She confessed to what she was really angry about.

What she hated most was that Loki had rushed into Thor's arms—and not hers.

Ever since their chat in the market she could think of nothing else—Loki's voice, Loki's eyes, Loki's bottom—yes, especially his bottom. She smiled ruefully. She had been so sure that he wanted her and now nothing.

There was a horse for Odin, a hug and a sing song for Thor, but not so much as a "Hello" for Carmel.

She looked up and saw Hod hurrying down the steps. Even that loser wasn't looking at her tonight.

What was wrong with her?

Reaching the top of the stairs, she headed for her room. She would shun him, that's what she would do, shun him. Let Loki know just what he was missing, he would soon come running if she ignored him. All men did.

With that reassuring thought in her head, Carmel stormed into her room and slammed the door shut behind her.

Knock, knock, knock!
That couldn't be her door, surely?
KNOCK, KNOCK, KNOCK!
The knocking was more insistent now.
"All right, Shhhh. I'm coming."
Carmel struggled out of bed and ran her hand through her tousled locks. It must be very late because she had been asleep for hours. Pulling on the first thing that came to hand, she stumbled over to the door.
"Who is it?" she called out, quietly.
"It's me," a voice answered in a loud and unhelpful whisper. It was followed by a fit of drunken giggling.
Carmel's heart skipped a beat. She knew who it was.
Suddenly she remembered she had no makeup on—and her hair was a mess.
"Wait a minute," She called again, trying to stifle her excitement. Her eyes frantically searched in the darkness for a hairbrush.
"It's me fair Carmel, fairest of all the Valkyries."
The voice was getting louder—and sillier.
Quickly she opened her door.
Loki stood there; swaying from side to side, his eyes glazed with alcohol.
"Come in, come in you idiot!"
Carmel hauled him through the door and he sprawled onto her floor, giggling hysterically. She stood over him. She knew she ought to be angry, and she had promised to ignore him. But—*oh, Loki!*
Next to Thor and Balder, he was the finest catch in all of Asgard and she longed to have him as her man. Kneeling down beside him, she stroked the curly, black locks away from his face.
What a state he was in.
"I've got a preshhhhent for you," Loki slurred, and with a half smile he tried to look up at her. His eyes refused to focus as the room span slowly around him. Fumbling madly, his hand went to a pocket and, at the third attempt; a small, brown, leather package fell out from it.
"Here, thishhh is for you. I mishhhed you."
His eyes closed as he lay his head on the floor; giggling inanely once more.

Carmel picked up the packet and opened it in the dim light. A heavy object glittered in the gentle glow from the embers in her fireplace.

She gasped.

In her hand was a heavy, gold necklace.

Carmel looked lovingly at Loki.

She knew he had a reputation as a lady's man, and had had more goddesses, Valkyries and Aesir women than she could ever dare to number. He was a wild and reckless rogue, heartless and thoughtless. He drank too much; he broke wind too often, and had stinky feet. Incidently; these were smelling right now.

"I'm shhhorry. I shhhhouldn't have come."

Loki smiled up at her once more.

"I'm no good for you, fair Carmel, I'm a bad, bad, bad, bad man."

He finished with a flourish and a giggle, and then tried to get up.

Carmel helped him.

"Shush. I know, I know." Carmel staggered with him over to the bed and Loki collapsed onto it, lying on his back.

The room was spinning faster now.

Carmel carefully lifted his legs up and then lay down beside him. She allowed her hand to slide slowly down his body, lingering lovingly over his manhood on its sensuous voyage of discovery.

Propping herself up on one elbow, she eyed him slowly up and down.

"It's lucky for you that I like bad men," she grinned knowingly.

Loki didn't hear her.

He was already fast asleep and snoring.

Carmel cuddled up beside him and laid her arm across his chest. Her man was staying there with her tonight; she smiled with a deep sense of satisfaction. Much later, when he awoke, she knew they'd make love.

After all; one nice gift deserved another.

26

A Chat with Mickey

Jess whistled quietly to herself as the officer helped her through the maze of corridors and stairs at the police station.

People in Midgard could be so helpful, she mused.

She had enjoyed looking at her reflection in the shiny metal door of a lift they had taken. She always felt she looked good in a uniform, and the pale blue shirt and navy blue trousers of the New York Police Department reinforced this impression. There was even a gun with her uniform, although it was unlikely she would ever use it.

Their tortuous walk down into the basement of the building took a long time, and as they reached the steel door to Mickey's cell, Jess shivered. It was cooler down here than in the rest of the station, but not as cold as the late December afternoon outside.

Jess always got caught out when she came on a mission to Midgard, forgetting that the weather was six months behind, or was that ahead, of Asgard. After seeing Mickey, she vowed her first stop would be to buy a good winter coat. Of course, she might not need to buy one at all; but that really depended on Mickey.

"Thank you officer," Jess beamed a warm smile at the officer when they finally arrived at the cell. He turned the key in the lock with a reassuringly heavy clunk. Opening the door, he ushered her inside.

"Would you like me to stay with you, ma'am?" he looked at her.

"No I'm sure that won't be necessary. I'm sure he won't be any trouble." Jess smiled disarmingly once again. The poor man was putty in her hands.

"Well don't forget he's a dangerous criminal, he's on a murder charge." The officer warned as he scowled menacingly in Mickey's direction.

"Thank you. I'll call if I need anything," Jess reassured him and motioned for him to leave.

"I'll be right outside the door, ma'am, just in case," he stressed this last point before closing the door behind him.

At last police officer Jessica O'Brien was alone with Michael Xavier Warren—Kat's murderer.

Jess quickly sized up the claustrophobic cell.

There was no obvious camera which was a relief. She looked at the man sitting on the bed. He had slowly risen from lying when they arrived, probably surprised to receive a visitor to his cell.

Jess scribbled a few lines of gobbledygook in a notebook she had been holding, shorthand should anyone ask, and then closed it and returned it to her breast pocket. This had been her ruse for getting in to see Mickey, her boss needed some details. No one had actually asked her who this boss was, nor had they checked her identity card properly.

Doors opened so easily if you happened to be wearing the right uniform.

Jess stood there for a few moments longer, carefully eyeing Mickey. His shoulders had slumped, and his gaze had returned to the floor when he saw that his visitor was a police officer. He obviously hadn't recognised her, but then in the state he was in, he probably wouldn't have recognised his own mother.

In one word, he looked pathetic.

Jess toyed with the dagger she had concealed in her pocket. Her eyes betrayed the troubled uncertainty she felt inside. She had begged Freyja to allow her to come back and kill Mickey, and she certainly didn't need him to attack her or perform some other act of evil to give her the right to take his soul.

He had killed Kat—that was enough.

He deserved to die, and that's what she had come here for; to kill him, and take his soul back. By Odin's sacred eye, he truly deserved to be punished. It was just now, looking at him sitting there; sweating and shaking, his body consumed by its need for a fix, she found she couldn't do it.

Not like this anyway.

Reluctantly, Jess turned and banged on the door. It opened instantly.

"Are you all right, ma'am?" the officer asked a bit too eagerly, hoping for an opportunity to prove his worth to his attractive and very welcome escort.

"I am, but he isn't," she indicated in Mickey's direction. "I think he needs a doctor."

"Already on his way, ma'am," he reassured her.

"Good."

Jess turned, and spoke to Mickey for the first time.

"I'll be seeing you again Mr. Warren, when you're feeling better."

And with that she left. Smiling sweetly and saying goodbye to all she had spoken to on her way inside the station.

An hour or so after Jess left, Marcus returned. He was tired as he entered the building, and in no mood to enter into small talk with the chatty receptionist at the front desk.

When he had left the building earlier that afternoon he had had a moment of inspiration. He wondered if the red headed lady who had entered the alley might have been a friend of Dr. Neal?

Hailing a cab, he had gone over to the hospital where Kat used to work. After a little bit of detective work, he had managed to track down and have a chat with one of Dr. Neal's friends who also worked there. Her name was Susy, and she seemed to have known her quite well. Certainly well enough to know Kat's friends from the past year or so.

Unfortunately, his journey had been a complete waste of time. Susy couldn't remember anyone with such unusual hair.

Disappointed with this dead end, he was returning now to finish up in the office. He wasn't on call, so as soon as the clock passed five, he would be out of there. It was approaching the hour now so he was in no mood to be delayed.

"Hello Detective Finch," chirped Mary or Daisy or whatever her name was.

"Hello," Marcus didn't stop. He flashed his identity card quickly at her.

"You're such a naughty boy," she scolded after him. "You haven't signed in."

Cursing under his breath, Marcus returned and hastily scribbled his name in the book. *Christ!* He was only going to be there five minutes.

"You know that man of yours—"

Oh shit, Marcus thought, *here we go.*

"Which one?" he sighed, resigning himself to waste another few precious minutes of his life.

"You know, your suspect, what's his name—" she started to click on the computer.

"Do you mean Mr. Warren?" Marcus was desperate to cut this short.

"Uh huh," she nodded and continued. "Well, he had an awfully pretty visitor this afternoon, a lovely lady."

Marcus was suddenly interested.

He had been wondering if Mickey's druggie girlfriend might put in an appearance. Maybe she had smartened herself up and popped in. Now that would be a stroke of luck and a much better way to end the day.

"Is she still here?" Marcus asked hopefully. He might even get 'Mary' some flowers. Finally, he'd remembered her name.

"Oh no, she didn't stay long, she left ages ago," Mary returned to her computer, gossip finished for the moment.

"Well thank you Mary, that was very helpful. I do hope you have a lovely weekend."

Dear God what was that woman on?

Why tell him this when she knew the woman had already left the building?

"Pointless chit chat, utterly, utterly pointless." Marcus muttered in exasperation as he started to walk away.

"Really pretty she was, really pretty."

He could still hear her prattling as he sped off down the corridor.

"Such lovely red hair—"

Marcus stopped dead in his tracks.

NO?

Now that would be too much of a coincidence.

27
Asgard's Wall

There was an extra spring in Carmel's step as she made her way out of the castle. She felt as if she was floating down the gentle slope, her feet oblivious of the ground below. There may have been clouds in the sky, but there were none in her heart. It was a wonderful morning, and she didn't want anything to disturb her happiness; at least not just yet.

When Loki awoke they had made love. It was the sort of furious, passionate kind when two kindred spirits finally come together. They were a good match—Carmel with her wild and fiery temper; and Loki with his free and wanton ways. The hunter and the quarry finally pitted against each other. One determined to ensnare, the other to evade.

For Carmel, it had been the finest night of passion she could remember, if she excluded the odd tryst with Freyr that is. This morning she felt complete; a long lost part of her had been found and put lovingly back in its rightful place.

As she walked she toyed with the thick, gold necklace around her neck. This was a little out of keeping with her warrior clothes, but she wanted to wear it. She wanted everyone to admire her new acquisition; both the jewellery—and her lover.

It was an exquisite piece, one made from thick, closely linked chains that ended in a large clasp of a jewelled swan performing an extravagant display of courtship. This is what made her know that Loki's passion was real. This was not some last minute trinket, a cheap gift to entice her into his bed. No; time and thought had gone into the making and buying of it, a sign of his sincerity.

"It was a necklace worthy of Freyja herself," Emile had exclaimed at breakfast this morning, proving her point exactly.

Carmel headed past the arenas and continued on toward Gladsheim. An orange flag was fluttering on the pole, a sign that trouble was brewing.

The flag system in Asgard was simple but effective.

Gold and silver flags meant good news. A hero or a new maid had arrived, both excuses for loud and joyous celebration. A black flag meant a prisoner for judgement, purple for good news, and a red one for immediate danger. This usually meant a call to arms for the warriors and their maids. Most days there wasn't a flag, and on these days the Aesir went about their businesses as usual.

Carmel suspected the flag today was linked to the smoke signals they had seen coming from the watchtower by the glacier. This watchtower was looked after by Heimdall, a trusted friend of Odin and a loyal defender of the realm. Fires were always lit when visitors from the mountain kingdom of Jotunheim came across the Bifrost Bridge.

Although there was no real need for Carmel to go to the hall, she was inquisitive. Like most of the inhabitants of Asgard, sometimes the need to be nosy was overwhelming. Besides, she really didn't feel like training this morning anyway.

Continuing her walk, Carmel turned her mind to another interesting piece of gossip. This had come from a most unexpected source.

Little Miss Goody-two-shoes, Kitty Kat, had pulled her into her bedroom and told her about her adventures of the night before. The story, and what Kat wanted to do about it, had changed Carmel's opinion about her.

Perhaps the wimpish kitten had claws after all.

Hod's bungled attempt at seduction had come as no surprise for Carmel. Her opinions about Hod were widely known. She despised his weakness and immaturity, and only spoke to him if she could mock or humiliate him. Now she was dying to see his face. She had a curious thrill to find out just how deeply the kitten's claws could scratch.

Kat's other news was equally impressive.

She had experienced the blood lust for the first time, but had struggled to control it. Carmel had reassured her that this emotion was normal for a Valkyrie, and that she would soon learn how to harness it. This purity of rage or passion was what made them so invincible, both in war and in bed.

Up until this moment in time, Carmel had found Kat of little interest.

She was a sweet girl, pleasant enough to talk to, but as a warrior in waiting, she seemed a complete disaster. Carmel had doubted she had a backbone. A spineless jellyfish incapable of carrying a sword and shield let alone walking into battle. However, the plan that Kat had suggested to save both her, and Hod, from disaster was enticing; and the role that she had suggested for Carmel was right up her street.

Maybe the kitten would make it as a Valkyrie after all?

Approaching the hall, Carmel could hear a loud voice booming from inside. It was the unmistakable resonance of Thor, and it sounded as though he was in a mighty rage. Outside the hall stood a large, chestnut horse, the property of the visitor who was no doubt causing the stir.

With mounting curiosity, Carmel went in.

"Loki!" Thor bellowed angrily. "I can't believe you could even consider such an outrageous suggestion. I don't know which skull to smash first, yours or your vile friend's."

Thor was pacing up and down, beating his hammer Mjollnir into his hand as he walked. His face was red with rage and his eyes flashed angrily, first to Loki and then to the visitor.

As Carmel entered the hall she caught Loki's eye and she mouthed "Hello." He turned and flashed a sheepish grin, the smile of a naughty schoolboy who has just been caught. She wondered what he could have done to upset Thor so badly. After all, they had been inseparable only the evening before. She nudged Emile who was watching the spectacle, and she kindly sketched out the details.

Apparently, Loki's friend was the master mason to the King of Jotunheim, and he had come to Asgard with a fine offer from his king. He would rebuild the shattered wall around around the town and he'd do this in a month.

Unfortunately the second part of the offer was as repugnant as the first part was pleasing.

All the king wanted in exchange for this work was the hand of Freyja in marriage. The Queen of the Valkyries would wed the King of Utgard, uniting the realms in an everlasting peace.

Thor didn't mind the truce, although he would rue the opportunities their animosity had given him to wield Mjollnir. The offer of harmony between the realms wasn't what had made him mad.

No; what filled him with rage was what Odin would say if he agreed to this deal.

It was no secret in Asgard that Odin and Freyja were lovers, and his hatred for the inhabitants of Jotunheim was eternal. For Odin, a union between the realms was as unthinkable as night not following day. It simply couldn't happen.

And then what about Freyja?

Thor dreaded putting this offer to her.

The people of Jotunheim were notoriously ugly and the king was no exception. He could see her cheerless face as she set off in her chariot toward the mountains, riding out to take her place as his new Queen; stepping up to a cold, stone throne in the frozen palaces of Utgard.

This was an unthinkable horror.

And what of Loki himself, how could his dear friend even think of coming to Asgard with such an outrageous idea?

He had to find out more.

Beckoning Loki toward him, Thor put a mighty arm around his shoulders and they walked toward the back of the hall. They quickly became engrossed in discussion, speaking in hushed voices that were impossible to hear.

"By Odin's beard Loki, what were you thinking of?" Thor hissed at him through clenched teeth. "I know you to be a trickster, but I would never have taken you for a fool."

"Listen, Thor, I don't think you have thought this offer through properly," Loki's voice sounded calm and confident, not the voice of a man who was expecting to get his head smashed in any time soon.

"Look at him; He's old and only one man."

They both turned and glanced at the mason. He was indeed greying and had a slight stoop to his once mighty shoulders.

"How can he possibly rebuild the wall in a month? It's impossible. You must agree to that, surely?"

Thor nodded.

"The worst that can happen with this deal is we only get part of the wall built, and that part will have been done for free!" Loki continued proudly with his justification.

Thor nodded again.

"I swear on my life that there is absolutely no way this mason can finish the job. Think about it, the joke's on their king—not you. Imagine how pleased Odin will be when he returns to find some of his wall repaired, hey? We all know the prophesy and what's coming."

Loki patted him on the shoulders. "Just think about it. This could be the best deal you've ever made."

Thor motioned for Loki to leave him, and stroked his beard long and thoughtfully.

Everything Loki said made good sense. The deal seemed water tight, a contract the mason could never complete. It seemed too good to be true—and there lay the rub. Thor knew Loki too well; and that was what worried him.

Loki never cut a deal without getting the edge somewhere down the line. There had to be some trick or magic going on, he was certain of it. Thor also reminded himself that Loki (and he still found this hard to believe) was the son of a former King and Queen of Jotunheim; although what freak of nature could have created a son so different from his parents was beyond even Odin's comprehension. Loki had divided loyalties—and that worried him. Still, he had to make a decision; and the deal could be so good for Asgard.

After what seemed an age, Thor finally turned and beckoned Loki and the mason forward.

"Here's the deal. You have one week and one week only to complete the task. That's my final offer." And with that Thor spat on his hand and stretched it out toward the mason.

"But my lord that's impossible!" Exclaimed the mason. "Not even I with all my strength and skill can finish this task in so short a time."

"Take it or leave it that's my final offer." Thor's voice boomed, and he motioned dismissively with his hand for the mason to be gone.

"I have an idea."

Loki stepped in abruptly, anxious that the deal he had so deviously forged in the halls of Jotunheim hadn't been in vain. "What if you had some assistance, say all the helpers your horse can bring in a cart? Would you then reconsider this deal?" he put this proposal to the mason, who was already marching out of the hall.

"Wait a minute," Thor was having none of this. "Let me see your horse first."

Thor and Loki chased after the mason, and the warriors and townsfolk filed out behind them. Everybody wanted to see the horse and consider this deal for themselves.

"Does your horse have a name?" Thor enquired, eyeing the large chestnut stallion suspiciously up and down. He was a big horse, but that was to be expected coming from the lofty mountain realm.

"Svadilfari," replied the mason and the horse whinnied obligingly. He looked well enough, but there was greyness around his muzzle and his back was bowed. Svadilfari was clearly a horse well past his prime.

"Somebody get me a pot of paint," Thor boomed.

After a disorganised and frantic search, a small boy eventually emerged and raced across the square, a pot of bright yellow paint slopping from his hands.

Thanking the boy for his help, and pressing a coin into his hand, Thor painted a large yellow 'S' on the rump of the horse. He then turned and looked Loki straight in the eye. He was certainly not going to let Loki change Svadilfari for a finer horse. This was a piece of trickery he felt sure his cunning friend had intended.

"All right, Mason, I agree."

The mason looked up in surprise.

"You have one week to rebuild the wall completely, and you can only have the assistance of Svadilfari here and all the colleagues he can draw in one cart from Jotunheim. And," Thor paused. "They must be here by noon tomorrow."

There was a flurry of conversation among the gathered audience, and then an approving handclap and cheers. No one could fault Thor's conditions. The task was impossible even if the mason and his horse could make ten journeys.

Freyja was safe and they would have a new wall.

The mason mulled the deal over for a few moments before speaking.

"This isn't the proposal I wanted, but if it's the best you can do then I guess I'll just have to accept it. We have a deal."

And with that both men spat on their hands and shook.

There was no going back now.

As the mason and his horse trotted away over the bridge and broke into a slow canter, Loki breathed a sigh of relief. His eyes were gleaming satisfied shades of green, a sight not missed by Thor.

What trick had the mischievous schemer got hidden up his sleeve?

Thor hoped he wouldn't live to regret his decision.

Much later that same day Carmel spied Hod in the distance, hanging around Jess's arena as usual. It was time to start her part of the plan.

"Hi Hod," She trotted over to him, her greeting catching him by surprise.

"How are you? Let me look at your face, Wow, that must have hurt," She feigned concern as Hod tried to hide his bruised cheek.

"Gosh! Did Kat really do that?" Carmel pulled Hod's face around, and pretended to study the marks compassionately.

"How do you know Kat did it?" Hod enquired crossly.

"Everybody knows! She's going round telling everybody about how she beat you up," Carmel lied deliberately, she loved winding him up.

"She wouldn't do that. She's not like you," Hod was angry now; he knew Carmel was making fun at his expense.

"Okay, so have it your way then if that's what you want to believe," Carmel shrugged and deliberately started to walk away.

"Hey! Wait up. What did she say, exactly?" Hod followed after her, a trace of uncertainty now creeping into his voice.

"Oh not much, just how you were a naughty boy, and how much she hates you." Carmel loved this, rubbing his nose in his misfortune.

"No way would she say that, she told me that she loves me. I caught her by surprise, that's all," Hod was being defensive now, trying to justify his foolishness of the night before.

"If you say so. Anyway she said something else as well, she said she liked another man; a REAL man." Carmel stressed the last words, she enjoyed making him wince.

"That's impossible. There's no way that could happen," Hod paused. "Did she say who he was?" He had to be sure Carmel was lying, just in case.

"No, but she really likes him, I can tell." Carmel was in her element, lie after lie trickling effortlessly from her lips.

"You're a liar! I don't believe you. You just want to make me mad and you won't succeed. Not today Carmel, you won't!" Hod shook his head in disbelief. It was all poison coming from her mouth, and he was having none of it.

"Have it your way, if that's what you want to believe then believe away. Frankly, I couldn't care less."

Carmel turned her back on him and walked away, a cheeky jaunt in her stride and a wicked grin on her face.

She had sowed the seeds of doubt in Hod's head and that was her job started. She knew the fear of a rival for Kat's affections would fester inside him. He would be back, she was certain of that, begging for more. His insecurity and jealousy would consume him, and he would have to find out more. Carmel would fan this little spark of jealousy until it roared into a raging fire.

Satisfied with upsetting Hod for the day, she turned her mind to another even more pleasing activity.

Now; where had that Loki gone?

28
Shopping

"That will be forty nine dollars and ninety nine cents please," the sales assistant rang up the sale with a satisfying 'kaching' on her old fashioned till.

"Did you say forty nine dollars and ninety nine cents?" Ruby enquired, as she opened her small leather purse.

"Yes Madam," she replied. "Would you like it gift wrapped?"

"No thank you very much, that's lovely as it is."

Ruby handed over the money and grabbed the brown paper bag. She wished the sales assistant good bye, and then left the shop and headed back down the side street to the more crowded mall ahead.

It had been two days since Elijah's killing and Ruby had kept herself deliberately busy; a desperate attempt to blot Elijah's swollen and bleeding face from her mind. It was difficult for her to stay focused, with so much anger and sorrow raging inside. She felt so responsible for his death.

Her guilt felt like a plague, ravaging her from within.

Cole of course, had insisted that she stay that night, and to prove he was the man, he had taken her repeatedly. She had tried not to show her emotions, but it had been difficult; even for her. Sex had been hard to stomach, which was why she was so relieved when Cole announced he was going away for a few days. A business trip, he had explained, reassuring her that his gang would be around to keep an eye on her. If ever Ruby had wanted an opportunity to make good her promise to "thank Slim," then this would be it. She couldn't believe her luck, and she thanked Odin for her good fortune.

Ruby had spent today shopping, crossing off a small list of things she wanted to buy. A list of toys she hoped to introduce to her sleazy, new best friend.

She had seen Slim at the club last night, and he seemed only too eager to accept her intriguing offer of a thank you, especially after a little flirtation on her behalf. "Whilst the cat is away, the mice will play." had crossed her mind as he scribbled his address enthusiastically on the back of a grubby beer mat.

A greedy smirk betrayed what he hoped her thanks would be.

Ruby had arranged to meet him secretly at his flat tonight, so they could share a drink or two together. She knew he would be alone and most probably drooling. There was no way he would tell anyone about their liaison, he was too smart to go the way of Elijah.

But as for honour amongst thieves, forget it.

Having the bosses 'bitch' whilst his back was turned was perfectly reasonable to him; it was just another perk of the trade.

Ruby checked her bag carefully.

There was a bottle of cheap scotch—nothing like a glass or two to get him in the mood—a pair of expensive cowboy boots with shiny metal heels and tips, duct tape, and of course her latest item—an antique, brass knuckleduster.

It had taken her a while to track this one down.

There were plenty of cheap, metal effect, plastic ones around which sold for a few dollars, but there was nothing like the feel of the good old fashioned original article. She fingered it lovingly, hoping that Slim would appreciate the effort she had made to buy this for him. After all, it was just like the one he had used, and imitation was the sincerest form of flattery.

With a smile on her face she checked her watch.

It was time to get ready.

It was almost that time of the week again, the time which Marcus dreaded—pruning time. He was standing at his desk holding Dr. Neal's file in his hand and trying to come to a sensible decision; the right decision.

The last forty eight hours had been productive.

Rose, Mickey's skinny girlfriend, had been tracked down.

The right question on the right street corner (backed by a twenty dollar bill) had led them to her with surprising ease. She had been very co-operative too, confirming what Marcus had guessed all along. Namely, that Dr. Neal had intervened in Mickey's attack on her, and despite beating the crap out of him, she had come to a tragic end. Rose would testify to this too, putting the final nail into the coffin of Mickey's argument that he had killed Dr. Neal in self defence.

The murder case was solved and he could now place the file officially in his out tray.

This unfortunately was what was proving to be his problem.

Sensible Marcus said put the file in the out tray and get on with other cases. These were—as usual—piling up.

Take for example the poor black kid, the boy with his throat cut. He had been dumped the other night on a street corner. A gangland killing if ever there was one. His body had been left as a warning to their rivals.

Our turf—keep out.

Marcus knew the area well and was a little surprised by the body's location.

The turf in question belonged to a villain known as Cole. He ran his patch with a ruthless efficiency that other gang leaders both admired as well as feared. It was unusual for anyone to cross him, particularly a young kid like this one. Marcus searched his memory for the victim's name. Elijah something or other. This was the sort of crime he should now be focusing on, the sort where he might be able to take down a really big fish, someone like Cole.

Unfortunately, there was his other side; the dark side of the force. Marcus the obsessive, Marcus the nitpicker; Marcus the dogged detective who had yet to explain the mystery of the knife.

This obsessive persona now had a possible witness; police officer Jessica O'Brien.

Unlike the restaurant CCTV footage, the cameras at the station were the latest in technology; providing pin sharp, detailed images and in full colour, too. He had several lovely stills of Officer O'Brien, and he had to agree with Mary at reception, she was indeed very attractive. A cascade of curly red hair, large pale blue eyes and a beautiful, wide smile.

She was absolutely stunning.

Sadly neither of the witnesses at the restaurant could definitely identify her as the headhead. She could be the woman who went up the alley, but she had been too far away from the restaurant for them to be absolutely sure. What he needed to do now was to talk to Officer O'brien, to confirm that she was indeed the red headed witness. She was a good match, and being a police officer meant he could track her down quickly.

Because of this he had done a little background checking and had stumbled upon a curious pattern.

Everything in her file seemed to be in order, but scratch the surface and you found absolutely nothing.

Officer O'Brien didn't have a life.

Take her parents, for example, they were both dead. Her references, one was dead and the other not contactable, his business had closed down. Her bank account too was extremely odd; regular monthly payments going in and cash withdrawals going out. These were all made in a monotonous and computer-like fashion. There were no random transactions, nothing haphazard as in his own disastrous account.

He had asked around the station and nobody seemed to recognise her face or know any of her friends. Perplexed, he had even telephoned the letting agent for the flat she was living in.

They hadn't heard of her or seen her around.

Everything on file looked correct and above board, but that was where it ended. She existed as a computer file—but nowhere else.

So here he was, about to make a decision—sensible Marcus or obsessive Marcus.

Out tray or in tray, the decision was black and white.

He took one last look at Dr. Neal's file.

He had written down Officer O'Brien's mobile number on the back of it. This had been on the computer, too. No doubt a dead number, but hey—it was worth a try.

Idly he dialed it.

"Hello, Jessica here."

The voice of a woman answered.

It had such a lovely Irish lilt.

29
Giants in Asgard

"Nice throw!" Emile exclaimed proudly as Kat's spear narrowly missed its target.

Kat was definitely improving, and her talent with the spear was beginning to draw attention. Other warriors and their maids would stop and watch her train, which Emile found extremely flattering.

Part of Kat's prowess was down to technique.

She had been good at athletics in high school and had learned the correct technique for throwing a javelin. This had translated into a style that allowed her to throw the spear nearly twice as far as the other Valkyries. Although at first she had been woefully inaccurate, this was improving dramatically. She was also getting a flatter trajectory, which meant losing some distance but increasing the speed and accuracy of her throws. Emile had previously been the best Valkyrie with this weapon, but she could see its crown slipping from her grasp.

Emile didn't mind. She was just pleased that with Jess away Kat was settled in and remained so contented. The story of her trouble with Hod had done the rounds and she was relieved that the incident hadn't damaged her confidence. If anything, she could see a new resolve.

They continued training in the arena for about an hour when a disturbance shook the town.

This started with the customary blowing of horns and beating of drums; but it was only when a red flag was raised above Gladsheim that they realised something more serious was afoot.

Grabbing her sword, spear, and shield, she beckoned for Kat to do likewise. After mounting their horses, they rode at a fast trot down to the main square. The sight that met them there was like no other Kat had seen before.

The Aesir were in a state of panic.

Women were screaming and crying and men were running around wildly waving pitchforks and shovels in the air. A bonfire had been lit, and the air was laden with acrid smoke.

Through the fire's haze Kat could make out a large chestnut stallion. He was hauling the biggest cart she had ever seen up the gentle rise from the bridge. Kat had not been in the hall yesterday when Thor had struck his deal with the mason. She had heard about it, but thought little of it at the time.

Now, seeing the cart and its extraordinary cargo, she was gripped by the same fear as the Aesir.

The spectacle was terrifying.

"I guess you've never seen giants before?" Carmel was at her side now and shouting excitedly in her ear.

"Aren't they hideous?"

Kat nodded slowly, she was dazed by the sight in front of her.

The cart slowly trundled up to the square and its occupants climbed out and formed a circle around it. A baying mob of townsfolk quickly surrounded them, poking crude, makeshift weapons menacingly in their faces. The noise and tension was increasing by the second, a tinderbox waiting to ignite.

For the moment there was a standoff, but one that wouldn't last long.

There was too much anger and resentment for the Aesir to hold back.

"SILENCE!"

Thor's mighty voice boomed above the noise.

The crowd fell silent immediately.

Thor strode forward and the Aesir parted obediently to create a pathway. Eventually he was standing in front of the mason and his horse.

As a hush descended, Kat was able to study the visitors from Jotunheim more closely.

The first thing she noticed, and she had to agree with Carmel's comment, was the fact that they were giants. Each individual stood at least two metres tall, with some rising to over two and a half metres in height. The men were heavily muscled with powerful arms and legs, and huge barrel shaped chests. They were all bare-chested and darkly tanned, although this might have been an illusion due to the dust and dirt from their journey and the dense, coarse hairs which swathed their bodies. Their faces were unusual, and reminded Kat of pictures she had seen back at medical school; artists' impressions of Neanderthals.

Each man had coarse features with a long broad nose and prominent eyebrows. This latter formed a single ridge across their foreheads. Their eyes were dark and deeply set, and they had long, matted hair and beards. None of them were wearing shoes, and they seemed to talk to each other in grunts, gestures, and facial expressions. They were ugly, but in a strange way they were beautiful; perfectly adapted to life in the cold and rarefied mountain air.

They were an awesome sight, and one Kat wouldn't have missed for all the world.

"SVADILFARI!"

Thor hollered the name of the horse and it whinnied in reply, turning its haunches obligingly to reveal the yellow 'S' he had painted yesterday.

"What trickery is this? Get me Loki at once."

Thor could see immediately he had been fooled.

The horse was indeed Svadilfari but not the greying beast with the weak back of yesterday. No, the stallion before him seemed fifteen years younger, and fifteen times stronger.

And what of the master mason?

Gone too was his grey hair and rounded shoulders, replaced by rippling muscles and a straight back.

"Loki!" Thor shouted at the top of his voice, and the thunder of a galloping horse told the crowd that he was on his way.

"What's the matter now?" Loki exclaimed nervously and breathlessly as he jumped down from his steed.

"You've tricked me for the last time." Thor was pulling his chain metal gloves from his belt in a very ominous manner. "This time you've gone too far."

"Where? What trickery? Show me Thor, show me?"

Kat had to admire Loki's nerve.

Far from turning tail and running, he was calling Thor's bluff. This was brave, but very foolish, too.

"Look at the mason and his horse, and look at all these giants!" Thor waved Mjollnir in their direction. As he did so, it glistened in the sunlight and seemed to grow in size.

"I can see them Thor, my dear friend, I've got eyes."

Loki was trying to soothe him now.

"They seem younger today I agree but that is not my doing. Perhaps they used charcoal or flour to appear older yesterday, but I swear I took no part in any such deception." He ended apologetically, and tried to sound as sincere as he possibly could be.

"And as for the other giants, why, they have been pulled by Svadilfari in a cart from Jotunheim, just as you agreed. One cart, but you didn't specify the size. That my dear friend is your mistake, not trickery nor treachery."

Loki stood back proudly, admiring the eloquence of his words.

Thor was flummoxed.

He scratched at his head, pulled at his beard, and battered Mjollnir into his hand. His desire to smash a few skulls was intense, but he was a god of the Aesir and his word was his bond. He would always honour an agreement, even one he might lose.

Still, there had been mischief and he had to know if Loki was involved. This issue was more than just about a wall; their very friendship was at stake.

"We need to have a word," Thor finally spoke as he pulled off his gloves and returned them, and Mjollnir, to his belt. He beckoned for Loki to come join him, and Loki did so with a very obvious look of relief on his face.

Thankfully, he wouldn't be meeting his end today.

Kat saw the two of them link arms and the flash of Thor's ring as he waved his hand across it. Within a heartbeat she saw a second flash. The two had been to Odin's garden and their faces now seemed much more relaxed. Clearly Loki had convinced Thor that there was still nothing to worry about.

Even with so many helpers, the task was still impossible.

"Come people of Asgard!" Thor bellowed as he stretched his arms out wide above his head.

"Make these citizens of Jotunheim welcome, they have much work to do."

Turning to Loki he slapped him hard upon the back.

"Come my dear friend, we must have a drink."

30
Officer O'Brien

With an intense buzz of excitement, Marcus hurried down the corridor from his office to reception. His visitor was already there, and the mystery surrounding Dr. Neal's case might finally be resolved.

By sheer fluke, police officer Jessica O'Brien had been on her way up to the station to see Mickey again. After a brief conversation over the phone, she had sounded delighted to stop by and have a chat with him first.

As he arrived at reception, he could see her waiting at the desk. The officer was simply breathtaking.

She had taken her hat off and her beautiful red hair hung exactly as he had imagined. Her uniform hugged her figure, and he could imagine the beautiful, toned body beneath. He tried to remember his inspector's words: "You can read the menu, so long as you don't order."

He also tried to remember that he was married to Anna.

"Hi, Detective Finch here," he held out his hand to the woman.

"Good afternoon," Jess smiled radiantly and shook his hand firmly. Her grip was as strong as it was steady.

"Would you mind coming up to my office for a minute?" Marcus enquired, hoping he didn't sound too eager with this request.

"Well of course not, detective," Jess replied reassuringly.

"Please call me Marcus, detective sounds far too formal."

Jess nodded, and invited Marcus to call her by her first name, too.

"There's just one little formality," Marcus indicated to the body scanner that stood next to the reception desk.

"Thank you," Jess removed her cuffs, gun, keys, and other metal objects and put them in a tray. As she did this, Marcus noticed a leather sheath amongst the items.

"May I ask what that is?" he enquired casually.

"Oh, a paper knife, it's sort of a family heirloom. I like to keep it about me for sentimental reasons, and back up in case my gun lets me down." Jess laughed, and patted her empty holster. "It's really very beautiful. Would you like to take a closer look?"

Marcus nodded and unsheathed the knife. It was a beautiful piece of craftsmanship. The knife was very light, and perfectly balanced between the blade, which was about eight centimetres long, and the handle. This latter was very ornate; being carved in the shape of a bird with a long neck. The creature was probably a swan, although he was no expert in these matters.

"It's lovely," Marcus observed turning the knife over appreciatively in his hands. "Is this a swan?"

"Absolutely right. My, you are so clever." Jess purred these words deliberately and they had the desired effect.

Marcus blushed; Jess teased him so beautifully. Her voice sounded like honey.

Overwhelmed by her charm, it wasn't until he had replaced the knife in its sheath that the penny finally dropped.

YOU IDIOT!

The words screamed like a siren.

Dr. Neal was stabbed with a knife!

He quickly looked at the blade again. Its size and width was a perfect match for the stab wound. It was the craziest possible notion, but instinct told him he was right.

Officer Jessica O'Brien—the redheaded witness—had become a suspect.

His mind reeled in shock, dazed by this stunning turn of events. He had to tread carefully and be guarded with what he said. He decided not to ask if she had been the witness–at least not until after he'd done some tests.

This was going to be tough.

"Officer O'Brien," he began once more with a nervous cough.

"Oh do please call me Jess," she reminded him jokingly and the warmth in her voice made him feel embarrassed for entertaining such a crazy thought. Still, he had to see it through; he had no alternative.

"Jess, I wonder, would you mind letting me borrow your knife briefly to give our lab a chance to look it over? This should only take a few minutes."

He studied her reaction.

"Of course not, that's no problem at all."

Jess flashed him a dazzling smile and he noticed that she didn't bat an eyelid.

Either he was barking mad, or this lady had to be the coolest customer he had ever encountered.

Marcus waved to another officer to take the knife up to the lab, and he escorted Jess to his office where they chatted pleasantly for about half an hour.

Marcus quickly learned she was working for the department of prisoner welfare, and her visit to see Mickey was part of a random sample. Prisoners they intended to use in an audit. They also discussed the unseasonably cold weather and the wonderful views of New York from her flat.

Finally, a lab technician returned the knife and he handed it back to Jess.

Their conversation was over, but he felt reluctant to end it there. She was one of the most charming women he had ever encountered and a breath of fresh air. So very different from the trash he usually associated with.

Finally Jess stood up and held out her hand.

"It's been a pleasure meeting you Marcus, thank you so much for your kind hospitality. I do hope your case for Dr. Neal goes well. By the way, would it be convenient for me to pop down now and see Mr. Warren?" She added hopefully.

"Oh, I'm so sorry, I'm afraid that won't be possible. He's in court today for his bail application and he won't be back until much later."

Marcus apologised for Mickey's absence.

"That's a shame, perhaps another day then. So charming to meet you," Jess shook Marcus's hand warmly, turned, and then walked out of the office.

Marcus followed her elegant departure with his eyes.

After she left, Marcus picked up the phone and dialled the lab. He had lied to Jess about Mickey being in court, just as Jess had lied to him about her apartment, the department of prisoner welfare, and her reasons for seeing Mickey.

As he waited on the phone he considered this unexpected twist.

There were two things he was now sure of.

One—that the knife in Jess's possession was the one that stabbed Dr. Neal.

Two—that Jessica O'Brien wasn't a police officer.

This really only left him with one mystery outstanding.

Who exactly was she?

31

A Thank You from Ruby

DING DONG!

Ruby rang the doorbell to Slim's flat.

It was eight thirty in the evening and she liked to be on time. She felt sure that Slim would appreciate her punctuality—as well as her outfit tonight.

Ruby had gone to quite some trouble to select a Dominatrix theme for her look this evening; tight, black leggings and black, strapless bustier with an extra wide belt. This was scarlet in colour, and buckled tightly to cinch her waist. She had tied her hair back too in a French tuck, and had bought a studded leather choker to complete the image. Oh yes, she had almost forgotten the best bit. The pointed cowboy boots with metal spiked heels.

Sadly for voyeurs, her fantasy outfit had been covered by a long, black leather coat. New York was well below freezing tonight.

"Hello Slim." Ruby smiled sweetly when he opened the door. Avoiding a welcoming hug, she strutted arrogantly past him.

Slim tittered lasciviously.

"Hey, what's in the bag?" he inquired as he closed the door behind her.

'Oh, just some toys, to help me say thank you."

His expression—what bliss—it was priceless!

Taking off her coat, she placed this and her bag on the sofa. Slim came across the room, eager to get his hands on her body. Intercepting these tactfully, she turned her cheek and allowed him a tiny peck.

"Ooooh, so much hurry and we have all night," she purred, pulling the bottle of scotch from her bag.

"Would you mind pouring us both a drink while I use your toilet?"

"Certainly, Legs."

Slim indicated the direction of the bathroom and took the bottle from her hands. He deliberately used Cole's nickname. With the boss out of the way, he was going to have fun. He was top dog in town and Ruby was his reward.

Fuck!

Cole's squeeze sure was a sexy bitch—and then some. She was into some seriously kinky stuff too by the looks of things. He was going to fuck her hard and it seemed almost a pity to kill her afterwards—what a waste. Still, he wasn't going to get his throat cut like that dumb-arsed, stupid kid. He wasn't that ignorant.

No matter what the bitch promised, no ho could hold her tongue. Cole wouldn't be pleased when he discovered that his fine piece of ass had disappeared; but then again, who really gave a shit?

He'd get over it.

Good ass was cheap and so easy to find.

Ruby walked slowly over to the bathroom, exaggerating the swing to her hips. She just hoped Slim wouldn't prematurely "pop his cork"—so to speak. Locking the door behind her, she relieved herself in his toilet. She had taken a laxative in the morning and had been holding it all day.

Feeling more comfortable, she took stock of her situation.

Like most thugs, Slim's name was a parody.

He was a middle aged white guy with grey balding hair. His stand out feature was his fatness, having a large pot belly and chubby limbs. He looked unfit and prematurely aged, but as Cole's right hand man she knew he would be strong and street wise.

It was always a danger to underestimate your opponent, and she had been around far too long to make that basic mistake. She would strike hard and fast, incapacitate him first before picking him off at her leisure.

The apartment was small with thin walls, so if she wanted to take her time she had to minimize the noise. Slim would certainly have a gun and this had to be taken into account. There was no easy escape route from the flat either, so she couldn't afford a mistake.

Her main weapon would be surprise.

Slim was blinded by lust; she wasn't by revenge.

Ruby focused briefly on Elijah's smile, and then his battered, bloodied face. An image of Joe flashed into her head. *Good.* She could feel the anger inside her beginning to simmer.

She was ready.

Without flushing the toilet, she returned to the room.

"I do hope you haven't peeked inside my bag. Have you Slim? Have you been a naughty little boy and taken a look?" she teased, picking her bag up from the settee.

Slim was giggling lecherously, hardly able to contain his excitement.

"Oh I did, I did. I have been bad, a really, really bad boy!" He practically drooled as he spoke.

"Good. I was so hoping you would say that. Now I want you to stand in the corner and look at the wall. I will tell you when to turn round. I think I will punish you before I give you your reward."

Oh sweet Odin this was such fun! She just hoped she could stop her self from laughing out loud.

Slim obediently did as she asked and she noted with quiet satisfaction his manhood sticking out from beneath his trousers. He was rock hard. Quietly, she slipped the knuckleduster onto her right hand and held it behind her back. She waited a few moments, allowing Slim's fantasies to run riot.

"You can turn round now."

Posing provocatively, hips thrust to one side and weight on one leg; Ruby beckoned with her finger for Slim to come closer.

"Come on, closer, closer, a little bit more—" she paused; Slim was foaming at the mouth.

WHOOMPH!

In a breath defying blur, Ruby's right hand connected hard with Slims stomach. He doubled up and exhaled loudly.

He was winded.

"What the fuck?" he gasped.

"Oh dear, and there I was thinking that you liked to play rough." Ruby taunted him.

"I do," he spluttered. "But that was—"

SMASH!

Slim didn't finish his sentence.

Ruby struck him hard across the face with the knuckleduster. He sprawled sideways, landing on his hands and knees. She hoped she'd broken his jaw.

Breathing heavily for a moment, Slim made a lunge for her legs.

Deftly, Ruby danced out of the way.

"Too slow, too slow, fat boy. Come on, you can do better than that."

She really hoped he could; she wanted him to make a decent fight of things and so far he was being a disappointment.

"I'm so going to fuckin' nail your arse, you fucking whore!" Slim cursed loudly as he staggered to his feet. His hand went for his holster, just as she'd anticipated.

Ruby waited until he had drawn his gun, and then sprung into action.

THWACK!

She flicked out a kick and the gun span from his hand and into a corner of the room. As soon as her foot landed, she moved forward turning sideways. Cocking her other leg high in the air, she bent her knee before thrusting the heel of her boot out beside her. Straight legged, the metal tip connected with his chest with a squelching thud.

It had penetrated the soft muscles between two ribs.

Slim howled and fell backward. As he landed Ruby, flicked another kick to his chest.

He rolled away, screaming in agony.

"You're so fuckin dead, you bitch! You wait 'til Cole hears about this." He gasped, hoping that his threat would put an end to her assault.

"Well now that's the thing," Ruby taunted him. "I'm not going to be telling Cole and you, fat boy, would have to be alive to do so."

She kicked him again in the same spot, the precision and ferocity making him howl.

"Why, fucking hell! What have I done to you, you fucking ho?" His voice was half pleading now.

Her assault had murderous intent and Slim didn't want to die. Thrusting a hand deep into a pocket, he fumbled with the buttons on his mobile phone. Cole would get to know what had gone on, even if this drug crazed bitch did finish him off tonight.

He found, and then pressed, the record button.

Ruby circled his writhing body. Revenge burned like a demon inside her.

"Not me—you idiot. Elijah! You killed my friend Elijah, and for that I will take your life and soul."

Bending forward, she punched him hard again in the face. His nose broke and blood gushed from it.

He began to whine and moan. Slim was a broken man, and no longer a threat.

"I'm sorry, I didn't know, I swear. Please, Ruby, please forgive me."

Slim begged for his life. He just hoped this bitch had a heart.

"I didn't notice you forgiving Elijah, did I? What did he ever do to hurt you?"

Her blood lust finally exploded and in a fury of revenge she delivered a hurricane of kicks and stamps. These rendered Slim almost unconscious.

"You have no idea who you are dealing with," Ruby sneered as she circled him, kicking and stamping at will. "I am Prudr, I am a Valkyrie, a warrior, an angel of death; I'm here to take your evil, rotten soul."

He was a dead man already, it didn't matter what she said or what he heard anymore.

Ruby continued to circle and kick for about ten minutes. Gradually his pleading and crying became weaker and more muffled as blood pooled in his mouth and nose. Finally, growing bored of his agony, she took the duct tape from her bag. She tied his hands and arms tightly behind his back.

Slim didn't resist, he was barely conscious.

"Come on, get up!"

Ruby pulled him roughly by his shirt collar and Slim half crawled, half shuffled behind her to the bathroom. This now smelt offensively.

Shutting the door, she ordered Slim to kneel in front of the toilet. She paused, lit a cigarette and then grabbed the scruff of his neck once more. She pushed his head, face first, deep into the bowl. He wretched and heaved at the stench.

"Do you smell this? Do you smell this excrement do you?" she bent down and snarled the words close behind his ear.

"Welcome to hell."

In a deft move, she raised his arms behind his back and plunged his face deep into the filthy water. He began to wriggle violently so she pressed her foot down hard on the back of his head, forcing his face to stay buried beneath the water.

Ruby smiled contentedly.

She loved the sound of him choking and gagging in her mess.

She was going to have some fun.

Playing with him, she let him up to gasp a quick gulp of air before forcing him deep into her filth. He wasn't going to drown just yet; he had to suffer like Elijah. She wanted him helpless in her hands, begging as he swallowed the shit around his face.

For a while, this became a little game; the more he swallowed the longer she let him live. Eventually, as his struggling began to weaken, she pulled the flush and watched the bowl fill up around his head.

It was time to die.

Ruby held Slim under water, arms high behind his back and her foot on his head, until his body had stopped struggling and she was certain he was dead. Finally she released him; and his lifeless corpse rolled from the toilet and landed heavily on the floor.

Returning to the sitting room, she collected her dagger and then stood over Slim once more.

"I'll be seeing you later," she spat as she plunged her knife deep into his heart.

Calmly she strolled back into the sitting room and picked up the phone.

She dialed 911.

"Hello, which emergency?" asked the operator.

"Police please."

"Just wait a minute while I connect you."

Ruby held.

"Hello, how can I help you?" a different voice enquired a few moments later.

"I would like to report a murder," Ruby replied calmly, lighting another cigarette.

"Are you sure it was murder?" the operator asked tactfully, trying to be helpful.

"Yes, absolutely; I've just killed the man."

Ruby put the phone down.

She preferred the police found Slim rather than any of Cole's goons; his thugs might just put two and two together.

Packing her bag, and after looking carefully around the room to make sure she hadn't left anything behind, Ruby finished her cigarette and then left.

Slim's mobile continued to record, long after the echoes of her footsteps had faded from the hall.

32

Odin Returns

Over the next few days a feeling of apprehension settled uncomfortably over Asgard. This hung in the air like a heavy blanket; stifling the usual merriment.

Everybody had only one thought on their minds, the progress of the men from Jotunheim; 'the giants'—as the Aesir referred to them.

Their daily toil quickly became a spectacle; a well-organised system of working that was orchestrated by the master mason.

On the first day, they cleared the debris and undergrowth that had covered the remnants of the old wall. They then chose which stones they wanted to keep.

On the second day, most of the giants disappeared to a quarry they had found. The noise which they made there was deafening. A constant barrage of chipping and chiselling that started just after dawn and ended just before dusk. The remaining giants cleaned and positioned the stones they'd chosen to use. Hour after hour they toiled, heaving and hauling them into place. Svadilfari played his part too, dragging the huge cart overflowing with freshly hewn rocks from the quarry to the wall. He worked without pause, and without complaint.

By the end of the third day a complete ring of the stone wall had been laid. This rose to about the height of a man's waist.

Thor watched their progress anxiously, pacing this way and that, stroking fretfully at his beard. He was a worried man, as was Queen Freyja.

Each day, in the early evening, she would trot down on her stallion to the wall, watch a while, before cantering swiftly back to the castle. Her face would be ashen and her brow deeply furrowed.

It was probably sometime on the second day that Thor told her the full extent of his deal and what that might mean for her. Kat felt quitely confident about this because Thor attended the evening's feast with a large, red welt on his cheek.

No doubt Freyja's opinion of his incompetence.

The townsfolk were kept busy too, with almost all of them being required to assist in one way or another. Thor had allowed the giants to set up camp in a field on the far side of the bridge, and he had agreed to feed them each night in Gladsheim; the only hall big enough to house them all.

Each day they consumed vast quantities of food and drink; forcing crops to be harvested early and keeping the huntsmen busy. These scoured the countryside hunting for deer, boar, pheasants, and other beasts to fill the giants' bellies.

The women too were kept busy, making porridge, bread, butter, ale, and mead. The giants ate at dawn and dusk, and no matter how much the Aesir laid on the table, they would finish every morsel.

The Valkyries and their maids couldn't avoid duties, either. Each day two warriors patrolled the wall and quarry, riding their horses in full battle dress. Each carried their sword, shield, spear, bow and quiver replete with arrows.

They were ready to fight at a moment's notice.

Kat, because of her inexperience, was spared this task; and she concentrated hard on improving her skills. She could now ride well in the saddle, but not bareback, and had progressed to sparring in armed combat with the other maids.

In a strange way this, and her problem with Hod, was bringing her closer to Carmel. The one maid she never thought she could grow to like.

With Silk busy on patrol, Carmel and she engaged in combat most days, using weapons carefully adapted to prevent serious injuries or death. Spears had their points filed down, axe heads were wrapped in leather and practice swords had their tips broken and their blades blunted and bound with thick twine.

Despite these measures, the weapons still had weight, and the maids battled each other ferociously until one of them submitted. Kat quickly had the better of Carmel with the spear, often using it like a staff to batter her. Carmel however reigned supreme with the axe and sword. She had strong arms and much of the skill of Silk.

During breaks between sessions the two girls would talk widely, gradually getting to know each other.

Carmel found Kat thoughtful and inquisitive, often forcing her to think about her life more deeply than she really cared to.

Kat in turn discovered that Carmel was quick witted and knowledgeable, knowing everything about the comings and goings of Asgard. With her keen nose for gossip, little passed Carmel by. They spoke often of Hod, although the arrival of the giants had forced a delay to Kat's plans. They both agreed that for now the danger posed by these visitors far outweighed her need to sort their relationship out. However, both girls decided to keep needling Hod.

Kat would keep avoiding him while Carmel would taunt him about her new lover.

Day by day, Hod was slowly becoming more jealous and suspicious. He was desperate to discover the identity of his rival for Kat's affection. Their plan was on target and all they needed to do now was to choose a day—and then pull the trigger.

At the end of the third day of work on the wall, a welcomed warmth returned to Asgard in the shape of Odin. He arrived as suddenly and unexpectedly as he had left; with no fanfare and no formalities.

Unlike his departure, however, Odin returned with company.

To everybody's relief he brought with him Prima, a warrior who had been patrolling along the far edge of the plain of Ida. Her return greatly eased the strain of keeping watch over the giants and her presence strengthened the number of warriors should there be trouble.

Along with the Prima, came two further guests, neither of whom was very pleasant.

Odin was accompanied by two dwarves.

They were brothers called Fjalar and Galar, who had journeyed from the court of their king. They came bearing a precious gift. In a cart pulled by two stout ponies, was a single heavy chest.

This was filled to bursting with gold coins.

Odin returned in excellent spirits, and even the shock of seeing giants in his kingdom couldn't dampen his joy. His love for gold was legendary, and he would be transporting their gift to Valhalla.

Rumour had it that this great hall dripped with gold.

Before feasting that evening, Odin decided to deal with some outstanding matters. First he took issue with Thor and then with Loki; whom he still hadn't forgiven for his wind breaking stunt.

Odin was very displeased with Thor's deal with the mason. It was a stupid and risky gamble and one that left him very disappointed. He felt so angry about Thor's foolishness that a cold silence fell between them; it was one that would last for many days.

Loki, on the other hand, was quickly forgiven and warmly welcomed at Odin's table. The gift of a horse so fine as Sleipnir could pardon many a misdemeanour.

The dwarves joined the feasting too that evening, sitting at Odin's table and speaking little to the other guests. They kept their own company, and no one was able to find out why they were here and with such an extravagant gift. Even a lap dance from the seductive and usually successful Carmel failed to loosen their tongues.

Despite ending the evening so drunk that they could hardly stand, the dwarves kept their silence.

As the partying slowly finished for the night, Kat stood at her window and gazed once more across the land beneath her. She felt a great relief and comfort now that Odin had returned.

What ever happened with the giants, she felt sure they would come to no harm.

The wolves were howling once more, a cheerless wail that echoed menacingly from the mountains. She dreaded their sound more than any other. It was hard to believe that both Odin and Loki kept such vicious beasts as pets.

As she turned to go to bed, Kat heard one howl rise high above the rest. It was Fenrir again, though he sounded much closer than she had ever heard him before.

She shivered for a while in the cool evening air, and then closed her window.

33

Two for the Price of One

Marcus sat at the small interview table absent mindedly stirring a cup of black coffee. He had been up all night and had a heavy head and the bags under his eyes to prove it.

In spite of his weariness, he had a contented smile on his face.

Quite possibly, the events of the last twelve hours had been the finest of his career. Events that could propel him into the position of inspector, with all the pay and perks that would offer. Two crimes solved, one criminal dead, and the other sitting in front of him now. Not a bad haul for one night's frenetic activity.

Marcus motioned with his hand to his assistant to switch the tape recorder on, and then he looked up slowly from his steaming cup of coffee.

He stared intently at the person sitting in handcuffs before him.

"Good morning Ms. Knight. I must apologise for dragging you out of bed at such an unreasonable hour," he paused, and then added as a poignant afterthought. "As you can see, your activities of yesterday have left me with little sleep, either."

The woman nodded empathetically, the uncombed locks of her tousled hair doing little to hide her beauty. She flashed a warm smile, and then spoke in a calm voice that echoed with an accent from the depths of Southern Virginia.

"I'm so sorry to have caused you so much trouble, Detective Finch."

Marcus sat back and eyed some of the contents of her room which they had seized. These had been laid out on the table between them.

Three items stood out from the rest, and with these in mind he tried to collect his thoughts.

His interrogation of Ms. Ruby Knight was certainly going to be interesting.

Ruby's phone call to the police the evening before set in motion a chain of events that surprised even Marcus in their speed and by their smoothness.

Once more Marcus found himself on call and with a murder on his patch.

Tonight, however, the crime sounded very different from the norm. His assistant, Dave, could barely suppress his excitement when he spoke to him on the phone, and he was even now hopping up and down, beckoning enthusiastically as Marcus parted the yellow and black police ticker tape that sealed the entrance to the flat.

"I've got something amazing for you to listen to," Dave exclaimed breathlessly as he brandished a small mobile phone under his nose. This had been neatly sealed in a transparent plastic bag and labeled as evidence.

"Just give me a minute, all right."

Marcus waved him away, irritated by this intrusion on his thinking space. He needed a moment to get his bearings; try to get a feeling for the sequence of events that had lead up to the brutal slaying in the bathroom.

He looked around the cramped room, surprised by its austerity and the squalor that greeted him. A week old, half empty carton of milk lay on a side board along with the partially eaten contents of a take away pizza. Cups of tea and coffee, half full and covered with mould, were scattered around the room like so many shabby ornaments.

Marcus already knew the victim's name, Vincent "Slim" Tucker; a notorious hard man and right hand thug to Cole Farra, the local crime lord. He would have thought Slim, with the amount of back-handers and crooked deals he had made over his illustrious career, could afford a much more up market pad. Maybe he had his money stashed away in a nice Miami condo, or some kind of off shore tax haven?

Either way, it didn't matter anymore.

Slim was dead; another vicious criminal Marcus could take off his 'Most wanted' list.

Marcus crossed over to the bathroom and immediately became nauseous. It wasn't the battered, blood spattered body that caused this sensation; it was the still potent smell of human excrement that hung heavily in the air. It wasn't a nice place to die, but probably appropriate for a piece of white trash like Slim.

"So, what's the story?"

Marcus turned toward Dave, hoping his appraisal of the crime scene matched his own.

"Well," Dave took a deep breath in as he tried to contain his excitement. "It looks like there was a bit of a struggle in the sitting room before the victim was bound and dragged to the bathroom. He was then stabbed in the chest and drowned in the toilet just there."

"Stabbed?" Marcus's curiosity was aroused, making him temporarily forget his nausea.

"Yes, stabbed."

Dave pointed to the entry point in Slim's body.

Blood still seeped from the wound.

Marcus crouched down and after taking a handkerchief from his pocket to cover his nose; he craned his neck forward to examine the neat incision more closely.

It looked identical to the one in Dr. Neal's case—same width, same position.

"Did you say stabbed and then drowned, or could it have been the other way round?"

"I dunno," Dave had been caught off guard by this question. To him, it made more sense to stab and incapacitate someone first before finishing them off by drowning.

"To be honest I don't know why they didn't use Slim's shooter. We found it in the corner of the room over there."

Dave indicated vaguely in the direction of the sitting room.

"Perhaps they didn't want to disturb anyone with the sound of a gun being fired?" Marcus mulled this over for a moment, then after standing up he changed the subject. "Why were you so excited about the phone?" he motioned toward the item. This was still in Dave's gloved hand.

"Because we know who the killer is, and we know why SHE killed him." Dave replied gleefully, like a cat that had eaten all the cream.

"Slim, he recorded it all. Listen."

Marcus ushered Dave away from the toilet, through the sitting room and into the kitchen. They needed some peace to hear the recording properly, not surrounded by the noisy comings and goings of police, photographers, forensic investigators and the like. Minute by minute the flat was becoming ever more crowded, like some badly organised circus ring.

Dave found the recording and switched it on. They stood close together side by side, each straining one ear to the phone. As the minutes of the recording rolled by, Marcus found his jaw dropping further and further down, leaving his mouth gapping ever wider. It was a gold mine, a complete confession and a cornucopia of other evidence.

Marcus quickly learned that Slim's killer was a woman called Ruby, that Slim already knew her, and that her reason for killing him was because he had killed Elijah Kelly. Marcus presumed Elijah must have been Ruby's lover.

In one stroke he had both the Kelly case solved and this one—brilliant!

The two detectives continued to listen as the woman ranted on about souls and being an angel of death. They both concluded that she had to be high on cocaine and alcohol or something. Her last words were strange too, "See you later."

Had she intended to return to the crime scene, and if so, why call the police?

This was odd, but junkies sometimes said and did the craziest of things.

Tracking Ruby down had taken minutes.

A quick phone call to one of the numbers on Slim's mobile confirmed that she was the latest squeeze of Cole, and that she worked at *The Candy Girls* club. This was just one block away from Slim's flat. A brief word with the manager there, and they had the address where she lived.

Marcus thought carefully about the badly beaten state of Slim's body.

This woman was fully drugged up and was obviously both strong and dangerous. He decided to call in a SWAT team to arrest her. He didn't want to take any chances. He was well past the age when he felt the need to go and heroically put the cuffs on himself. He left that to the experts these days.

At 4 am precisely, the team hit the motel. Ruby was handcuffed and in the back of a heavily armoured van before she had even opened her eyes.

Job well done—job very well done indeed.

In the small hours, Marcus returned home but found yet again he was unable to sleep. He was too excited, too pleased with their collective success. Pulling on a fresh shirt and trousers, he had headed back down to the station and begun sifting through the items found in Ruby's room.

Among the usual jumble of clothes, lipstick, toothpaste, and money, three items stood out and vied for his attention.

The first was in Ruby's small leather purse, mixed in with a credit card and some money. It stood out like a shiny beacon; an unusual yellow-coloured coin, one which looked both old and new at the same time. It was about the size of a quarter, rough milled and stamped in a very old fashioned manner. It felt soft, like gold, and shone as though it were new.

Marcus had no explanation for this as yet.

The second item was a worn, leather bound flask with a cork stopper. This was about one third filled with a red coloured liquid, which smelt mildly of alcohol. Marcus guessed that this would turn out to be a dizzy cocktail of drugs and booze, the substance she no doubt was high on when she had murdered Slim. He decided to send this off to the labs in the morning, he was sure they would have fun with it.

The final item, and the one that almost stopped his heart from beating, was the knife he was now turning over and over in his hands. This was identical in every way to the one he had examined yesterday, the one which belonged to Ms. O'Brien. Indeed, it probably was the same knife, and this was what excited him so much.

Perhaps she, and Ms. O'Brien, were both in some strange type of drug-based cult; a cult that got its kicks on violence and ritualistic killings?

This was only a hunch, but it felt like a good one. If he was right and he could expose them, then he would hit the big time and make some serious money.

Secretive, drug crazed women running riot in the city, wielding knives, evading the law, and stabbing people through the heart?

Ka-ching!

The story was mind blowing.

Good bye boring old police station and hello Oprah and the glamour of day time TV.

Trying to hold his fantasies in check, he looked up once more from the knife to Ruby. She sat there calm and composed, a stark contrast to his exhausted and nervous state.

"Perhaps, Ms. Knight, you could begin by telling me something about this knife?"

34

Chamomile and Lavender

By the sixth day of wall building, the air of apprehension that had gripped Asgard had descended into one of gloom. People went about their work almost in silence, the only sounds to be heard coming from the giants as they chiselled and heaved the last stone blocks into place.

The wall was already as high as the previous one, and only one row of stones and a gateway was left to build.

Among the giants a carnival atmosphere was growing. They knew they could complete the job, and they had time to spare showing off and playing games. The Aesir looked on in horror as they entertained themselves, throwing huge boulders at grazing cattle, or seeing how many children they could swing beneath their outstretched arms.

Without Odin's intervention, it seemed certain that tomorrow they would lose their beloved Queen.

It was against this backdrop that Carmel stood in the Hall of Gladsheim and waited nervously for Thor to arrive. He had especially requested a private meeting with her today, and she was at a loss to explain why. Under normal circumstances, she would have been proud of such an invitation. But today was not a normal day, and she couldn't help but feel that their meeting had something to do with the wall. Quite why he wanted to discuss this with her was beyond her imagination.

Thor strode through the doorway in a state of nervous agitation. He was chewing at his fingers and mumbling noisily to himself. As he drew near, he managed to force a watery smile, or something that might just about pass for one.

"Please come near, fair Carmel."

Thor sat on one of the thrones and beckoned for her to join him.

"Has Loki said anything to you about this mess?" he waved his hand in the general direction of the building works.

"No my lord, we haven't spoken about it."

Suddenly the lights came on and Carmel knew why she was there. Pillow talk. Her relationship with Loki had blossomed since his return and they were a recognised item around the town. This had obviously been noted by Thor.

"Nothing at all?" Thor probed hopefully. "Not even in bed?" He was clutching at straws now.

"No my Lord, nothing," Carmel spoke with honesty and without fear. When she and Loki were together, the problems of Asgard were the last things on their minds.

"Oh sweet Odin." Thor placed his chin on his chest and tugged slowly at his beard. "Loki promised they wouldn't be able to finish it, he swore they wouldn't—he swore they couldn't," he was half talking and half thinking out loud.

"My Lord, as the giants were deceitful surely your deal with them is null and void? They can finish the wall and you can chase them away with your mighty hammer. Isn't that possible?"

Carmel tried to sound encouraging. She felt uneasy seeing Thor so down in the dumps.

"Oh fair Carmel. I wish it were that simple. Without proof of mischief I cannot go back on my word. To do so would be the undoing of the gods. Hasn't Loki hinted anything to you, any weakness of his kinsmen we could exploit, use against them to stop them finishing the wall?" He spoke in tones of desperation, having little hope that Carmel could have a solution to his predicament.

"No my Lord, he hasn't. I'm so sorry."

Carmel truly wished she could be more helpful. She felt awful. The life of her Queen was at stake and she had always had a soft spot for Thor. He was a good man, an honest man; the sort Loki could run rings round. He didn't deserve this humiliation.

"Oh well, at least you tried. Thank you for talking to me anyway," he slapped his thighs with both hands and slumped back into the throne. He looked the picture of despair.

Carmel wished she could do something.

"I think Freyja wishes to see all the Valkyries and their maids in her chambers soon, so I'd better not delay you any further. Thank you for your help, fairest Carmel." Thor gave her leave to go, and she trudged out of the hall with her shoulders slumped.

She had never felt so helpless since her arrival in Asgard.

As she walked she thought about what Thor had said. The giants were deceitful, so why can't we be, too? They must have a weakness, all men do.

"AH HAH!"

Carmel shouted loudly as she leapt excitedly into the air.

She had had a brain wave.

All men do have a weakness, and in that moment she knew exactly how to stop the giants from completing their task.

Changing direction, she hurried back into town to collect some supplies. She felt sure Freyja and the other Valkyries wouldn't mind her being late.

"Thank you my Valkyries for coming and seeing me today." Freyja spoke slowly and with great dignity to the gathering. She gazed slowly around her sumptuous bedroom and felt a great sorrow—but she didn't show it. She was determined that if she had to leave for the realm of Jotunheim tomorrow, she would do so with her head held high.

This was her right, her duty as the Queen of the Valkyries.

"It seems inevitable that the giants will soon complete their task, and tomorrow I will have to take my leave of you all." The room fell silent as she spoke. "If any of you have any requests or wishes you would like me to fulfil before I go, would you please speak now. I may not have much time later."

She felt tears welling in her eyes, but she refused to shed them. Not now, not in front of her warriors.

The girls looked at each other. Each wanted to say words of comfort, but none chose to be the first to break the silence. The atmosphere was leaden, reeking with the scent of despair. There seemed no way to save their Queen from her fate.

"Hi everybody," Carmel burst into the room, grinning broadly from ear to ear and brandishing something in her hand. "I'm so sorry for being late!" She exclaimed loudly and brashly, oblivious to the outrage her entry had caused the sombre meeting.

"Here, in my hands, lies the key to our salvation."

She tossed the small brown bottle from hand to hand, laughing cheerily as she did so.

"My Queen, your worries are over. Have no fear, you will not be marrying the giant king, and you will definitely not be going to Jotunheim tomorrow, that is, unless of course you want to." Carmel finished her little speech with a triumphant flourish.

The room around her erupted as each girl fought desperately to see what was in the bottle, and how it could possibly help their Queen. Carmel swiftly uncorked the vessel and passed it round, each girl taking it in turns to sniff the pungent liquid inside.

"Well, what is it?" Emile asked once the bottle had done its tour.

"That, my dear sisters, is a mixture of chamomile and lavender. The Aesir use it as a sleeping potion, and that is how we will stop the giants." She looked round the room expectantly, waiting for cheers and a round of applause.

She didn't get one.

"Um," it was Emile again. "This sounds like a good idea, but there is one small snag. How exactly are we going to get this potion into the giants in the first place? They'll smell it a mile off."

There was a chorus of agreement from the other girls. The lavender in particular was very pungent.

"Ah, well, now that's the clever part," and with that Carmel explained the detail of her plan to her rapt audience. Everybody agreed it was inspired, and they all left to get ready in high spirits, that is, with one exception—Kat.

"Come with me," Kat pulled Carmel into her room as they were leaving. "Look!" she pointed angrily at a large bunch of flowers on her dresser.

"Are they from who I think they are?" Carmel asked nosily, anticipating the answer.

"Yes, and it gets worse. He wants to see me tonight."

"Interesting, this could be the moment to set our little plan in motion. Would you like me to make the call?" Carmel felt excited; she was growing bored of just upsetting Hod, she wanted to see some action.

"I, I'm not sure," Kat paused, suddenly feeling nervous and indecisive. "Do you think Freyja's brother will like me? You know; find me attractive?"

"Don't be so daft. You're gorgeous," Carmel laughed; she knew Freyr would be delighted with such an attractive date.

"Are you sure?" Kat needed to hear her reassurance one more time.

"Yes, positive. Don't worry about a thing. I will arrange for both of them to be there as planned."

Carmel patted her on the arm.

"Okay. Well so long as you're certain then let's do it," Kat pulled away and folded her arms resolutely.

The flowers were beautiful, but they were from Hod. She didn't have the heart to throw them away, but she felt bad accepting them before she had sorted things out. He was still chasing after her, forcing himself upon her in a way that felt suffocating. She had intended to wait until the giants had gone, but this was an opportunity too good to miss.

"Are you sure Hod will come, too?"

Kat was fretting now.

"Stop worrying. By the time I've finished with him wild horses wouldn't keep him away. Just relax and trust me."

Carmel laughed as she left the room.

She knew Kat would have fun tonight, and she wished she could be there, too. Hod's face when he saw her with Freyr would be a picture.

Later that evening, as the sun set over Asgard, the men from Jotunheim assembled as usual in the great hall of Gladsheim for their supper. As they took to their seats a strange procession headed down toward them from the castle. It was lead by the Valkyrie warriors and their maids. Each was elegantly dressed in their best evening gowns, and they had had their hair freshly washed and elaborately styled. They wore fine necklaces and ear-rings, and the warriors wore jewelled silver crowns on their heads. They were a wondrous sight, and the Aesir quickly flocked to the roadside to marvel at their beauty.

Behind the girls came Balder, Tyr and Kvasir with his harp. They would help provide the entertainment for the evening. Finally, at the back of the procession was a cart bearing a large vessel overflowing with mead.

This had been brewed all afternoon and made especially for the occasion.

With a flourish, Balder threw open the doors to the hall and made an announcement to the hungry guests. To thank them for their wonderful work, they would be throwing a party in their honour. The likes of this party would be beyond their wildest dreams.

To the astonishment of the giants, the warriors and maids fanned out among them and filled their empty flagons with the mead they had brought.

"Come!" cried Balder. "Let's all drink a toast to the King of Jotunheim. Let's celebrate his triumph with the finest mead from the halls of Valhalla."

The giants let out a mighty roar, and in one long draft they drained their flagons. They hadn't tasted mead from Valhalla before so this had to be a great honour, regardless of its peculiar taste and smell. Sitting back down, their empty flagons were quickly refilled by the helpful Valkyries.

Kvasir struck up his harp, and the ladies began to dance for the giants, who were dazzled by their beauty. Deftly the girls weaved in and out of the tables, avoiding lustful hands that yearned to squeeze their slender waists and pinch their shapely behinds.

As the giants began to eat, Balder told them bold and daring tales, and Tyr cracked wicked jokes. These made them cry with laughter. As the giants enjoyed the show, the Valkyries plied them with mead from their vessel. Not one soul commented on its unusual flavour or smell.

Confident that they only had a few hours work left tomorrow, the giants let their hair down and enjoyed the party to the full. Some even tried to dance, which provided yet more amusement for their friends.

Slowly, as the hours passed by, the mead laced with the sleeping potion began to take its effect; and as the evening drew late into the night, one by one the giants fell happily into a deep and dreamless sleep.

Tomorrow, the men from Jotunheim would surely bask in their triumph.

35

Epiphany

After helping the other girls get ready for the night's festivities, Kat returned quietly and alone to her room. She wanted to go with them, join them in their fun, but she had to settle things with Hod. Quickly she changed into her warrior tunic. She didn't know why she felt like wearing this tonight, but somehow it just seemed right.

After a while, there was a gentle knock at her door.

"Come in," Kat called a little nervously. She didn't know what to expect.

Freyr entered, and Kat felt a huge wave of relief. He was exactly how she had hoped he would be; chiselled and hunky. The perfect man of her dreams, if she could ever remember having one. Her former life now seemed so long ago, a fading dot on a distant horizon.

He walked slowly over toward her, and as he did so she tried to stifle a laugh.

Now Kat knew why the other girls had all been giggling when they talked about him. She could see that below the waist he was well endowed.

Actually, she corrected herself, he was enormous!

Freyr followed the line of her eyes and quickly understood her mirth.

"Oh I'm sorry, didn't the other ladies explain who I am?" he too was now chuckling.

"No!" Kat was laughing more loudly now, welcoming the release of her nervous tension.

"I'm a fertility god, a god of love. I go round helping women and couples who need some assistance," he pointed to his groin. "This is, well, sort of my job description."

Kat collapsed in tears, howling with laughter—giants, dwarves, slaves, and now this—the Asgard equivalent of a sex counsellor! She really felt she had seen it all.

Freyr joined in the joke, and as their laughter subsided he told her more about himself.

He explained that just like Loki he could change shape, and that he had taken the form and character of a man whom Kat would feel comfortable with. His gift was to know a woman's desires, and adapt his appearance and manner to fulfil them. He was always available to those in Asgard who had need of him, especially those at the castle. Finally, he asked if she still wanted to use his services.

"Yes, but not all of them, and not here. Could we go to Odin's garden, please?"

"Of course we can," Freyr took her by the hand, and with a wave of his they vanished from the room.

Arriving in the garden, Kat led Freyr to Yggdrasill and they lay down gingerly beside each other. They talked at first and Kat was thrilled by his charming manner. His company was perfection.

After a while, they began to slowly kiss and caress each other, cautiously and delicately at first. Being with him felt so good, so joyous. He made her feel more relaxed than at any time since Jess had gone away.

A powerful emotion rose swiftly within Kat.

It was the blood lust and it hungered now for passion—not war.

Kat knew she should resist it, but its potency was too intoxicating. The plan had been for Hod to see some gentle petting, nothing more; just enough to crush his love; not destroy his soul.

Now, faced with a tidal wave of desire, Kat couldn't hold back.

Forgetting the problems around her, the giants, Carmel, Jess, Hod; she made love to Freyr in a frenzy of wild and unfettered passion. She wanted him, she needed him, and this time she was in control.

The blood lust was hers and she bathed joyously in its fire.

Kat had no idea how long their love making lasted and she didn't really care. All she knew was that when they were done, it had been the best she'd ever known.

Exhausted, she rolled over and lay by his side; basking in the contentment he had given her. His powerful eruption lay deep inside her and her heart felt complete. The lust had been quenched and she could rest now in peace.

Eventually, Freyr got up and dressed.

"Mmmm. Thank you so much," Kat murmured through half closed eyes.

"You're most welcome. Would you like me to take you back?" he enquired holding out a hand.

"No, that won't be necessary; I think I might have other arrangements."

Kat had forgotten about Hod until now, and she wanted to savour this moment just a little longer.

Freyr wished her well, and with a wave of his hand he was gone.

After a few more minutes Kat propped herself up on her elbows. She prayed Hod hadn't come, but an instinct told her he was around.

"Hod," she whispered quietly—there was no reply.

"Hod," she called out more loudly. This time, she was sure she saw a bush shake.

"Hod!" she finally hissed. "Come out please, I know you're there."

After a few moments Hod emerged slowly from the undergrowth. His head was hanging and he wouldn't look at her.

"Have you been there long?" Kat asked.

He didn't reply.

"Did you see," she hesitated, not knowing quite how to put it. "Did you see everything?"

Hod nodded.

"Look at me, Hod."

He looked up, and Kat could see large tears rolling down his cheeks. His bright red eyes told her that he had been sobbing for some time. Mesmerised, and too shocked to run away, Hod had done the only thing he could. Watched and wept as the woman he craved made love to another man.

Kat had prepared an angry speech for Hod, but seeing his bloodshot eyes and tear-stained face, she knew this wouldn't be necessary. He had suffered a harsh lesson, a crushing humiliation far more painful than she'd intended. She felt a wave of sympathy for him, but surprisingly; no regret.

What was done was done; and Freyr had been magnificent.

Wow! What a mighty lover. Part of her felt like screaming with joy—but she knew she mustn't. That would be gloating—and far too cruel.

Hod was in agony.

Slowly Kat got up and walked over to him. She laid his head on her shoulder and hugged him gently, patting him as he sobbed uncontrollably. Although it was she who wasn't wearing any clothes, he was the one who was naked. Stripped of his manhood, his pride had been destroyed.

Somehow she would have to rebuild this.

As his tears subsided, Kat encouraged him to help her dress. He was hesitant at first, too shocked and grief stricken to control his trembling hands. Gently she persuaded him, tenderly coaxing him to overcome his new found fear of womanhood.

Little by little, the warmth of her praise soothed his shattered nerves. His hands began to move more freely, and he helped her fasten her skirt and then lace her bodice the way she liked it done. The terrible tension that had raged between them slowly faded, and Hod found that he could talk again, faltering at first but gradually gaining in confidence.

He knew now that Kat didn't love him, but he could see that she cared. Her compassion at his distress touched him more than the terrible pain he had endured.

He had deserved this disgrace.

He had brought this misery upon himself.

He felt so ashamed now about his clumsy and egotistic courtship, his lack of consideration and arrogant, godly conceit. He vowed he would mend his ways. He wanted to win her love now more than ever, but he knew he would have to earn it first. She was his equal; she was a woman he must respect.

Finally, Kat was ready.

"How do I look?" she grinned cheekily as she stood in front of Hod.

"You look lovely, fairest Kat," Hod replied; now almost smiling, too.

"Thank you; you've done a great job. Now will you please take me back to my room?"

Hod took her hand and with a wave of his, they were back in her chambers.

Hod didn't stay long, he didn't need to. Kat kissed him tenderly on the cheek as she wished him good night. Opening the door to leave, Hod turned and spoke once more.

"Thank you dearest Kat, thank you for everything."

He wasn't entirely sure why he had said this, but somehow it just seemed right.

"You're very welcome."
Kat flashed him a smile, one filled with confidence and strength.
It was the smile of a powerful woman.
It was the smile of a Valkyrie.

36

A Close Shave

Jess stood beside the trash can with a large carrier bag in her hand. The early morning streets of New York were grinding slowly into life. A steady flow of commuters passed her by, their cold hands buried deep in pockets, and collars pulled up high. Their numbers were swelling by the minute.

Jess handled the bag longingly; she hated throwing her police uniform away, but sadly it had to go.

After her meeting with Detective Marcus Finch she knew that her disguise had been blown. She could see it in his eyes as she was leaving, handsome blue eyes but ones now clouded with distrust. It was the knife that had given her away, the one she had stabbed Kat with. It was an unfortunate coincidence to bump into the detective working on her case, but what a clever man to connect her to Kat.

She guessed it was Mickey.

He must have blamed her.

She knew that she should have worn a disguise, her unusual red hair was too distinctive; it always had been. Briefly she reflected on the rolling fields of rural Ireland, the caches of arms—and her torture.

Her hair had been her undoing then, too.

Jess was certain that the analysis of her knife would reveal traces of Kat's blood. She had cleaned it, and some time had passed since she had saved Kat's soul, but there were clever people here in Midgard and they had cunning equipment which seemed to perform miracles. They could detect the tiniest pin pricks of blood and identify it. She couldn't risk walking back into the police station wearing that uniform again, just in case. No; it was better to ditch it and think of some other way to get to Mickey. Perhaps a wig, pretend she was his girlfriend or something like that. She only needed a minute and it would all be over.

As these thoughts, a mix of memories past and present, drifted through her mind, something caught her attention. It was an image on a television screen in the rental shop window.

There it was again.

Hastily Jess pushed past the bustling office workers and pressed her face against the glass.

It was the early morning news, a breaking story. Amidst the flashing lights of police cars and ambulances she could make out the figure of a woman being man-handled into a van, her hands cuffed tightly behind her back. She was a black woman, distinctive, her head held high. Then the picture that had caught her eye came on the screen again. It was a still shot of the woman's face.

It was Prudr.

Jess reeled with the shock.

The Valkyries usually undertook their missions alone, and she had no idea another was here in Midgard at this moment in time; and in the same city, too. She stared at the screen once more. This time the woman was being bustled into a police station, her police station.

The co-incidence seemed absurd.

Of all the cities in all the countries Prudr was here, barely four blocks from where she was standing now. She was also in trouble, and Jess knew she had to help her, and help her fast. She wouldn't last long in chains; Ruby needed the mead more than any of the other warriors.

Jess thought quickly.

This was breaking news, so Prudr would still be in interrogation. There was bound to be some confusion at the station with so many comings and goings. These would make good distractions that could conceal a snatch operation—a quick in and out. No frills, no fancy trickery.

She looked at the carrier bag.

It was unlikely Marcus would have issued a warrant for her arrest or alerted the station yet. He was a detective, methodical, and he would almost certainly wait until he had the results from the blood on her knife. It had to be done; she had to take the risk.

Police Officer Jessica O'Brien had one last duty to perform.

"What exactly would you like to know detective?" Ruby returned the gaze of the man sitting across the table from her.

She was tired and she couldn't remember his name.

"Where you got it, what you have done with it; anything that might be of help."

Marcus was offering her an open question, hoping she would reciprocate with an answer rich in detail. She was clearly an intelligent woman, and no longer high on whatever she had taken the evening before. He felt certain that with the right approach she would co-operate.

Ruby paused for thought.

She needed to tell him enough to get this interrogation over with quickly. The more she gave the more likely he was to relax, and give her an opportunity to escape. She glanced casually at the items on the table—her knife, her leather purse, the gold coin, and the leather flask. It would only take a minute, and she would be free once more. All she needed was to get these handcuffs off while she was in sight of her belongings; before her interrogation ended and she was moved to a prison cell.

It was a tough call.

The detective looked tired and a bit edgy, but he seemed a reasonable sort of man. The sort who might just loosen or release her cuffs if she complained they were too tight.

Firstly, she had to humour him. Get him to trust her.

"Well?"

Marcus spoke again. Patience had never been his strong point, and this morning tired and pumped up on too many cups of coffee he was struggling to be polite. All he wanted to do now was to go home and get into his nice cosy bed.

The woman opposite him, Ruby Knight, was his only obstacle. He wanted answers, and he wanted these fast. He could see she was organising her thoughts and this was not what he needed. An honest, quick fire answer; that was his goal.

There was a loud knock on the door. It sounded urgent.

"Shit! What now?" He blurted explosively.

The door opened and a receptionist popped her head through the crack.

"Telephone call for you Detective Finch."

"Can't it wait? Tell them I'm busy and I'll call them back."

"Sorry sir, the caller was most insistent. He asked me to mention his name, Agent Woods—said you knew him."

Marcus waved his hands in the air and stood up, heaving a loud sigh of exasperation. He hurried past Ruby and out of the door, waving the receptionist to follow him. He walked quickly to the phone as she trotted to keep up.

"Hello, Finch here."

"Good morning, Finch. I understand you have detained another murder suspect?" Woods' voice sounded calm and methodical, just like his previous call. There was obvious background noise; he must be in a car and moving fast.

"Yes. I am interrogating her at this moment." Marcus hoped he would get the hint.

"Very good, excellent, I understand the murderer used a knife. Did the wound strike you as similar to the one in the Neal case?"

There was the slightest hint of excitement now in Woods voice.

"Yes, identical. In fact I have the knife in my possession even as we speak."

Marcus was surprised that Woods had details of the case so soon. There must be a mole somewhere, and he obviously knew more than he was letting on. Before Woods spoke again, Marcus heard a sharp intake of breath.

Something had struck a nerve.

"Do you have any other items of interest, any unusual artifacts?" Woods voice was now openly agitated, unable to mask the intensity of his interest any longer.

"Yes, several; a purse, a strange coin, and an old leather flask filled with some sort of a druggie cocktail."

Now please, Marcus begged, get off the phone and let me get on with my work.

There was a long pause.

"Thank you for your excellent work Detective Finch. This is now a matter of national security and I will be coming there immediately to take the girl into FBI custody. Please don't interrogate her further, and place her in a cell with maximum security." Woods spoke quickly and decisively. "I hope I've made myself clear on these points. Do not speak to her, and hold her with all possible precautions. She's extremely dangerous."

Marcus nodded obediently, murmured good bye, and put the phone down.

He was gob smacked; all his hard work, his dreams of fame, all gone up in smoke. His brilliant detective work hijacked by the Feds.

Some days, life could be such a shit.

Suddenly his tiredness was overwhelming. All he wanted to do now was flick two fingers at the station and fuck off home to bed.

Thanks, he thought, *for nothing.*

Slowly he returned to the interrogation room. Barging through the door, he slumped into his chair. Ruby could see the hallmarks of surrender.

What was going on?

"I'm so sorry Ms. Knight," Marcus began, but he didn't finish. There was another knock on the door. This time it sounded even louder and more urgent than the last.

"Oh fuck!"

Marcus slammed his fist furiously into the table.

"COME IN!" he hollered, deafening Ruby and his assistant.

"I'm so sorry to bother you," the same receptionist peeked nervously around the door this time. She had heard the bellow, and was fearful of something being thrown.

"There's a police officer on her way down to see you. She said it couldn't wait."

"Who the hell is she?" he screamed furiously.

"Officer O'Brien sir, I did say you were busy and mustn't be disturbed, but she was awfully insistent. Simply wouldn't take no for an answer."

Marcus wasn't listening anymore.

He was already by the door and had unholstered his gun. He motioned with his hand for the girl to go and she raced away down the corridor, ducking her head as she went.

Instinct told Marcus this was no coincidence, and her presence here spelled trouble. He had been right about the knife; Jess must have given it to her. Ruby and Officer O'Brien were in this together, both members of a cult bound by macabre blood rituals.

This was getting dangerous, he had to be careful.

Footsteps were coming his way, and a shock of red hair emerged from around the corner.

He levelled his gun.

"FREEZE!"

Jess didn't stop.

"FREEZE NOW!"

Marcus released the safety and took aim. One more step and he knew he would fire.

Jess stopped, and then smiled at him.

"Drop your gun and put your hands in the air."

Marcus gave his statutory warning loudly and clearly. If he was going to drop her in the station, he would be doing it by the book.

Carefully Jessica took her gun from the holster, and holding it with her fingertips, she crouched and placed it on the floor in front of her. As she rose, she pushed it in his direction with her foot.

"Please Marcus," she spoke in a clear and calm voice. "There's no need for your gun. I'm here to give myself up. I know you are holding my friend Prudr."

Marcus looked blankly at her, his expression showed he hadn't recognised this name.

"I beg your pardon, my friend Ruby." Jess corrected herself, and then continued. "If you would be kind enough to take me to her I will explain everything to you. She's ill, and she needs my help."

Marcus took a moment.

He didn't want to do this but something in her voice, her look, her manner screamed at him to trust her. He felt instinctively she was a good person, and just possibly would give the answers he so desperately needed. To hell with Woods. Jess's arrival changed everything. He had to get to the bottom of this.

He had to know the truth.

Keeping his gun pointed at her, he motioned for her to enter the room.

He followed her in.

"Brynhildr!" Ruby rose, calling her name out in astonishment. No more welcome a person could have arrived than had it been Odin himself.

"Prudr," Jess acknowledged her comrade in arms.

"Are you well?"

Jess knew the answer already.

Just by looking at her she could see that Ruby was tired. Grey hairs were showing on her head, and laughter lines around her eyes and furrows on her forehead were growing at an alarming rate. She had obviously not taken her mead for at least a day.

Jess turned to Marcus.

"Please Marcus, will you allow me to give her some of the liquid from her flask?" she indicated toward the item on the table. "'It contains a medicine that she needs. Without it she'll die."

Marcus paused, a wave of uncertainty visible on his face. The flask contained drugs not medicine. One swig and Ms. Knight could turn into a crazed killer once more. He couldn't take the risk.

"No, I'm sorry." He shook his head.

"Very well, perhaps you might reconsider this if I show you my knife?"

To Marcus's astonishment, Jess pulled a sheath from her pocket and offered it to him. He withdrew the knife; it was identical to the one already on the table. He sat down slowly, gazing intently at the weapon.

"You see, Marcus," Jess wandered cautiously round the table to stand next to him. "This is the knife I stabbed Katarina with. It looks identical, doesn't it; just like the one you already have on the table. But if you look carefully, it isn't the same. If you look closely you will see mine has my name inscribed on the hilt. It says Brynhildr. Look, just there." Jess pointed at the hilt and Marcus squinted. He craned his head forward trying to make out the inscription.

"Please forgive me," Jess murmured softy in his ear.

THUD!

Those were the last words Marcus would hear for a while.

Jess had smashed his head down hard on the table and he slumped unconscious to the floor below.

Dave went for his gun—and then froze.

Jess had already picked up Marcus's weapon and had it levelled at him. She motioned to him to come over and stand next to her.

"Sorry," Jess shrugged as she smiled apologetically. Bringing the butt of the gun down hard on the back of his head, he too sank unconscious to the floor. Jess searched Marcus's pockets and after finding his keys, she quickly found the one to undo Ruby's cuffs.

"Drink!" Jess ordered, but Ruby needed no further encouragement. Gratefully she took a large gulp from her flask. The soothing mead coursed through her veins and she felt its warmth rejuvenate her aching body.

"Do you have a plan?"

Ruby glanced at Jess. She was too confused to be able to think clearly right now.

"Yeh. Hostage situation."

Jess motioned to Ruby to twist her arm behind her back and take her hostage. "We need to get to the cell where Mickey Warren is held captive."

"Your mission?"

"Uh huh," Jess grunted.

Hastily they gathered Ruby's possessions from the table and clattered their way noisily out of the room.

"Nobody move!" Ruby yelled loudly at the first police officer she saw in the corridor. She waved her gun threateningly at Jess. "Take me to the cells, now."

The man nodded nervously, and hastily took them along the corridors and down the stairs to the cells.

A small but growing crowd followed them at a distance. The station had been put in lockdown, the highest state of emergency. A SWAT team was already arming itself to take Ruby down. Every second counted.

Quickly Ruby demanded that a guard open Mickey Warren's cell, and after a brief pause, the door was unlocked.

"Throw the keys inside and stand back."

She barked the instructions and the man obliged. Bundling Jess in, she slammed the door shut. Jess grabbed the keys and turned the lock.

For now, they were safe and secure.

Outside the crowd pressed closer. No one could believe their luck. The fool had taken her hostage into a dead end. Ruby would be going nowhere, she was a sitting duck.

Inside the cell Mickey was already on his feet, stunned by their violent intrusion.

"Hello Mickey."

Jess strode over to him and grabbed him tightly by his balls.

"Katarina says hi!"

She twisted his testicles sharply and he sank groaning to his knees. Bending down beside him, Jess grabbed his hair and then smashed his head against the floor.

He was stunned.

"Is that your mission?" Ruby asked scornfully, the man looked pathetic.

"Ah hah."

Jess stood over him now and and pulled his arms up tightly behind his back.

"What about yours?" She inquired as she raised his arms up straight and pressed her foot down hard on his neck.

Mickey's face squashed to one side and he gurgled an anguished cry.

"Incomplete. I need to get back out there now and find him." Ruby motioned to the door.

"Don't be stupid Prudr."

Jess chastised her as she pressed down harder on Mickey's neck. Twisting both his arms, she forced them higher still. He howled in agony, his arms and neck contorting unnaturally as they stretched close to their breaking points.

"We have to get home, now." She continued as she pushed harder still against his neck and arms. They were now at an impossible angle, something had to give.

Without warning, a sudden muffled, satisfying snap told her she had broken Mickey's neck.

His body went limp as his lungs exhaled their final breath.

Mickey was dead.

"I can't, I can't go home without finishing my mission." Ruby tried to plead her case, but in her heart she knew that Jess was right. She had never failed in a mission before, never.

"Let's get our things ready."

Jess fumbled in her pocket for her leather wallet. Finding it, she took out her gold coin.

"Wallet, check, coin check, mead check, knives check." The girls spoke aloud as they went through a mental list of things they needed.

"Thank you, I almost forgot," Jess smiled before rolling Mickey over with her foot.

"Kat will be dying to meet you," she quipped as she plunged her knife deep into his heart. She felt the sudden warmth in its handle, and saw the brief, brilliant flash of light.

Mickey's evil soul was on its way to Asgard.

Standing up, the girls turned to face each other and clasped their coins firmly between their hands. They closed their eyes then chanted quietly, in a strange and unfamiliar tongue; ancient words long lost to the people of Midgard.

When the chanting ended, they were gone.

Two dazzling bursts of light returned to the Chamber of the Valkyries.

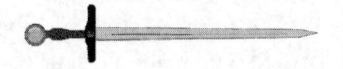

Woods arrived at the station shortly after Marcus regained consciousness.

Marcus knew it was him, as he staggered out of the interrogation room. The dark suite, the tie, the ear piece; all hallmarks of an FBI agent; and one who was striding quickly down the corridor toward him.

Marcus's head was splitting, his vision was blurred, and he felt like shit.

"Where is she?" Woods barked angrily. There was no pretence of politeness now. He had been contacted en route about the disturbance at the station and he knew Ruby was at the bottom of it.

"Don't worry; she's safe, locked up in a cell or something," Marcus began to explain. This had been reported to him only moments ago.

"And the artifacts?" Woods enquired hastily.

"Gone with them."

"Idiots!" Woods exclaimed loudly. He could feel Ruby slipping from his grasp.

"Take me to the cell, now."

Woods strode off rapidly and Marcus staggered behind him, trying desperately to keep up. Woods was tall and thin, Marcus would guess a metre ninety five or thereabouts, and his legs made short work of the walk along the corridors. When they arrived, Woods motioned to the gathered crowd to let them past. They did so, but not quickly enough to avoid a push or a shove as he barged his way through.

"Open the door, there's no escape."

Woods banged loudly on the cell door. The sound echoed ominously along the corridor.

There was no reply from inside.

"Open up at once!" He banged again; he was in too much of a hurry to snatch a look through the peep hole.

Still no reply.

Woods turned and motioned to a guard.

"Get this door open." He spoke calmly and with authority.

The guard hesitated, unsure if he should accept his command.

"Do it now. That's an order Officer." Woods tone of voice reeked with menace. He was not a man to be toyed with.

Meekly the guard did as he was told.

Door unlocked, Woods turned the handle and pushed it open. It swung inward, creaking softly as it did so.

Mickey's body lay on the floor. A slick of blood seeped down the side of his chest and formed a growing pool at his side.

He was dead, no doubt about that.

Marcus stared; he checked the walls, the bed, and the ceiling.

Jess and Ruby were gone. Vanished into thin air.

Woods took one last look around the room, and then sighed deeply. As he turned to go, he beckoned for Marcus to follow him.

"We need to talk."

Woods spoke now in a more measured voice. Though it gutted him, he accepted his defeat gracefully. Ruby was gone, slipping through his fingers just like last time.

What the fuck had these stupid cops been playing at?

He'd warned them that she was dangerous—why couldn't they have listened?

He glared angrily at Marcus—Marcus gulped.

37

The Silver Line

THUD, THUD!

There was a heavy knock on a distant door.

"Wake up ladies, this isn't a rehearsal."

THUD, THUD!

The knock was getting closer.

"Time to get up, full battle dress."

Kat felt vaguely annoyed at her rude awakening. She had been in the middle of a particularly nice dream about Freyr, and the next ten minutes or so had promised to be pleasant, very pleasant indeed. What a pity it had to end so unfulfilled.

She listened intently to the knocking on doors, the zig-zagging of footsteps coming closer down the corridor, and the unmistakable voice of Silk.

THUD, THUD!

"The giants will be up soon, and they'll be mad as hell."

THUD, THUD!

Oh dear God!

Kat froze in her bed; the knock was on her door now.

Opening the door without an invitation, Silk popped her head round.

"Wakey, wakey Kitty Kat."

Silk smiled slyly in the direction of the mound of bedding under which she knew Kat was lying.

"You're up today girl; time to get bloodied."

Closing the door behind her, Silk continued down the corridor, her noisy banging and running commentary wakening the remaining sleeping Valkyries.

Kat was wide awake and sitting bolt upright in bed.

If she had a beating heart, it would be pounding round about now. This was it. The moment she had been training for. There could be trouble today, and she would be playing her part along with the other maids and warriors. As Silk had said, this wasn't a rehearsal. She scarcely dared imagine how enraged the giants were going to be.

It was a frightening prospect and her hands trembled as she struggled clumsily into her leather tunic. Yesterday this had felt so cosy and natural, today it felt hostile and alien. It was as though she was putting it on for the first time.

Standing in front of her mirror, she suddenly felt so small and insignificant. How could she, a twenty five year old, one sixty five centimetre, and fifty four kilo woman with three weeks training possibly fight with huge giants?

It all seemed so absurd.

Suddenly her legs felt very weak and insecure. *Just don't faint!* She silently begged her body not to humiliate her today.

Whatever happened, she mustn't show any fear.

With teeth close to chattering, Kat made her way downstairs to the hall for breakfast. Fortunately the sight that greeted her helped sooth her jangling nerves.

"Kitty Kat!" Carmel hailed her excitedly and waved for her to join them.

The tables were in a state of uproar and there was a party atmosphere amongst the Valkyries. Girls were laughing and joking, messing with each other's clothes and weaponry. Everybody seemed relaxed and exuberant about the day ahead, welcoming the opportunity to fight alongside each other.

"You'll be fine, don't worry. Just stick with Carmel, she'll look after you." Emile slapped her heartily on the back as she made her way over.

Kat tried to smile; she wasn't quite yet ready to join the surreal party mood.

"Feeling nervous? Don't worry, that's normal," Carmel reassured her as Kat sat down beside her.

"Hey Kitty Kat, we'll have fun today!" Zara pushed a bowl of porridge across the table to her, and then carried on her conversation with Mika.

"Just stick with me," Carmel explained as she turned to her, and for a moment the expression on her face became serious. "Do exactly as I say, when I say it. One rule and one rule only. Don't get separated, do you understand. Do not get separated."

Carmel laughed loudly and then hugged her.

Kat could have kissed her.

Her reassuring hug meant the world today. If she remembered Carmel's words, she knew she'd be all right.

A horn blew loudly outside; it was a long, high pitched blast.

The girls quietened immediately.

"Ladies, the giants are up—it's time to go to work."

Silk's voice was calm and collected.

Hastily scooping up a few mouthfuls of porridge, Kat followed the rest out to the stables.

It was time to face the foe.

The men from Jotunheim stood outside Gladsheim and glared angrily at the Aesir.

The townsfolk had formed into small clusters dotted thinly around the edges of the square. The bravado of yesterday was gone, replaced by nervous tension and distrustful loathing. They whispered quietly among themselves, not wanting to attract attention.

The giants were armed, some with pitchforks and axes stolen from the townsfolk, others with huge double headed axes and swords they had brought with them from Jotunheim. These had been hidden under the cart drawn by Svadilfari.

They looked mean and angry and their mood matched their looks. Their huge bodies seemed to fill the square; a vast army, one strong enough to sack the town should they choose.

For the moment, the mason's men waited patiently, eager to hear from Thor. He was the one god whom they feared, and the only one who might persuade them to leave Asgard without a fight.

The procession that headed down from the castle gates to the square seemed miniscule.

Six Valkyrie warriors rode abreast at the front, their horses trotting slowly and their helmets gleaming in the bright morning sunlight. It was a glittering, silver line that stood between the giants and their Queen.

Behind the warriors marched the nine maids. They walked in a line, shoulder to shoulder, shields raised and spears in their hands. Kat was on the far right, walking next to Carmel. Silk had placed her there deliberately, away from the centre of the action and under Carmel's watchful eye.

"See that no harm comes to her."

These had been Silk's parting words before she mounted her horse. Silk was tough, hard as nails; but she cared passionately for her sisters. She loved them all—even Kat—though she would never say as much.

Behind the maids was a chariot and in it stood Freyja. Beside her strode Thor, Balder and Tyr.

As they reached the edge of the square, the procession stopped, and the warriors dismounted; sending their horses cantering back up the hill. Swiftly the Valkyries formed up in two lines to face the giants, who stood only metres away.

If it came to a fight, it would be hand to hand at close quarters. This was to the girls liking, the preferred style of the Valkyries.

Kat stared at the host facing them.

They were so close she could almost taste their fetid breath and sweating bodies. They seemed immense, a living, seething wall of flesh, muscle, and hair.

"It's so one sided," she muttered under her breath, feeling hopelessly outnumbered.

"You're right," Carmel had overheard her. "Too many warriors, we maids won't see any action today I'm afraid."

Kat looked at her in amazement.

She was joking, right?

"MASON!"

Thor's loud voice cut through the hush that had descended upon the square.

The mason strode forward and stood at the front of his host.

"Thor, you have tricked us and your Queen is forfeit. Give her to me at once and we will leave in peace."

The mason had his arms folded across his chest and he spoke with an air of measured confidence. The sheer size of his comrades must surely intimidate the gathered warriors into a bloodless surrender of their Queen.

"Mason, you tricked us first. You've lost the deal and I offer you now a chance to go, before you all loose your lives."

Thor spoke loudly, matching the mason's arrogance. He stood without fear. He knew that although the Valkyries were few in number, they were battle hardened and skilled.

The mason hawked, and then spat a huge wad of spittle onto the ground in front of him.

"Why don't we settle this, you and I Thor; god to giant, right here, right now?"

Thor chuckled.

"I won't unleash Mjollnir on you or your friends. My warriors will escort you from Asgard."

The mason sneered.

"What, the great Thor too scared to fight? Oh look everybody, he's leaving his fighting to his little girls!"

Waving his arm disparagingly in the direction of the warriors, he laughed heartily and his fellow giants joining in.

This was a very stupid thing to do.

Thor saw red, the insult was too much.

Mjollnir was in his hand and without hesitating, he threw it at the mason's face.

His throw was dead on target.

The mason's head exploded, showering those nearby in shards of blood, brains, and bone.

With a hideous roar, the giants raised their weapons and began to lumber toward the warriors. They would avenge their leader's death.

"NOW!"

Silk's voice shrilled high above the commotion of the attack.

As one, the warriors unleashed a volley of spears into the attacking enemy and then dropped to the floor.

"Take the one on the far right!" Carmel yelled at Kat as she raised her spear and took aim with the other maids.

"NOW!"

Silk cried once more, and a second wave of spears from the maids flew into the baying mob.

Giants staggered and fell, at least eight of their number injured or killed by the two deadly volleys.

Kat didn't know if she had hit her target, she was mesmerised, her body moving in automatic mode as the mob lumbered toward her. She didn't feel fear or excitement; she didn't feel anything.

It was all happening in a dream.

The warriors were on their feet the instant the second volley of spears had left their maids' hands. Gripped by the insatiable blood lust and with terrifying screams and battle cries, they tore into the host—swords and axes flashing in the sun.

Swiftly they hacked their way deep into their ranks.

It was a hideous and beautiful sight, both at the same time.

The giants were pitiful; hopelessly out manoeuvred by the speed and cat like agility of the Valkyries.

As the men from Jotunheim swung their huge axes, the girls darted this way and that, dodging each mighty blow before counter attacking with wasp-like stings from their swords. They thrust these deep into the giants' bodies before withdrawing their blades in one smooth, flowing motion.

The giants fell like flies; twisting this way and that, the living trying desperately to avoid the Valkyries' blades.

Carmel's predictions about the fight might have been right, had it not been for two giants who, defying the odds, started to shamble toward her and Kat.

"Take the one on the right!" Carmel yelled as she rushed forward to kill her foe.

A quick dodge, then a thrust, and it was all over. The giant collapsed in a groaning heap at her feet.

Her sword—dripping with blood—was back at her side before his body even hit the ground.

Carmel looked over to Kat.

Kat's eyes were fixed on the monster coming toward her. His massive axe was swinging around above his head and he bellowed loudly. She could see his yellow teeth and fixed, hideous snarl as he drew near.

She wasn't afraid, she wasn't excited. An eerie calmness gripped her.

She could see herself fighting in slow motion.

First, she raised her shield and braced herself, preparing for the impact of the giant's axe. This would surely cleave her shield and arm in two. As the axe scythed through the air, she watched herself move deftly to the side, smiling as her enemy staggered forward, stumbling off balance and burying his axe deep into the ground in front of him.

She heard herself scream, a terrifying, blood curdling war cry. Then she thrust forward, lunging murderously with her blade.

She marvelled as this cut so deeply into his body, like a red hot knife through freshly churned butter, it sliced all the way up to its hilt. The motion felt sublime, so smooth and wondrous in its power. His life had been lost so easily, taken effortlessly by her hands.

As she withdrew her blade, she watched his dying body fall face first into the ground. He was lying at her feet, twitching death's final dance.

It was over.

Kat had killed her first man.

A horn blew close by, and with a jolt she returned to the fray.

It seemed like hours, but after only a few minutes Frejya had signalled for the horn to end the battle.

It had been a rout.

As the Valkyries stopped fighting, the full horror they had inflicted became apparent.

Less than a dozen giants remained standing.

They looked dazed and confused; their eyes wide open and striken with fear as they faced certain death. Around them lay the dead and dying, few would survive the terrible wounds the Valkyries had inflicted.

Frejya hadn't relished a blood bath.

The slaughter of ill equipped and untrained giants was not a battle worthy of her mighty warriors. All she wanted was for the men of Jotunheim to leave Asgard in peace. Their deaths had been pointless and futile, brought about by the mason's vanity and his ignorance of her Valkyries. She felt a sorrow for the survivors, and for the families of the dead who would grieve their wasted lives.

Slowly the Valkyries departed the battle field and made their way up the hill. None had suffered serious injury and spirits were at boiling point. They were eager to get inside the castle and to begin their celebrations.

It was difficult to walk slowly, but they had to appear sombre, show their respect for the slain. Dignity was a must; they were proud and fearless warriors, defenders of Odin's law.

However, once concealed behind the castle's walls—things would be very different.

It would be party time; a wild and drunken celebration of their victory and their comradeship.

As the girls climbed up the hill, Kat spotted two lonely figures standing at the gates of the castle. She recognised one of them instantly.

"HEY!"

With a loud whoop of delight, she broke ranks and flew toward the figure who had opened her arms wide.

It was Jess, returned at last, safe and sound from her mission.

The two girls embraced, kissing passionately, not caring who saw their deep affection. Tears streamed down Kat's cheeks as she clung on for dear life. Closing her eyes tightly, she thanked Odin for their safe deliverances.

Enveloped in the victory of war, few of the jubilant party noted the rainbow forming in the skies over Asgard, nor did they see the black flag or hear the slow drum beat coming from Gladsheim.

Along with Brynhildr and Prudr, prisoners had arrived from Midgard.

38

Musa Qala

Jameela hated to admit it, but she was feeling rather bored and frustrated. She had been going through the same routine for over a week now, and she was beginning to wonder if she'd been right to volunteer for this mission.

At first she'd been very excited.

The prospect of any mission in Midgard was always greeted enthusiastically by the Valkyries, and this one to bring back a fallen hero was particularly pleasing. Personally, she had little taste for disposing of villains and she already had chosen her wonderful maid Alexandria. She loved the feelings that came with the rescue of a hero's soul and, as Freyja had put it, her cultural background was perfect for this task.

Standing as she was now, with a large group of women and boys in the main square of Musa Qala, she was beginning to wish that weren't so.

It was a cold day, just past the winter solstice, and a fierce wind was blowing freezing air down the valley; air that hugged the course of the river. Mountains festooned in snow rose high all around them, and the sky was heavy with clouds that promised still more to come. Flurries were falling intermittently and she had wound her silk Hijab tightly around her mouth and nose. Today only her eyes were showing. Many of the women and girls standing with her were clothed in full chadris, which she now regretted not wearing today. At least her thick woollen pashmina, and silk churidar suit, would keep the worst of the icy blasts from reaching her body.

In the drab winter landscape, in a town shattered beyond repair, the gathering of two hundred or so shivering souls made for a wretched sight.

They had been stood in the square—for their betterment—for over an hour now, with Taliban officials ranting and raving in front of the three tier monument which marked the town's centre.

Jameela understood little of what was being said.

The Pashto language was alien to her and only occasional words sounded similar to her native Hindi tongue. Luckily, two of the daughters of her adoptive family were standing next to her, and both Amal and Farah kept her updated whenever a watchful guard briefly turned his gaze away.

The childrens' rushed interpretations were always the same. A rabid mix of cursing the British and American infidels, misquoting from the Koran, and passing Sharia law judgements on some hapless soul paraded in front of them. So far today they had been spared a beheading, a hand amputation or even a flogging.

Jameela presumed they must be running out of local officials to persecute for co-operating with the "British sons and daughters of Satan."

What she hated most about the performance each morning was its futility.

These men were bullies, strong only because they held a Kalashnikov or RPG launcher in their hands. Most of them came from local Afghan families, humble and poor, just like the gathering in the square today.

Why did these monsters persecute their brethren?

There was no easy answer to the question that churned frequently in Jameela's head.

At best perhaps, weeks and months of warped indoctrination had turned the young men into fervent, Islamic idealists. At worst, the lure of wealth from the cash rich poppy fields had bought their souls; making them brutal and sadistic killers.

It made her blood boil; watching vicious beatings of women and boys and needless executions of innocent farmers. She struggled to suppress her Valkyrie instincts. Her name Herja, 'The Devastator,' had not been chosen by chance.

In full flow, she was second only to Prudr in her ferocity.

In contrast to her anger with the Taliban, she felt a huge warmth and respect for the small family who had so kindly taken her in. They were sheltering her from detection. Odin himself had met with local officials, and a few thousand dollars in cash had bought their loyalty and silence. They didn't know her mission, only her need to blend in and to be treated as part of the community.

Jameela was sharing a small, mud brick dwelling with a family of five. This lay only a few hundred metres from the square. The mother was the head of the household. She was a widow in her early forties, though she looked much older. She was worn down by the stress of staying alive, and keeping her family warm and free from starvation.

Her husband had been killed two years ago while working in the fields. A stray bomb from a jet had blown him and five others to smithereens. There was little of any of them left to bury. Surprisingly, she bore no resentment toward the Americans, choosing to blame the Taliban for his death.

She hated these evil brutes with a vengeance, and along with the death of her spouse, she had other reasons for hating them, too.

Her eldest son, Mohammed, had been taken shortly after her husband was killed; press ganged into joining their guerrilla army. It had been eighteen months since she'd last seen him, and she feared he was now one of the monsters who terrorised towns like theirs.

She wondered if she would recognise him or worse—if he would recognise her.

Amal, her seventeen-year-old daughter who was currently hugging Jameela for warmth, was sixteen weeks pregnant.

Her baby was a souvenir from some nameless fighter who had taken a shine to her face. The family could say or do nothing, just bear the humiliation it would bring with their usual stoic pride. To be honest, the boy hadn't actually raped her; it was just hard for Amal to say "No" with an AK-47 pointed at her head.

Her biggest fear now was that her youngest son Amir would be recruited by the Taliban, too. He was just ten-years-old and they were already courting him. Encouraging him to fire their rifles and letting him join in when they listened to football matches on the radio.

Absurd as it might seem, many of the Taliban were fervent supporters of British teams. The lone picture on the wall of their communal bedroom bore testament to this strange paradox. Amir had become a fan of Manchester United, and his most treasured possession was the faded poster of *Ronaldo* he had stuck above his rusty bed.

The Taliban fought the British with a hatred and fervour that made them formidable and yet, at a stroke, they followed their British football teams with a passion equal to any home grown fan.

Such was the irony of waging war in a globalized world.

A distant sound of droning dragged Jameela back from her daydreaming and into the square.

Men were beginning to shout and cock their rifles.

The noise was getting closer and the crowd was being roughly ordered and pushed away from the square. The show was over for today—*Odin be praised.*

Jameela followed her friends slowly toward their home. She kept turning round; craning her neck to see what was causing the odd noise that had sent such a panic amongst the men. Guns were being fired now, random shots hosed wildly into the air.

Suddenly she saw what they were shooting at.

An impossibly small plane cruised by overhead. It was too small for a pilot, having a bulbous head at the front and a propeller at its rear. She had been hearing about these craft all week, and its presence here today sparked a flame of hope among the citizens of Musa Qala.

The machine was a drone plane and it was spying out the land and the strength of the Taliban numbers.

The British were coming—and amongst them Jameela prayed she would find her hero.

39
The Mead of Poetry

A hush spread like a slow ripple around the hall. It crept from person to person as each in turn realized that Odin had joined the feast.

As was his custom, Odin arrived quietly, beckoning the serfs not to announce his presence with a fanfare of horns. He much preferred a cloak of anonymity, allowing him to mingle unnoticed and catch the unwary off their guard.

Tonight, fortunately, no one needed to be concerned. He was among his loyal friends and this was an evening of celebration. Slowly making his way toward the head table, he congratulated each warrior and maid in turn on their part in the victory that morning. Behind him came the two dwarves, Fjalar and Galar, and the musician Kvasir.

He went to his harp and made ready to play.

The four of them had spent the day together, watching the battle unfold from the comfort of Odin's citadel. They had admired the skill and ferocity of the Valkyries, and lamented the hopelessness of the giants. After the battle, the dwarves had stayed on, listening intently as Kvasir played for them. They were entranced by his music and by his beauty as a boy. They fingered his hair lovingly and greedily stroked his arms and face with their hands.

Their motives weren't driven by love—but by lust.

They believed that Kvasir could bring them the riches they desired.

They were merchants, traders of any item they could get their hands on. Kvasir was the reason for their long journey from beneath the mountains of Jotunheim. Through him, and his gifts for music and poetry, they believed they could unlock the vaults of Nidavellir. Here was stored the vast wealth of their kingdom, and it was jealously guarded by their king, Modsognir. They hoped that the seductive power in Kvasir's song would loosen the treasure chamber's keys from his fingers; even from a grasp as tight as his.

Eventually Odin reached the head table and stood beside Freyja, Thor, Balder, Tyr, and Silk. He raised his hands and motioned that he was about to make a speech. A silence fell, and the gathering craned their necks forward. Nobody wanted to miss the words that would fall so softly from his lips.

"My noble Queen, dear friends, and warriors; I propose a toast to your marvellous victory today."

He raised his horn which was overflowing with mead.

"HAIL VICTORY! HAIL VALOUR! HAIL ODIN!"

The gathering cheered wildly with each salutation, and it was some time before they had quietened down sufficiently for Odin to continue.

"You will have noticed that we have two ambassadors from the court of Modsognir. May I introduce Fjalar and Galar."

There was a polite ripple of applause as the two dwarves stood on their stools and bowed deeply. There was much suspicion and distrust among the Aesir for the sons of Nidavellir. Their hunger for gold bred treachery and deceit and because of this, their kind was seldom made welcome in Asgard.

Odin spoke once more.

"I have agreed to lend them Kvasir for two weeks. They would like him to play at their King's birthday feast, and for that honour they have paid a very generous price."

Odin's mind briefly fingered its way through the heavy chest of gold coins.

"As part of our agreement, I have requested safe passage for a Valkyrie to escort them; both as their companion and as their guard. Who will volunteer for this auspicious role?"

Odin threw his arms open and a fierce debate raged amongst the warriors as to who would be best suited for the task. In the end Emile was chosen. Her shorter stature gave her the edge over her sisters. The tunnels between the caves of the dwarf kingdom were notoriously narrow and low.

After stressing that the party would not depart for another day or two, Odin finished what he had to say and sat down.

Seizing the opportunity, Thor leapt to his feet.

"Fair Kat where are you?"

Thor's voice echoed around the hall.

Stunned by his unexpected call, Kat dutifully rose to her feet.

"I understand you were bloodied today?"

Thor's question was immediately overwhelmed by a chorus of wild cheering and foot stamping. Her first kill had already been widely toasted that evening.

"Come, you must name your sword, I insist. Slave, bring Kat her sword," he shouted loudly as a slave scurried swiftly from the hall.

Oh God!

Kat could already feel her face turning red. She had completely forgotten about this tradition.

The people of Asgard had a habit of naming their belongings. They didn't have much so what they did have they valued. Naming what they owned gave their possessions an identity, a value, a personality to be cherished. Out of all the things a warrior could own, her sword was the most important. Kat's now needed a name—and a good one to boot.

She tried desperately to think.

Her mind had gone a complete blank. She was rubbish at these things.

Think, damn it!

She remembered her pet rabbit many years ago back in Midgard. She had pathetically called him 'Bunny Cuddles.' Her teddy bear too, 'Teddy Edwards' screamed for lack of imagination.

Desperately she searched her mind for something clever.

She played with the letters that made up the word sword: words, srodw, dowrs—*damn!* These were all garbage.

Looking around her table, her eyes pleaded for inspiration.

Jess and Ruby smiled blankly back at her. So too did Carmel, Mika, and Emile. They all felt her predicament, and were revelling in it. She swore she would pay them back for their lack of helpfulness some day.

Eventually her sword arrived and it was pressed eagerly into her hands. She held it tentatively before raising it slowly above her head.

Help!

She still didn't have a name.

"I name this sword—" she paused, a spark of inspiration flashed across her mind. They had been discussing Jameela's chack ram, sword and other weapons in her room, what word did she use—?

"I name this sword—" she found the word at last.

"TALWAAR!"

"All hail the mighty Talwaar!" Thor cheered loudly and the room erupted into a rousing chorus of drunken cheering, foot stamping and whistling.

As Kat sat down, overwhelmed with relief, Ruby turned cheekily to her.

"Congratulations dear Kat, you've just named your sword—Mr. Sword."

The girls all howled with laughter as Ruby explained that 'Talwaar' was in fact the Hindi word for sword. Still, for Kat that didn't matter. The name sounded good and nobody else seemed to know or care about its true meaning. She joined in their laughter, and slowly the conversation turned to other things.

"Did you feel it?"

It was Jess's turn to speak and her question was directed at Ruby.

"What?" Ruby replied absently. She was only half paying attention, still too depressed and ruing her first failed mission in Midgard.

"The aura, Marcus's aura. You remember?"

"Oh yes," the memory jolted Ruby back into the room. "Wow, that was strong. I mean, it was really strong."

"Mmm, I know. Not quite ready yet, but definitely one for the future," Jess spoke almost dreamily, with a look of longing to her eyes.

Interest aroused by this unusual exchange, Kat inquired as to what exactly they were talking about.

"Ah," Jess began. Sometimes they forgot that Kat still had so much to learn about the ways of the Valkyries. "When we go to Midgard in search of heroes or a maid we can sense them by their aura. The stronger it is, the nearer they are to joining us."

"Did I have one?" Kat enquired hopefully.

"Sweet Odin, are you kidding? Wow! When I bumped into you on the street it was like being sucked into a whirlpool. It was fabulous; you were so ripe and so ready."

"What does it feel like?"

Kat was blushing now, taken aback by Jess's description of the attraction that had pulled her toward her. She was curious too, being sucked into a whirlpool wasn't an easy emotion to visualise.

There was some discussion amongst the warriors before finally Ruby spoke.

"Sex!"

The others all laughed as they agreed. The feelings were so strong that any other word just seemed inadequate. It also helped explain why with the passage of time the warriors would yearn so desperately for Valhalla. With each hero they saved, their desire to join them grew until eventually it overwhelmed them.

Ruby's ability to resist this craving was unique.

She had been a Valkyrie for two hundred years, twice as long as her nearest sister. Someday she too would succumb, but for now a part of her remained unfulfilled. She didn't know what it was that she lacked, but she knew that when she found it, she would joyously go to Valhalla and join the rest of the Valkyries.

As the girls continued to chat, Carmel fell silent.

Loki was nowhere in sight and she was missing him. Signalling for a slave, she whispered something in his ear. He left; his task was simple.

Find Loki, and tell her where he was.

Carmel looked over at Kat and Jess's happiness and felt a pang of jealousy.

She had enjoyed the days she had spent with Kat, and it hurt to see her cozying up to Jess once more. She remembered how she had disliked her at first, but there was something about Kat, a certain charm, a certain warmth, that attracted all around her. They were like moths to a flame and she could now understand how Hod's wings had been so badly burned.

And here she was too, like that love sick idiot of a god, all gooing and gushing as she hurried to the back of Kat's fan club.

Damn! This was so nauseating. She had to get out of there.

Rising from her chair, she made an excuse and left the room. Outside the hall she slumped back against a cold, stone wall, and closed her eyes.

Where in Asgard was Loki?

Within moments the slave returned. Loki was in the stables preparing to leave. Hurriedly, she checked her hair in a mirror before hastened down to meet him.

"Loki," Carmel exclaimed loudly, making him startle. "Where are you going at so late an hour?"

Loki looked around, surprised and embarrassed to be caught so unawares.

Even in the dimness of the torchlight he could see how fabulous Carmel looked tonight. A sheer silk dress, peach in colour, hung from one shoulder before being gathered tightly at her waist. It then fell in shimmering pleats to the ground, a deep slit up the right side revealing glimpses of a shapely, tanned leg. On her forehead was a large tiara, a spray of silver feathers fanning backward from a cluster of sparkling emeralds. Below these dangled ribbons of pearls.

Looking at her, dressed in such splendour, Loki knew why he had been leaving so secretly. He couldn't resist her, the one great beauty that kept his heart firmly anchored in the realm.

"Forgive my manners, fairest Carmel. I fear I'm in no mood for merriment tonight."

Carmel moved closer and placed her hand upon his face. She stroked it lovingly as he kissed her palm. She knew his parents were giants, and understood the mixed emotions he must feel about the deaths of his kinsmen.

Without saying a word, Loki pulled her tightly against him, squeezing her waist firmly against his groin. He kissed her lips gently and slowly at first, then more swiftly and passionately as their hunger grew. Clasping his hands tightly around her bottom, he could feel the warmth of her breasts heaving close to his chest.

This was too much for Carmel.

She drew back, pulling Loki roughly down into the straw on top of her. Her hand was in his trousers, searching for the manhood that had pressed against her so firmly. Finding it, she withdrew her hands and then ran her fingers through his hair. She could feel his hot breath as he nibbled at an earlobe before caressing her swan like neck. Closing her eyes, she clawed her fingers down his back, digging her nails in deeply and drawing crimson blood from his flesh.

Loki exhaled sharply, his breath filled with both ecstasy and great pain.

There, in the stalls beneath his horse, they made love. Their bodies writhing and convulsing as they were consumed by passion's fire.

Their rapturous embrace would continue long into the night.

Ruby left the feast shortly after Carmel. She too was consumed with a need, but it wasn't for love, nor was it for companionship.

Dressing quickly into her leather tunic, and commanding two slaves to follow behind her, she strode purposefully toward her arena. In one hand she held her coiled whip and in the other a leather gag.

Unfinished business had arrived from Midgard, and she was in just the right mood to deal with it. Even on a moonless night, the darkness couldn't disguise the thunder in her scowl.

She had failed in her mission to Midgard and Odin had requested that she join him for a private audience tomorrow. Neither of these matters gave her joy, and the reason for both would soon be tied naked between two posts.

Slim would be experiencing Valkyrie justice tonight, and her gag should ensure his screams didn't wake the neighbours.

Ruby prayed silently she didn't kill him again.

She didn't want to send his bloodied corpse to Niflheim; well, at least, not just yet.

40
Forty Commando

With the arrival of the drone plane, Jameela and the girls quickly returned to their home and barricaded themselves in. They spoke little as they turned their dwelling into a fortress. Jameela watched their well-rehearsed survival routine and helped them where she could.

First the double bed was dragged into the middle of the room. Basic food, water, and warm blankets were laid on the floor underneath it. The table was then turned upside down and placed on top of the iron bedstead. Other mattresses and items of furniture were then stacked tightly around it. Finally the doors were locked and bolted; and they all crawled into their tiny shelter. Jameela joined them, taking the side nearest the front door. She could protect them in the event of an unwelcome intrusion.

Neither their mother, nor their brother Amir had returned to the house with them.

Jameela guessed that Amir had been taken by the Taliban, and he would be as safe with them as he could be anywhere else. She prayed that they didn't use him as a runner or a spotter, ferrying ammunition or calling out troop positions for the fighters. This would put his life in terrible danger; not that the Taliban cared.

As a child he was disposable, just like everyone else.

Of more concern to Jameela was the whereabouts of the girls' mother. She had definitely seen her leaving the square, and it was unlike her not to come home. She could see from the girls frightened expressions that they missed her.

Jameela was now in charge, the temporary head of this fragile family.

Silently, she studied the girls' faces.

They were all beautiful, with deep, chocolate brown eyes, long curly hair and large gleaming, white teeth. Amal, was the oldest. She was pregnant, but her sisters didn't know this yet. Farah was fourteen and Asbah was only eight.

She smiled at the irony of their names—Hope, Joy, and Pure.

Whatever else the world might think of Afghanistan and its people, no one could dispute their optimism and their courage. In a country so ravaged by war, they still managed to give their children names filled with such optimism. This had to be worth something.

She looked around the tiny home.

It was a simple dwelling; a hut really, with a concrete floor and a corrugated iron roof. The front door was aged but solid, and the windows a mixture of wooden boards and broken glass. A naked bulb hung from the ceiling, but it didn't work. There hadn't been electricity or running water for years.

Despite their intense poverty, the family had a simple routine that kept them clean and adequately fed.

Farah would sweep the floor morning and evening, and Asbah would collect wood and twigs each day for the cooker. Amal collected water at least twice a day. She carried it in two heavy plastic containers which swung either side of a yolk. She carried this across her shoulders. Their mother toiled in the fields, watering a meagre crop, foraging for roots and other edibles, and tending the few goats they possessed. Each day the whole family would bathe using water warmed in buckets on the stove.

The constant fighting may have robbed them of the most basic of amenities, but it could never take away their pride. Jameela, smiled, and then kissed Asbah on the forehead as she hugged her close.

She would do her best to keep them safe today.

Time passed slowly.

For many hours after the drone had gone, all they could hear was the scurrying of footsteps, loud shouting, and the clicking of magazines being loaded into rifles.

They were fortunate that no fighters chose to use their house as a base, and they kept their fingers crossed that it would stay this way.

Eventually a loud 'WHOOSH' heralded the start of the attack.

A jet had passed low over the town, looking for targets. They could hear the 'Whirr' of helicopter blades and short, saw like bursts from its powerful machine guns. At least one such burst sprayed their street, sending shards of shattered concrete spattering against their front door.

Finally, they heard gunfire; short, staccato bursts of automatic weapons. Each burst sounded louder than the last as the battlefront inched closer to their home.

Jameela cradled Asbah's head against her chest, and listened intently as the sound of warfare stuttered up their street. She felt an excitement and a warmth growing deep inside her.

She could sense the presence of her hero.

Spurts of muzzle flames and loud, thunderclap gunshots now ricocheted around their room.

The fighting was right outside.

With a loud crash, the front door splintered and then caved in. A solitary soldier stumbled through and flashed a torch around the room. He said something in broken Pashto, and Amal answered him in English.

"Don't shoot, we're civilians."

"How many?" came a clipped reply. Jameela could see the soldier crouching by the door, eyes darting between the street and their room.

"Four," Jameela replied this time, crawling out from under the bed. She wanted to take a good look at this man.

"Get back under there!" The man scolded as he looked at her in alarm. "It's not safe to come out just yet." He hissed the words urgently and hoped she would do as he said.

Jameela didn't.

Cautiously she made her way over and crouched behind him. Despite the camouflage paint on his face, she could see that he was very young. His face was boyish and rounded, with bright brown eyes that flashed with excitement as well as fear. She glanced at his name badge, Lance Corporal Benjamin Lee, and then at the motif on his combat fatigues. It was a simple dagger and the name of his unit, *Forty Commando Royal Marines*. The feelings inside her were unmistakeable now.

She had found her hero.

A loud burst of gunfire startled them as it splintered the wood and concrete of the doorframe. Taliban fighters had spotted the soldier and they now had him pinned down inside the house. The soldier shepherded her deeper into the room before crawling back to the front door.

"Is there a back door?" he whispered coarsely.

"Yes. I can show you if you like," this time Farah's voice answered from their shelter.

"I'll check to see if it's clear, and then I'll escort you down the road to safety." He motioned to the girls to stay put. They were poking their heads out excitedly from under the bed.

He needed to make a quick reconnaissance first.

"Can I help?" Jameela offered. She wanted to stay close to her hero.

"Just stay here, please, and keep them safe."

The soldier unleashed a spray of gunfire from the door then made his way quickly to the back. The Taliban fighters would try to retake the house if he showed any weakness, so each second was precious. Opening the back door, he threw his back pack across the street—nothing. There was no spatter of bullets from a trigger happy sniper.

The exit seemed clear.

"Come on, quickly!" He snapped with his hand, and the three girls crawled out and made their way hurriedly toward him. He pointed to a cart, some thirty metres away.

"When I say run, you run and wait for me there, do you understand?"

They nodded.

"You too," he looked directly at Jameela for the first time. Only her eyes were visible through the slit in her Hijab, but he could see they were large and beautiful.

She nodded as well.

"NOW!"

The soldier rose up and sprayed the street with gunfire. The girls ran like three startled rabbits and made it safely to the cart. Now it was her turn. Jameela prepared to make her run, and then heard a loud 'Whoosh!'

It was the sound of an RPG, a rocket propelled grenade.

It was heading straight toward them.

"NOOO!"

Jameela heard the soldier cry out as he threw himself on top of her, shielding her body from its blast.

The ground shook and thunder exploded inside her head. For a moment she couldn't see or hear anything. The air was dense, filled with smoke, dust, and debris. The acrid cordite made her choke.

For what seemed an age they lay together stunned, the soldier lying motionless on top of her. Gunshots whistled around them, ricocheted off what was left of the rear wall to her home.

"Oooh!"

Jameela heard the soldier groan softly, he was injured.

Moving her hands carefully she could feel a hot, ragged shard of shrapnel sticking out from his body armour. The metal had penetrated this and was now embedded firmly in his chest. He was badly injured, but alive. She had to find them shelter and fast.

Pushing him off, she crouched down and tugged at his arms. Desperately, she dragged him back toward the remnants of the house.

Showers of bullets landed thick and fast around them.

One round sliced through her left arm. She barely felt it. At least two further bullets embedded themselves in the soldier's legs; they made a sickly, squelching sound as they buried themselves deep under his flesh.

His blood splattered her, but she didn't care. She was struggling to save his life.

Finally, they were back behind the shattered walls, a temporary haven from the deadly barrage.

Jameela quickly pulled his helmet off and cradled his head in her lap. He had such beautiful hair; short, ginger, and curly; and his face still had pimples. His eyes were roaming, focusing poorly. She could tell he was drifting in and out of consciousness; he was an innocent little boy, not some burly, macho soldier fighting a war.

Without hesitating, she pulled the leather flask from her belt and pressed it urgently to his lips.

"Here, drink please, you'll feel better." Jameela whispered the words gently and to her relief, he took a large gulp and then swallowed.

"Thank Odin," She breathed quietly. He had saved her life today, and she wasn't ready to take his soul to Valhalla just yet.

Bullets continued to whine over their heads and then they stopped. The battle front had changed direction and it brought a welcome lull in the intense fighting.

Remaining huddled closely together, Jameela cradled his head, humming softly as she did so. She offered him sips of her mead when he was able to take them, and stroked his forehead when he couldn't. He was breathing more peacefully now, and she felt a contentment deep inside.

It was a joy to help her hero, especially in his hour of need.

The peaceful moments they shared seemed to last for hours, but she knew they couldn't last. The Taliban were all around, and they knew the British soldier was injured and close by. This gave them an opportunity, one they were eager to exploit.

His capture would bring them glory.

Where were his comrades?

She could hear heavy gun fire on the street, but the rest of his company were still too far away. She prayed to Odin to give them strength and hurry to his rescue.

Suddenly, she heard footsteps. They were creeping stealthily up behind her. Before Jameela could turn around, a gun was pressed hard against her neck. The steel of its barrel brought a cold shock to her skin. She could smell the breath of the man as he shouted something to her in Pashto.

She didn't respond.

There was a pause.

"Hands up, English filth!" the man spoke once more but in broken English.

Jameela lifted the soldier's head from her lap and then slowly stood up. The smoke and dust was clearing from the shattered room, and stealing a brief glance, she could make out the forms of three heavily armed fighters. She knew her hero would be okay, a live British hostage was worth more than gold bullion. They would sacrifice themselves, if it was needed, to get him back behind their lines.

As for herself, they would execute her on the spot.

She had no worth.

A bullet through her head, and that would be that.

"Do you speak good English?" Jameela enquired calmly, surprising the men with her question and her lack of fear.

As far as they were concerned, she was already dead.

"Why?" one of them sneered contemptuously. "Any last requests before you die? You filthy, traitor whore."

He spat at her.

"Yes, but please wait just one moment."

Jameela spoke confidently and with growing menace.

Slowly she removed her hijab and took off her pashmina, dropping these to the floor. The men gasped, taken aback by this bizarre and unexpected move. Shaking her head, her long, black locks of hair fell loosely around her shoulders.

Jameela turned around, and the fighters murmured appreciatively at her beauty. Casting their eyes admiringly down her shapely figure, these widened dramatically as they alighted on the rusting machete and dagger she had tucked into her belt.

"Can you all see me?"

Jameela spoke loudly and with authority as she raised herself up to her full height. The men nodded slowly as smiles lit up their faces. The girl was good looking and maybe they'd have some fun before she died.

"Good, then listen carefully and make peace with your gods. I am the Valkyrie Herja and today I send you to your doom."

Her eyes flashed angrily as the fury raging inside her finally exploded out of control.

She was Herja the Devastator and she knew only two things.

People were going to die—and she wasn't going to be one of them.

41

Odin's Rings

Loki escorted Carmel back to her room after they had finished making love. Then, after kissing her tenderly goodnight, he left the castle and trotted slowly off into the night.

Breaking his horse into a canter, showers of sparks flew from his hooves. They were crossing the narrow bridge over the river Iving, and the metal shoes flashed as they struck the brittle flints on the road. It would be a long ride to Utgard, the capital of Jotunheim, and he was determined to make it there before the cart load of dead and injured giants.

He knew he would have some explaining to do.

Thrym, the King of the giants, wouldn't be pleased.

As he rode, he let his mind wander. He was trying to focus on a new plan to capture the Valkyrie Queen, but thinking wasn't going to be easy tonight. The taste and smell of Carmel pervaded his thoughts, their smouldering passion distracting him from his scheming.

Still, it would be a long ride, and he felt sure that the cold, grey light of dawn would extinguish his lingering ardour.

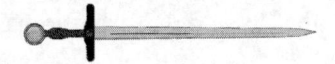

Kat spent a blissful night with Jess.

It was wonderful to be back in her arms; and in her bed. She no longer cared who saw them together, or when. However, as Jess had pointed out, if you thought about it, no one really took any notice of them anyway. The people of Asgard were hot-blooded, and the gods were even more so. In a typical night there was usually so much bed hopping that by morning time, it was anybody's guess who would come out of which bedroom.

Gods made fickle lovers.

After enjoying a leisurely breakfast together, Jess announced that she would be busy for most of the day in Gladsheim, passing judgements with Freyja.

Kat had anticipated this; the black flag still hung limply over the hall reminded her that at least one of the prisoners who had arrived yesterday was Jess's responsibility.

After parting company with an affectionate kiss, Kat wandered wistfully down the road and into the town. It was market day, and the bustling streets would fill the emptiness now that Jess was gone for the day.

"Hey, Hod!"

Kat spied him in the distance, and she called to attract his attention. He turned away, pretending not to notice her.

Stupid boy.

Hod hadn't been at the celebration last night, and Kat had noticed his absence. She thought they had settled things and that they were friends. She really didn't want a rift to grow between them now. Hod was hurt and his pain could consume him.

"Hey Hod," she called again. "Hey wait up, don't be a stranger."

Trotting briskly through the crowded street, she caught up with him and tugged at his arm.

"Oh. Hi, I didn't see you there." Hod tried to act surprised, but Kat knew that he was lying.

"Are you okay?" she felt concerned, so she turned him to face her when she asked.

He was sulking.

"Yeh, sure. Just, you know, keeping out of your way now that you've got a new boyfriend and told everybody about what happened …" his voice trailed off. He so didn't want to have this conversation with her today.

"Excuse me," Kat exclaimed indignantly. "I haven't said a word, nor will I. What happened is our business, just yours and mine, I promise." She grabbed his hand and squeezed it hard. She meant it. She wasn't like Carmel, the gossip queen.

"Yeh, yours and mine—and Freyr's, too," he retorted grumpily. "I expect you'll be seeing lots of him," he added ruefully.

"Of course," Kat answered without really thinking. That was none of his business.

"Why?"

This was such an idiotic, knee-jerk question that Hod wished immediately he hadn't asked it. He knew the painful answer already and didn't need his face slapping with it.

"Because he's a fabulous lover, that's why. Don't be so stupid."

Ouch!

Even Kat had to admit she shouldn't have said that, it really was quite bitchy. She decided to change the subject.

"Look, we're still friends, aren't we? I mean, I thought we'd made up? Anyway, I was hoping you would take me out hunting today. I'm getting so much better at riding; I bet I can even beat you to that thicket over there."

Kat pointed to a small copse of trees across the bridge. To her relief, Hod took the bait.

"I'll bet you can't. You're so going to lose."

He smiled as he looked at her. He really did want them to stay friends, and he was relieved that she hadn't told anyone. He knew he could trust her, and deep down he was delighted that she wanted to spend the day with him. He still loved her madly, and prayed one day she would feel the same way, too. He really hoped so.

"You're so on," Kat gave him a friendly shove. "Go on, get your horse and meet me at the bridge. We have a little wager to settle."

They departed quickly to get ready, both pleased at the prospect of spending a day in each other's company.

Ruby knocked hard, and then waited nervously outside the black wooden door at the bottom of Odin's citadel. Odin had requested she meet him there when he had spoken to her last night; and she felt sure it wasn't to compliment her on the failure of her mission.

As she waited, she cast a wary glance to her right.

Freki was sleeping, but Geri was wide awake and had his beady eyes set on her, which made her feel uncomfortable. This was always the pattern with Odin's wolves. One stayed on guard while the other one slept. No one could escape their watchful presence, and no one would dare cross the bridge without an invitation.

Suddenly, and with a loud creak, the door began to open and she stepped reluctantly inside.

WHOOSH!

She hated that feeling, the moment when you go too fast over a hump back bridge, or hit the top of a roller coaster. The moment when your stomach leaps up into your mouth and you really wish you hadn't eaten such a big breakfast.

There was no staircase in the citadel, just a heady rush as you were whisked up to the chamber at the top. It was a bit like the feeling when she travelled to Midgard, but probably not so bad; and it certainly didn't last as long. She blinked, and rubbed her eyes as she became accustomed to the brightness inside Odin's chamber.

Ruby looked quickly around her. Everything was exactly as it always had been.

The nine long, arched windows with their low sills, and the raised central platform on which stood Odin's, slender wooden throne. He had been sitting there, and was now standing and beckoning her to come and join him on one of the chairs which lay in a semi circle before his.

Gulping nervously, she made her way across the floor. This was richly carpeted, covered with brightly patterned rugs made of wool and silk. These felt deep and luxurious beneath her feet. She looked tentatively at a cask that stood on a small table beside the throne. This was beautifully fashioned from gold and decorated with a delicate silver tracery. The four sides of the vessel had been carved into an intricate lattice, a network of entwined leaves, berries and flowers. These left tiny holes, pores so fine that you couldn't see inside. You could, however, smell occasional wafts of a sickly sweet odour that came from within.

She prayed Odin wouldn't open the cask today.

Its contents gave her nightmares.

"Come, Prudr. Come sit and tell me all about your trip to Midgard."

Odin bade her sit down and he listened intently as she recounted her tale. From time to time he interrupted her with questions, which occasionally she struggled to answer. There was a long pause when she finally explained her reasons for killing Slim, and her decision to return to Asgard with Jess.

"You understand why you were sent to Midgard?" Odin enquired.

"Yes, my Lord. It was to bring Cole's soul back to you." She felt uncomfortable, having to spell out her failure like this.

"And you let me down, didn't you?" Odin continued as darkness clouded his eye.

"Yes, my Lord." Ruby looked down at her feet.

This was so humiliating.

A tremor struck the citadel and the surrounding hills. It felt like a small earthquake. Odin tried to control his anger, and as this subsided so too did the shudders. For all their sakes, he mustn't lose his temper today.

"What you don't seem to understand was the importance of your mission, which was why I specifically entrusted it to you."

He stared angrily at her, his eye remained unblinking.

"I did my lord, I truly did." Ruby still hadn't look up.

"Then why did you let your emotions get the better of you? Why didn't you complete the mission instead of getting sidetracked in some petty vendetta?"

Odin wanted her to feel his frustration and she seemed to be getting the message.

"I don't know my lord, I really don't. I'm sorry, very sorry for everything."

Ruby wanted to cry, but that would be an unthinkable humiliation for a Valkyrie warrior.

"Did you forget the prophesy? Did you not remember me saying that from a Midgard apple, black and rotten to his core; a man would spark a fire that would rage so fierce as to consume us all?" Odin practically quoted the prophesy word for word to her. She had to understand its terrible significance.

Ruby nodded miserably.

The apple was New York of course, and Odin believed that the black and rotten person was Cole. He fitted the bill perfectly.

"Please, my lord, let me try again. I swear on my honour I won't let you down." She looked up and Odin saw a hunger burning in her eyes.

"Maybe yes, maybe no, perhaps it's time for you to go to Valhalla?" Odin studied her face intently, he was testing her resolve.

"No my lord, I know I'm not ready yet. Let me try once more, please, I beg of you."

Odin sat back in his throne and stroked thoughtfully at his beard.

Prudr was one of his greatest Valkyries and he wanted her to travel to Valhalla with all the accolades she deserved. He didn't want her to arrive as a failure. He would give her a second chance, but for a while he'd let her stew.

"Hmmm, let me think about it. I will let you know my decision when I have made one."

Odin waved one hand over his ring, and Ruby found herself standing once more at the bottom of the citadel. Her ordeal was over, and she breathed a deep sigh of relief.

For now, all she could do was wait and keep her fingers crossed.

Kat lost her wager, but not by as much as Hod had expected. Reluctantly, he had to admit that she was becoming a fine horse woman. With her long blond hair flowing wildly behind her as she galloped excitedly across the fields, she looked every inch a noble Valkyrie.

They spent the afternoon together, both joyously hunting.

They waded neck deep through musty ferns, and crawled on their bellies in undergrowth laden with the fragrance of summer flowers. The sunlight danced on the forest floor around them and the canopy was filled with the excited calls of startled pheasants. These flapped hastily away from them.

On a hot summer's day, the woods surrounding Asgard were Kat's favourite place. It didn't matter if they caught something or not, it was the peace and beauty she adored—the cool shade of the trees, and the warm sunshine in the glades. It was a feast for her senses, and she avidly drank all of them in. Sometimes, she would close her eyes and focus on the woodland sounds. At other times she would cover her ears too, honing her sense of smell on its rich tapestry of fragrances.

It was days like these she wished would last forever, and made Asgard the sweetest heaven.

Eventually the two of them came to a small pool in a dip in the forest. It was surrounded on three sides by dense undergrowth, but on the fourth was a small, muddy clearing where a stream meandered from it. Here they decided to wait and lie in ambush. As the shadows lengthened, a small family of wild boar came to drink and wallow in the mud. Seizing the moment, they let loose a flurry of arrows. To their great excitement they bagged a young suckling boar, and instead of riding straight home they settled down and held an impromptu barbecue in the woods. As the sun began to set, they lay back and rested their aching stomachs.

They had gorged themselves to bursting on meat, berries, and wild mushrooms.

"Fair Kat," Hod began cautiously. "I want to tell you something, and I want you to promise me you won't laugh."

Kat eyed him suspiciously with a naughty smile on her lips.

"If you're going to tell me you're still a virgin then don't worry, I'd already guessed," she giggled, cheekily.

"No I, I—" he thought about denying it, and then decided better. "Actually, what I wanted to say was, would you teach me how to fight?"

"What?" Kat sat up, taken aback by this admission. "I thought everybody here knew how to fight, especially the gods. You can shoot a bow and arrow, so surely you know how to wield a sword or an axe?"

"No I can't. My mother won't let me just in case I get hurt."

"What do you mean? You can't get hurt because you're a god. I've shot arrows into Balder myself and I know he can't be killed."

This was true.

Balder often allowed the maids to use him as target practice, pulling their arrows out afterwards one by one. He delighted in telling them which ones stung and which ones didn't.

"Ah, that's because he's special. Mum had him enchanted because of what will happen to Thor. All the rest of us, including Odin, we can be killed just as easily as any mortal."

Kat was intrigued now. This was unexpected news and she pressed Hod to tell her more.

He did so.

Apparently Thor, who was actually adopted by Frigg and not her natural son, had been cursed at birth. He was fated to die in the last, great battle for Asgard. Terrified at this prospect, Frigg had woven an enchantment to protect Balder from death by any object native to Asgard. She had also forbidden Hod to learn how to fight, and often kept him confined to Valhalla. He was "Grounded" as Kat so tactlessly put it. There, he would be close by and safe from harms way.

"Well, if you can die, then tell me this. Why don't you grow old? Surely you can't have one without the other?"

Kat's curiosity was well and truly aroused. She loved learning about the gods' secrets.

"We can grow old, if we want to," Hod began. "Although we do age much more slowly than you. We can also stop growing older altogether if we choose."

"How do you do that?" Kat interrupted. She was thirsty now for answers.

"By eating Idun's apples; that's why all the gods go to Odin's garden to eat them. They stop us from growing old."

"And if you stop eating them?"

Kat was delighted with what she was hearing. It explained the laughter when she had offered Odin and Freyja some wild strawberries instead of apples.

"Our age will catch up with us. The older we should be, the quicker this progresses." He replied.

"And what about the Valkyries, we're undead so we can't grow old and we can't be killed. In some ways, we're more god-like than the gods." Kat hoped she hadn't sounded too arrogant. What she said had come out wrong, but she hoped he got her point.

"My dear Kat," Hod exclaimed loudly, sounding surprised. "Hasn't anyone told you? The mead you drink each night, the mead from Valhalla? If you don't drink that then you too will rot and die—just as surely as the gods would without their apples."

Kat sat back astonished.

She felt for her heart again; still not beating.

A frightening thought began to dawn on her and it was one that would colour the rest of her stay in Asgard.

If what Hod said was true, and she could see no possible reason for him to lie, then Odin had all the Valkyries and the gods over a barrel. The mead came from Valhalla and the apples from Idun. Odin controlled both these sources. If he chose, he could easily stop their supply and let them all die. Worse, he could threaten them with that possibility.

In a very real sense, the gods and the Valkyries were no better than the prisoners. They were all hostage to Odin's whim.

Kat felt an icy chill.

Odin seemed so kind and so generous, but what if he had some secret, a dark, hidden agenda for them all?

This thought scared her and she sat back, pretending to cough. She didn't want Hod to see the apprehension in her face, and this idea was probably nonsense anyway.

She decided to pay more attention, however, to what went on around her. She would use Hod, and anyone else for that matter, to learn as much as she could about Odin and his world. Knowledge was power, and she had to acquire it—quickly and secretively.

She wondered briefly once more about the mead.

If it stopped their bodies from aging, perhaps it did other things to them as well? What if it messed with their minds, altering these in some way?

This was an intriguing possibility, but she didn't dwell on it. Her mind felt too clear and razor sharp, so that couldn't be true, surely?

"Tell me about your ring."

Kat deliberately decided to change the subject.

"You, Thor, and Balder, you all have three diamonds in your rings. What does that mean?"

"Well, each one takes us to a different realm. This one takes us to Odin's garden," he looked at her, smiling sheepishly. "But you already know that. This one here takes me back to my Mum."

"You mean Valhalla?"

Hod nodded at her clarification.

"Yes, and this one, well it doesn't seem to work. Look." Hod waved his hand back and forth over it, to emphasis his point.

"Has it ever worked?" Kat enquired thoughtfully.

"No, not for me; it used to work for my brothers, but not anymore. Odin has blocked their access to this place, too. He said we couldn't use it until the realm was ready for us once more. He said this should be sometime soon."

Oh my God!

Kat's mind raced wildly, her ridiculous notion just might be correct. Odin really did have them all, even his sons, under his thumb. He was controlling all their lives.

This power didn't feel right, not right at all.

"Any idea when it stopped working for your brothers?" she enquired once more, trying to make her question sound casual.

"Oh years ago, hundreds, maybe even a thousand." He shrugged; he was getting bored with this line of conversation.

Kat had an impulsive thought, the sort where one and one just had to make two. She bet the blocked realm was Midgard. The time when they used to go there was perfect. It coincided exactly with the period on earth when myths about Odin, Thor, and the other gods were all the rage.

What worried her now was the last thing Hod had said.

That they would be going back and sometime soon.

She really wanted to press him further on this point, but she felt that she couldn't. She didn't want to arouse his suspicions. That might be dangerous, particularly if he mentioned this conversation to Odin or his brothers.

"What about Loki. He's got two diamonds. One obviously takes him to Odin's garden, but where does the other one go?" Kat changed the subject once more, hoping it would encourage him to tell her more about the rings.

Hod gave her a very strange look.

"You really don't want to know that answer, fairest Kat."

"Why?"

"Because—"

His look became stranger and she knew there was no way she could let him leave her like this, dangling in suspense.

"Oh go on, you can't do this to me." Rolling over, she playfully punched him.

For a while they wrestled together, laughing and joking as Kat tried to tickle the answer from him.

"I can't, I really can't," he cried with laughter as he tried to wriggle out of her interrogation.

"I won't teach you how to fight."

Kat threatened him while keeping up her assault. To her immense surprise, Hod took her threat seriously. He suddenly stopped messing around and sobered up.

"Okay, but you must prepare yourself." Hod looked her straight in the eye as he said this.

Kat brushed herself down and tried to put on a sombre face.

"The other diamond takes him to Niflheim, the realm of the dead. This is where people who aren't heroes go when they die." He looked at her, expecting to see shock in her face.

"Why?" Kat was too bemused to be afraid. "Why would anybody want to go to such a dreadful place?"

"To see his daughter."

This time Kat did look surprised. She had no idea that Loki had a child so she pressed Hod to tell her more.

"Well, Loki's daughter was banished from Asgard a long time ago. She was a Valkyrie once, but she turned evil and became very powerful. She was so powerful in fact that even Odin came to fear her. We gave her a nickname, one we whispered behind her back. We called her The Black Valkyrie. Eventually Odin had enough of her violence and he banished her to that terrible realm. It was the worst fate imaginably but amazingly, fortune smiled upon her. To his dismay, she thrived in its evil and is now the kingdom's Queen. Loki's daughter is the ruler of Niflheim; she is the Queen of the dead."

Kat and Hod made their way back home slowly under the stars; they spoke little as they trotted. Kat's head was reeling with Hod's revelations. It would take many days for her to make sense of them all, and she couldn't share her thoughts with anyone, not even Jess.

Odin's incredible control, the mead, apples, and the rings—Loki's daughter. *Wow!* These thoughts blew her mind. She knew she wouldn't sleep tonight.

As they journeyed homeward the wolves howled. They were the closest she had ever heard them. Their horses twitched and pranced nervously and it was with some relief when they finally arrived safely in the castle stables. Bidding Hod goodnight with a little peck on his cheek, Kat hurried inside.

Unfortunately, there was one last surprise waiting for her that evening.

"Hello," said an overly-clean gentleman. He had emerged from the steps leading down to the Chamber of the Valkyries.

"Hello," said another gentleman, who had also come up the steps.

He looked just like the first, a reflection in the mirror. Identical in every detail, even down to their clothes.

Kat stopped and drew her sword.

"Explain yourselves?" she commanded angrily of the intruders. "No stranger to this castle dares enter the Chamber of the Valkyries."

She moved forward, pointing her sword menacingly in their direction.

"Oh yes, quite, I see. Please may we introduce ourselves. Fair, fair—?" one of the gentlemen searched politely, hoping she would tell him her name.

"Fair Kat; I am maid to the Valkyrie Brynhildr."

Kat introduced herself with pride. A few weeks ago she wouldn't have uttered such words, but now these came naturally. She was proud of her status, even though tonight she looked a proper mess. Her legs, arms, face and tunic were all covered in mud; and her hair was tangled and matted with twigs and leaves from the woods.

"Well, fair Kat," the gentleman stepped forward, offering out his hand to shake hers.

"My name is Vili."

"And my name is Ve," offered the other gentleman as he also extended his hand.

"We're Odin's brothers, would you let him know that we've arrived?"

42

Black Hawk Down

"Excuse me, what did you say your name was?" the lieutenant stared hard at the petite young lady, squatting on the floor in front of him.

"Jameela sir, Jameela Masood."

"Thank you. I do apologise for the unpleasantness back there," he continued as he stared blankly back at her. He was mulling over the extraordinary sights and sounds he had witnessed barely an hour or so ago.

The fight to retake the street where Lance Corporal Lee was trapped had been ferocious. Their comrade had been cut off from the rest of his platoon for nearly an hour and they had all feared the worst. Several RPG rocket rounds had landed around the building and it had taken at least one direct hit. Eventually, when they regained control of the street, they found Lee and the girl inside the building's shattered carcase. They were huddled together, both smothered in blood. The girl had been cradling Lee's head in her arms.

Lee was lying now on a stretcher, waiting to be airlifted back to base. Multiple bullets had pierced his legs and arms, and blood was haemorrhaging into his lungs from a piece of shrapnel. This had pierced his body armour. He was lucky to be alive, and the lieutenant hoped they could keep him so until he reached the main hospital. A drip had been set up, and he was being pumped full of morphine.

Forty Commando had suffered enough casualties during this tour of duty, and he didn't want to add Lee to his 'Killed in action' list.

As he considered Lee's fate, the lieutenant's mind drifted back to what had happened. It had been strange finding a woman there, surrounded by so much gore.

The girl seemed so timid, slight of stature and shy when she spoke. It must have been terrible, witnessing the slaughter that had taken place.

Even from down the street, the soldiers had heard the screaming. This had risen high above the staccatoed bursts of automatic gun fire and the heavy thud of mortar rounds.

The screams were terrified, desperate yells, the hideous sound of men as they died in terrible agony. Mingled with their torment had been another cry. It was one he had never heard before, but one he would never forget.

The sound was terrifying—and difficult to describe.

It had been unearthly, the high pitched wail of someone possessed by a demon. It was not a cry of pain, nor a cry of fear. It was a battlecry, and it had come from a woman's throat.

A woman crazed with elation, intoxicated by the ecstasy of waging war.

When the soldiers had finally stormed the house, they found the two of them, Lee and the girl, lying in a blood bath. The mutilated bodies of three fighters lay strewn all around them. The men had been butchered, hacked to pieces in a frenzy of violence. He'd only ever seen an explosion cause such carnage before.

He could easily understand their screams, and the agony they must have suffered. Looking at the gentle mannered girl before him, this now left him with a problem. It was impossible that she could have done such a terrible deed, but this caused a major headache.

If she hadn't committed the atrocity, then who on earth had?

Jameela tried to avoid the Lieutenant's gaze.

She knew he was searching for answers and she was determined he wouldn't find them. She tried desperately not to smile, which was hard given the circumstances.

She felt satiated; a warrior who had gorged her blood lust on the battlefield. She always felt a guilty pleasure after a good fight, and the three Taliban guerillas had fought bravely. Jameela silently saluted their courage. They had been worthy opponents and had died with great honour.

Jameela always felt regret after such a battle. Killing men in the horrific way she did. She couldn't control herself, hence her Valkyrie name. The battle always became such a blur, the boundary between victory and carnage fusing into one. She couldn't help it. Much as she hated her harsh nickname, she knew it was well deserved. She was 'The Berserker,' because she lost control as these enemies did.

Berserkers were the one group of warriors that the Valkyries dreaded fighting. They charged ferociously into battle, flaying wildly with their minds high on a cocktail of religious fervour and psychedelic drugs—magic mushrooms and bog myrtle stirring their reality into hell. They fought without fear and possessed impossible strength.

This was Jameela's reincarnation too when gripped by the blood lust.

"What will happen to Benjamin now?"

Jameela broke the awkward silence that had descended upon the safe house. The distant echoes of gunfire could still be heard, but the centre of Musa Qala was now firmly back under British control. She had decided to call her hero by his first name, she couldn't keep calling him 'soldier' and Lee seemed so impersonal. Until he was awake, she decided that this was what she'd call him.

"We'll be airlifting him to our field hospital as soon as a helicopter becomes available," Lieutenant Ashwood reassured her.

"May I go with him?" she enquired hopefully. She really didn't want to be separated from him now.

"I'm sorry. You'll have to stay here. We only airlift casualties and foreign nationals to safety. You'll have to return to your family when you're ready."

"But I'm an American citizen," Jameela announced suddenly.

"What? Do you have any proof, where's your passport?"

Ashwood eyed her suspiciously. He was surprised she had left it this long to tell him that. Besides, what the hell was an American girl doing out here and all alone?

"Yes, just a minute," Jameela got out her small leather purse and opened it in her hand. "Here's my American passport."

She spoke slowly and deliberately over her purse, and as it opened a badly folded and slightly crumpled document fell into her hands. Ashwood took it and scrutinised it carefully. He jotted down the number, and contact details of her next of kin. Her Visa, photograph and other biometrics, they all seemed to be in order.

"You should take better care of this," he handed it back to her, pointing at the crease in the middle. "What on earth are you doing here?"

Aah!

Jameela had rehearsed this many times.

"My parents sent me here to meet my future husband, to have an arranged marriage." She looked up into his eyes; her story had found his soft spot. A poor, little rich kid sent abroad by extremist parents. The image tugged at all the right heart strings.

"Oh my dear, I'm so sorry. Have you been treated well?" Ashwood suddenly felt a wave of sympathy. He would get in touch with the U.S. authorities as soon as he could. The girl must feel so lost in this bloody hell hole.

"Yes, his family, they've been lovely, but I need to leave. I can't stay; my parents want the marriage as soon as…" she trailed her voice off as she faked a small tear.

Ashwood was about to speak, but the whirr of helicopter blades approaching told them that their lift had arrived.

A small party, Jameela, Benjamin, and two stretcher bearers fought against the windy blast from the rotor blades as they boarded the chopper. It was heavy going. Jameela had never been in such a machine before. Looking out of the small window as they took off, her eyes opened wide with amazement.

Banking steeply, the helicopter sprayed burning flares from either side as they left; the pilot weaving a crooked course. The town may belong to the British, but the surrounding countryside was all Taliban. Their fighters were heavily armed, with missiles that could easily bring a helicopter down.

As the noisy craft swept low over the barren valley and away from the town, Jameela turned her attention to Benjamin.

He was stirring once more.

Tenderly, she stroked his forehead and offered him another sip from her flask. It was just as she was finishing this and resealing her flask, that a loud explosion shook their machine.

KABOOM!

The helicopter had been hit.

Lights went out as the fuselage filled with acrid smoke. This scorched her lungs. With a sickening lunge the vessel lurched downward, spinning slowly before gathering momentum as gravity seized control.

They were going down.

The last thing Jameela could remember before the sickening impact was squeezing Benjamin's hand hard.

He had opened his eyes and was looking straight at her.

They were such beautiful, clear brown eyes.

43

A Breakfast Date

Odin was pacing up and down, tugging angrily at his beard. He was not a happy god, and he had plenty of reasons not to be so.

It was a few hours after midnight, and he had been woken by the sound of Gjall—the ringing horn of Heimdall. He already knew why this had been blown, but what he didn't know was how to deal with the problem it heralded.

Torches had been hastily lit, and already the occupants of the castle were trickling into the shadows of the great hall of Gladsheim. They were arriving in dribs and drabs and in various states of attire. The scene was a bit like a late night fire drill in a large Midgard hotel. Guests slowly arriving at the assembly point, politely but begrudgingly. Each wondering if they could have stayed in bed, their absence going unnoticed.

As he paced he reflected on his problems. There would be trouble with Thrym, the giants' king. He wouldn't be happy with so many slain and injured brethren returning to Jotunheim. Prudr had failed to bring Cole back to Asgard and now his brothers, Vili and Ve, had arrived. How typical of those two idiots to turn up unannounced.

He hated it when they visited.

They were always so nosey and inquisitive. Questioning him about this and that, and poking their noses into all the comings and goings of his realm. They treated it as though it were their own, which hardly seemed fair.

Okay, so he admitted that the three of them had worked with Mimir to create Asgard, but his brothers had chosen not to live there. It annoyed him intensely that they still took so much interest in his kingdom. Whatever he did, whatever he said, they always claimed they could have done better; which he knew to be absurd. The two might be geniuses—but they lacked one iota of common sense. Why couldn't they give him some appreciation, a crumb of gratitude, or toss him a carrot now and then?

"Is this what I think it's all about?"

Thor's voice echoed loudly around the hall, jolting Odin away from his thoughts.

"Yes, of course," Odin raised his hands and coughed loudly, hoping to get the attention of the assembling warriors and maids.

"Fellow gods and warriors," he began. "I'm sure you've all heard the horn of Gjall."

They nodded politely. Everybody in the realm would have heard it, because that was what it was for. In the event of an invasion, or deadly foe crossing the Bifrost Bridge, this was Heimdall's alarm call. That was why he lived in the watchtower, patiently keeping an eye on all who came from the mountains of Jotunheim.

"I'm equally sure you have all noticed Fenrir and his pack of wolves are getting closer to Asgard."

There was a murmur amongst the gathering; they had all heard the howls of the wolves growing louder, night by night.

"I believe Fenrir has crossed over the bridge, and is now hunting in the realm of Vanaheim. It will not be long before he, and his pack, are at the walls of Asgard."

Odin raised his voice for the last few words, a point not lost on his audience. He must indeed be worried for such a rarity to occur.

"Let me handle him. Mjollnir will smash Fenrir's head to smithereens!"

Thor bellowed loudly as he pulled his hammer from his belt.

"No Thor, No." Odin wagged his finger at him. "You know the prophesy as well as I do. Fenrir must not be killed."

"Well, can't I just maim him a little bit?" Thor played wistfully with his hammer. There was nothing he loved more than wielding it in a good fight.

"No Thor. I don't trust you."

Odin knew he was right. The power Mjollnir could draw from the Well was almost without limit. Thor couldn't be trusted. Even Odin had trouble sometimes, controlling the energy when he used Gungnir.

"Then what can we do?" Thor threw his arms open wide, and posed this question to the gathering.

There followed a swelling chorus of answers, everybody had their own ideas about how to stop Fenrir and they all wanted these to be heard at the same time.

Slowly Odin settled the hubbub, waving his arms downward in an attempt to bring some order to the chaos. Somewhere in the cacophony he had heard what he wanted, and he pointed to Tyr who was standing next to Prudr. He motioned for him to speak up once more.

"We should bind him, and then lock him up in a dungeon forever. That way he isn't dead and the prophesy can't be fulfilled." Tyr spoke loudly and with confidence, making sure everybody heard and understood what he was saying.

More discussions broke out, and after what seemed an age, a gradual chorus of approval came from the warriors. A tired and disjointed handclap followed.

Tyr's plan was clever thinking.

"Excellent idea!" Thor boomed as he strode over and clapped Tyr on the back. "Leave it to us," he squeezed Tyr tightly against him, not bothering to ask if he wanted to be involved.

"I'll make some chains so strong that when Fenrir's bound he won't move a muscle. Come my dear friend, we have work to do."

Thor strode out of the hall as he spoke, dragging Tyr in his wake.

Debates continued among the remaining Valkyries and gods for some time. But the hour was late, and no-one really wanted to hang around for too long. Chatting quietly amongst themselves, they left Gladsheim as they had come, returning to their beds in dribs and drabs.

It was unlikely many would go back to sleep.

Thor was true to his word.

As soon as he left the hall he went straight to his foundry and started a raging fire in his furnace. Making a tremendous noise, he set about creating the thickest and strongest chains he could imagine. He worked tirelessly throughout the night, the noise preventing all but the soundest sleepers from getting any rest.

Kat was one of the many who couldn't go back to sleep. She dreaded the wolves, and knowing that they were so close made her very uncomfortable. She cuddled Jess hard and held her close.

Eventually, as the first rays of light crept across their bedroom floor, Kat got up and went down to the courtyard.

The hammering had finally ceased and Jess was asleep. She didn't want to wake her sister with her incessant tossing and turning.

Arriving in the courtyard, the scene that greeted her was most unusual for this time of day.

Instead of a few sleepy slaves going about their duties, the cobbled courtyard was a hive of industry. Thor's chariot was being loaded, with four slaves straining under the weight of the chains he had made. In one corner of the yard Tyr was sitting at a grindstone, busily sharpening his sword. Sprays of sparks flashed around him as he beavered industriously.

Kat noticed another cart had been made ready, and Kvasir's harp, bound in leather skins stuffed with straw, had already been stowed on the back. Fjalar and Galar were at the front with Kvasir sitting in between them. Beside them, on her beautiful horse, was Emile. She would be their escort for the trip, and she looked magnificent in her full battle dress.

Kat felt a pang of embarrassment.

She had pulled on the first clothes she could find, and thrown a thick, scruffy cloak over them. Her hair was uncombed and she still had sleep in her eyes.

How could she ever become such a noble Valkyrie as Hlokk?

There was a clatter of hooves behind her and she turned to see who the approaching horseman was.

Hod waved excitedly to her.

"Hod!" she exclaimed loudly, surprised at seeing him up so early in the day. "What are you doing here?"

"Fair Kat, how lovely to see you," he beamed down warmly from his horse. "I ride with Fjalar and Galar to Nidavellir."

"Don't be so silly," Kat replied crossly. "It could be dangerous, especially with Fenrir on the loose." She suddenly felt concerned for his safety, particularly after his revelation in the woods. He couldn't fight and that made him a liability.

"I'll be fine with Emile here to protect me. Don't worry, I need to break loose and have an adventure. I need to become a man!"

Hod pulled his sword from his side and flourished it enthusiastically in the air. He wanted to impress her, and the dwarves obligingly clapped and praised his little display.

"Farewell, dearest Kat. I'll see you again soon." Hod blew her an exaggerated kiss as he waved a cheery goodbye; and with a swish of a whip; the cart, Emile, and Hod slowly trundled away.

Kat stood there with her hands on her hips. She was furious, and also scared.

This was all her fault.

If she hadn't humiliated him and pushed him around, he would never have dared to set off on such a perilous journey.

What could she do?

Part of her wanted to race after them, drag him from his horse and slap some sense into his silly head. The other part of her was secretly proud of his determination. With a shock, she realised how much she really did care for him. She knew that she would miss him and would worry every day until his safe return.

Reluctantly, she raised her hand and waved a fond farewell.

Turning around to make her way back inside the castle, she noticed a stranger had arrived in the courtyard. The person had been standing behind her, and her appearance was by far the oddest thing she had yet encountered in Asgard.

The woman, who was also waving goodbye, was dressed in the most immaculate cream, Armani suit. She had designer sunglasses perched on top of her forehead and on her arm was a matching handbag. Dressed so exquisitely; she practically glowed in the pale grey light of dawn.

With a sudden shock, Kat realised that the woman was coming toward her and offering her hand.

"My dear Katarina. I have heard so much about you. It's so lovely to finally meet you."

The woman spoke with a flawless, English accent, one heavily laden with the inflections of aristocracy.

Kat shook her hand cautiously. She hadn't a clue who she was.

"Oh dear me, you don't know who I am, do you? How rude of me. My name's Frigg, I'm Hod's mother."

"Would you care to join me for a spot of breakfast?" she added warmly.

44

Frigg

Kat had pretty much got used to the magical mystery tours of the gods by now. So it didn't come as too much of a surprise when, after accepting the breakfast invitation and with a single wave of Frigg's hand, she was transported somewhere completely different.

Looking slowly around her, she had to admit she liked her new surroundings very much.

She was standing in a large room that had been lavishly decorated and styled in a feminine and cosy manner. It was a sort of cross between a Victorian sitting room and a French boudoir. The room had two large picture windows, heavily screened with rich velvet curtains and swathes of lace netting. The ceiling was ornately plastered, and the floor was covered with a deep, luxurious carpet. A large fireplace adorned one wall and a small fire glowed in its hearth. This was just sufficient to give the room its cosiness, and take the edge from the chill of an early summer's morning.

Around the hearth were several, studded leather armchairs and a sofa. Each of these was festooned with beautiful silk cushions. Kat could have sworn that on the coffee table was a copy of *Vogue* or *Elle* or some such quality woman's magazine.

At the far end of the room and standing next to the doorway, was a circular table with four elegant dining chairs. An antique silver coffee jug and some fine porcelain crockery lay invitingly upon this.

"Tea or coffee?" Frigg asked politely, moving toward the table.

"Tea please," Kat replied hungrily. A lovely cup of Earl Grey was just what she fancied, that, and a nice slice of toast all dripping with fresh butter.

"Would Earl Grey do?" Frigg asked, beckoning for Kat to sit down, and offering her a slice of hot toast from the toast rack in front of her. A large bowl of butter materialised abruptly on the table.

Kat sensed something odd was going on.

Allowing the image of a pot of strawberry jam to float across her mind, this dutifully appeared on the table as well.

Frigg smiled self consciously at her.

"Yes, I can."

"You can read my thoughts, can't you?" Kat enquired, realising too late that Frigg had already answered the question.

"Oh do please forgive me. It's such a nasty habit and I really must try to stop it." Frigg squeezed her hand apologetically as she sat down next to her. "That's partly the reason why I've invited you here my dear," she continued with a merry twinkle.

Kat helped herself to some toast and butter, and cast a wary eye over the woman sitting beside her. She knew already that as Hod's mother, Frigg was also Odin's wife. With this thought in her mind, she took some time and studied her closely.

She had to be important with powers as great as hers.

Frigg had long, straight, ash blond hair that flowed gracefully down to the middle of her back. Her face was beautiful in a timeless, classical style. She had deep-set blue eyes, and high cheek bones which were accentuated by the pale, almost alabaster colour of her skin. Around her neck she wore a single stranded necklace of black pearls, complimenting the cut and colour of her impeccable suit. This accentuated her full, womanly figure and wasp-like, slender waist. She clearly spent a lot of time keeping in shape, and this showed.

Frigg oozed style and elegance, and was the sort of woman Kat hoped she might become one day.

"Why, you're so complimentary my dear Kat."

Kat blushed.

Frigg had been reading her thoughts again.

"Do you like my Jimmy Choo's?" Frigg enquired enthusiastically, pushing an elegant, cream stiletto in her direction.

Kat nodded appreciatively. "Can all the gods read peoples' minds?"

"Gracious me no. Thank goodness," Frigg laughed at such a notion. "It's my little gift," she explained before continuing. "I really wanted to thank you for being so nice to my little Hod. He has told me so much about you, he really likes you an awful lot and I'm so glad you like him, too. Not like some of those other nasty girls at the castle. They can be so spiteful. I could tell that you really cared for him, I read your thoughts as he was leaving."

Kat was about to say something, but Frigg spoke once more. She really was extremely chatty.

"But, you know, you mustn't feel responsible for his little adventure. If anything, I blame myself. I've been far too over protective; he's just being such a rebel. I'm sure he'll get into some trouble or other whilst he's away, so when he gets back we can both take it in turns to give my little Hodikins a good spanking."

At that silly notion, they both fell about laughing. Kat felt a great sense of relief that Frigg didn't blame her for his rashness, although she still felt partly responsible.

"By the way, I really must apologise for his awful behaviour. I kept telling him to ask you out, but he wouldn't. He's so shy and awkward, just like his father used to be. And then to go and get the Norn singing, honestly, what a stupid little boy. If you hadn't gone and slapped him, then I know I would have done. He can be such an idiot sometimes, but I do love him so."

Kat was giggling continuously. It was bizarre to hear Frigg talk like this, not only about Hod but also Odin. She was so funny, treating them both like naughty boys; she sounded just like a proper mum.

"Now tell me dear Kat, how are you settling in?"

Finally, Frigg was going to let her speak.

"Oh, pretty good really. It's very different here, but the warriors and maids are really rather nice, and they've have done their best to make me feel at home." She began.

"That's lovely. I expect you know why I don't spend much time here?" Frigg looked carefully at Kat and she nodded that she did.

"The other wives and I, we tend to stay in Valhalla, looking after Odin's army of heroes. He wastes such a lot of effort and money on it, you know; it's his pride and joy. I don't have the heart to tell him it's a complete waste of time."

"Wives?"

Kat felt rude, but she had to interrupt at this point.

"Oh yes, all the boys are married, didn't you know? There's Thor's wife, Sif, and his daughter, Thrud; Balder's wife Nanna and Sigyn. She's Loki's wife, he gives her such a hard time."

Frigg touched Kat's hand at this moment, in a knowing, best friend's sort of way.

"I'm so sorry," Kat began. "I'm finding this all rather confusing. I didn't know any of the gods were married, other than Odin that is.

How do you, you know, put up with all their…" she struggled for a polite way to put what she wanted to say.

"Mistresses and girlfriends?"

Frigg decided to help her out.

"They're naughty boys the lot of them, but what can you do? We let them have their fun here in Asgard, and we turn a blind eye to it. When they're ready, they come home with their tails between their legs. Husbands always do."

She winked and smiled tellingly at Kat. Frigg had a secret, but she didn't know Kat well enough to talk about him just yet.

"I would really love for you to meet the other goddesses some time. They're such a fun crowd. Perhaps I could arrange an afternoon tea here or something? I'm so sorry I can't invite you back to Valhalla, it's just one of Odin's silly little rules."

"Wow. I would love that, thank you, thank you very much." Kat was delighted at the thought of meeting the 'First Wives Club.' Other than Freyja, it was the first time she had met any of the goddesses, and she was relieved to know that there quite a few of them around.

"By the way, where exactly are we?"

Kat suddenly realised that she hadn't asked Frigg where they were.

"This is Fensalir, my little pied-a-terre when I'm here in Asgard. You won't have seen it before because I like to keep it well hidden, behind a lovely waterfall in fact. I seldom invite guests here, but you are a very special girl Katarina, and I have high hopes for you."

"I beg your pardon?"

Kat was taken aback by her sudden use of her full name, and her expression of hope. She would love to know what this meant.

"You're a very clever girl, dear Kat, very clever indeed," Frigg patted her affectionately on her head. "You've already worked out many of the mysteries of Asgard, and I hope you'll be able to stop some of the silliness that is gripping Odin and the boys."

Kat had a horrible thought.

Did she know about her thoughts in the wood the other evening when she was with Hod?

"The answer to your question is yes," Frigg was holding her hand now. "And please don't worry; that can be our little secret. You are right to be afraid, there are dark days coming and I need an ally here in Asgard. Someone I can trust, someone I can depend on."

Suddenly Kat felt an urge to hug Frigg, and she did so, holding her close.

"Please forgive me," she whispered. "You're just such a lovely lady. Hod is so lucky to have a mum like you."

To her great relief, Frigg reciprocated her gesture. She too seemed relieved to have someone at the castle she could talk to.

"You know," Frigg decided to change the subject. "When you become a warrior, you really must join me on a shopping trip in Midgard. I do so love the clothes the women wear nowadays."

"I didn't know you could bring things back to Asgard?"

Kat was surprised by this revelation, but it did explain her wonderful clothes and the magazines on the table.

"You can't, my dear; but Odin and I can," she waggled the ring on her finger in Kat's direction. It had as many diamonds as Odin's.

Delighted by this very pleasing discovery, Kat settled into a long and detailed conversation about shoes and dresses, make up and bags, and practically every other sort of girly shopping you could imagine. Time rolled by and eventually, with a great deal of reluctance, Kat admitted that she really ought to be getting back to the castle.

"What time would you like to return for?" Frigg tapped at an expensive watch she was wearing around her wrist.

"About mid-morning, if that's okay with you." Kat was amazed by this offer. Frigg was a remarkably powerful woman; and she wouldn't be surprised if she didn't pull a mobile phone from her hand bag and place a call ahead to the castle.

Frigg looked at her and smiled. She had read her thoughts again.

"Unfortunately there isn't any reception here. But don't worry, I'm working on it."

They both laughed heartily at her little joke, and then with a wave of her hand, Frigg returned Kat to the castle.

After she'd gone, Frigg settled back into one of her comfy armchairs and thumbed through a magazine from the table. She smiled as she did so. Their meeting had gone very well and she'd said all the right things. She'd engineered a budding friendship, and the mead was working nicely on Kat's mind.

With a bit more manipulation, perhaps one day she might take advantage of the clever, yet oh-so-naïve Kat?

45

Debriefing

It was a long drive from New York to the FBI headquarters in Washington DC, but after four hours Marcus was finally nearing his destination. As he turned into Pennsylvania Avenue and headed for the imposing concrete and glass J Edgar Hoover building, he felt butterflies in his stomach.

It had been several days since the disappearance of Officer O'Brien and Ms. Knight, and Marcus was now feeling comfortable about having a chat with Agent Woods.

Woods had finally cooled down.

Marcus would have liked to have had their conversation sooner, but to his embarrassment, he had collapsed in the corridor on that fateful day. After twenty four hours of observation at the local hospital, a combination of tiredness, stress, too much caffeine, and a tendency to being a hypochondriac were pronounced as the diagnoses.

This pretty much agreed his own verdict.

Having excluded the possibility of a heart attack, he had been discharged on some blood pressure pills, and advice to avoid coffee. Both of these were now contributing to his sense of lethargy, and a headache which was proving hard to shift.

From his bed, Marcus had been impressed by Woods efficiency as the FBI tidied up the muddle left behind at the police station.

Officer Jessica O'Brien disappeared from the computer database, and effectively ceased to exist. Ms. Ruby Knight was officially transferred to FBI custody, with a stand in agent exiting the station under a blanket to give the story some media credibility. Ms. Knight would eventually become forgotten, lost in the tortuous system of prisoner processing somewhere down the line.

The inconvenient death of Mickey Warren in police custody was dealt with extremely smoothly.

He became the victim of a fatal drug overdose, drugs which somehow had evaded detection and ended up in his cell. The stab wound to his chest would never appear on the post mortem report.

Everything was totally plausible, and a highly satisfactory cover up to the debacle.

"Good morning Finch, do take a seat."

Agent Woods greeted Marcus at his door and showed him into his small office.

Woods was wearing exactly the same clothes as he was wearing the other day—black suite, black tie and a freshly laundered white cotton shirt. His room matched his manner; minimalist, clean, and functional. Not one picture on the wall betrayed anything of his life. If he had a wife and children, Agent Woods left these at home when he came to work, and no doubt did the opposite when he went home.

Woods was a consummate professional, clinical in his efficiency and with an intellect as sharp as a razor. He would make a formidable adversary if you were unlucky enough to be on the wrong side of the law.

"Coffee?" Woods offered politely.

"Tea, please."

Marcus would have killed for a strong black cup, but he had to heed his doctor's advice.

"You do realise," Woods began, as they sat down either side of his pristine desk. "That you're now an official world expert on Valkyries?"

"Valkyries?"

Marcus's blank face betrayed his ignorance of that word.

"Yes, Valkyries; the 'choosers of the slain,' if you believe in Viking mythology. That's what we think Officer O'Brien and Ms. Knight consider themselves to be. I've been tracking them and others on and off for at least a decade."

Marcus sat back and took a deep breath in.

Wow! This was going to be an interesting conversation.

Slowly Agent Woods explained the information that they had, and more importantly, emphasised how much they didn't.

Like Marcus, the agency had concluded that the women were part of an all female cult, headquarters unknown. They were already aware of the particular style of knife and the flask of liquid that they used, but the coin was a revelation and Woods made detailed notes of Marcus' limited description of it.

The cult appeared to be world-wide, because the only way the agency had been able to track their activities was by investigating murders that involved a knife. They specifically looked at those where the knife penetrated the heart, and of these, over ninety nine percent could be excluded for various other reasons.

From the possible attacks that could have be done by Valkyries, they had found them occurring all around the world. Interestingly, they tended to cluster around wars or outbreaks of violence. The cardinal sign of a Valkyrie attack was ambiguity over the cause of death. All the victims were either killed by some other means before being knifed through the heart, or vice versa. What Woods was keen to stress, however, was that the frequency of these attacks had risen dramatically over the last ten years; and how the motive behind the slayings was now changing.

"How do you know their motives?" Marcus interrupted Woods on this point.

"The cult seems to have taken the mythology literally. Almost all attacks prior to the nineteen nineties occurred on heroes or heroines. They chose only people who would be decorated for their valour and bravery."

"So in what way has this changed?" Marcus understood what Woods was suggesting, but he wanted further clarification.

"Let's take for example the three cases you've been involved in, Dr. Neal's case, Slim's case, and the Warren case. Dr. Neal was an innocent woman, Slim was an out and out villain, and Mr. Warren was a down and out junkie. Absolutely none of these fit the classic image of a hero, but I still think there's a link." Woods added confidently.

Marcus nodded. He was interested to hear what Woods thought might be their connection.

"Dr. Neal died heroically, defending a woman from a villain. Here is our heroine. Officer O'Brien kills her before knifing her in the usual Valkyrie fashion. Ms. Knight killed Slim because he had murdered her lover Elijah Kelly. This seems like a revenge slaying, nothing more, nothing less. Ms Knight then gets caught; Officer O'Brien comes to her rescue and kills Mr. Warren because he witnessed her murdering Dr. Neal. It all fits rather nicely don't you think?"

Marcus nodded. His explanation sounded a bit garbled and detailed but the motives seemed to make sense, although they didn't explain one fundamental question.

"Why are they doing this?"

He felt almost embarrassed asking such an obvious question.

"And why are the FBI interested?" he added for good measure.

These were a tiny number of vigilante style killings. Surely it was unworthy of an FBI investigation spanning decades?

Woods sat back in his chair and clasped his hands tightly across his chest. This was the money shot. Suddenly he looked up, smiled and laughed; in a totally uncharacteristic manner.

"The first question you asked Finch is what we don't know ourselves. We have theories, but that's all they are. Until we can get hold of a cult member, and ask them these questions, that's all we're left with—theories, nothing more."

"And my second question, about the FBI involvement?"

Marcus wasn't going to let him off the hook with this one. There had to be something important for the FBI to throw money at the case.

"I can best answer that by showing you some photographs."

Woods went over to a filing cabinet and took out two files. One was old and weathered; the other seemed fresher and more recent. Marcus noted the names attached to the files. Prudr and Brynhildr; the names Ms. Knight and Officer O'Brien had used for each other.

Woods removed a picture from each file, and pushed them across the table to Marcus.

"See if you recognise these."

To his astonishment, Marcus found himself looking at a faded colour Polaroid of Officer O'Brien in a British military uniform and a black and white picture of Ms. Knight in a nineteen fifties style outfit.

"Fancy dress?" he enquired optimistically.

"Look at the dates on the back please."

Marcus checked—1971 and 1956 respectively.

"Their mothers?" he enquired more tentatively, hoping for both their sakes that he was correct.

"Clever thinking, but no. We believe these are the same people. We have checked the fingerprints you had on file for Officer O'Brien, and they match those of this Lieutenant in the British Army. She was a woman who served with the British Intelligence Services in Ireland during the IRA troubles of the nineteen sixties and nineteen seventies.

We can't match Ms. Knight's fingerprints, but obviously her photograph goes back a lot earlier."

There was a long pause while Marcus digested the impossibility of what Woods had shown him.

Eternal youth, resurrection, aliens from outer space?

All manner of crazy ideas swirled in his head. He was speechless and looked pathetically at Woods for the answers.

Woods smiled.

He was pleased to see that Marcus was as flummoxed as he had been when he first took over the files some ten years ago. He let him flounder a little longer before putting him out of his misery.

"Cloning, that's what we think this is all about, cloning." He watched Marcus's face for a reaction, and was disappointed to see the same blankness he had seen earlier. Clearly Finch didn't keep up to date on scientific matters.

"I expect you're thinking about elixirs of youth and resurrection, but I'm afraid we can exclude those. The lieutenant was brutally murdered shortly after that photo was taken and her body was cremated. No. The only possible explanation is cloning."

Once again, Agent Woods went into an elaborate explanation of the reasons behind his conclusion.

He believed that the cult members stabbed their victims to collect a small blood sample. White blood cells could be isolated from these, turned into stem cells and the victims could then be cloned. Their bodies would be identical in every detail, right down to finger prints and retinal eye scans. It was likely that Dr. Neal had been chosen, as a heroic woman, to replace a cult member who may have died.

The other heroes he wasn't so sure about.

Clearly their genes must have some value. Perhaps the cult was building a genetic library to sell? It seemed impossible that the cult could have cloned and raised so many people in secret. The occasional Valkyrie women yes, but not a whole army of cloned men?

That just wasn't possible.

The FBI's interest and indeed that of the American government was now obvious.

This sort of technology still didn't exist, so getting hold of it 'off the shelf' was a mouth watering prospect.

As he spoke Marcus became increasingly impressed. Woods had taken a nonsensical situation and tried to make it rational and understandable. He wasn't totally convinced about the whole cloning idea, but as Woods had said; this was just a theory.

As Woods finished talking, Marcus asked the one remaining question that stuck out like a sore thumb.

"So how did they escape from the cell?"

In many ways, this was the single most important answer he had wanted from this trip. He had seen inside the cell with his own two eyes. The two women had gone, completely vanished into thin air.

"Ah," Agent Woods sighed conspiratorially as he rested his elbows on the table and drew himself closer.

Marcus could tell this was going to be the highlight of his talk today.

"Meta-materials."

46

Reprisals

Following her breakfast with Frigg, Kat struggled to concentrate for the rest of the day. For Jess's sake she tried, but it was difficult to wield a sword with conviction when your head was swimming with Armani suits and Jimmy Choo's. The thought of shopping in Midgard was an overwhelming joy, and no amount of bullying by Jess could stop her blissful daydreaming. Even the bribe of a surprise that evening did little to shake her distraction. Finally Jess gave up, and they called an early end to the day's training.

It wasn't until after supper, when Jess took her and Carmel to the arena that Kat's mind finally returned to Asgard.

When it did so, it was with an almighty bump.

Approaching the arena, Kat saw the figure of a man spread-eagled between the whipping posts. Illuminated as he was by a few slaves holding torches, she could tell that he was a skinny individual, with a head of matted, curly brown locks. This was lolling to one side. She realised at once that this must be Jess's surprise, and the reason behind her recent mission.

She recognized the man too, and guessed immediately what was expected of her.

"Hello Mickey. Do you recognise me?"

Kat had stood for some minutes wondering quite how to introduce herself. *What do you say to the odious monster who murdered you?* Words seemed somehow inadequate.

Slowly he raised his eyes, and she could see that they were rolling. He seemed dazed, demented even, his mind dangling unhinged and divorced from reality.

"Well hello sexy lady," he laughed abruptly and explosively. It was a horrible, sinister noise, one laden with malice. "So what are you doing down here in hell with me?" he sneered, emphasising their location.

He motioned with his head for her to draw nearer and she did so.

"You're still a fucking bitch!" He swore loudly and then spat at her face, missing a cheek by only a few millimetres.

He howled with laughter.

"I fucking killed you, bitch, and now you're here in hell with me." He screamed, baring his teeth as he glared at her face. His eyes were now open wide and filled with hatred.

Kat stood impassively.

The vicious bully hadn't changed.

She hoped he would have done so for his sake, not hers. Any hint of remorse would have been helpful, but no. Not our Mickey. He was bad to the core.

Kat smiled icily. She still hated that word he used and now she could do something about it.

"Do you have your whip handy?"

Kat looked over to Carmel who was caught off guard by her inquiry. Carmel indicated that she didn't, but sent a slave racing back to the castle to fetch it. As she did this, Kat turned once more to the man.

"I'm going to whip you tonight, Mickey do you understand? I'm going to whip you and whip you and hard."

She looked at him, hoping he would beg her for mercy, and give her a reason for clemency.

"Do your worst you fucking bitch!"

He spat at her again.

"I'm fucking dead, bitch! You can't hurt me no more." He swung on his ropes, laughing demonically at his brave defiance.

"Trust me Mickey, I can, and I will, hurt you. And when you have recovered from my whipping, I'm going to make you regret using that word. I'm going to turn you into a bitch, do you understand me? I want you to think about that; that's my promise to you."

Kat's mind was made up.

He had got the better of her back in Midgard but she was in charge here. He hadn't changed, and still had no respect for her or any other woman for that matter. Carmel and Jess were right, as was the Valkyrie creed. Flogging and castration were the only solutions for scumbags like Mickey. He was mad and bad; and would always be so.

He was beyond redemption.

For a while Kat chatted calmly with Jess and Carmel, and finally when the slave returned, she laid into Mickey good and hard. It was the first time she'd given a whipping, and she did so without mercy.

It wasn't the hardest of floggings, nor was it the longest. But as Jess and Carmel watched Kat flex her arm, still dressed in her evening finery, they reflected with satisfaction on how far she had come. The little girl who couldn't even watch Carmel was now a powerful woman.

Jess had been right.

The blood lust had changed Kat, just as it did all the other maids. Crime demands punishment, and violence begets violence. That was the Valkyrie way.

Kat was learning fast.

A few days later, in the cells beneath the arena, Kat made good her promise to Mickey. Under Jess's watchful instruction, she emasculated him. She felt no pity or anger as her hands took his manhood, just a deep sense of satisfaction that he would never hurt or abuse a woman ever again.

While Kat flogged Mickey, Loki was finally arriving at the great hall of Thrym. His journey had been long and arduous, but spurred by necessity; he had travelled quickly and with little rest.

He had galloped hard through the previous day, crossing the plain of Ida in near record time. He took care skirting the villages of the Vanir that dotted the marshlands and foothills; their attentions would have slowed him down. Making excellent progress, by nightfall he had arrived at Heimdall's watchtower. Deciding that discretion was the better part of valour, he bedded down there for the night. The Bifrost Bridge over the glacier was dangerous to cross even by day, and would be lethal in the darkness.

He too awoke to the sound of Gjall ringing out at some time during the night. Its warning call blew far and wide across the realm of Asgard. He also heard the howls of Fenrir and his pack of wolves, and he rejoiced at their bravery. He knew the prophesy, and knew that Odin wouldn't dare kill him. A little harassment by his beloved pet would serve him well, avenging the blood of giants that had been spilt in the town.

With the first light of dawn, Loki set out across the glacier.

In the summer heat with its freeze-thaw conditions, the route was extremely treacherous; a series of precarious ice and wooden bridges marked by poles that zig-zagged their way across the deep crevasses of the glacier. The route changed almost daily, as some bridges collapsed and others reformed. It was a path fraught with danger, but it was the only way to reach the realm of Jotunheim.

An hour or so after he had started, Loki made it safely to the other side. Saddling up his horse once more, he wound his way slowly up the mountain trail to Utgard, the capital of the realm.

Hour by hour he climbed, the fierce heat of the summer sun countered by frequent gusts of cold air, these blew down from the mountains ahead.

At first, the climb ascended through beautiful, shaded forests of magnificent giant sequoias and Monterey pines. The air was heavy with the scent of cones dripping resins, and the calls of wood pigeons and pheasants echoed through the trees. Occasional log cabins stood in great clearings, places where woodsmen would shelter at night. These ancient forests were dangerous places. Along with the wolves, there were giant cave bears and smilodons (sabre toothed tigers); all being skilled and ferocious predators.

Finally, ascending above the tree line, he reached a rocky pass, one that brought him down to the first of many great mountain plateaus. Here the air was cold and thin, but grass and heather lay deep and springy underfoot. Breaking into a canter, he marvelled at the great herds of musk ox, giant elk, and woolly mammoths that roamed these remote pastures. Here was the real treasure trove of Jotunheim, a realm rich enough in meat and berries to feed the hungry stomachs of the giants.

As daylight began to fade, he reached the far side of the plateau and descended once more through woodlands to a large lake. Beside this lay Utgard, the capital of Jotunheim. Making his way by torchlight, he followed winding streets paved with broken slabs until he stood before the huge doors of Lyr. Knocking boldly, he entered.

Inside was Thrym, the last surviving frost giant.

Here at last was the King of the giants' realm.

"I'm surprised you dare show your face here."

Thrym's voice growled from somewhere in the depths of the room.

Loki blinked, letting his eyes adjust slowly to the dimness. The hall was vast and beautifully warm, heated by a huge fire that raged at one end. Its name Lyr, meant "holder of warmth," and the hall was made from a double skin of stone separated by a layer packed with moss and lichen. The roof was made of slate slabs laid on pine logs, and then covered with a thick carpet of sedum. Birds nested there during the summer months, their eggs and young safe from rats, weasels, and other vermin. Throughout the hall were long tables with equally long stools running beside them. These stools rose almost to Loki's waist, which gave a good impression as to the size of fellows who would dine there most evenings.

In the centre of the hall stood a huge cauldron, this nestled upon a small fire. In the cauldron was a potent alcoholic beverage—a mixture of berries, mead, cider, and whisky. This was served hot, with cloves and other spices. It tasted not unlike Gluwein, a drink found in Midgard.

Growing bolder, Loki stepped forward. He could make out the shadow of Thrym now; he was sitting at the table nearest the fire.

Thrym was the great grandson of Ymir, the very first frost giant of the realm. Ymir had been murdered by Odin and his brothers at the very dawn of time, and the grudge the giants bore them for his death endured to this day. Thrym could speak well, a gift that was rare amongst their kind. Most giants had great difficulty in uttering more than occasional simple words. His ability suggested he had mixed blood in his veins; but this was a slur he vehemently denied.

"Greetings noble King."

Loki bowed low, hoping a show of humility would carry good favour.

It didn't.

"Give me one good reason why I don't kill you this very instant?" Thrym growled again. His yellow teeth gleamed menacingly in the half light, and he spoke with a voice so deep that his words became lost in the booming echoes reverberating around the hall.

"I bring good news," Loki started optimistically. "News of a plan that will bring about the fall of Asgard."

"I have no need for any more of your rotten plans," Thrym interrupted him angrily.

"I have no desire to see more of my fine kinsmen return as rotting carrion."

He spoke with passion and fire in his belly; and spittle flew from his lips. In his hand was a large thigh bone from a bison, thick with fatty meat. He tore great chunks from this with his teeth, eating as he spoke.

"But this plan is as cunning as a weasel and as stealthy as a fox," Loki tried once more, a desperate effort to redeem himself.

"Enough!" cried Thrym.

Wiping his mouth with the back of a hand, he pointed the bone threateningly at Loki.

"I too have a plan and you will do as I bid, do you understand?" he leaned forward, and Loki saw the whites of his eyes flashing at him.

He nodded respectfully.

Thrym was indeed in a foul mood.

"You will go to Odin and challenge Thor to a duel. Tell him that if he doesn't accept, he will be cursed forever as a coward. Let him know that if he wins, no giant will ever step foot into Asgard again. Finally, warn him that if he loses, he will forfeit Freyja as my wife."

Thrym thumped his fist down hard on the table. The whole hall seemed to shake with its force.

"But my noble king, Thor has Mjollnir and no giant can withstand its mighty blows."

Loki was bemused by Thrym's lame challenge. *Hadn't enough giants been killed already for him to have learnt this simple lesson?*

"Loki, do you take me for a fool?" Thrym leaned forward, a twisted smile upon his lips. "Hrungnir will be my champion, and he will be enchanted by Gullveig. Not even mighty Mjollnir can overcome her great magic."

"Gullveig?"

Loki seemed shaken by the mention of this name. He had not heard it uttered for millennia, and many now doubted the witch had ever existed.

"Yes, you heard correctly. Gullveig," Thrym repeated her name, relishing the awe it brought to Loki's face.

"But my Liege that's not possible. Odin burned that dark creature, not once, not twice, but three times at the stake. When she still didn't die, he banished her from this world for all eternity, binding her with charms so strong that she could never return."

"Banished yes, but not for all eternity and nor did she leave this realm. All this time she's been sheltered by the black elves living deep below the dwarves. A place so dark and forgotten that even Odin cannot see into their realm. She is here, now, in Utgard, this very moment. With her help I shall kill Thor and seize Freyja as my prize."

Thrym sat back, watching as Loki slowly choked on the genius of his plan. It was rare indeed that anyone could up stage Loki. After all, he was the self-confessed master of deception and trickster extraordinaire.

"I will do as you bid my King. If what you say is true, then Odin and his realm will soon be yours."

Loki bowed low. He believed that Thrym was bluffing about Gullveig, but it was useless to argue further. Contrition would ensure his safety while in Jotunheim, and he so very much wanted to see Carmel again.

Thrym sat back at last and bade Loki to eat and drink.

He was contented.

The death of Thor would be a bonus to his plans. Freyja was the real prize. With her came the key to Mimir's Well, and with the well came limitless power.

Should the final battle take place, he alone would emerge victorious. He would be ruler not only of Asgard but also Midgard, a realm fabled to be fabulously rich in food, slaves, and strange creations. He had heard rumours of machines that could fly, voices that could be heard from the other side of the world, and weapons that could flatten mountains. He slobbered at the prospect of possessing such wonders.

When Loki had eaten his fill, Thrym bade him leave to sleep the night in Utgard. As Loki turned to leave the hall, Thrym couldn't resist one last jibe.

"Look at you, Loki, you're a disgrace," he sneered wickedly. "Your father, Farbauti, would be ashamed of you if he were still alive. Cavorting with the Valkyries; our sworn bitter foe? Yes Loki, bad news travels fast. I know of your love for Carmel, fair maid to the cursed Gunnr. It was she who brought about the defeat of your plans. Have you no shame?"

Content with the humiliation his final brutal insult had caused, Thrym leaned forward. Hawking loudly, he spat a huge wad of spittle into the fire.

This spattered and fizzled in the heat of the flames.

47

Invisible Thoughts

Marcus declined Agent Woods' offer of an overnight stay at an all expenses paid hotel. He preferred instead to take the four hour plus drive back to New York the same day. He knew he would arrive home close to midnight, but he felt a terrible need to get back to his wife, to Anna; and the 'real' world.

The lengthy conversation with Woods had left him a little shell shocked, and the drive was an ideal opportunity for him to get things sorted in his head.

He was quite exhilarated to be called a 'world authority' on the Valkyries. He had never been an authority on anything before, but according to Woods, other than the two of them and a select few at the agency, no one else in the world was even aware of their existence. Anyone who had the misfortune of running into one always ended up dead. To have met two and lived to tell the tale was, well, simply put– unique.

Not that his new scholarly status would come to much.

Marcus had been sworn to secrecy.

Woods himself had only ever met one Valkyrie and that had been Ruby. He hadn't elaborated further on their encounter, and Marcus hadn't pressed him on the point. It probably wasn't relevant to their case anyway.

The fact that both he and Woods had reached the same conclusion about the girls being part of a cult came as something of a relief. It suggested Marcus still had a sharp mind, which was something he often doubted as he waded through the tedium of day to day work.

What he wasn't sure about was this whole idea of cloning. It all seemed a bit too elaborate and flimsy to his way of thinking.

Killing people and then stabbing them just for a drop of blood?

This seemed excessive for the potential reward.

Although Marcus didn't like to admit it, he had struggled to come up with a better idea. Most criminals, or cults, were all about making money; and he suspected the Valkyries would be no different.

Megabucks had to be the reason behind their killings.

What about obtaining the cells to create illegal eggs for fertility clinics?

He could imagine a thriving black market for the hunky hero type of baby so he decided to run with this idea.

How about taking this one stage further, and implanting the eggs in surrogate mothers?

If they did this in Third World countries the cult would have a steady supply of cheap, designer babies ready for adoption. There was a desperate need for these, and that could be very profitable.

The idea was sound, and certainly no worse than Woods proposal for an 'army of clones.' However, as a motive for murder it still didn't feel quite right. They were missing something, something important.

Intuitively, Marcus knew that they were wrong.

They were barking up the wrong tree.

You had to have a really big motive for killing people, and to be brutally honest, for the Valkyries—they didn't have one.

This left a big puzzle, one with a gaping hole right through the middle.

What were the girls up to?

Marcus scratched his head.

Perhaps Woods was lying and knew more than he was letting on?

This thought was intriguing and he mulled it over for a while.

Woods was a 'Fed' and they seldom dealt from the top of the pack. One and one weren't making two and that made Marcus uneasy. Woods had told a good story—*but was that all it had been?*

A fairy-tale spun for his edification, to distract him from a deeper truth?

Feeling a little unsettled with this notion and without having any proof, Marcus decided to return to issues that were more firmly rooted in fact.

One thing that wasn't in dispute, and the matter they had agreed on most, was the need to get hold of a Valkyrie for questioning. This was a priority and he liked the scheme that Woods had proposed.

Vincent 'Slim' Tucker had been a fat, small fry, petty crook from New York. Not really the sort of premium cell donor a Valkyrie would go after. No, he agreed with Wood's suggestion that the real target must have been Cole. It was possible either Jess or Ruby would be back to have a second crack at him.

Marcus liked the idea of placing Cole under surveillance; they could then capture a Valkyrie should one of them pop up. There were other appealing dividends in this option. He might just catch Cole doing any of the myriad of illegal activities he got up to. To date, Cole had been such a slippery operator the muck had never stuck.

Twenty four hour, covert surveillance might just change all that.

Unfortunately, Marcus wasn't at all happy with another of Wood's ideas, the option of recruiting Cole to aid them in a capture. The thought of offering him an amnesty made Marcus choke.

Cole was a hard-nosed, low life, verminous thug who was responsible for countless crimes and murders. The sooner he was off the streets and banged up for life the better. He had told Woods that he didn't agree with this proposal and he would fight it with a vengeance.

Finally, what about the bizarre meta-materials?

The disappearance of Jess and Ruby from the police cell had been the toughest part of the case for Marcus to swallow.

This was an impossibility.

The walls of the cell were solid, and no amount of "Open Sesame" was going to reveal some secret passageway tunnelling its way out of there.

Wood's explanation for their disappearance was as brilliant as it was simple.

The girls hadn't vanished from the cell; they only appeared to have done so. He suggested that they had remained hidden in the cell under some sort of 'Harry Potter' style cloak of invisibility. They could then have left much later, when the coast was clear.

Marcus would have dismissed Wood's proposal as lunacy had he not been shown some recent and remarkable video footage.

The science fiction that was quickly becoming science fact was being made possible by progress in the development of meta-materials. These were bizarre, man-made materials that could bend light inside them, rather than reflecting it back from their surface.

By making fabrics from tiny beads of these materials, you could bend light around an object hidden underneath it. Light hitting the fabric on one side would enter the beads, and then curve from bead to bead as it passed around the object. Once on the opposite side, the light would re-emerge just as though it had passed in a straight line through it. This made the object underneath the fabric appear invisible.

The video he had been shown was of a material doing exactly that.

A piece of cloth made from a meta-material had been placed over a small microphone and 'Hey presto'—the microphone disappeared from view.

If this cult was capable of cloning people, and both Jess and Ruby seemed living proof that they could; then creating a cloak from such a fabric might not be such an outrageous suggestion after all.

As dusk slowly faded into night, Marcus continued on his long drive home. Gradually his thoughts of clones and meta-materials drifted to those of the beautiful redhead, Jess.

He really wouldn't mind meeting this Valkyrie again; and he had a funny feeling that someday he would.

48
The Binding of Fenrir—Part One

The day after Thor had set out to capture Fenrir broke with fine, pink tufts of clouds drifting lazily up in the sky. There was a heavy dew on the fields around Asgard, but a lightness in the people's hearts.

As dawn broke, the Aesir woke to the news that during the night, Thor, Tyr, and Balder had captured Fenrir. Horns began to blow, drums were beaten and a purple flag was raised high above Gladsheim. From early morning, a noisy crowd began to gather in the main square, everybody was eager to see the captured beast.

An atmosphere began to grow, one tense with excitement and fear.

Few had ever seen Fenrir, and the stories that were told about his monstrous deeds were packed with blood and gore. To have him finally bound and behind bars would indeed make today one they would all remember.

Carmel joined the other warriors and maids in a procession that headed down to the hall much later in the morning. A servant had reported seeing dust rising from the horses and carts of the hunting party. This was now drawing near to the town.

At Silk's suggestion, all the party wore full battle dress, with shields, swords, axes, and spears. Even bound, Fenrir could prove a handful, and they needed to be on their guard.

As they neared the hall, Carmel looked round wistfully; she was hoping to spy Loki somewhere in the crowd. She felt sure that news of his pet's capture would have reached him, no matter how far away he was.

Before he had left, Loki had told her that he was going to the realm of Jotunheim, but he hadn't elaborated further. Carmel didn't mind where he went, and she really couldn't care what he got up to. As long as he loved her, that was all that mattered. She toyed with his necklace, and smiled at the thought of the passion they had enjoyed. A terrible yearning was growing, a need to feel him deep inside her once more. She couldn't help this urge.

Her blood still held its hot, Latino fervour.

Reaching the edge of the gathered throng, the warriors struggled to part the crowd and make their way through to the front. Eventually, they took their places on the steps of Gladsheim and watched the hunting party's slow progression up the hill.

"HAIL WAR! HAIL VALOUR! HAIL ODIN!"

Three triumphant cheers roared from the crowd as they greeted the exhausted heroes when they finally arrived in the square. The crowd surged forward, and the Valkyries had to use their shields to clear a space around the hall. Eventually, when enough room had been made, the horses of Balder and Tyr, the chariot of Thor and the cart on which Fenrir was laid, were brought in front of Gladsheim. Odin and Freyja, who had been waiting inside, came out to greet the party, congratulating them warmly on their success.

"Would you like to see the beast?"

Thor bellowed triumphantly to the crowd, raising Mjollnir above his head and waving it jubilantly around. A mighty roar was his reply, and despite his tiredness, Thor was in a playful mood.

He was going to have some fun.

"What was that, I can't hear you?" he exalted the crowd once more.

They responded eagerly, roaring even louder than before.

"Are you ready?" he roared victoriously as he prepared to show them the beast.

Thor was loving this moment of triumph.

It had been well earned.

During the night, he, Tyr, and Balder had encountered Fenrir and his wolves in the heart of the plain of Ida. To their surprise, the pack hadn't turned and run away from them.

They did the opposite.

With Fenrir taking the lead, the wolves had surrounded the gods; snapping ferociously with their ears pinned back and teeth bared such that the roots of their fangs were clearly visible.

The wolves' hatred and rage came without fear, and a terrible battle soon ensued.

Swords and axes rose and fell, and fangs dripped red with the blood of the three warriors. A writhing sea of fur and teeth surrounded the trio, and the demonic noise of the fray could be heard for miles around. The battle could have been lost, were it not for the power of Mjollnir and the might of Thor's arm. Finally, when the ranks of the wolves broke, and the rest of the pack had turned tail and fled, the gods cornered Fenrir.

They bound him fast with the heavy iron chains Thor had fashioned.

All three men now stood before the crowd, dripping with blood and viscera from head to toe. Some was their own, but most came from the score or so wolves that had been slain. Thor himself had accounted for at least a dozen of these. His chest, arms, and face were smothered with their congealed remains.

With a final joyful roar from the crowd, the three men took hold of the chains and heaved Fenrir from the back of the cart. He landed heavily with a mighty thud on the cobbles.

Dust rose all around him.

Now the crowd could finally see the horror of this monstrous beast.

Fenrir was huge; at least four times the size of an average wolf. His fur was jet black, forming a thick and glossy pelt. His eyes were large and green, but they seemed to change colour as his head swung from side to side.

His eyes darted menacing daggers deep into the crowd.

Fenrir's legs were long with muscled haunches, and as the men hauled him across the stones to Odin's feet, he snarled and squirmed. Lunging both left and right, he snapped at the air with his hideous, long, white fangs. Dribbles of foam dripped from the corners of his mouth, which was fixed in a sardonic snarl.

He looked every inch a demon from Niflheim.

With Fenrir at his feet, Odin begged the crowd for silence.

"It is a great day," he began in his habitually quiet voice. The crowd pressed forward, eager to hear his words.

"We must all praise the valour of Thor, Balder and Tyr, and give thanks to Yggdrasill for their safe return."

The crowd erupted once more with cheers, clapping, horn blowing, and drum beating. It would be many minutes before a hush fell, allowing Odin to speak once more.

"Now Fenrir," Odin turned his words to the mighty wolf writhing at his feet.

"You can make mischief no more. You will be taken to cage where you will remain for the rest of your life. This will allow us to all live in peace and safety."

As he spoke, Fenrir watched Odin closely.

He seemed to understand what was being said.

He began to pant.

Slowly at first, he started to tense, and then relax the muscles in each of his legs in turn. He was testing the strength of the chains that bound him. Faster and faster he repeated this process, each time the chains creaking and clanking a little bit louder.

A murmur arose in the crowd and began to grow in its intensity. Those nearest the wolf tried to back away. They felt uneasy. The chains were strong, but so too was Fenrir. A wicked glint in his eyes suggested that his reign of terror was not yet over.

A wave of panic gripped the crowd.

The victory that had seemed so certain only minutes before might yet be undone.

GHAARRRH!

With a mighty snarl, and the crunch of bursting metal, Fenrir broke his chains, and leapt to his feet. He was free at last, and the people of Asgard would pay for his humiliation with their blood.

The Valkyries quickly raised their shields and levelled their spears, forming a deadly barricade between him and the crowd. This latter was dispersing rapidly, people screaming and crying hysterically as they fled from the square.

Fenrir snarled, snapping left and right with his mighty jaws. Seeing an opportunity, he lunged at Odin and opened his mouth wide.

Fenrir leapt toward his neck.

"NOOO!"

Seeing his lord in danger, Tyr shouted as he hurled himself in front of the leaping wolf. He buried his fist deep inside Fenrir's mouth.

Odin was saved.

Frustrated by his failure, Fenrir sank his razor sharp fangs deep into Tyr's arm. He still demanded a prize.

Lashing this way and that, he tore Tyr's arm from his body and he collapsed, bleeding heavily, onto the cobbled floor.

His arm had been severed at the elbow.

Brandishing his trophy triumphantly and with his head held high, Fenrir catapulted himself toward the wall of shields and spears.

"YIELD!" Silk yelled at the warriors, and their ranks divided. Fenrir was allowed to pass harmlessly through.

Thor raised his hammer, but Odin grabbed his arm; stopping him in mid throw.

"NO! Let him go. Remember the prophesy; he mustn't be killed."

To their agony, the warriors watched as Fenrir bounded down the road and across the bridge. Gathering pace, he headed for the trees and disappeared into the woods. They knew that he would regroup his pack within the hour; and tonight he would once again bring terror and destruction to the land.

With a heavy heart, Thor turned to Odin.

"I have failed you, father."

Thor hung his head mournfully, and Odin, in an effort to console him, placed his hand upon his shoulder.

"What can we do now?" Thor spoke softly for once, his voice laden with the misery of defeat.

Odin looked around.

Apart from himself, the warriors and their maids, few people were left in the square. Where once had been a crowd intoxicated with the joy of victory, there now stood a silent and deserted square.

Their conquest had turned to despair.

No bonds could harness the evil beast.

"You're going to need more than mead for that my lad," Balder jested somewhat cruelly, pointing to Tyr's bleeding stump and trying to bring some light relief to the gathering's mood. Tyr tried to force a grin, but he was slipping into unconsciousness. Kat was already by his side, busy binding his arm tightly to stem the loss of blood.

"It can't be done," Thor continued dejectedly. "No chains can be made that will ever hold Fenrir. He's just too strong."

"I can do it."

A voice strong and confident rose from amongst the warriors. It was Silk and she stepped forward boldly.

"Where you boys have failed, we women will be victorious."

Looking at each god in turn, she stared icely at Thor, Tyr, and Balder. Silk was laying down a challenge, and they could see a steely coldness in her eyes.

"Brains and not brawn, that's how we will capture Fenrir," she raised her spear, and turned to face the warriors and maids once more. They cheered loudly, desperately hoping that she had a plan and wasn't merely bluffing.

"The guile of women will capture Fenrir, not the strength of men. Come sisters, there is much work to be done."

Striding resolutely off across the square, Silk beckoned for the Valkyries to follow her. They did so, and as they walked Silk whispered hasty instructions to each in turn.

Odin watched and a smile formed across his face. He saw her dispatching warriors and maids in all directions, and wondered what cunning plan was underway. He noticed too that Silk had her arm around Carmel, and they were talking intently as they walked.

He tried to eavesdrop on their conversation, but from this distance, the only word he managed to catch was "chamomile."

49

Hostages

The good news for Lance-corporal Benjamin Lee and Jameela was that they survived the crash of their helicopter. The bad news was it hit the ground in Taliban-controlled territory.

Instead of arriving in the warmth and security of Kandahar airport, they crashed into a field close to a guerrilla position. A lucky strike from an RPG had blown the tail off the helicopter, forcing it to spiral out of control and into the ground. Only four people on board survived, and they were all quickly captured by the jubilant fighters. Downing a helicopter was big news, and they would be local heroes.

Hostages meant even more, big cash bonuses for them all.

Jameela, had she been conscious, would not have believed her continuing good fortune. For the third time that day lady luck showered her with her favour.

The three captured British soldiers had an obvious cash value, but the little Afghan girl, pretty though she was, was barely worth the cost of the bullet that would dispatch her. With a gun cocked and pressed against the back of her head, and an assassin's finger squeezing on the trigger, a cry suddenly ordered him not to shoot. They had been rifling through her possessions, robbing her, and had found her American passport. Suddenly the girl's life had a value, and she was hauled along with the others into the back of a battered four by four.

The fighters worked quickly, a downed helicopter would attract British soldiers and spotter aircraft like moths to a flame. Within minutes, the three vehicles, two laden with captives and one mounted with a heavy machine gun, were speeding away from the crash site.

Bouncing and bumping crazily along a frozen and rutted track, they were already climbing into the mountains by the time the first attack helicopters arrived on the scene. Arriving at a junction, the men stopped the cars and split into two groups, dividing the hostages between them.

Jameela and Benjamin were tied up, wrapped in blankets, and bundled over the backs of pack horses. Theirs would be a slow, treacherous journey up a narrow, twisting mountain trail.

The other two hostages were transferred to another vehicle, which sped on up the valley. Their journey would be faster but unfortunately shorter. A spy satellite high in the skies picked up their trail; and two fighter jets were dispatched. Less than an hour after their rescue from the helicopter, the men were killed by a missile strike. The pilots were unaware of the captives' presence in the vehicle, and the accidental nature of their deaths was never made public.

Just like the Taliban, lives had a value for the allies.

Their value was measured in publicity, not money.

Deaths from friendly fire were about as welcome as a summer cold.

Jameela remembered little of the first day's trek up into the mountains. She drifted in and out of consciousness, waking only for short periods, whenever a particularly sharp jolt ripped through her body like a dagger. She knew her collar bone was broken, and she could taste blood in her mouth. This, she quickly realised, was seeping from a deep gash in her chin. She could move her arms and legs; just enough to determine that no other bones had been broken.

The blankets she was swaddled in, used to conceal her presence, kept her mercifully warm. The temperature was below freezing, and the fighters continued to climb well into the night. The tiny trail they were following was almost invisible to the human eye, but the men and the pack horses knew it like the back of their hands. It was one of a network of countless supply routes that criss-crossed the mountainsides. Arteries that made it all but impossible for the allies to stem the flow of guns, rockets, and mortars which fortified the Taliban strongholds. Sometime around midnight, the fighters eventually stopped and made camp. It was on a tiny area of flatness, sheltered beneath a large and fissured rocky overhang. They warmed up food, which they carried in tiffins, over a small camp fire.

To her immense surprise and relief, both she and Benjamin were taken from the pack horses and their wrists were untied. At least two of their captors spoke passable English, and they were offered food and warm drinks.

In a strange way, their captors were fascinated by them and eager to converse. They wanted to know all about where they came from, and in Benjamin's case, which football team he supported. This peculiar camaraderie, high in the freezing mountains of Afghanistan, brought an even more welcome surprise for Jameela. Her precious flask was among the possessions they had looted from the helicopter, and she managed to persuade them that it contained medicine that she needed to take every day. Two gulps of the soothing mead refreshed her immediately, and when the fighters weren't looking, she managed to give Benjamin a couple of sips, too.

Benjamin was in a bad way, but even with the limited amount of mead he had drunk, he was in much better shape than he should have been. For the first time they managed to hold a small conversation, and he spent much of it apologising for getting her into this mess.

Jameela learned that he was twenty one, and that he lived in a small town in Devon in England. He had a pet dog called Biscuit, and he also wanted her to call him Ben.

She did so with great delight.

Spitting on a piece of rag, she cleaned their faces up as best she could. They both looked a mess, but at least they were still alive and their captors seemed in no hurry to kill them. For now they were safe, and that was all that mattered. After a while the conversation around the camp fire lulled, and she cuddled up close to Ben. Their thick blankets, and shared bodily warmth, ensured that they both slept peacefully for a few hours, and didn't freeze to death.

When dawn arrived it was snowing, and the party broke camp quickly and set off early without eating breakfast. Jameela was allowed to sit upon her horse, but Ben remained bundled up across the back of his. He was still too weak to sit unaided.

The trail continued to climb higher, and with the snow came increased danger. At first it fell gently as leafy flakes, carpeting the broken rocks beneath them in a fine layer that muffled the sound of the horse's hooves. It was slippery work, and Jameela quickly persuaded the fighters to let her walk beside her horse. She could go nowhere, because there was nowhere to go. The falling snow reduced their visibility to almost zero, and the risk of injuring a pack horse burdened with an unnecessary passenger outweighed their fear of losing a captive. Indeed, as they climbed higher, their battle became more one of survival against the elements; all of them together, pitted against the forces of nature.

A vicious, swirling wind picked up and gusted down the side of the mountain. The large, Christmas card snowflakes turned into blasts of icy pellets. These stung like needles as they lashed against their faces. The snow beneath their feet became deeper, and began to drift. The horses struggled now to find a foot hold on the rocks. These lay buried and hidden in the deep snow beneath their hooves. Their progress became slower and slower, but just when it looked as though they would have to turn back, the party reached the narrow mountain pass they had been heading toward. Crossing this, they carried on down the other side for a few hundred metres, where they came upon a shallow cave.

In here they took a brief, but welcome, break.

The fighters, using dry kindling which they carried with them, lit a fire. Expertly they sheltered it with their bodies until it had gained sufficient strength to survive the icy gusts which swirled all around them. They brewed a pot of sweet, black tea, and offered dry biscuits and corned beef which Jameela gratefully gulped down. She took another sip of mead, and managed yet again to get some into Ben without being noticed. She desperately wanted to rest there longer, but barely an hour after their arrival, they were on the trail again.

This time, they were going downhill.

If climbing up had been difficult, the descent was nigh impossible. Blinded by the blizzard; Jameela felt, rather than saw, her way down the slope. Clinging on to her horse for dear life, she prayed to Odin that they would all reach the bottom safely. The fighters shouted words of encouragement to each other and their horses, as they picked their way cautiously down the treacherous ravine.

As dusk approached, the blizzard began to abate and Jameela could see once more.

They were in a valley, one that was narrow with impossibly steep sides and littered with huge boulders. Some of these were the size of small houses. A frozen stream descended steeply down the valley's floor, its frozen waters forming cascades of icicles as it twisted and turned along its route.

Following the stream's course, their trail approached a particularly large, rocky outcrop. To Jameela surprise, she heard the distinctive, low pitched hum of an electricity generator coming from behind it. As they rounded these final, craggy boulders, a large, well lit cavern came abruptly into view.

Concealed by the rocks, and invisible to the outside world, she concluded this would be where she and Ben were going to be held captive.

The fighters unloaded their horses and ushered her and Ben inside.

50

The Binding of Fenrir—Part Two

Despite the crushing disappointment of their failure earlier to bind Fenrir, there were one or two things that gave Odin some cause for comfort.

The first of these was the absence of his brothers, Vili and Ve, from the morning. He was delighted that they had missed Fenrir's escape. They would have scoffed and gloated at his misery in a manner that would have made them even more unbearable. He wasn't sure where they were at this moment in time, but he had his suspicions.

They had spent yesterday very pleasantly together, inspecting Odin's army in Valhalla. This was the one thing guaranteed to gain their admiration although they wouldn't say as much. It was more their quietness and subtle jibes that gave away their jealousy. He knew they longed to have such a host at their disposal, but there was no way he would ever share it with them, no matter what their need.

Later that same evening his brothers had enjoyed the feasting. They had spent some time chatting to, or rather chatting up, the latest Valkyrie maid—fair Kat.

Both Vili and Ve were partial to blonds, which was why they always spent so much time with Frigg when they visited. He knew that she was part of the reason for their brotherly rivalry, and why they hadn't settled in Asgard.

Long before time itself had begun, they had all chased her as suitors. Odin had been the victor, gaining her hand in marriage. Vili and Ve made no pretence of their disappointment when they wed.

Even now, he suspected that given half a chance they would try their hands.

One thing he did take note of were their comments about fair Kat. Yes, they admired her beauty very much, but they urged him caution when speaking to her. She was far too intelligent for their liking, absorbing what they said like a sponge. To their minds, beauty was fine in a woman, but brains weren't. It was a chauvinistic view perhaps, but in a world like Asgard this advice needed to be heeded.

The last thing Odin could afford was trouble among his loyal Valkyries. He would keep a watchful eye on her, and a better guard upon his tongue.

Earlier this morning Vili and Ve had spent some time beneath the castle checking Mimir's Well. To his discomfort, they had also spent an hour alone in the citadel with the cask. He hated this, and it would no doubt take him a long time to find out what they might have gleaned and discussed in his absence. The citadel was where Odin was now, and he opened a window and held out his hand. Huginn, one of his two beloved ravens, was first to arrive. He landed gently, pecking at some food Odin held out for him.

Climbing onto his shoulder, Huginn nibbled tenderly at his ear.

The second cause for comfort was the activity he could see in the courtyard below, activity which was spreading throughout the town. He was impressed with the way Gunnr had taken charge, but very disappointed with his favourite Valkyrie—Prudr.

Since her failure in Midgard she had retired into herself, and become a shadow of the warrior he admired so greatly. The Valkyrie he knew and loved would never have permitted Gunnr to take control of such an important task.

It was because of this, that he had invited Prudr to his chambers half an hour or so ago. He had informed her of his decision to let her return to Midgard. Almost before the words had left his lips, her depression lifted. He cautioned her to be patient, trying to stop her zeal from clouding her judgement. When the time was right, he would allow her to return and get a second chance to capture Cole's soul.

He just hoped, for all their sakes, that this time she would be successful.

The day passed quickly for Silk and the ladies of Asgard. Six cattle were slaughtered and butchered, and a large cauldron of Chamomile and lavender was brewed under Carmel's careful instruction. Every seamstress in the town was utilised, and a steady stream of badly wrapped bundles were passed around, each time growing fewer in number but larger in size. Eventually, as dusk began to fade, a single large bundle lay in the back of the cart, along with the marinated remains of the six animals.

Preparations complete, Silk chose the final party who would venture forth.

To make it fair, and to maximise the boys' humiliation, she would be taking only two other warriors. Where the muscled might of Thor, Tyr, and Balder had failed; she was certain she, Carmel, and one other warrior would succeed.

Competition to be chosen was fierce, as she expected. With Carmel's place assured, the last member of the party was decided by an arm wrestling competition. It was close, but Zara just beat Jess in the final round. Silk did however make one concession for their party. She decided to take three strong slaves with them. They would be needed to haul Fenrir onto the cart; when they eventually captured him.

With high hopes for success, the three Valkyries set off in the direction of the plain. They could hear their quarry in the distance, the wolves howling loudly into the night. They were celebrating the return of Fenrir, and baying their defiance of Odin and the people of Asgard.

Silk's plan for the capture of Fenrir was simple but ingenious.

Taking a leaf from Carmel's victory over the giants, they had brewed a strong potion of chamomile and lavender, and then marinated the butchered meat in it. She knew the wolves would be hungry tonight. They would have eaten little yesterday, lying low after the thrashing they had received from Thor. With a slight breeze in the air tonight, they wouldn't even need to get too close for the pack to pick up the scent of their poisoned bait.

Hauling the meat from the cart, and laying it out in an open field, they withdrew to the shelter of a hillside copse and waited.

Spurred on by their hunger, the wolves descended upon their surprise feast almost before the party had reached the safety of the trees.

With Fenrir leading the way, they tore into the meat, ripping and gorging themselves on the tasty flesh. It was hard to say if they noticed the distinctive scent and flavour of the sleeping potion. Even if they did, any suspicions they might have had couldn't stop the instinctive greed to fill their hungry bellies. Satiated, and having eaten every last morsel of food; the pack settled down to rest.

Barely two hours after their arrival, Silk, Zara, and Carmel were able to pick their way safely through the unconscious beasts.

As they walked among the sleeping animals they speared each creature in turn. They took their time, making sure each wolf was killed. Finally, arriving at the centre of the pack, they found Fenrir.

Eyes tightly shut, he lay snoring like a baby.

With no more difficulty than if she was tying her boot laces, Silk bound Fenrir's legs tightly with the fabric the seamstresses of Asgard had worked so hard on all day.

This was a combination of fibres; silk, cotton and wool, all spun and woven together into a braided thread that was strong yet supple. When Fenrir would eventually wake, the harder he struggled against his bonds, the more firmly they would bind. The thread would give as he flexed his muscles against them, and then rebound firmly when he relaxed. Satisfied that his legs were at last secure, Silk bound his muzzle tightly as well. They would do well to avoid a repeat of Tyr's mishap.

With some difficulty, the warriors and slaves heaved Fenrir into the back of the cart. He didn't stir, so potent had been their sleeping draught. They travelled swiftly back to Asgard, and shortly after midnight Fenrir was placed gently on a pile of fresh straw in the centre of the hall of Gladsheim. Locking the doors behind them, and leaving the slaves on guard, the warriors returned tired, but jubilant, to the castle.

After a quick wash, Silk slipped into her bed and snuggled up next to Balder. She hugged him closely, smiling with satisfaction at the expression he would have on his face tomorrow.

Without a single drop of the girls' blood being shed, they had finished off the wolf pack and now had Fenrir securely under lock and key.

Lovingly, she stroked Balder's head and manly chest before she fell asleep.

Such silly boys, she thought as she drifted into sleep.

Never send a man to do a woman's work.

A terrible howling erupted from Gladsheim the following morning, and it was with some trepidation that the townsfolk peered through the windows at the unwelcome guest inside. Thrashing weakly this way and that, Fenrir appeared to be in a drunken stupor. He was furious at his bonds, but unable to work out quite what to do about them.

He remained this way, until Odin, and an excited host from the castle, unlocked the doors and entered the hall.

"Good morning," Odin beamed at the mass of black hair writhing in the hall. "How lovely to see you again."

With gleeful delight, Odin danced around Fenrir, occasionally drawing close and gazing deeply into his malevolent eyes. Fenrir fumed and foamed, wide rivulets of saliva drooled from the corners of his fettered mouth; but he could do nothing. Try as he might, the more he struggled the tighter his bindings became.

He was captive, and in his fiendish heart he knew that his life of freedom was over.

Magnanimous in their defeat, Thor, Balder, and Tyr congratulated the warriors on their success. Silk didn't say a word, the cheeky grin of satisfaction she had when Balder kissed her said it all.

She loved besting the gods, and today she had done that with style.

After some debate, it was decided to throw Fenrir into the cells of a fortress on the Island of Lyngvi. This lay a few leagues out in Middle Sea and to the south of Asgard. A large cart was summoned, and to jubilant cheers from the waiting crowd, Fenrir was bundled on board. His journey to the prison would take the rest of the day, and to ensure there were no further mishaps, Thor kindly volunteered to travel with the party.

There was even more good news that morning for Odin.

Just as he was bidding Thor farewell, Vili and Ve joined the gathering in the square. He could barely control his pleasure as he recounted the capture of Fenrir. They seemed pleased with his success, but, as always, they enjoyed sowing a little sourness.

"What will happen when Loki hears of this?" they whispered in his ear.

Odin barely heard them, and certainly paid no attention to their provocative question. Tonight would be a night for great celebrations, and he ordered everyone to wear their finest clothes for an evening of great merriment.

The feasting did indeed live up to Odin's expectations.

The finest foods and ale were prepared, and in Kvasir's absence, a troop of travelling musicians and actors gave a spirited re-enactment of the tale. The guests all howled with laughter when Tyr had his arm ripped off, and the actor playing the part of Fenrir bounded from the hall with a leg of ham between his teeth. Even Tyr smiled, but whether or not he really appreciated the joke he kept to himself. He was a noble warrior, and he wouldn't let his feelings spoil the night's entertainment.

Silk and the other Valkyries were resplendent in their finest gowns. No training had taken place all day, so they all had plenty of time to bath, groom and tie their hair up in all kinds of pleasing fashions. Silk spent much of the evening sitting on Balder's knees. They kissed and cuddled openly, which was unusual for Silk as she usually liked to keep an air of secrecy about their relationship. Perhaps a little too much mead had passed her lips, but Balder didn't complain. He relished her show of affection and gladly reciprocated her caresses.

It was not until much later in the festivities, when some had already left for bed, that the doors to the hall flew open and Loki marched angrily into the gathering.

A silence fell immediately, and the girls watched anxiously as his eyes darted their way slowly round the room. They flashed red, purple and green in a display of rage that sent shivers down Carmel's spine.

She had never seen him like this before, and she feared for their safety.

"Where's Fenrir?" Loki hissed quietly, but no one answered.

"Where is Fenrir?" he spoke more loudly and slowly, stepping forward menacingly.

Still no one spoke.

"WHERE'S FENRIR?" he snapped and with one bound grabbed the maid Lara, placing his sword at her throat.

"There's no need for violence Loki," Odin rose slowly and spoke softly from his table. "He's safe and hasn't been harmed. Come, lay your sword down and join us, for the night is still young."

He had half expected Loki to make an appearance, and had brought Gungnir as a precaution. He had the weapon now in his hand, and he knew that Loki wouldn't dare to challenge the power it could unleash. Just like Mjollnir in Thor's hands, Gungnir wielded a similar destructive force in his.

Loki slowly released Lara, and she returned gratefully to her seat.

"You have insulted me," Loki spat venomously at Odin. "You have made a grave error in capturing my beloved Fenrir, and you'll pay dearly for this, all of you."

He turned around slowly, waving his sword at the gathering.

Nobody spoke.

A silence as deathly as a graveyard had descended upon the hall.

For all his naughtiness, most of those present enjoyed Loki's company. They hated to see him so angry and upset. They knew that Fenrir was his favourite pet but they also understood that the wolf had to be behind bars. Perhaps Loki would one day realise this, too? For now, they prayed he wouldn't say or do anything too stupid.

Words he might utter that he would later regret.

Loki gazed once more at them in turn. He nodded as he met and held the stares of Silk, Prudr, Goll, and fair Carmel. Even her presence couldn't stem the terrible rage that burned inside him.

He would have his revenge, regardless of his love for her.

"You know the prophesy Odin."

Loki spoke once more, but this time more calmly. He had decided what he wanted to say, and none now could stop his fateful words.

"And you have chosen to ignore it. By your own hands you have forged your doom."

And with that he turned to the assembly and raised himself to his full height.

"RAGNAROK HAS BEGUN!"

The forbidden words tumbled from Loki's tongue, and Odin fell back shocked into his chair.

His face was ashen and his hands were trembling.

51

Afternoon Tea

If someone had told Cole that he would be spending the afternoon sipping tea in his penthouse suite with three federal agents, he would probably have laughed. Either that, or punched their lights out. As it happens, that was exactly what he was doing this very afternoon in the Viceroy Hotel in Miami.

Business had been good for Cole, and despite the death of Slim, he had decided to stay on longer in Miami. From the camouflage and safety of his five star accommodation, he had concluded several important drug deals, and networked with some influential Hispanic dealers. They seemed to control a supply of high quality cocaine coming from Colombia, and he was anxious to get his hands on their merchandise. He had also partied hard, enjoying the balmy climate down south. Mild weather usually persisted here throughout the long, miserable winter months. If his patch in New York wasn't so damn profitable, he might even have considered moving here permanently. Ostentatious displays of wealth suited his lifestyle, and the hotel had a magnificent spa where he could relax and sculpt his body.

"Do we understand each other?"

Agent Woods spoke slowly and deliberately between bites of a delicate cucumber sandwich. These really were extremely tasty, the type where the slices of cucumber were wafer thin and juicy, and the bread was pearly white and had had all the crusts carefully removed before serving. They were one of the few British exports he considered worthy of his patronage, along perhaps with an Aston Martin DB9. Something he knew he would never be able to afford.

Woods never drank alcohol while on duty, and this was the closest he, and the likes of Cole Farra, would ever get to socialising together. He hated offering scum like him an amnesty, but he was so sure that Ruby would make contact with him; and he had to get him on board. He knew he had promised Finch he wouldn't do this, but time was pressing, and he couldn't afford to miss this opportunity. Surveillance was one thing, but with Ruby likely to kill Cole and probably vice versa, he really had little choice.

He couldn't risk either of them dying prematurely.

"I need her alive, and with all her artifacts. You must call me as soon as you have her," Woods held Cole's gaze with his steely blue eyes.

"Cool," Cole grinned at him. "Slate wiped clean?"

"Slate wiped clean."

Woods emphasised this point by running his arm slowly across the coffee table, and pushing an imaginary file off the end.

"Sweet," Cole enjoyed his colourful metaphor.

"And my men?" He indicated to his body guards, standing either side of him. He rather hoped Woods would repeat the gesture, just one more time for his amusement.

"Once Ruby is in safe custody, and you have all the artifacts, everything is up for negotiation."

Woods folded his hands together, which rather disappointed Cole.

Cole sat back and considered his options.

To be honest, he couldn't care less about the amnesty. He didn't need it and he didn't want it. They had fuck all on him, and if they ever tried to drag him into court on some trumped up charges, he could skip the country in a heart beat. He had plenty of cash stashed away, and the contacts to make him disappear from view. Even, perhaps, from the extreme binocular vision of the FBI.

What was making him consider this offer were the reasons behind it.

Cole had learned of Slim's killing by his woman almost before the police did. He had been momentarily sorry. Ruby was a fine piece of ass, and he had been looking forward to enjoying her booty for quite a bit longer. He was, however, a realist.

A good lay was easy to find—loyalty wasn't.

Legs really had seemed too good to be true, and he had intended to reward her vicious betrayal in person. Slitting her throat when he returned to New York would have been appropriate. Unfortunately, the stupid bitch had gotten herself banged up that very night, putting an end to this notion.

What, however, had really got his attention, and was making him consider this offer, was the revelation by Woods that Ruby had escaped from FBI custody. And there was more. The Feds were interested in her, very interested indeed if they were prepared to make him a deal.

She must have something very important that they wanted; and that, of course, made him interested, too.

Cole was street wise—and no fool.

He didn't buy for one instant the story that she was some dangerous terrorist from a fanatical cult. They wouldn't be offering him a peach of an amnesty just for that. No; there was much more to this than Woods was letting on.

Take the artifacts for example.

Woods had gone into some detail about a dagger, a coin, a flask filled with juice and an oversized coat or cloak. Crazy stuff, but Cole was a business man. If the FBI were prepared to offer a high price for these items, he knew he could find someone who was willing to pay higher. Sure, he wouldn't kill Ruby, maybe cut her up a little, but he wasn't going to just hand her, or any artefacts, over to these fancy mother fuckers until he knew their true worth.

"So, what happens if we can't deliver?" Cole asked, his teeth flashing a brilliant white in the fading afternoon winter sun.

"Then you'll find I'm not a very nice man to mess with," Woods paused, and noticed that Cole hadn't reacted.

He needed to offer a sterner warning.

"Let me put it another way. You try to fuck me over and you'll find my foot so far up your arse you'll be using my toes for teeth!"

He leaned forward and stared coldly at Cole's eyes, invisible behind his sunglasses.

"Sweet," Cole continued to grin. He must remember that phrase, too. It was a good one.

"You have my numbers. Do we have a deal?" Woods stood up and offered Cole his hand.

"Sure," Cole got up too, but he didn't shake Woods hand.

As Woods indicated to his colleagues that it was time to go, he decided to re-iterate what he wanted one last time. He didn't trust Cole any further than he could chuck him, and that wasn't very far.

"Remember. She mustn't be harmed and we want all her possessions. Keep in touch," he made a mobile gesture pointedly with his hand.

"Sweet," Cole kept his smile firmly fixed until the door had closed behind the trio.

"Fuck these!" he scoffed as he sat down and imitated Wood's gesture; pushing the handsome platter off the end of the table.

"Now where's my Jack D?"

52

Behind Enemy Lines

The irony of the location for their captivity wasn't lost on Ben.

He was now more often awake than unconscious, and he could smile wryly at the solid but rusting doors that gave them shelter from the snow outside. A string of naked electric light bulbs, hanging like a pearl necklace along one wall, led gently downwards, and away from, the entrance to this particular Taliban stronghold. The walls of the passageway were blasted from solid rock and then roughly hewn; and its cracked and dusty floor had been cast in reinforced concrete.

With absolute certainty; Ben knew that their aging, remote, hostile prison had been paid for—lock, stock and barrel—by the American taxpayer.

The camaraderie that had once existed between the fighters and their hostages, uniting them against the elements, evaporated as they crossed the threshold to the caves. Ben and Jameela's wrists were tied once more, and they were roughly pushed and prodded by gun barrels as they walked down the twisting tunnel. All around them lay the nostalgic reminders of this stronghold's heritage, a legacy left over from the soviet invasion in nineteen seventy nine.

It was a fortress bought, and furnished, by the CIA.

In those days, the guerrillas' fathers had been welcomed as freedom fighters, the Mujahedeen. A resistance movement tasked to withstand the might of an invading Soviet empire. Who would have thought then, that less than thirty years later their sons and daughters would be treated so very differently?

Branded now as insurgents, terrorists, and murderous Al Qaeda fanatics.

Somewhere in the back of Ben's mind, the history of the caves gave him hope. He smiled encouragingly at Jameela. It was highly likely that the intelligence services had detailed plans of this labyrinth tucked away somewhere. Sticklers for detail, every penny spent on this project would have been painstakingly recorded by their fastidious operatives. If they could just unearth these details, a rescue mission might be launched for them.

Jameela shyly returned his smile, and Ben already knew that he fancied her. Her eyes were the biggest and darkest almonds he had ever seen, smouldering with a fiery beauty. Her face appeared sullen, with hamster-like cheeks. These gave her the look of a perpetual scowl but far from being unattractive, this heaviness enhanced the beauty of her pouting lips.

What really made his heart race, however, was when she smiled.

Her face then lit up with the radiance of a summer's day.

Ben felt an instinctive confidence in her, and realised, with a blush, that he could not have wanted for a more gorgeous cell mate. She was his guardian angel, and his inspiration to remain brave and courageous.

Eventually they were pushed down some steps and into a small cavern. This branched directly off the main tunnel. The room was well lit and warm, like the rest of the hidden complex. On the far wall was a large black flag with a central yellow circle and yellow Arabic text. This read: No deity but Allah and Muhammad is Allah's messenger. This was the flag of Al Qaeda, and before it stood a simple chair on a carpeted, wooden platform. They were forced to kneel before this, faces pressed roughly against the bare concrete floor. Ben tried to whisper to Jameela, but he was rewarded with a sharp kick from one of their captors.

After what seemed an age, but was probably no more than ten minutes, they heard footsteps, and watched as a pair of heavy duty, black leather boots make their way slowly round to stand in front of them.

"Allah hu akbar, la illaha illah-lah," the man chanted. "Allah is great; there is no God but Allah." He did this for several minutes, and then spoke to them in English. His voice bore a heavy Arabic accent.

"Get up you filthy infidel dogs."

Jameela and Ben rose slowly, their knees aching from their prolonged and unnatural posture. Before them stood a balding, fat, middle aged man with a long, unkempt and greying beard. They knew instinctively that he was going to be in charge of their captivity, and from his words that he was probably a sadistic bastard. Later they learned his name was Mohammed Aqbal, and that he was a local drug-dealing war lord. For now though, these details were irrelevant.

"Where are you from, English pig?"

The commandant stuffed a paan (folded leaf containing beetle leaves and tobacco) into his mouth, and chewed it greedily. He ground it loudly between his teeth.

Ben gave his name, rank and serial number, and the leader repeated his question. When Ben replied with the same answer once more, the man slapped him hard across the face. Ben staggered to the floor; a bead of blood dribbling from the corner of his mouth.

The commandant then turned his attention to Jameela.

"And what about you, you filthy American whore?" he grabbed her cheeks between his fingers and held them like a vice.

Jameela said nothing but held his stare, trying to control her rage. She had already decided to take his soul should an opportunity present itself.

"You're a feisty cur," he pushed her roughly away, and then addressed the pair of them.

"I hate you, you American arsehole and your English Poodle dog. I hope your countries never pay your ransoms. I want to hack off your heads and feed them to the crows."

He spat on the floor in front of them, and then beckoned for the guards to take them to their cells.

His point had been made.

After they had been taken to their cells, they were left alone for a while. To Ben's great relief, these lay side by side. They were able to see and touch each other through their iron bars. Gratefully he accepted Jameela's offer to wipe the blood from his mouth, and they held hands tightly.

"We'll be all right," he tried to reassure her, without sounding terribly convincing.

"I know we will."

Jameela pressed his hands between hers and kissed his knuckles tenderly.

This act was so kind and impromptu, Ben prayed he wouldn't burst into tears.

Christ! She was lovely.

He sniffed as he tried to pull himself together.

"All we've got to do now is find a way out of here," he proposed, and then chuckled at his impossible suggestion. They were buried hundreds of metres beneath a mountain of solid rock, and surrounded by guards. Even if they did escape, where exactly would they go in the freezing winter air?

They wouldn't last twenty four hours on the run.

Jameela smiled, as if she had read his thoughts. She liked her hero, and was glad that the guards were posted outside their prison cave and not inside.

Despite the harshness of the commandant's words, and his obvious hatred for his captives, they were treated a little more kindly by his minions. They both enjoyed a spicy meal of curried goat with rice, and even managed to share a naan bread between them. As they finished their meal, scrapping their tin plates clean, a visitor arrived in their cell. He introduced himself as Dr. Nyran Unadkat, and announced that he had come to perform their medical examinations. He spoke with an Oxford English accent, and chose to take Jameela with him to his examination room—ladies going first and all that.

With a heaviness inside her, Jameela followed him back down the twisting tunnel. To her surprise, when they arrived at his 'Surgery' it was both clean and modern. There was a well furnished medicine cabinet and an operating table in the room complete with a functioning anaesthetic trolley. Young and naive he might look, but he clearly was well trained and skilled. A surprise find in this wilderness of poorly educated and impoverished people.

"I understand you take medicine every day for epilepsy. What is its name?" he asked, writing as he spoke.

"Phenytoin," she replied politely. This was well rehearsed, a standard cover for the contents of the Valkyrie flasks.

"Any other ailments?"

"No, nothing, Dr. Unadkat."

"Please call me Dr. Nyran, everybody else does around here," he looked up, and smiled briefly. "I need to examine you now, your wrist please." He motioned for her to extend her forearm.

"I'm sure that won't be necessary, I'm really quite fit and healthy."

Jameela tried to encourage him not to examine her, but she felt a tenseness in the pit of her stomach. This was not what she needed tonight.

"I'm afraid I really must insist. I have to document your exact state of health. When you are released, this will prove that any problems you have were not inflicted by my friends." He nodded toward the door to emphasis the point. A burly guard with a Kalashnikov was posted outside.

"Oh dear, you really aren't going to like this," Jameela pushed her arm forward, and watched with some amusement as the doctor struggled to find her pulse.

Laughing awkwardly at his failure, he motioned to her to let him try her other arm—still no success. He pressed his fingers to her carotid artery, and when this failed he placed his stethoscope upon her chest and repositioned it six or seven times, both left and right sides.

He couldn't hear a thing.

Maybe the diaphragm to his stethoscope was broken or his ears were full of wax?

Dr. Nyran was perplexed.

"I really am most awfully sorry Ms. Masood, but I don't seem to be able to hear your heartbeat. I'm afraid you must be dead." He slumped back into his chair, laughing at his witty but preposterous conclusion.

Jameela joined in.

That was absurd.

"Don't worry doctor; you're not the first to have this difficulty. I have low blood pressure; it runs in my family. I can reassure you that I am well and truly alive." And with that they laughed once more.

It was strange how often Valkyries passed medical examinations. Doctors simply couldn't believe their findings. You couldn't be alive without a pulse, and therefore they either had to have made a mistake or their equipment was faulty.

"Jai Swami Narayan."

Jameela leaned forward unexpectedly, catching Dr. Nyran off guard as she whispered an excited, religious, Hindu greeting. She made a prayer shape with her hands as she did so. She had spotted his double necklace of tulasi wood, and she felt an overwhelming urge to share the common bond of their guru.

"Jai Swami Narayan," he replied gently, a warm smile of recognition spreading swiftly across his face. This was an extraordinary coincidence.

For a brief moment Jameela felt ashamed.

She had drunk alcohol and eaten meat, garlic, and onions for the last fifty years or so since her death; breaching the strict code of the guru she had worshipped and adored in her previous and forgotten life. The sight of his necklace had suddenly brought those memories alive and starkly into focus. Her disrespect hadn't been her fault, she rationalised. It was a necessity of living in Asgard amongst pagan meat lovers and adulterors, people who offered her no other choice.

Jameela and Dr. Nyran chatted eagerly for several minutes, united in a shared devotion. They spoke quickly in Hindi, and in hushed whispers. What on earth was he doing there, a Hindu, alone amongst so many fervent Muslim extremists?

Dr. Nyran didn't have time to answer; the guard was already knocking on the door. As she made to go, Jameela thanked Odin for giving her a friend and ally among so many enemies.

"Just remember, Doctor," she patted her chest knowingly and pressed her finger against her lips.

"This is our little secret."

53
Balder's Dream

Balder awoke with a start. His heart was pounding, and he was bathed in a pool of sweat. It was one of those awful moments when you pinch yourself in a desperate hurry to prove that you are still alive, and that your nightmare is really over.

Sliding carefully out of bed, he walked over to the French windows and threw these wide open. Gratefully, he gulped down the cool air that greeted him, sighing deeply. Beads of sweat glistened like tiny pearls on his naked chest, the full moon casting his long shadow across the interior of the room.

Silk had heard him get up.

She was already awake, woken earlier by his tossing and turning. Quietly, she slipped out of bed and joined him at the window. Pressing her naked body against his back, she wrapped her arms tightly around his waist.

"Are you all right?"

Pulling him close, she felt the cold, sweaty, clamminess of his body.

"Uh huh."

"Was it the dream again?"

"Uh huh." Balder didn't want to say more, he hated being so vulnerable.

"Shush." Silk nibbled at his earlobe, and massaged his strong shoulders with her powerful hands. She knew he was embarrassed by his dream, but she was worried for him.

Several days had passed since Fenrir had been bound and imprisoned, and Balder's nightmare had started soon afterwards. It was always the same; a poorly remembered terror, a dream that left him breathless, sweating, and filled with great dread.

It always started with a shadowy figure, or possibly two, a presence or presences that he could feel rather than see. Then came a terrible pain in his chest, a stabbing, burning sensation, rather like being hit by a bolt of lightning. The pain was so fierce, so intense that it took his breath away, hijacking all his senses.

The worst part of the dream was what happened next.

He felt a coldness that spread slowly from the inside out. A slow, creeping frost that travelled down his arms and legs, paralysing him as it spread. He would try to shout, but his lungs were empty, and no sound came from his mouth. Finally, as his fingers and toes turned to icicles, he would start to fall; slowly at first and then gathering pace. Faster and faster, a stomach churning ride, spinning toward oblivion—or the point where he would mercifully wake up.

Gasping for air, and drenched in a cold sweat.

The dream was getting worse, becoming stronger and more vivid with each retelling. It recurred now every time he fell asleep. The shadows in the dream were becoming darker, and the sense of pain and coldness growing stronger. The shadowy figures remained vague, but their evil intent was coming ever closer.

Even to Silk, Balder's dream was obvious.

He was visualising death, and most probably his own. Herein however, lay a paradox. She knew he had been enchanted since a baby, invulnerable to death from any object native to Asgard. Of all the gods he was the only one who couldn't be killed, *so why was he dreaming of death?*

There was no doubt his dream heralded impending doom—but for whom?

Gently, as he calmed in the cool, fresh air of a summer's night, she coaxed him back to her bed. She made love to him, tenderly and with passion; her body on top as she preferred. Pinning his arms above his head, she ground her body against his, clasping his thighs strongly between her legs. She bore down hard upon his groin, thrusting her hips forcefully against his in violent spasms, challenging his body to match her lustful rhythm. Eagerly she took his manhood and buried his strength deep inside her. His proud member thrilled her as she fought to control its might; taming his manly power and forcing its vigour to do her will. She yearned to take his explosive warmth, but only when she bid.

These were the terms by which Silk made love, and they were non-negotiable.

Captivated by the beauty of the body which rose and fell above him, Balder let his horror take flight. He allowed his terror to lose itself in the ecstasy of their love making. Following her lead, they shared their moment of climax together, each bursting in an explosion of brilliant colours.

Exhausted at last, Balder laid his head against her chest. He allowed the soothing caress of her hand to finally send him forth into a fitful sleep.

As Balder's breathing became easier, and his body told her that he was asleep, Silk came to a decision. She would talk to Freyja in the morning, and if that didn't help, she might consider giving him some chamomile and lavender potion. The worsening distress of his nightmare hurt her deeply, and she felt his pain. She wouldn't admit her love for him to anyone, but inside, his torment was breaking her heart.

She prayed to Odin it would end soon.

After Loki had uttered those fateful words and stormed out of the hall, it felt as though Ragnarok might come that very night. Odin left almost immediately, and as soon as he had gone, the others melted away to their beds. Few slept, as all were fearful that they may not live to see the sun rise again.

Taking some by surprise; dawn did break the following morning—and they all awoke to see its majesty.

With the name of the final battle now spoken, a strange peace descended upon the people of Asgard. Freed from fear, they were able at last to openly discuss the prophesies that surrounded it. Fierce debates raged up and down the land, as gods, Valkyries, and common folk discussed what was known, and more importantly, what wasn't. The whole prophesy was laid open, and found to be awash with vagueries and subtle ambiguity.

Some parts were authoritative and not in dispute.

There would be a battle, and the world would end. Most would die. These words were clear and precise. It was known that Thor and the wolf Fenrir would be killed, but some, like Loki, were destined to survive.

The date and time of the battle were less clear.

It was not known if it would be days, weeks, months, or even tens of years from the uttering of Ragnarok to when the battle would take place. Similarly, although the world would end, exactly which world was the prophesy referring to?

Did it mean just the realm of Asgard, or could it be all the realms of their world, or even the world of Midgard?

The prophesy didn't say.

In a similar way the prophesy spoke of a battle, but it didn't name the combatants, nor its outcome. The Aesir usually took it to mean a battle between them and the giants, but it could just as easily be with the evil dead of Niflheim, or even the realm of Midgard. Some thought it could be a battle between the elements. Fire and lava verses the snow and ice of Jotunheim, just as it had been at the dawn of time.

Unfortunately, one fact about the prophesy was only too clear. Mimir, the only person who knew it in its entirety, was too incapacitated to tell them his knowledge.

Mimir had learned what he knew from the well that stood beneath the castle. Odin had tried to read the well too, but he had paid a terrible price to acquire what little snippets of knowledge he had gleaned.

The well held the key to unlocking the mysteries of Ragnarok, and because it lay safely in their land, the people of Asgard were content. Its awesome power, and vast store of knowledge, gave them the advantage should any war come to pass.

Carmel joined in these debates, but divided her time between the castle and consoling Loki. He had chosen to sleep rough when he left. Preferring to pass the nights outside, he lay under the warm summer skies rather than in the castle with his enemies.

At first he took the imprisonment of his wolf very badly, blaming the warriors for his fate. He shouted to her to go away, and even threw stones at her, too. But Carmel, true to her Latin temperament, wasn't one to give up easily.

Subtly she gained his confidence and soothed his rage. "Stroking my ego and plumping my pillows," he would begrudgingly put it when they spoke.

Little by little, she overcame the impossible, and Loki returned once more to the feasting tables. He also returned to her bed, which was of far more importance to Carmel. For this, she rewarded him with many favours.

Kat too entered into the debates, eager to learn all she could about Asgard and its people. Mimir and his well intrigued her, making her more determined than ever to become a warrior as soon as possible. Only they, and the most senior of the gods, were allowed access to the chamber beneath the castle.

She knew that in that place lay the answers to her many questions.

Tonight, Kat stood alone on her balcony, gazing out at the moonlit town and surrounding fields. Without the sound of Fenrir and his wolves, the world seemed a calmer and more peaceful place. It seemed impossible that sometime soon it would all be torn apart by an apocalypse. As she stood, she waited for the sound she knew would come. The rumbling that told her a warrior had left the chamber and started their journey. She knew that tonight Ruby was going back to Midgard to complete her mission. This was why Jess wasn't standing beside her now, embracing her with her strong arms.

The vibration finally passed; a gentle rumble that lasted less than thirty seconds. It rose slowly to a crescendo, then fell again more rapidly. Somehow she knew that this noise was linked to Mimir's Well. It had to be.

As she turned to go to bed, she paused, and took one last look out of the window.

She wondered how Hod was, and if he was enjoying the adventure he had yearned for.

Far beyond Kat's view, and in the heart of the plain of Ida, a lonely chestnut mare plodded slowly toward Asgard. Her footsteps were measured and methodical, rhythmically counting down the miles until she arrived safely home.

The mare had travelled all the way from the caverns under Jotunheim, the hidden realm of the dwarves. She had crossed the treacherous ice of the Bifrost Bridge on her own, passing untroubled by the guards of the watchtower. A horse without a rider was harmless and of little consequence to them.

Her progress was slow, because she was heavily laden. A bundle of rags hung down from her back, and lay on either side of her flanks. The rags stank of filth and looked infested with maggots and disease.

If the guards had risked the stench and bothered to look more closely, they would have seen that the rags concealed a body, a figure trussed up tightly with arms tied behind their back and legs bound all the way to the hips.

The body hung there motionless, but it was still breathing; just.

54

Problems with Propaganda

"Thank you for your cooperation and understanding."

Agent Woods put the phone down with a huge grin. Today was a lovely day, one to be savoured to its full. "Valkyries were just like buses," he chuckled to himself. "You waited ages for one, and then all of a sudden, two would come along together."

He was referring of course to foreign events that had unfolded over the last two or three days. From these, by his clever use of intelligence filtering, he had gleaned some very valuable information.

The main role of the Valkyrie cult was to stalk battlefields in search of heroes, and the current areas of conflict in the world were Iraq and Afghanistan. Woods always studied reports coming from these locations very carefully, looking for signs of unusual activity. It had therefore been easy to spot the details of an alleged American citizen who had been caught up in the conflict in Musa Qala.

The person was a woman, and she was now missing following a British helicopter crash. Her name was Jameela Masood, and her passport claimed that she came from the town of Detroit. Woods had instantly recognized the name Jameela, being one of the six or so Valkyrie aliases he held on his database. Her parents were unsurprisingly dead, and she didn't live at the address in Detroit when he checked it out.

He was fairly confident that she was a cult member, and the circumstances around her rescue cemented this belief.

He had had an interesting conversation with Lieutenant Ashwood, the officer in charge of the British platoon that wrested control of the town from the Taliban. The Lieutenant had spoken about the injured British soldier, and the bloodbath in the building where they found him, lying wounded in the arms of Ms. Masood. He had spoken at length about the blood curdling cries emanating from the building, and the mutilated bodies they'd found there. The only missing feature from his story was the absence of a stab wound to the chest in any of the dead fighters. Unfortunately, due to the severity of their other injuries, the soldiers hadn't bothered checking for these and other subtle wounds.

It didn't really matter; Woods knew he had found a Valkyrie.

Having a fairly senior position in the ranks of the FBI, and with clandestine connections that went much higher still, Woods had access to some fairly hefty privileges. One of these was the power to order a news blackout of the incident.

Even though there were three British service men missing with Ms. Masood, all presumed captured, he was able to gag the media. This had been done in the interests of national security, or so he had claimed. Woods led the press to believe that Ms. Masood was an undercover operative, working deep in the heart of the Taliban command structure. She just might hold the key to the whereabouts of Osama Bin Laden, a name that always got their attention. To blow her cover would mean certain death and an end to this promising lead.

Woods had bought their silence on the understanding that he knew where they were being held, and a covert rescue operation was imminent. The Western press had given him a week to deliver the goods, before they blew the story wide open. It was just too juicy for them to resist. British war heroes captured with a beautiful, American girl—their "damsel in distress." That headline alone was worth millions to them.

The trouble now for Woods was making good on his promise; finding and freeing the captives.

Using connections in the CIA and other intelligence services, Woods had drawn up a large scale map of the area; everything within a fifty kilometre radius of the crash site. He reasoned that with the terrible winter weather, the Taliban would be holding their hostages nearby. Spy satellites, which he had been pinning his hopes on, had sadly been useless. Dense clouds had covered the area shortly after the helicopter crash, causing the heavy snow storms that had engulfed Jameela and Ben. Lacking this crucial intelligence, he had to follow a different approach, one that required as much luck as it did judgement.

He used his contacts to gather details of all the known Taliban strongholds in the area, particularly those that were underground. Woods knew that the U.S. had helped in the construction of a network of safe havens for the Mujahedeen during the war with the Russians. He felt strangely confident that one of these was where the hostages would be taken.

Using his best judgement and hoping that they kept to pony trails, Woods followed a ten kilometre sweep into the mountains and valleys nearest the point of the crash. His luck held. There were two documented underground networks buried in his chosen, precipitous valleys.

Throwing caution to the wind and with agreement from his contacts at the very top of the FBI, he had been given authority to order a rescue operation using Apache helicopters and a detail of U.S. Rangers. These were the toughest fighting infantry in the American army. They were now making final preparations for their assaults, and Woods prayed that the poor weather would continue. He knew that as soon as it lifted, the Taliban would move their hostages further afield.

He desperately wanted to catch them now, before they had a chance to bury their captives deeper in their labyrinthine networks.

If he was very lucky, and the captives were rescued intact, Woods would be the hero of the hour. If he wasn't, and the soldiers found nothing but mountain goats on their multi-million dollar rescue flop, it would be his head, and his alone, that would end up on the sacrificial chopping block.

This was a sobering thought.

Ben surprised Jameela by passing his medical examination by Dr. Nyran. Helped by her mead, he was healing rapidly. The deadly piece of shrapnel that had blasted through his body armour had been forcibly removed long ago. Ripped violently from his body when his flak jacket was stolen, a useful trophy seized by the fighters who had found them at the downed helicopter. Luckily the mead, and his youth, had saved him from bleeding to death.

Pulling their rough straw beds together, they had slept side by side during the chilly night; their bodies huddled as close as the iron bars that separated their cells permitted. Two bowls of cold rice arrived in the morning, leftovers from the meal last night. These, and a glass of apple tea, were their breakfast.

To her dismay, Ben had been taken from his cell by the guards soon after their meagre meal, and it was his footsteps that she was now retracing.

The structure to their prison complex was easy to learn.

A single, long winding central tunnel led down from the iron entrance door. This gave rise to shorter tunnels, each being a cul de sac that ended in a cave. Dr. Nyran's surgery was out of their prison cell, turn left and two passageways down on the right. The headquarters of their captors' commander was two passageways up in the opposite direction.

Unfortunately they were now taking her somewhere different, and she felt uneasy.

Arriving at another heavy iron door, they entered a spacious cavern lit by a single central light bulb. At one end was a wooden table with two chairs; and at the other was Ben.

Jameela gasped in horror when she realised it was him.

Dangling naked from chains looped through a ceiling ring, he was half conscious and moaning. She could tell, even in the dim light, that he was being tortured, and assumed that that would be her fate, too.

The two guards chained her up in a similar style, but left her clothed. Then, to her surprise, they left her dangling and returned to Ben. They set to work on his body with obvious relish; beating him methodically with heavy wooden sticks. They struck him randomly from his chest right down to his knees, and then back up again.

The guards hit him with all their might, the sticks cleverly weighted to cause maximum pain, but with minimal risk of rupturing internal organs. Ben took his beating well, shouting and groaning through clenched teeth as little as was humanly possible.

Eventually the pain and shock of their blows overwhelmed him, and he slumped into unconsciousness. The guards stopped when they saw this happen, and sent for Dr. Nyran. To her horror, he came and checked Ben's pupils, pulse, and blood pressure, before indicating to his torturers that it was all right for them to continue.

As he left, Jameela made dagger eyes at him, and he looked away in embarrassment.

He had lied to her yesterday.

The medical was not to document injuries, merely to ascertain how much torture they could withstand. She spat on the floor as he passed, making sure he knew what she thought of him.

How could he, a Hindu and follower of her own guru, assist these monsters in their brutality?

The guards waited a while before throwing a bucket of cold water over Ben. He yelled, and then went limp again. The shock hadn't roused him, which was exactly what his tormentors had hoped for. Gleefully they attached electrodes, and watched as his body danced in agony to their vicious, electronic tune. Jameela screamed at them to stop, she couldn't help herself. He had suffered so much already, and she prayed that they would start on her now. At least that would give him some respite.

They stopped, but didn't start on her. The door to the cavern had swung open and their commander stepped through with two further guards. He spoke to them briefly in Arabic before turning to Jameela.

"So much unnecessary pain for your stupid, pig-dog boyfriend no?" He gloated as he sneered at her.

She didn't reply.

"All I want is for him to talk on a little tiny video and what does he say—name, rank and number. It's so stupid, no? All this beating for nothing."

He indicated for the guards to untie Jameela and bring her over to the desk. She saw his hand go to his trousers, and with a woman's intuition, she guessed what was about to happen.

Coldly, she analysed their situation and the probability of escape.

With a bit of luck, she could take the four guards and Mohammed. What she couldn't rely on though was Ben not getting killed in the crossfire. Even if they both survived, they would still have to exit the tunnel system. Being buried so deep inside the caves, and lacking a proper plan, she didn't fancy their chances of escape. She could probably do it on her own, but he was too weak from his hours of torture to be able to help her.

With reluctance, she decided to accept her fate, and wait for a better opportunity.

"So now my friend," Mohammed turned to Ben. "I will have to fuck your American, bitch-whore girlfriend. That's good, yes?"

He indicated to the two guards to strip her leggings, and then spread her over the table, face down. Jameela didn't resist, and raising her head, she tried to smile weakly at Ben. She wanted to let him know that she was all right.

"YOU FUCKING BASTARD LEAVE HER ALONE!"

Ben screamed—exactly the reaction Mohammed had wanted.

"I'll talk all right; I promise I'll talk—just leave her alone!"

Ben was begging now and Mohammed was revelling in it.

"Oh you'll talk all right, but first I fuck her good like this."

Spreading Jameela's legs wide apart, he flipped up her top and then penetrated her from behind. He pounded her arse hard, right from the start. Jameela didn't utter a sound. She lay there passively, depriving him of any show of distress.

He wasn't going to get any satisfaction from her rape; she would make sure of that.

"See! Your American slut-whore, she like my big cock, look," he waved at his men to silence Ben who was still shouting obscenities at him. They hit him again and again with their sticks but he wouldn't stop.

Jameela blessed him for his courage.

He was indeed a hero.

"I fuck her good and tomorrow I fuck you too hey, English pussy boy? You like that? I fuck you good like her."

He was loving his moment of power, hurling insults as he climaxed abruptly inside her.

Finished at last, and with a satisfied grunt, he came round and stuck a gun to Jameela's temple. He wanted her to clean his phallus with her mouth. She resisted, keeping it shut; knowing that he couldn't kill her. He knew this too, so he did the next best thing to humiliate her further.

Ordering his guards to hold her head up, he urinated on her face, and then pulled his zipper up. The guards grinned hopefully at him, but their dreams of a gang bang were quickly quashed.

For now, Mohammed was keeping Jameela to himself.

Show over for the day, the guards returned the two of them to their cells.

One good thing came out of this, and Jameela smiled as she clung on to this thought.

She had at least been given some clean clothes to wear.

For many hours after their return to the cells, Ben lay on his bed semi-conscious. Finally, Jameela saw his shoulders heave and heard him sobbing. She pushed her arms through the bars to comfort him, but he pulled away.

"Are you badly hurt?"

Jameela hated to hear him cry.

"No," he rasped through clenched teeth. He couldn't face her, he felt too ashamed to let her see his unmanly tears.

"I'm so sorry I couldn't stop him. I can't forgive myself for what they did to you. It's my fault; I'm so sorry—so very, very sorry."

Jameela stretched her arm through the bars as far as she could, and stroked the back of his head. "Don't worry, it isn't your fault. Besides, he didn't hurt me," she smiled with satisfaction.

"He was tiny!"

With this silly thought in their heads, they both laughed and hugged each other. Ben winced, his ribs hurt like stink, throbbing as they embraced.

"Don't worry. Here, have some of this."

Jameela pulled her flask of mead from her mattress. She had hidden this and her purse there as a precaution. Together they sipped at the bottle, and clasped each other's hands.

"We have to get away," Jameela looked him squarely in his eyes. "You won't be able to take much more of this."

Ben nodded. "We must make a plan."

Ben was right.

Jameela had more than one reason for urgency in their escape.

She was running low on mead, and her Valkyrie knife was missing. She would have to return to Asgard soon, and she wasn't going to leave him alone in this stinking hell hole.

Even if it meant her own death, she wouldn't abandon Ben now.

55

Flight of the Valkyries

"AARGH!"

Kat, like the rest of the inhabitants at the castle, was woken shortly after dawn.

She awoke to the sound of a woman screaming, and the gong being frantically beaten. Leaping out of bed, she rushed downstairs and out into the courtyard.

At first, the scene that greeted her didn't seem all that unusual.

A chestnut mare was standing peacefully, snorting and twitching her ears irritably at the noise of the woman causing the commotion. The wailing was beginning to distress her. That same woman was now kneeling beside a pile of dirty linen. This had slipped off the horse's back, and was lying on the cobblestones. She was crying and screaming hysterically, desperately trying to pick through the jumble of filthy rags in front of her.

More and more people were beginning to crowd into the courtyard.

Taking the initiative, Kat moved closer and bent down beside the woman. The pile of rags moved, and to Kat's horror she could make out the shape of a body. Following its contours she arrived at what she thought was the head. This was heavily bandaged down to the nose, and the lips that were just visible were parched and cracked from days without food or water. Rivulets of dried blood ran from the bandaged eyes and congealed on the stubbled cheeks.

These cheeks were unmistakably those of a man.

Kat suddenly felt sick.

An overwhelming wave of nausea told her that she had to vomit. Doubled up and urging, she struggled over to the side of the courtyard and threw up.

She knew the man.

It was Hod.

Horns were blowing now, and the whole castle had sprung into life. She could see Jess kneeling beside Hod, pressing mead to his lips. Servants were hastily bringing a stretcher through the crowd and Balder was frantically giving orders, not that anyone seemed to be listening. Trying to take control of her senses, Kat staggered back to the throng, and fought her way back to Jess's side.

"Please, take him to my room," Kat gasped in her ear, and then staggered off to be sick once more. This was the first time she could ever remember throwing up at the sight of trauma, but it was also the first time she had ever seen a friend so hideously injured.

Fifteen minutes later, Hod was lying on her bed.

Jess, Silk and Mika were beside him, gently coaxing mead between his ulcerated lips. He was slowly coming round, and from his hand gestures he was desperate to talk.

The room was almost full.

Odin and Thor were already there, as was Freyja and Balder. Frigg arrived in a panic, her hair tied back in a plait. She was wearing jodhpurs and had obviously been riding in Valhalla when the news had reached her. Kat could see tears welling in her eyes, and the gathering parted sympathetically to let her through. Jess moved, and she sat down upon the bed beside Hod, cradling his head in her lap.

Slowly at first, and with a husky voice laden with emotion, Hod began to tell his tale of their trip to Nidavellir—the realm of the dwarves.

It had taken the party two days to reach the entrance to the mountain caves where the dwarves lived. Fjalar and Galar had been good hosts on the journey, almost generous in their hospitality. They had arrived late in the afternoon, and it took them at least another hour to travel deep inside the mountain to the hall where the feast was to be held. The journey through the mountain passageways had been slow and difficult. The tunnels twisted this way and that, with frequent flights of steps going both upwards and downwards. The passages were rough hewn, fashioned by generations of dwarves in a random, meandering manner. Some were wide and well lit, while others were desperately gloomy and narrow such that they were hard to squeeze through. Countless openings revealed caverns and tunnels branching off in all directions.

Without an experienced guide, it would be impossible to find your way around the tortuous maze.

Eventually the party arrived in a large, well lit hall. This was richly decorated and littered with long wooden tables and benches. Here was where the celebrations for their king were due to take place. The two dwarves set up Kvasir's harp, but before they let him play they encouraged their guests to sit and eat. They had prepared a feast in their honour.

The food and ale were excellent and they all dined heartily. The dwarves plied them with drinks as they ate. It was not until Hod was almost full that he felt a terrible tiredness, and a desperate need to sleep. The urge was overwhelming, and he could see that Kvasir and Emile were feeling the same. Realising too late that they had been drugged, they sank into unconsciousness where they sat.

Hod had no idea how long he was out for; only that when he awoke he was in a much smaller room—and tied to a chair. Emile was lying before him, tied to a bed and still deeply asleep.

Kvasir was nowhere in sight.

At this point in his story Hod's voice broke and he sobbed uncontrollably. It was going to be desperately difficult for him to recount the next part of his story, and it took all the kindness and gentleness of Frigg to coax the words from his lips. He had to finish his tale.

Hesitantly, between breathless, gulped sobs, he continued.

The two dwarves told him that Kvasir would be staying with them, and that they would mix his blood into a honeyed potion to gain the soothing power of his voice. They said that he would be sent home as a warning to Odin and his Valkyries, not to try and rescue Kvasir.

Then, in a hideous act of spite, the evil dwarves did the unimaginable.

While she still slept, they hacked Emile's head off, and then put out Hod's eyes.

Emile's headless corpse was the last sight he would ever see.

Kat's bedroom fell deathly silent when these odious words finally came from Hod's tortured lips. Not only had the cowards murdered Emile, they had denied her the right of a Valkyrie to enter Valhalla. Decapitation was one of the few ways a Valkyrie could be permanently slain.

The castle began to shake violently, and for a few minutes it looked as though the world might come to an end. Odin was locked in a desperate battle to control his rage, the like of which he hadn't experienced before. He clung desperately to Balder, fighting to regain his composure. After what seemed an age, the ground began to shake less strongly, and he nodded, letting them know that he had command of his emotions once more.

"We have to go there, now."

It was Freyja's voice that finally broke the terrible silence.

"We have to rescue Kvasir, if he's still alive. We must bring back the body of Hlokk, and kill every last dirty, stinking, rotten, little dwarf we can find."

There was a mighty roar when she spoke of revenge, and Thor's hammer was already above his head, swinging malevolently.

"WAIT!" Odin shouted anxiously. The sound of his raised voice shocking the gathering back into silence.

"Did you not hear Hod's words? We cannot raise an army and crush them; they have a weapon in Kvasir's blood; his voice, those silken poems and songs. If they turn his words against us we may not be able to fight at all."

"Is that possible?" Silk enquired uncomfortably.

"I don't know," Odin shook his head. "But we can't afford the risk of finding out."

"Won't they be affected by their own voices, too?" Mika spoke now.

"No," Hod replied. "They're immune to his charm and eloquence. That was why they came here; to see if Kvasir's voice would affected them. Apparently it didn't."

The room fell silent, mulling over their strange predicament. They had to retrieve the bodies. Not to avenge their deaths was unthinkable. There had to be a way to do this.

"Wax."

This time it was Kat who broke the silence and she spoke in a quiet voice.

"What?" Silk enquired.

"We can use wax. If we fashion ear plugs from wax, and shout battle cries as we fight, we won't hear their voices."

After a moments silence, a loud ripple of approval reverberated around the room. Thor clapped his arm around her and praised her warmly.

"We need to go now, and quickly. Catch them by surprise."

It was Silk once more, putting a plan together swiftly in her head. This was a great skill of hers, one admired even by Odin.

"A small group, just four of us, the passageways are too narrow to make a larger force effective."

There was a general chorus of agreement. Everybody wanted to join the war party, but they could see the logic behind her reasoning.

"We will travel fast, Valkyrie style," Silk looked knowingly around the room and the warriors and Freyja nodded. Kat didn't understand quite what she meant, but she was determined to be part of the posse.

She had to avenge Hod's torment.

"Please, may I come?" Kat enquired hesitantly, her voice timid yet resolute.

"No. I'm sorry. You're not a warrior and you'll not be able to travel as we intend to."

Freyja spoke, drawing attention to a difference between a maid and a warrior.

"She could go," this was Frigg, and in a vanishingly rare moment she spoke directly to Freyja, her rival for Odin's love.

"If she wears your necklace."

An audible gasp went round the room.

The necklace she was referring to was *The Necklace of the Brisings*—Freyja's most valuable and powerful treasure. Rumours abounded as to how she acquired this fabulous possession, and other than around her neck, it never left the Chamber of the Valkyries.

"Please?"

Frigg pleaded with Freyja.

"I can feel her strength. She can control the blood lust and I know she won't let you down. Please, for Hod's sake; for a mother's sake; please let her go."

Freyja looked slowly around the room, and then to her surprise she found herself nodding yes. She knew she wouldn't lend her necklace for Hod or for Frigg either. However, she couldn't refuse the desperate plea of a mother.

"Right," Silk barked her orders. "Brynhildr, Skogul, and fair Kat—swords, knives and axes. Goll please bring you cloak. My room, let's go—now."

Within moments Kat's room had emptied, and trembling excitedly she put on her leather tunic and tucked Talwaar into its scabbard. Her sword gleamed expectantly in the light, and she kissed the blade affectionately. Turning to Frigg, who had remained on her bed beside Hod, she thanked her.

"My dear Kat, you will make me proud. Go now, and avenge our little Hod."

Frigg clasped her hands and kissed her on both cheeks. Kat reciprocated, before hugging and kissing Hod on his cheek.

"Be here when I return," she whispered tearfully as she left.

Kat joined Silk, Jess, Zara, and Freyja in Silk's room. Feeling a little shaky, she nervously wrapped the cloak of swans' feathers around her shoulders. She looked around the group, hoping to find answers in their faces. Finding none, she plucked up the courage and spoke.

"What exactly did you mean when you said we would be travelling Valkyrie style?"

To her surprise and relief, the warriors, and even Freyja herself, smiled and laughed warmly.

"My dear Kat," Jess replied. "We're going to fly of course. What do you think these cloaks are for?"

Kat's jaw hit the ground.

She had to be joking?

Freyja walked toward her and opened a gold cask in which lay the most beautiful necklace Kat had ever seen. It was fashioned from nine strands of heavy gold chains, each festooned with delicate leaves and effigies of animals. In the centre of the chains was a large, flawless white diamond. This was the size of a ripe plum.

Carefully Freyja placed it around her neck. It felt heavy, and looked indescribably beautiful.

"You must guard this with your life," she implored solemnly. "The pain and humiliation I endured to get this is beyond imagination."

Kat nodded, and then the four girls, wrapped in their cloaks, held hands and formed a circle. Silk instructed her to repeat the strange words of the chant that she and the other warriors uttered. Kat did so, still incredulous at Jess's words.

At the end of the incantation, nothing seemed to have happened.

Kat was about to say something when a peculiar warmth spread rapidly from the diamond in the necklace.

Then came a blinding flash of light.

Blinking at its brightness, Kat realised everything had changed.

She was shorter, much shorter, and the room positively reeked of perfume and body odours—each of which she could easily identify. Her eyesight was incredible, but to her amazement instead of seeing Jess, Silk, and Zara; she saw three white swans.

The warriors had obviously changed into them.

Wow! How strange was that?
She marvelled at this absurdity.

Kat spoke, but all that came from her throat was a terrible honking sound. She waved her hands in surprise and nearly toppled over. A tremendous pressure had forced her body backward. Stumbling drunkenly, her legs felt weird and stumpy. It seemed as though she was trying to walk on her knees and she could barely keep her balance.

"Sweet Odin!" She cried loudly, with the realization that she too was now a swan.

Her ears heard a honking noise from the other birds, but in her head she could heard the sound of laughter, and then Jess's voice.

"Do you realise," Jess exclaimed. "You've just sworn your first oath on Odin?"

It was true. She was a Valkyrie now.

"Do be careful, it will take a few minutes to adjust. Just think the words as you speak, and we will hear your voice," Zara spoke, trying to reassure Kat.

"Come ladies, we must away. It's a long flight to the mountains and time is precious." Silk honked as Kat realised that she could easily tell which swan was which. They all looked so different; subtle, individual markings now revealed by her fabulous vision.

Leading the way, Silk led the elegant, swan procession down the stairs and out into the courtyard. To Kat's horror, a large party had assembled to bid them farewell.

"Right," Jess whooped encouragingly. "Do exactly as Zara tells you, wave your arms when she does and run as fast as you can. Try not to think too much, just look straight ahead. Let your instincts take over, flying will come naturally."

Kat looked around her, without turning her neck. She could see almost all the way behind her head and in such detail, too. The crowd were parting to create a runway, and she watched as Silk waddled forward, flapping her wings and gathering speed. Suddenly she was airborne, and banking away to circle the castle.

"Come on!" Kat heard her honk impatiently.

"You'll be fine," Zara nibbled encouragingly at her neck with her beak, and then the two of them lined up and began their take off. Kat flapped as hard as she could and felt her body lifting from the ground. She froze, and then bounced head over heels as Zara soared above her.

The crowd roared with delight.

This is so embarrassing, she thought, shaking her neck with dismay as she waddled dejectedly back up the runway.

"Just relax, nobody takes off the first time," it was Jess's voice inside her head. "I'll wait for you. Now try again, and good luck."

Kat tried once more.

She started her waddling-run, gaining speed as her knees moved faster and faster beneath her. Flapping her arms rhythmically, she felt the weight of her body lifting as she focused her eyes on a distant clump of trees.

"One, two, three, four—"

Kat concentrated on counting her arm beats; flapping these more slowly now as she felt the weight and the movement of air on their underside. Hearing a cheer from below, she realised, with an intense wave of elation; that she too was now flying.

"Five, six, seven—" Kat continued to count, she didn't dare to stop.

"Hey, slow down!" It was Jess again; and turning her head slightly, she could see her flapping hard to catch up.

"This is awesome," Kat whooped ecstatically, feeling the air rushing by her face.

"Form up ladies, and follow my lead," Silk took control. "Oh and by the way, congratulations on getting airborne Kitty Kat."

Carefully Kat dropped behind her wing and changed direction. As the crowd watched and waved goodbye, the four swans formed a 'V' formation before heading off toward the mountains.

Their flight took approximately two hours. Kat was tired when they arrived, but exhilarated by the experience.

She had seen so much as they flew; picking out individual people and animals on the ground. Fabulous smells too, drifted up from below. Scents she had never experienced before, light, fragrant and so rich in detail. Finally, arriving at the mountains, she followed the other girls down to land, which she did very badly.

Without question, the flight had been the most wonderful experience of her time so far in Asgard.

The girls landed on a broken and rocky area and after repeating the chant, the four warriors quickly returned to human form.

Silk had chosen their landing site with care. It was out of view of the main entrance to Nidavellir, and they had flown low over the glacier and mountain foothills as they approached. This, she hoped, would give them the element of surprise. Stowing their cloaks under rocks, and putting wax earplugs in their ears, they made their way toward the tunnel's opening.

To their relief, Silk's plan caught the dwarves unawares.

There were only four of them on duty and they were totally overcome at the sight of the Valkyries. Keeping one as their guide, they sent the others packing, encouraging them to flee as fast as they could into the surrounding hills.

Cautiously the girls entered the caves, and made good progress at first. The dwarves offered no resistance. Caught off guard, they scampered away shouting and screaming with terror.

As they travelled deeper into the mountain, things began to change. The dwarves mounted a stern defence, firing thick wooden bolts from short, stubby crossbows. These were an ideal weapon to use in the narrow tunnels. All four warriors picked up injuries, and they took it in turns to take the lead. Each time they were attacked, they charged the dwarves; killing them easily with their swords and axes. Close up, the dwarves could offer little resistance to the overwhelming strength of the powerful women.

As they fought deeper into the mountain, they picked up small shields and crossbows from their slain enemies. Lighting some of the bolts from the torches that lit the passageways, they fired these at the dwarves. This terrified them once more, and the stiff opposition that they had encountered earlier rapidly melted away. They carried on more swiftly again, and soon arrived at the chamber where, according to their guide, Hod, Kvasir, and Emile had dined so fatefully.

The cavern was empty.

"Where are they? Where are Fjalar and Galar?" Silk hissed menacingly, pressing the tip of her sword deep into their guide's throat.

He gulped nervously.

"I don't know, I swear I don't," he pleaded, his voice sounding sincere.

As he spoke, they heard the dull thud of an object falling. It came from a room on the far side of the cavern. The warriors raced swiftly in the direction of the noise and came to a wooden door. This had been hastily forced shut and was now locked.

Instinct told them they would find the dwarves behind it.

Attacking the door with their axes, Jess and Zara smashed at it in a frenzy of anger. Despite its thickness, the door couldn't withstand the ferocity of the enraged Valkyries. It quickly yielded, and the pair crashed through its shattered carcase.

They were right.

Cowering in the corner of the room were the two evil dwarves, and on a bed beside them lay the dismembered remains of Emile.

Words couldn't describe the emotions they felt in that hideously, vile chamber. Slumped dead in a chair was Kvasir, his body a ghostly shade of white. It had been completely drained of blood. Beside him lay two large bodns, earthenware vessels filled with a mixture of his blood, honey, and mead.

The evil room stank of death, and blood was spattered everywhere.

The blood of Kvasir, Emile, and Hod.

The room was so wretched that when the warriors had finally forced the dwarves to remove the bodies and the bodns, they set it on fire, hoping the flames would incinerate it from existence.

Rounding up other dwarves from the surrounding caves, the warriors forced Fjalar, Galar, and their colleagues to carry the bodies to the surface of the mountain.

This was slow and dangerous work, and the party was attacked time and again by angry dwarves now stung into action. Each time they attacked, the Valkyries fought back, returning their hails of bolts with accurate burning ones of their own. These sped along the corridors like tracers, landing amongst their foe and scattering them into the shadows. Any who dared stand their ground were quickly put to the sword.

Utterly exhausted, the girls finally reached the surface. The sun was low in the sky and to their amazement they had all made it out alive. Blood oozed from their many puncture holes, and their press-ganged party of helpers had been decimated by the ferocity of the close quarter fighting.

A cart was commandeered, and Kvasir, Emile, and the bodns were reverently laid amongst straw which was piled high around them. The Valkyries were in no mood to take prisoners, and after some debate, they encouraged some of the dwarves to find rope in exchange for their freedom. They did so eagerly, and then departed.

They were grateful that their lives had been spared.

Unfortunately for Fjalar and Galar, their fate wouldn't be so lucky.

Silk knew that they should take them back to Asgard, but so sickened were the party by the horror of the room, they decided to kill them there and then.

Pleading and begging for their lives as they worked, the Valkyries forced the two dwarves to fashion nooses from the rope. After throwing these over a stout branch of a nearby hawthorn tree, the women hanged the wicked pair.

Kat gleefully helped with this task, using the weight of her body and the strength of her arms to hoist one of them high into the air. She held on tightly, revelling in the jerking, spasmed, torment of his dying body. This was her retribution; a personal 'thank you' for Hod's suffering.

The warriors held the dwarves like this, dangling high as they watched with satisfaction their desperate, wriggling death throws. When eventually the dwarfs' bodies fell still, the girls tied the ropes and left them swinging from the bough.

This was a potent reminder.

Here hung Valkyrie justice.

56

A Break for Freedom

"Oh my God, look, please help her!"

Two guards had entered the cave where Ben and Jameela's cells were, and one was now frantically trying to open the door to her cell.

The guards had come again for Ben, and he guessed that it must be the next morning. They had slept fitfully for some hours, but with a constantly burning light bulb and no watch, it was hard to say what time it really was.

Day or night made no difference, held captive in a windowless cave.

During the long period since their return to the cells, Ben and Jameela had hatched an escape plan. It was a simple scheme, and much would be made up as they went along. What was certain was that Ben's body couldn't take too many more beatings, and he couldn't cope with them torturing her, either. No matter how bad the weather was outside, they fancied their chances more on the rocky mountain slopes than being cooped up here with their sadistic jailer.

Jameela's feigned epileptic fit was the first part of their plan, and the rest was now in motion.

Both guards had initially opened the door to Ben's cell. Once they were both inside that had been Jameela's cue to fall to the floor; arching her back and shaking her limbs in a feigned epileptic fit. Ben had to admit, she was giving a very convincing performance.

For the moment, she had the guards' full attention.

"Please, loosen her shirt, she'll choke to death."

Ben wasn't sure if these guards understood English, but by focusing their minds on her convulsing body, he could creep closer to the guard who had stayed behind in his cell.

As the other guard drew nearer to Jameela, she lashed out with a foot, kicking him in the shin just below the knee.

He yelped with pain and doubled up.

This was Ben's cue.

Stepping forward, he brought his fist down hard on the back of the neck of his guard. Stunned, the man slumped to the floor.

Ben relieved him of his rifle.

Jameela sprang into action.

After her disabling kick, she rose swiftly to her feet and leapt onto the back of her guard, wrapping one arm tightly around his neck and locking her legs around his waist. The guard staggered under her weight, toppling sideways to the floor. As they landed, she rolled onto her back, flipping him belly up on top of her. With his neck squeezed in the crook of one arm, she clamped her free hand over his nose and mouth.

He started to suffocate; thrashing his arms and legs helplessly, unable to prise her murderous arms from his body.

His fate now lay in her hands.

"Don't move a fucking muscle," Ben hissed as he took a pistol and the keys from his guard's belt. "Hands behind your head—now!"

He motioned with the gun and the guard understood his gesture.

"What the hell are you doing?" he whispered loudly into Jameela's cell. He could see her locked in a death roll, the guard jerking violently in his final efforts to wrestle free from her deadly embrace.

"We only need one guard," Jameela replied harshly through clenched teeth. She had a half smile on her face—the blood lust was rising fast in her Valkyrie veins.

"Do you have to kill him?" he hissed.

Ben couldn't believe his eyes.

Jameela didn't answer.

It was a silly question and one that was about to become past tense.

"Check the door," Jameela nodded curtly and Ben shuffled over toward it, pushing his guard in front of him. "Almost finished," she added, feeling the man go limp beneath her vice-like grip. She continued to hold him tightly, counting slowly in her head until his lungs finally gave up their desperate struggle for air. Pushing him off, she quickly frisked his body for weapons and ammunition.

"Oh sweet Odin be praised!" she exclaimed more loudly than she would have liked to.

There, in his pocket was her Valkyrie knife.

It must have been with him since the helicopter crash, where he had claimed it as his prize. Finding it so fortuitously had to be a good omen. Surely today would be their lucky day.

"What did you say?" Ben muttered curiously. "Keep the noise down, please." He added, still shocked by the sight of her taking a man's life.

This deed unsettled him.

Perhaps his damsel in distress wasn't so helpless after all?

"Nothing," Jameela called back as she removed a short, ceremonial, scimitar-like blade from the dead man's belt. This was more her style of weapon, and another welcome surprise this morning.

Odin was indeed smiling on them.

Gathering themselves at the door, they instructed the guard to take them to the commandant. This was the second phase of their plan, to seize their commander and use him as their hostage. No one would give a moment's thought to killing the guard they were currently holding, but they would definitely think twice if they had his commander in their sights. Using him as a human shield, they might just be able to force their way out of the caves. It was a high risk strategy, but they hadn't come up with anything better.

The guard appeared to understand their request, and they hurried him along the corridor, Ben keeping a cocked pistol pressed into his back. The tunnel was deserted. Clearly the base was so well concealed that there was little need for security. Within a few minutes, they had arrived at a heavy iron door.

It was the room where they had first met their jailor.

It was the room with the flag.

Pausing to regroup, and looking at each other as they did so, they counted slowly to three before forcing the door open. They burst inside, bundling the guard before them.

Mohammed looked up in surprise.

He was sitting with Dr. Nyran at a table eating his breakfast. On either side of them were two guards.

For a brief moment there was a stunned silence. A deadly race began between the attackers—and the attacked.

Who would strike first?

"KILL THEM!"

It was Mohammed who made the first move. Standing up, he screamed the command in English to the two guards.

Ben crouched behind his hostage, and took aim with his pistol at the guard on the right. He could see him level his Kalashnikov in his direction and loose off three deafening rounds. He felt their impact on his human shield, who thrashed wildly, screaming as he fell dying to the floor.

Ben fired once, and the guard dropped to the floor like a sack of potatoes.

One shot—two holes.

A small entry wound dead centre forehead and a large exit wound at the back. This splattered blood and brains onto the flag behind it.

"NOOO!"

Ben screamed as he looked to his left and saw the blurred motion of Jameela tearing toward the other guard. He heard the man loose off two or three automatic rounds from his rifle, and saw the spatters of blood as her body jerked.

The bullets had smashed into her chest.

She must have died instantly, but her body continued to race forward; running the guard through with her sword.

Jameela was dead.

Three blood spattered bullet holes in the middle of her chest told him so.

But she was alive—still standing, and screaming now for his help.

It was impossible, but there wasn't time to deal with that now. Mohammed had his pistol in his hand and he was taking aim at her head.

Ben lunged forward and lashed frantically at his arm. Mohammed snatched at the trigger, but the deflected bullet whistling harmlessly over Jameela's shoulder and ricocheted off the wall behind.

Locking Mohammed's wrist tightly in his hand, Ben punched him hard in the stomach. He doubled over, and as he did so, Ben struck him again in the face.

The fight was over.

Mohammed's gun fell from his hand and he collapsed onto the floor. He was bleeding heavily from his nose and mouth.

"Lock the door!" Jameela yelled at Nyran who was crouched and cowering against the flag. His hands were clasped above his head and his eyes were screwed tightly shut.

"NOW!" she screamed.

Stung into action by the force of her command, Nyran raced over to the iron door and slammed it shut. The keys were fortunately still in the lock. As he turned the heavy tumblers, a loud banging and shouting erupted on the other side.

Relief had arrived for Mohammed, but it was moments too late. For now, he and Dr. Nyran were Ben and Jameela's hostages.

The captives were now captors.

"GET UP!"

Wiping the sweat from her forehead, Jameela yelled to Mohammed to get up from the floor and onto his knees. He did so, unable to take his eyes off her. Blood was oozing from the wounds in her chest, wounds that should have killed her instantly.

Slowly Jameela walked around behind him before yanking his head up. She held her blade to his neck, pressing its razor sharp edge tightly against his throat. Beads of blood trickled from his skin.

"Urinate on him!" Jameela spat at Mohammed, but her order was for Ben.

"What? I, I can't," Ben stammered, reeling at her insane request.

"Do I have to do it?" Jameela fumed angrily, the tone of her voice telling Ben that this was not an empty threat. Mohammed had pissed on her and she yearned to return the favour.

"No, please, I just can't, you know, pee on request," Ben stuttered to answer her question, but the resounding clang of bullets slamming into the iron door interrupted them.

"You are lucky, you evil, filthy dog!" Jameela bent forward and whispered viciously in Mohammed's ear. Her body and mind were completely consumed by the blood lust.

"I will see you again soon."

Jameela drew the blade deeply across Mohammed's throat, and he fell to the floor gurgling and drowning in his own blood. She let out a chilling war cry; one that echoed harshly around the cave.

"OPEN THE DOOR—LET ME KILL THEM ALL!" She screamed fanatically.

Foaming at the mouth, Ben could see flecks of saliva dribbling from Jameela's lips as her eyes rolled wildly in her head. She seemed in a trance, and as she raced toward the door he grabbed her arms from behind and pulled her close. She struggled violently for a few minutes, enraged that her thirst for bloodshed had been so cruelly interrupted.

Slowly, as her breathing became less rapid she began to calm. Ben's embrace soothed her soul and her efforts to struggle free grew steadily weaker.

More gun shots rang out and bullets ricocheted around the door. Ben didn't hear them. His thoughts were only for the beautiful woman in his arms; the hell cat who had cheated death.

When at last Jameela was still, he pushed her gently away before turning her to face him. Holding her hands in his, he gazed incredulously at the three gaping holes in her chest.

Blood was trickling down her clothes, dripping onto the concrete floor beneath her.

This wasn't possible.

This wasn't happening—but he still had to ask.

"Just who the hell are you?"

57

The Journey Home

It was with a great heaviness in their hearts that the warriors started their journey home from the gates of Nidavellir. Zara was sent on ahead, flying as swiftly as she could to inform Odin of Kvasir's death and the success of their mission to recover their friends' bodies.

The sun had begun to set, and already a chill breeze was blowing across the barren mountainside. They were exhausted, but none had the stomach to stay the night where they were. The Valkyries didn't fear further attacks by any remaining dwarves; rather they knew that they wouldn't be able sleep.

The fate of their fallen friends, now lying silent and still in the cart beside them, was too close to allow them the luxury of slumber.

Taking big gulps from their flasks of mead, the girls toiled beside the cart, helping the ponies drag their heavy load toward the Bifrost Bridge.

It was backbreaking work.

The path was poorly marked, and deeply rutted with unseen boulders strewn across its surface. Luckily it was a cloudless night, and the moon still held some strength. Lighting torches, and coaxing the reluctant ponies forward with handfuls of straw and carrots; they eased the cart through the broken scrubland which lay all around them.

The path they travelled lay in the foothills of Jotunheim, and they prayed to Odin that they didn't come across a patrol of sleeping giants. They had had their fill of fighting and killing for the day, and the prospect of a further battle was unwelcome.

Wolves howled all around them, eager to feast on the stench of death that drifted from the cart. The girls, dripping with blood from their many bolt wounds, smelled equally appetising.

Time and again the warriors could see clusters of green and yellow eyes, at first stalking, and then circling them. In the moonlight they could make out the dark silhouettes of the wolves as they skulking between the boulders and clumps of gorse, their paws falling as silently as ghosts. At times the wolves ventured so close that they could hear the beasts panting, their breath fast with excitement and foetid with anticipation.

Fortunately, the wolves didn't attack.

The unmistakable shapes of Valkyrie warriors and the glint of their swords and axes deterred them. The news of the capture of Fenrir and the slaughter of his pack travelled fast, and they had no desire to join their fallen brethren. Reluctantly, the wolves retreated, and continued their foraging for easier prey.

Pausing only for an hour's troubled rest; the party reached the far side of the Bifrost Bridge as dawn broke. They had sweated hard during the night, and beads of perspiration now soaked their clothes and bodies. In the coldest hour before dawn, this dampness chilled them to the bone.

Holding her horn to her lips, Silk let out six short blasts, paused; and then repeated the call. To their great relief, a horn called out from the fortress on the other side. They were expected, and swiftly a team of experienced serfs and peasants came and helped them across the treacherous glacier. Within the hour they were at the watchtower, and Heimdall himself came out to greet them.

He congratulated them warmly, and after muttering a brief prayer over the bodies in the cart, he placed a sprig of fresh pine needles on top of each. With great relief, the girls bathed, put on fresh clothes, and dined heartedly on a magnificent hot breakfast which had been prepared for them.

They wanted to travel on immediately, but Heimdall persuaded them to stay. A party was heading toward them from the castle, and would arrive around midday. He begged them to wait and rest awhile before setting off once more.

Secretly grateful for his insistence, the girls climbed the steep spiral staircase to the bedrooms. They lay their weary heads down on soft pillows stuffed with eider feathers, and then pulled fresh linen sheets up around their noses. Within minutes they were all asleep, and wouldn't wake again until the sun had passed its zenith.

It was the sound of horns blowing that finally awakened them. Combing their tousled hair, and wiping sleep from tired eyes, the girls made their way stiffly down the stairs, blinking as they stepped out into the bright midday sun.

"Greetings Gunnr, Brynhildr, and the fair Kat," it was Odin and he embraced each one in turn. Kat felt like crying at the sight of his friendly face. It had been the longest twenty four hours of her life, and she felt grateful to be alive.

"We will take over your sorrowful task now." He indicated toward the bodies and the bodns that had now been transferred into two gilded chariots. These gleamed in the sun, their cargoes visible inside their splendour.

Each of the bodies was shrouded in a scarlet, silken sheet, with lilies scattered around them. A crown of silver oak leaves had been placed on the chest of Emile, and a gold leafed crown on that of Kvasir. A sword and shield had also been placed by the side of Emile. At last, the remains of their fallen friends could lie in a manner befitting their noble statures.

"We have brought you fresh horses, and if you make haste you will be at the castle before sundown." Odin spoke kindly, giving them his permission, and his blessing, to leave.

The girls needed no further invitation.

Thanking Thor, Tyr, Juliet, and Mika who had kindly travelled out to relieve them, they sped off across the plain of Ida. Refreshed by the food and the few hours' sleep that they had snatched, they made good progress. The hot sun on their backs and the cool wind in their faces brought smiles from the Valkyries as they galloped across the grassy plain. Small herds of fallow deer, goats, and wild horses startled out of their way as the girls thundered over the ground.

They whooped and shouted with delight now that their heavy burden had been lifted.

By sundown the warriors had arrived at Asgard, and they dined once more in the feasting hall. Kat ate quickly, anxious to get upstairs.

"Do you mind if I go and see Hod now?" she asked Jess, feeling a little guilty at her eagerness.

"Of course not," Jess smiled warmly, sensing the awkwardness in Kat's voice. "He needs you. Spend as much time as you want and send him all our best wishes." She kissed Kat tenderly on the lips before bidding her to go.

Kat leapt up the stairs two at a time and raced along the corridor. Without knocking, she flung open the door to her room and entered. She hoped he would still be there.

Hod was.

Sitting up in bed, his head now had fresh, clean bandages wrapped around his eyes. He called her name out hesitantly, and she bounded across the room kissing him warmly on the cheek.

"Fair Kat, how lovely to see you."

It was Frigg's voice and she rose stiffly from where she'd been lying. She'd been dozing beside Hod, and looked utterly exhausted. She still wore the clothes she had arrived in yesterday, and had obviously not left her son's side since arriving at the castle.

"I know your journey was successful. Thank you so much for everything," Frigg smiled and stroked her face gently with the back of her hand. Tears welled in Kat's eyes. She still felt so responsible for Hod's ill fated trip, and his terrible injuries.

"Oh please, don't cry. None of this is your fault, you mustn't blame yourself."

Frigg held her close and Kat sobbed into her chest. Her tears weren't for herself, but for the terrible future that lay ahead for Hod. He was blind and would never see again.

She felt so guilty.

Gradually, as Kat's tears subsided, Frigg spoke once more.

"I'll go now. Please look after him tonight. I'll see you both again very soon." Frigg, kissed both their heads, then, after waving her hand over her ring, she was gone.

"Are you feeling better?"

Kat turned to Hod and tried to read the answer in his face.

"Yes much. Are you hurt?" Hod's voice sounded anxious, he was more concerned for her than for himself. He certainly looked better, copious amounts of mead and apples had obviously restored much of his energy and strength.

"Nothing serious," Kat looked at him, and felt a glow in her heart. He looked so small and boyish all alone in her big bed.

Jess was right.

He needed her and she had to be there for him.

"May I stay here with you tonight?"

It felt strange asking his permission to sleep in her bed, but it seemed improper not to do so.

"Of course," Hod pulled the sheets back enthusiastically and beckoned for her to join him.

Kat signalled for a servant to extinguish the candles and after he had left the room, she quickly removing her clothes and snuggled up next to him. Placing her arm around his chest, she pulled him close.

"Hey! No funny stuff now," Hod jested. He could feel her sensuous body and it made his heart burst with joy.

Kat turned his head toward her, and playfully tapped at his cheek.

"Shush. You're supposed to be sick, remember?" She laughed before kissed him tenderly on the lips. She wasn't ready to take him as a lover, but her kiss lingered a moment too long, giving a tantalising hope that this might come.

Parting slowly from their embrace, they felt a distant rumble that grew steadily stronger until the whole castle shook violently. Candles crashed from the walls around them, and they could hear concerned voices in the corridor outside.

It was an earthquake, the strongest one for many years. Gradually the tremors subsided, but smaller aftershocks continued throughout the night.

After greeting the warriors and handing over responsibility for the safe transport of the bodies to Thor, Odin travelled on alone toward the gates of Nidavellir. There he had pulled his hat down over his eyes, and wrapped his blue cloak around his shoulders.

Invisible to the eye, he had journeyed deep into the dwarfs' realm, deeper even than the blood soaked room which had reeked with horror and death.

Arriving finally in the very heart of the kingdom, Odin slammed Gungnir down upon the rocky floor, opening Mimir's Well as he did so. He opened this wider than he had ever done before, channelling its huge surge of energy through his spear and into the ground beneath.

That night, Odin unleashed such a mighty quake upon Nidavellir that the death and destruction it caused left the realm in ruins for many years to come.

It would be a long time before dwarves would venture above ground again.

Satisfied that at last he had avenged their evil deed, Odin waved his hand across his ring and returned to his citadel.

He had a long and painful night ahead.

Bowing his weary head in his hands, Odin struggled to determine what to do with Kvasir's enchanted blood.

58

Friendly Fire

"**I** am the Valkyrie Herja, and I mean you no harm."

When Jameela eventually responded to Ben's question, it was in a calm and measured voice.

"I don't understand," Ben pointed to the bullet wounds in her chest. "Why aren't you dead?"

"Because I'm not really alive, look," Jameela picked up Ben's hand and placed it where her heart should have been beating. He held it there, hoping that everything would make sense. It didn't.

"This is fucking crazy!"

He shook his head and looked away from her gaze.

He was being held captive somewhere deep in Afghanistan and facing almost certain death. The woman he had fallen in love with now turned out to be some sort of pulse-less, American, terminator-styled cyborg. It was the only way he could explain this lunacy, other than a bad dream—and he hurt too much for that to be true.

Ben sighed deeply.

What a crazy, fucked up mess!

Jameela studied Ben's expression. He had taken her revelation well.

Since they had first met, Jameela's attraction toward Ben had been growing steadily stronger. It was inexorable, her fate to be drawn to him as his death grew ever closer. The intensity of this feeling had now reached its peak. Bubbling over with emotion—Jameela was totally consumed by its force.

She could resist it no longer.

Pulling Ben toward her, she grasped his face in both hands and kissed him passionately on the lips, forcing her tongue deep inside his mouth.

Taken by surprise, Ben hesitated, and then returned her fire.

It was a moment that stretched to eternity. A moment when they both knew they were in love, and that the other felt the same way, too. It was life changing—pent up emotions exploding in their embrace. A love that had been so carefully held in check could finally roam free.

As they kissed, the enemy around them lost their menace, and the hopelessness of their situation became of little consequence. All that mattered was the love they felt in each other's arms.

With great reluctance, but with an even greater sense of calm, their lips parted, and the world came crashing harshly back into existence.

The fighters had enlisted a heavy battering ram, and they were now pounding at the door. With each swing, the bolts and hinges were getting looser and weaker.

"So what do we do now?" Ben spoke first, smiling at the calmness in his voice. "You've killed our star hostage, should we use the doctor instead?"

Jameela shrugged at his suggestion as Dr. Nyran shrank even smaller into the wall.

KABOOMB!

A massive, muffled explosion shook the cave, then another, and then another.

Three one thousand pound bombs landed almost simultaneously, each one exploding nearer than the last and sending massive shock waves deep into the tunnels. The third and last explosion shook the room so violently that for a moment the lights flickered, went out, and then came back on again.

The base was under attack.

The bombs had landed precisely around the cave entrance, shattering the heavy iron doors as though they were made of matchwood. Allied troops in winter combat fatigues were already rushing up the slopes toward the opening, and an apache assault helicopter had begun firing murderous missiles and large calibre tracer rounds into the gaping void. Nothing in the first thirty metres of the tunnel complex would survive this ferocious onslaught.

"HURRAY!"

Ben cheered loudly and then almost as soon as he had done so he wished he hadn't. Yes they could be saved, but equally they could be buried alive. One thing was certain; their problems had just multiplied and were no longer confined to their Taliban captors. Now they had a trigger happy allied assault to avoid, soldiers who could easily mistake them for fighters in the smoky, cordite laden confusion of the complex.

"We have to get out of here, now," Ben shouted, his voice sounding strangely too loud. The hammering at the iron door had ceased. The fighters had either taking flight or were preparing to battle a more deadly foe.

"Please, take me with you."

Ben turned round. He could see Dr. Nyran looking at him, pleading with his eyes. He sort of understood the doctor's position. Jameela had told Ben that he was Indian, and a Hindu; and had been caught up accidentally in the fighting. He clearly had no allegiance to either side, his only interest being himself.

Dr. Nyran's goal was simple—to stay alive at any the cost.

If that meant changing flags with the ebb and flow of battle and doing whatever was asked of him—then so be it. The only thing that mattered was self preservation and to make it out of there in one piece.

Ben had sympathy for this point of view. He had no quarrel with Dr. Nyran, and bore him no malice. Unfortunately, this was more than could be said for Jameela; who was now striding purposefully in his direction.

"Don't kill him!" Ben shouted desperately.

THUMP!

Jameela's fist connected squarely with the tip of Dr. Nyran's upturned chin, and he collapsed dazed onto the floor.

"Oh please. Would I do that? He wasn't armed," she looked up with a wicked grin.

Ben laughed; a moments light relief in their desperate struggle to stay alive.

"Come on, let's go. I'll take the lead," Jameela walked briskly toward the door.

Ben intercepted her.

"Hang on a minute. I thought I was the hero," he teased, grabbing her arm and pulling her back behind him. "Anyway, you're my guardian angel so what can possibly go wrong?"

Jameela pulled Ben close.

What he was saying was only partially true. She wasn't here to prevent his death. He had to know that, he had to make the right decisions. His life depended on it.

She decided to speak up, let Ben know the truth.

"If you go out of the door first, I can't promise that you'll remain alive. What I can promise, and I swear this on Odin's sacred spear, is that if you fall, I will take you to Valhalla. Here you will live for all eternity in the hall of mighty heroes."

"Are you talking about heaven?" Ben enquired absently. He hadn't really heard what she was saying, because he didn't really care. He knew that with his undead, warrior angel beside him—he'd be all right, come what may.

"Yes."

For Jameela, heaven and Valhalla were the same.

Leaving Dr. Nyran dazed and alone in the room, the two of them snaked their way down the tunnel toward the entrance. They took it in turns to lead. Crouching, checking ahead, and then running forward and crouching once more.

On several occasions they encountered fighters behind makeshift barricades. The men were facing the entrance, unprepared for an assault from behind. Ben shot them with the Kalashnikov he had requisitioned. He had no choice. If they didn't escape the cave complex, they were as dead as the fighters soon would be.

Finally, the two of them reached some shattered crates barely ten metres from the cave's entrance. The air was heavy with acrid fumes and smoke, and their eyes streamed with tears. Amongst the arsenal of weapons thrown against the stronghold were canisters of tear gas. These burnt their lungs and made their eyes, mouths, and throats feel as though they were on fire. Explosions and gun shots burst all around them; some from behind, some from in front.

Hell itself could be no less welcoming.

"Do you have something white?" Ben shouted in Jameela's ear. She shook her head. He had hoped to wave a flag of surrender.

Shit!

Ben knew he would just have to chance it. He hoped they would see his tattered uniform and hear his English accent before a sniper took a shot at him. *Christ!* How he wished he still had his body armour—and his helmet.

"DON'T SHOOT! ENGLISH! DON'T SHOOT!"

Ben stumbled forward, running in zig-zags as fast as he could. Crouching and shouting as he ran, he made his way toward a large crop of boulders, five metres from the cave's entrance.

TAK–TAK–TAK–TAK–TAK!

A burst of machine gun fire drew a line that bisected his flight. The bullets sent a spray of shattered stones and concrete spluttering around his feet. He seemed to stumble, and then crashed headlong a metre short of safety.

Ben hadn't made it.

Two rounds struck him in the chest as he fell short of his goal. He was dead before he hit the ground; heart and aorta shredded as the hot, fragmenting bullets ripped through his chest.

Jameela sprinted forward, knife ready in her hand. She had felt his death and had to make good her oath. She cursed as she stumbled, falling inches short of Ben's upturned body. A burst of automatic fire whistled past her ear, three rounds from an M16 assault rifle pinging from the ground close behind her head.

She had to move on; she had to save Ben's soul.

Looking up, she could make out the shape of her assailant. His hunched figure was crouched behind a rock; his rifle was aimed at her.

Holding her breath, she lunged forward once more. Reaching out at full stretch, she plunged her knife deep into Ben's heart. She held it there, hanging on grimly with both hands. To her relief, the knife glowed warmly, and then flashed a single, intense pulse of white light.

Ben was saved.

His soul had gone to Asgard.

Laughing now with her mission accomplished, Jameela looked up. The soldier was moving toward her, rifle aimed and finger poised on the trigger. A round in the head would surely kill her, but that didn't matter anymore.

She had done her duty.

Ben was saved and it was a good day to die. She could stare death in the face and smile.

Jameela grinned as she watched the soldier approach. Tears streamed down her cheeks, her eyes still burning from the CS gas. The man's face was covered in a mask, and his gun remained levelled at her head. He was a killer without expression; a nameless, faceless monster hungry to steal her soul.

"Take your hands away from the knife, ma'am."

Caught by surprise, Jameela did as she was told.

His voice, with its heavy, American drawl, had replaced the bullet she had been expecting.

59

No Guns

Click–click–click.

The spiked metal heels of Ruby's stilettos echoed loudly as she walked confidently across the marble floor of the foyer to the Viceroy Hotel. She was looking great, and feeling even better. Today was the day for her showdown with Cole, and whatever the outcome, she was not returning to Asgard without him. The humiliation of her last return was etched too deeply in her mind, and it was one she vowed never to repeat.

As she walked, heads from the few guests milling around the foyer turned and gazed appreciatively at her. Some stared openly; while others cast their admiring looks more furtively.

It was mid afternoon, and Ruby had spent the morning shopping and getting ready. She had taken advantage of the vast shopping malls in Miami to purchase the shortest, white, denim mini skirt she could buy. To compliment this, she had bought a sleeveless black body and short sleeved bomber jacket. Distracting Cole was not the only object of her skimpy outfit. Its minimalist form gave maximum freedom of movement, and she expected she would be needing this before the day was done. Black ankle boots, pink sun visor and hair tied back in a simple pony tail completed her killer look; the irony of the metaphor not being lost on her.

Either she or Cole was going to die today. Of that she was certain.

Having obtained directions to Mr. Farra's penthouse suite, and after begging the receptionist to keep her visit as a surprise, she crossed the floor to the lifts. Out of the corner of her eye she noted a man in a suit talking hurriedly on a mobile phone. He stood out from the other garishly coloured, Hawaiian shirted, guests. He must be one of Cole's goons, warning him of her arrival. It didn't matter. Cole knew that she had killed Slim, and he would want to see her as much as she wanted to see him.

To quote his own words, Ruby's continuing existence would be "Bad for business."

Arriving at the twelfth floor, Ruby walked down the spacious corridor and knocked on the apartment door. It opened immediately, and she strolled in.

Click–click–click.

This time it wasn't the sound of Ruby's heels.

This was the noise of the safety catches being released on his guards' automatic weapons. It was nice to know she had been expected and was being made to feel at home.

"Hey Legs," Cole looked up from his cream coloured, leather sofa and waved for her to join him.

Crossing the room, Ruby noticed the two Latino types sitting opposite him and the two black leather attaché cases on the coffee table—cocaine and cash—or vice versa. Either way Cole looked pleased, it must have been a good deal for him.

Ruby sat down and nodded curtly to the two gentlemen. They weren't introduced, and after a brief exchange of handshakes they grunted their goodbyes and left with one of the cases. She sat back, and Cole offered her a cigarette which she gratefully accepted. It was the first of the day—*now wasn't she being a good girl?*

"You know Legs; you've been a bit naughty," Cole grinned at her, big white teeth gleaming devilishly in her direction.

"Depends what you mean by naughty," she began slowly. "Some might say I did you a favour." She paused, wanting to gauge his response to her excuse for killing Slim.

Cole said nothing and neither did his expression change. He took a sip from his glass of Jack D before starting a different line of conversation.

"I've got some new friends who are dying to meet you."

Ruby laughed. She wondered if he was referring to the detective who had arrested her back in New York? It was funny, the thought of Cole having a police officer as a friend. The notion was surreal.

"You know, I could say the same thing." She retorted, her thoughts turning briefly to Odin—and her arena.

"Sweet," this time it was Cole's turn to chuckle. He had no idea why some fantasy cult would have an interest in him, but he had no intention of finding out, either.

They finished their cigarettes in silence, and then as Cole drained his tumbler he spoke once more.

"So Legs, how are we going to do this? The easy way, or the hard way?" he motioned with his hand to the three guards.

"Well, you know me sugar, bit of a sucker for the hard way."

Ruby flashed him a smile before rising slowly to her feet.

There was no time like the present.

"What do you reckon? Just you and me, one to one? Winner takes all so to speak?" it was Ruby's turn to make a proposal, and she could tell from Cole's face that he liked what she was suggesting.

"Fine by me," he rose slowly, and started to take his jacket off.

Cole chuckled; this would be a bit of a laugh, duking it out with the crazy fucked up bitch, seeing how tough she really was. Who knew, he might just get to bang her, too, for old times sake.

"Just one thing—no guns."

Ruby pointed to his shoulder holster which was now visible. Thankfully, Cole took the gun out and laid it on the coffee table.

"No knives either, hey?" he looked up from the table.

"Touché."

Ruby smiled at his request, and after opening her shoulder bag she produced a blade. She placed this neatly on the coffee table beside his gun.

"Where?" Ruby had started to take her jacket off before she paused. She didn't want his goons to shoot her if things went badly for Cole.

"Oh Legs, so little faith. Come on, let's go," Cole made his way over to the bedroom door and opened it; motioning for her to follow him. It seemed rather an appropriate place for their relationship to end.

After holding the door open, Cole closed and locked it behind her. Ruby placed her jacket and bag on the bed, and they turned to face each other.

This was it.

Show time.

Slowly they began to circle each other, fists raised, ready to strike. Cole made the first move, a long, lazy roundhouse hook which was easy to avoid. He was testing her, playing with her. She may have been able to take a fat slob like Slim, but Cole knew there was no way a sassy ho could take him down, no fucking way at all.

His ego was way too big for that sort of shit.

Ruby ducked, and stepping inside his reach she threw a hard upper cut to his midriff. He barely flinched, his abs were like iron. Begrudgingly, Ruby had to admit that his physique matched those of Balder and Tyr. He was fit and strong, and obviously well versed in the art of boxing.

She had to be careful, very careful.

"Nice shot Legs." Cole acknowledged the force of her blow. She had power, and obviously knew how to fight. He was going to enjoy this bout.

"Glad you noticed." Ruby grunted, feigning jabs at his head as she talked. She was trying to coax him into throwing a punch so she could judge his reach more accurately.

She didn't have long to wait.

Feigning two jabs in return; Cole ducked sideways before lunging forward, unleashing a massive hook that caught her squarely on her ribs. Unbalanced, Ruby flew sideways and sprawled across the floor.

Sweet Odin! He hit hard.

"Nice punch, you won't get so lucky next time," she gasped, winded by the blow.

Ruby rose slowly to her feet, grateful that he hadn't followed his blow with another. He could have finished her off there and then if he had wanted to, but his confidence was sky high and he was still treating this fight as a joke.

Big mistake.

They began circling once more, both twitching jabs to the head. Ruby struck next, feigning a big hook to his midriff with her left hand, Cole lowered his guard defensively. Seizing the opportunity, Ruby threw a powerful clubbing blow with her right hand to the side of his head. It connected, and he shuddered with the force of its impact.

To her surprise, he didn't go down.

"Sweet," Cole shook his head, reeling his dazed senses in. He had never fought a woman like this before, and Ruby was surprising him. Skilled and strong, it would be a pity to kill her if it came to that.

Cole stepped forward, unleashing a combination of well thought out jabs and upper cuts. Ruby was forced backward, ducking left and right to avoid the onslaught. Eventually, reaching the wall she crouched down and let him move closer. Launching herself upward, she rammed an uppercut hard into his groin.

He collapsed to his knees, groaning with the pain of her illegal blow.

"How'd that feel?" Ruby taunted him, smirking as she looked down at his huddled sprawl. It amazed Ruby how a woman could ever loose a fight with a man. Their masculinity was just too easy a target—a design flaw; its position chosen by a god with a sense of humour.

"Now Legs, that punch was definitely bad for business."

Cole was rising slowly to his feet, He had a small gun in his hand and this was aimed at Ruby's heart. It was his back up, a weapon he kept tucked into one of his socks.

He pulled the trigger and fired twice.

Both shots were on target and he watched with satisfaction as Ruby recoiled under their impact before collapsing to the ground. Blood oozed from their entry wounds.

He didn't give two fucks anymore about his deal with Woods, or about her worth. She'd killed Slim and tried to fuck him over, the psychotic bitch.

She had to die, no question about that.

Standing up once more, he walked around her body and aimed the gun at her forehead. Always put one slug in the head, just to be sure. As he began to squeeze the trigger, there was a loud knocking on the door.

"Are you all right boss?"

It was the guards, startled by the sound of gunshots. Cole relaxed his finger, and placed the gun on the dresser.

She was dead, why waste the bullet?

"Yeh fine. Just taking care of business."

Cole walked over to the bathroom and ran the taps to the basin. Carefully he washed his hands, and then splashed his face with the tepid water to freshen himself up. Towelling himself down, he returned relaxed to the room.

Click!

Cole heard the sound of the gun being cocked and felt the cold steel of its muzzle pressed against his neck.

"I thought we agreed. No guns."

He could hear Ruby's voice hissing from behind him. It was her hand on the trigger.

How could that be?

What the FUCK was going on?

Reaching behind her back, Ruby withdrew her Valkyrie knife. She had tucked this under the waistband of her skirt before entering the hotel. The knife on the table had been a decoy.

Just like Cole, she liked to have a back up.

Slowly Ruby drew the razor sharp blade across Cole's throat. It felt like a feather caressing his skin, but the blood that gushed from its wake told a very different story.

Ruby cut deeply; there would be no mistake this time. Dropping the gun, she covered his mouth and eased Cole's jerking, dying body to the carpet. She didn't want the guards to hear his blood-choked cries, nor feel the thud of his body hitting the floor.

Holding his head against her as he died, she loved the look of shock on his face, the chaos of his confusion.

His death, her resurrection?

There were so many questions that went unanswered as he slipped, gurgling and choking into death's bitter embrace.

Waiting patiently until his body was still, Ruby plunged her dagger into his silent heart.

His soul was hers now.

She stood up slowly, and then made her way into the bathroom. It was her turn to wash her hands and to wipe her knife clean on a hotel towel.

Finally, with one last look around the room, she took the coin from her purse and began to chant. Sacred words spoken, an imploding, flash of brilliant light signalled her departure.

By the time the guards had finally figured out something was wrong and had battered the door down—Ruby was gone.

60

A Funeral for Friends

It was a sombre party that set off early the next morning from the castle. The journey south to Middle Sea would take most of the day, and was through land that became progressively more rugged as they journeyed toward the coast.

The funeral procession was lead by Thor. He stood in his beloved chariot, with Hod alongside him. Hod had turned down Kat's offer of riding with her on her horse. He was still nervous about her skills, and he really didn't want to hurt himself today.

Thor's chariot had once been an object of great amusement for Kat. It was pulled by two goats, Tanngnost and Tanngrisni, and she had vowed she would never be seen dead in it. The embarrassment would be too great. However, like so many things in Asgard, all was not as it seemed. The goats were enchanted, and could pull his chariot as swiftly and as smoothly as any team of horses.

They also had other more extraordinary talents, but Kat would learn more about these at a later date.

Beside Thor's chariot rode Odin, Balder, Tyr, and Freyja. Odin looked tired and distracted. He had been up most of the night fretting over the fate of Kvasir's blood. In the wrong hands, the enchanted potion could be very dangerous indeed.

For the time being, Odin had decided that the safest place for the bodns was in his citadel. Only he had access to his chamber and he could keep a good eye on them there.

Behind the party of gods were the two gilt chariots.

The talented seamstresses of Asgard had undertaken the gruesome task of sewing Emile's head back onto her body. They had done this brilliantly, placing a jewelled choker around her neck which concealed their needlework. A little make up and the faces of both bodies looked serene; more asleep than at life's end.

Lying on their beds of straw, their bodies covered by red silk sheets and surrounded by white lilies, they would ride in state to the fishing village on the coast.

The Valkyries rode behind the chariots.

As a mark of respect, they wore full battle dress but with ceremonial tunics dyed black. The warriors wore crowns made from plaited strands of silver that were festooned with delicate clusters of silver oak leaves; and their maids wore matching tiaras. As they trotted on their horses, these gleamed and sparkled in the bright morning sun.

Behind the Valkyries walked a crowd of serfs and townsfolk, their numbers swelling throughout the day as people from hamlets and villages joined the respectful band of mourners.

Slowly they followed the well beaten road south to the coast. It twisted this way and that, all the time rising through dense forests of beech, oak and elm trees. These eventually gave way to craggy scrubland, thick with gorse and heather.

At first the conversations amongst the party were subdued, filled with tales of the achievements of Hlokk and Kvasir. As the journey wore on, and the heat of the day intensified, conversations turned to lighter topics.

One item in particular, was at the top of everyone's agenda.

Who would be the victor of the next Valkyrie tournament?

Now that Emile had died, a place was vacant for a maid to become a warrior. This process would begin with a knock out tournament in which all the maids could take part. Kat spent some time discussing the ins and outs of this with Jess, and she noticed that the warriors were pairing off with their respective maids as they rode. Conversations were hushed, as each couple discussed the competition and individual tactics. There was fierce rivalry between the warriors, each wanting their maid to be victorious.

Vicki, Lara and Alex rode together. They were the maids of Emile, Ruby and Jameela; the three warriors who were either dead or absent from the party today.

Everyone had a word of sympathy for Vicki; hers was surely the most difficult role. The tournament would be to replace her Valkyrie mistress and succession would not automatically be hers by right.

Amongst all those discussing the contest there was universal agreement that the most likely successor would be Carmel. She had come second in the last tournament, and it surprised Kat to learn that the winner of that had been Jess.

At last she understood the hostility that had existed between her and Carmel when she arrived in Asgard.

Discussion about the tournament's outcome wasn't limited to the Valkyries. Indeed, it formed the bulk of conversations amongst the gods and the commoners.

The Aesir loved to gamble, and they could do this on almost any subject you could imagine.

They would bet on sensible things, such as the winner of a horse race or a joisting competition; or they would make more ridiculous wagers on say how far Thor could throw Mjollnir? Or how many gold coins it would take to fill Odin's hall in Valhalla?

Already bets were being placed on the winner and odds were quickly shortening. It came as no surprise to Kat to learn that her odds were the longest, and they would remain obstinately so. She even suggested to Jess that it was pointless for her to enter, but Jess insisted otherwise. It would be good experience and besides, Kat had brains, and not just brawn.

Kat had an outside chance of winning if she could only figure out a way to beat Carmel.

As they rode, Hod whistled cheerfully to her and she cantered ahead to ride beside him for a while. He was improving in strength day by day, and he was now wearing a simple black band over his eyes.

The reason for his cheer, he explained, was he had placed a bet on her to win. He had been given odds of one hundred to one. Kat laughed, imploring him not to get his hopes up. She had been in Asgard almost eight weeks, although at times it felt so much longer. Looking around her, she could hardly believe how quickly she had made friends, so many dear friends, amongst the warriors and maids.

Some days, it felt as though she were still living a dream, the happiest dream anyone could ever imagine.

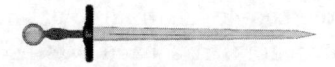

"What would you say if I made you the Queen of the Valkyries?"

Loki posed this question to Carmel, as they strolled arm in arm through the meadowed banks of the river Iving. They had elected to stay behind at the castle today, keeping guard because somebody had to.

In truth, this was an excuse.

Loki had been out of sorts since the imprisonment of Fenrir, and they had spent little time together. Today was a perfect opportunity for them to catch up and do just that.

"Don't be so silly," Carmel slapped his arm playfully while watching the expression on his face. She couldn't tell if he was joking, but the idea was too absurd to even consider.

Loki poked his tongue out cheekily before running away; and Carmel chased after him. Arriving under the shade of a willow tree, Loki stopped and allowed her to fall into his arms.

Pushing him to the ground, Carmel play wrestled him for a while. They were both confident that she would win the tournament as her only credible opponent was Prudr's maid, Lara. She was strong and experienced, but Carmel had never lost a sparring match to her yet. If you were going to place only one bet on the competition, then Carmel was the maid to go with.

The outcome seemed assured.

In two days time, Carmel would be crowned the next Valkyrie warrior.

Loki's impudent question, however, had not been made in jest. He was testing her, gauging her allegiance to Odin and Freyja.

Loki's hatred for Odin was well known and he had many good reasons for his disdain.

The murder of one of his forefathers, the first frost giant Ymir, the binding of his wolf Fenrir and most importantly, the treatment of his daughter when she had been a Valkyrie.

He still hated Odin's harsh nick name—The Black Valkyrie—and her banishment to Niflheim. She had been treated cruelly and unfairly, and this punishment was too severe.

Odin was arrogant and aloof, a man who looked after his own and cared little for those beneath him. He was a true aristocrat and an autocrat, so unlike his son Thor, whom Loki had great affection for. Thor was a man of the people, unafraid to get his hands dirty and to muck in with the townsfolk. If a hand was needed in the fields at harvest time, he was always the first to offer; and usually the last to finish; often labouring late into the night.

Loki had known for some years how to get rid of Odin. Indeed, he knew how to harm or destroy all the gods, easily and without bloodshed. They had one fatal weakness, one that had been staring him in the face for many years.

The golden apples.

The gods' very existence depended on these, and they only came from Idun's orchard. Kidnap Idun—and the gods would be at his mercy.

Simple.

In theory this looked like child's play, but in practice it would be very difficult. However, Loki had an ace hidden up his sleeve; one that made this crime a real possibility.

He could capture and imprison Idun if he took her to his daughter. Niflheim was a realm beyond Odin's reach, and his daughter despised Odin even more passionately than he did.

Once Loki had worked this out, he marvelled at how stupid he had been not to have seen this sooner. Thor, and now Carmel, were the only reasons why he held back, and why he was still holding back.

As they play wrestled, Loki decided he would wait a little longer to start his plan. He would let the outcome of the tournament decide Odin's fate.

If Carmel won, he would leave the gods alone.

If Carmel lost, then he would swing into action and make good on his pledge. Carmel would become Queen of the Valkyries, his Queen, and ruler beside him over all of Asgard.

Growing tired of fighting, Carmel rolled onto her front and lay with her hands folded under her head. It was too hot to continue, and she loved the feel of Loki as he ran a reed teasingly down her back. She tingled unbearably at its delicate touch. Putting the reed down, Loki massaged her firm bottom before sliding his fingers slowly but firmly down the outside—and then up the inside—of her powerful thighs. He pressed his hand suggestively upon her bottom once more and felt it arch invitingly upward against his hand.

Some things, it seemed, it was never too hot for.

Rolling on top of her and pinning her face down to the ground, he grasped her outstretched fingers between his. He thrilled at the perfect fit of her muscular, upturned bottom in the pit of his stomach. Slowly they moved up and down, pressing their bodies hungrily against each other as they savoured the erotic sensations in their groins.

Hidden from view by the willow tree, they made love in slow motion; their bodies arching gracefully and rhythmically together.

Locked in an intimate dance of love, their movements grew ever stronger until their final, powerful jerks told them this had come to an abrupt end. Their passion had reached its climax, and they could relax once more into the warmth of their embrace. They lay together like this for some time, locked tightly as one, sharing the ecstasy of their union.

It was the sound of drums beating, and a rising crescendo of horns that eventually brought their bliss to an end.

Hastily getting up, Carmel parted the fronds of the willow trees. Not one, but two bright rainbows filled the sky. She called eagerly to Loki to join her; the excitement in her voice was uncontrollable. The drums signified a prisoner had arrived but the horns meant so much more.

With nine Valkyrie maids accounted for, a hero must have come from Midgard.

Quickly brushing themselves down, they hurried back to the town. The day had just got even better.

It was mid afternoon when the funeral party rounded a steep rocky outcrop, and the path they had been following plunged sharply down toward the sea.

It was the first time Kat had seen Middle Sea, the ocean that lay in the middle of their world, and she wasn't disappointed by its magnificence.

Beneath them and stretching down toward the shore, lay a narrow, steep sided valley. This was laced with weathered, wooden cottages that followed the road as it twisted toward a curved and shallow bay.

Lying on wooden rollers in the centre of this lay a large, gilded long boat. This shimmered exquisitely in the late afternoon haze; although its graceful, curving form seemed strangely out of place amongst the muddled sprawl of angular fishermen's huts that lay clustered all around it.

The long boat lay on a shingle beach which rose gently from the sea. It did so in broad, sweeping folds that followed the contours of the bay. White marquees of various shapes and sizes had been hastily erected on these shingle banks in preparation for the funeral. The party would be staying the night here in this sheltered cove, before returning to Asgard tomorrow.

As the village drew closer, Kat was able to appreciate more fully the true splendour of the vessel.

Its sail was furled, but along each side of the deck lay a single row of round shields. Each bore the colours of the nine Valkyrie warriors. The prow and stern rose majestically and symmetrically at either end of the ship. The prow was carved in the form of a swan's head, and the stern into the shape of a serpent's tail. Upon the deck lay a deep bed of straw, and it was here that the bodies of Emile and Kvasir would finally be laid to rest.

Tired from their journey, the party settled on the beach for refreshments and to wait for the sun to lose its strength. The funeral would take place at sunset, but before this, the party would pay their last respects to their fallen friends.

With the bodies reverently laid upon their final beds, Odin was the first to do this. He kissed the foreheads of Emile and Kvasir gently, before placing a white rose beside each body. Freyja followed next; bending low and chanting ancient words into the ears of each in turn. She spoke in a whisper, her voice breaking from time to time. Her words were intended only for the souls of her friends, her last offering before their final journey. As she spoke, tears fell from her eyes; and as these fell they turned into tiny flakes of gold, which sparkled and twinkled like a myriad stars.

One by one the gods, warriors, maids, and townsfolk followed, each saying their sad goodbyes until at last all were done.

As the setting sun turned from gold, to yellow and then on to a deepest, crimson red; Thor and the other men gathered up the thick ropes and hauled the boat down into the water. Balder unfurled the sail, and catching the slightest breeze, the boat gently glided out to sea.

"HAIL WAR! HAIL VALOUR! HAIL ODIN!"

Thor's voice bellowed the tributes.

Horns blew, drums beat and the crowd cheered wildly as the vessel drifted further from the shore. Freyja raised her arm, and on her signal the Valkyries unleashed a hail of flaming arrows from their taut bowstrings.

The arrows arched gracefully into the evening air, stalling momentarily at their apex before plummeting swiftly downward and into the deck of the vessel. Tinder dry from the long hot summer, this burst speedily into flames.

As they watched the vessel burn, the cheers from the crowd rapidly subsided. Quietly and sombrely, each bid their friends a silent and fond adieu.

When the flames reached the water line, the sea around the vessel began to foam and churn. Something deep below the waters was rising rapidly to the surface. With a great roar and plume of spray, the serpent Jormungard raised its head above the water. Summoned by Odin, the huge creature grabbed the ropes attached to the boat's prow, and pulled the remains of the vessel out to deeper waters. With a final swish of its tail, the monster dived, dragging the long boat down into the ocean's depths.

When the churning waters finally settled, all that remained on the surface were a few charred remains; pieces of driftwood smoking lazily in the twilit sky.

The funeral was complete, and the party headed soberly back toward the waiting marquees.

In contrast to the tearful ceremony, the feast that followed was a riotous affair. The food was excellent and abundant; and mead and ale flowed freely. As the gathering ate and drank, the gods took it in turns to tell silly stories of valour and fanciful deeds. When eventually they became too drunk to recount further tales, party games began. Arm wrestling, feats of strength and a raucous drinking game loosely based on *Simon Says* which everybody took part in.

Of all the games played on such occasions, Kat's favourite was one they called 'Valhalla.'

Tables and benches would be lined up in a long row, and the men would sit down opposite the women. A coin would be passed secretly from hand to hand under the table by one side, while a caller would be chosen by the other. When the caller cried "Valhalla" the men or women passing the coin would place their elbows on the table, holding their clenched fists in the air. The coin would be hidden in one of their hands.

The caller would then ask them to bring their hands down flat onto the table. This could be done in one of two ways; either very quickly and loudly as a "Grand Slam," or slowly and stealthily as a "Creepy crawly."

The caller's side would listen intently as the opposition brought their hands down; each hoped to hear the tell tale tinkle of the coin in the hand that would be covering it on the table. The opponents would do the opposite, making a terrible racket to mask the coin's sound.

Then came a wild and frenzied melee.

All the players would yell at the caller, encouraging them to take different hands off the table. The besieged caller would try to do this one by one, praying he or she didn't loose the game by revealing the hidden coin. Eventually, when the caller was certain he knew where the coin lay, he would cry "Tip it" and the opponent would reveal if the coin was indeed under the chosen hand.

If the caller's guess was correct, then their side had won the round.

It was a peculiarly silly battle of the sexes, and a game that played better the more who took part. People cheated and couples conspired to thwart each other in a wickedly, delicious game of high spirits.

Tiring slowly as the festivities drew to a close, the party drifted in their ones and twos toward their beds.

Hod retired early, spending the night in his mother's tent. He was exhausted, and hit harder than most by the funeral. He felt his body should have lain alongside Kvasir's and Hlokk's. Somehow, he felt a deep injustice that his life had been spared and theirs hadn't.

Perhaps he was destined for a greater purpose?

Hod would often return to this thought in months to come.

Kat spent the night with Jess.

They cuddled closely together, whispering quietly so not to disturb the other sleeping guests. Despite her growing friendship with Hod, Kat was relieved that her relationship with Jess hadn't suffered. If anything it was stronger, and both girls revelling in a night of intimacy together. Their tender kisses and joyous, stifled moans continued late into the morning hours.

As the night wore on, and when everyone else had fallen asleep, Balder awoke. Startled; he burst sweating and gasping into wakefulness.

Silk stirred beside him. She had hoped his dreams of death and doom were linked to Kvasir, and that the funeral would bring an end to this torment.

With a growing sense of foreboding, she realised that his nightly journey to Niflheim would continue. This left her torn and helpless; only able to offer him her caresses and words of soothing comfort.

As she watched him now, fighting his inner demons, a single question burned inside her heart.

If Balder's dream hadn't heralded Kvasir's death, then whose death did it foretell?

61
Work

"Telephone call for you, sir."

"Uh huh," Marcus grunted his acknowledgement, but didn't look up from behind his desk. The last few weeks had seen a steady deterioration in his mental health, a deterioration he was decidedly unhappy with.

Before Christmas and the New Year he had been his usual self. Stressed and frustrated, pissed off with a never ending workload. Now, looking at the files before him, he just felt bored and depressed. These were unexpected feelings, and ones he found more unbearable and oppressive than the anger that had gone before.

Take for example the file in his hand—a hold up at a local liquor store.

In the years he had worked the area, this same store had been held up five times. The criminals, victims and witnesses were different, but the crime remained the same. He knew that he would fingerprint the same till, and he would watch the same surveillance footage. The camera was in the wrong place, so there would be no clear view of the thief and the till was flimsy and easy to jemmy open. He had told the owners repeatedly to move the camera and change the till. But had they done this? Hell no! Even if he solved this crime, he bet a pound to the dollar that he would be back sorting out an identical one within a year.

What was the point?

He tossed the file to one side and picked up another. Ah yes. He recognized the location.

Without opening this file he knew the crime would be a mugging. He knew the street and he knew the exact spot on the street where the mugging would have taken place. He visited this spot every six months or so. The money and goods stolen varied, as did the ages and sex of the victims; but the location didn't. A brighter street light or a CCTV camera pointing in the right direction would prevent this file from ever finding its way back to his desk. Sadly, until that merciful day arrived, the same pointless crime would keep recurring.

Christ!

He was just like some bastard hamster, crawling wearily out of bed to get onto some mindless tread wheel. Running faster round and round, but only ever managing to stand still.

The saddest part about his nightmare was that every bloody day was the same.

No wonder he felt so fucking down.

"Would you like them to call you back, sir? Only they did say it was important."

It was the same receptionist again, dragging Marcus away from his melancholy contemplations.

"Who is it?" he asked wearily.

"Agent Woods, well at least, I think that's who he said he was."

Marcus sat bolt upright. It was as if he'd been electrocuted. He had heard of Coles killing in Miami the other day, and had drooled at the prospect of a call from Woods. The mysteries surrounding the Dr. Neal and Slim Tucker cases, these were the only files that shone a ray of hope into his dreary existence.

"Put him through right away, please."

Marcus fumbled with his phone, palms sweating with excitement.

"Agent Woods here. I expect you've heard about the killing of Mr. Farra?"

Woods clipped voice resonated down the line. He got straight to the point as usual; no messing about.

"Yes indeed. Do you have—" Marcus paused for a moment, trying to think what names he should use. "Ruby or Jessica?"

"No I'm afraid not. The fool decided to go toe to toe with Ruby and paid the price. She slit his throat, before stabbing him Valkyrie style through the heart. He managed to wound her though, and for that we should be grateful. At least we now have a blood sample and her DNA on file."

"Any artifacts?"

Marcus couldn't hide his disappointment at this news. He had been looking forward to meeting them again, especially Jessica.

"No. Nothing from her I'm afraid. However, it isn't all bad news." He added hastily with a sly chuckle.

Marcus could sense excitement in his voice. *Was the calm and methodical Agent Wood's playing with him?* He got a feeling that something momentous was about to be said.

"A situation came up in Afghanistan, a young lady by the name of Jameela Masood. She claimed to be a U.S. citizen and got herself taken hostage with a British serviceman."

Marcus expressed surprised at this. A hostage situation should have made the national news, but Woods didn't go into the politics behind the affair. He had far more important things to talk about.

"Anyway, the upshot of this situation was that the soldier got killed and the woman escaped." Woods continued.

"I'm not sure I'm following you," Marcus couldn't quite see where this story was going, or its relationship to Ruby or Jessica.

"Ah yes. I should have mentioned this earlier. We have a captured Taliban fighter. He likes to go by the name of Dr. Nyran. He's on a military flight to America as we speak, with an artifact. That's the reason why I'm calling you."

Wow!

Marcus nearly fell off his chair.

"What artifact?" he almost breathed down the phone.

"A knife; I believe it's a Valkyrie knife. Dr. Nyran wants to make a deal. He claims he has some vital information that he will only share in exchange for American citizenship. I would have dismissed this out of hand, if it weren't for two important details."

Go on!

Marcus felt like screaming these words at Woods. His slow and precise narration was too slow for Marcus's liking. He wanted the punch line, and he wanted it now.

"First, the girl called herself the Valkyrie Herja. Not exactly the sort of name someone would make up on the spur of the moment. This is one of the cult names we already have on file," he paused, giving Marcus time to let the information sink in.

"Second," he continued methodically. "One of the army rangers who stormed the stronghold gave a very detailed account as to what she did, and how she escaped after he'd captured her."

Marcus grunted and indicated urgently for Woods to continue. This was getting more interesting by the second.

"Apparently the British serviceman was down and injured, and he saw the girl leap forward and plunge a knife into his chest."

"Bloody hell!"

Marcus couldn't help his loud expletive. This news was extraordinary, an eyewitness account of a Valkyrie slaying. He was desperate for Woods to go on, but obsession compelled him to ask the obvious question.

"How did she escape?"

That didn't make sense. You can't just stab a guy and bugger off, not when there's a fully kitted U.S. ranger standing over you with a gun.

Surely that was impossible?

"An act of total incompetence," Woods fumed. "Apparently he got the girl to release her hand from the knife, but instead of handcuffing her straight away, he allowed her to say a prayer over the dead soldier's body. Can you believe that? She asked him to let her say a prayer! She vanished, there and then, right in front of his eyes. In his own words, she disappeared like a flash-bang in reverse."

Marcus sat back, and toyed with this image in his head.

He knew what a flash-bang was all right. It was an explosive device the army and counter terrorist units used when flushing out a building. You threw it in a room, and it exploded with a loud bang and a dazzling flash of light. This would temporarily blind and stun any terrorists inside, making entry less of a death trap. He couldn't quite understand what he meant by "In reverse" and he asked Woods to clarify this point.

"Ah yes, an implosion; instead of the bright light expanding from the point of the explosion, it contracts back to that point. That's an implosion."

Marcus paused before replying.

"Does that fit in with your funny Harry potter style cloak of invisibility?" He enquired curiously. He had forgotten the fancy scientific name Woods had used to describe such a device.

This time there was a longer pause, and when Woods spoke it was slowly, and with deliberation.

"No, not really. And that's the puzzle. A meta-material would behave differently."

Marcus noticed that he didn't offer an alternative explanation, so he took the initiative.

"So, how can I help you?"

"I was just getting to that," Woods replied impassively. "Could you possibly come over to my office the day after tomorrow? I would like you to confirm the identity of the knife, and would welcome your thoughts when I interview Dr. Nyran."

Marcus confirmed his acceptance of the invitation, and agreed to the date and time. Putting the phone down, he sat back in his chair.

A huge, cheesy grin spread across his face, one that stretched from ear to ear.

Perhaps his job wasn't so tedious after all?

62

Preparations

It was while the funeral party slept through the night, that the news of the return of Prudr and Herja travelled south to greet them. By breakfast time, the camp was on fire with the gossip. Some was true, and some was utter nonsense.

It was clear that a hero had come to Asgard, and possibly two or three prisoners. However, like some giant game of Chinese whispers, the details of these arrivals varied according to which 'reliable' source you heard it from. Some said that the hero had been so badly injured not even the mead of Valhalla could revive him. Others spoke of a giant black monster that had to be hunted down by twenty horsemen. The camp seethed with expectation, as claim and counter claim grew wilder and more exaggerated.

Imaginations ran riot, and all who had horses set off as soon as possible to return to Asgard. A wild, cross country race ensued with maid chasing warrior, and warrior chasing god. This raged for hours, as they galloped madly homewards along the twisting trail. It was Odin, riding upon Sleipnir, who eventually reached the castle first. He was of course elated.

Finally Cole, the great black apple and starter of Ragnarok, was safely in his hands. Better still; the rumours as regards the fallen hero were unfounded. Yes, he was injured, but he was recovering slowly in a fashion very similar to Kat's arrival. Lying tucked beneath soft sheets and attended by a doting warrior.

The remainder of the mounted company arrived soon after Odin, and all crowded into the castle eager to greet the new hero. A gold flag flew over Gladsheim and the town was in a state of frenzy. Not only were they celebrating his arrival, but also preparing for the Valkyrie tournament tomorrow.

It was a bit like the Winter Solstice and the Summer Solstice both arriving at once. No one knew which way to turn.

Prudr was the first to be greeted by the warriors. She looked tired and badly injured, and had needed a lot of mead since her return. Although the warriors were undead, and wounds that didn't scramble their brains or decapitate them couldn't kill them, they were wounds nevertheless.

They still hurt like crazy.

Odin was delighted to greet her, and hugged her enthusiastically. They departed to her arena together, Odin eager to meet his nemesis at last.

Of course, the rumours about his arrival had been exaggerated as well.

It was true that he had limped some distance from the point of his arrival, but the farmers had easily tracked his trail of blood using large wolf hounds. When finally cornered, he had offered little resistance. Safely locked in a cell beneath Ruby's arena, he now awaited her pleasure. Ensuring that he was given just enough mead to stay alive, Ruby discussed his fate with Odin.

Odin was afraid of him.

His link to Ragnarok, the war that would end all worlds, seemed to scare him and he admitted as such to her. He urged Ruby to emasculate Cole, remove his virility and his appetite for aggression. Ruby, however, was reluctant to do this; she was hesitant to deprive herself of such a magnificent foe.

Ruby was a true warrior, which was why she was so feared. Her pleasure was in breaking prisoners, both mentally and physically. Only when their will was destroyed, would she allow them the luxury of emasculation and the 'comfort' of slavery. Until that point, she whipped and sparred with them without mercy.

Cole was her enigma.

Their fight had been inconclusive, cut short by necessity and by their cheating. She yearned to find out which of them was the greater and until she did, he would stay her prisoner and remain whole.

Another god who had an interest in Cole was Loki, and his jaded point of view was unique in all of Asgard.

The enemy of his enemy was his friend.

He knew about the predictions of Ragnarok, and he was eager to gauge the ferocity of Odin's adversary. He couldn't do that safely here and he already had a plan to get his hands on Cole. Like his scheme to destroy the gods, whether or not he would seize him and take him to Niflheim depended on the outcome of the tournament.

As the day progressed, the atmosphere around the castle became more tense and fragmented; the Valkyries dividing their time between last minute practising for tomorrow's showdown, and visiting Jameela's hero.

All agreed Ben was one of the most handsome men who had ever come from Midgard, and there was much jealousy and jostling for his attention. This eventually became so silly that Balder and Tyr took it in turns to stand guard over Jameela's chamber, questioning all who wanted to enter. The wealth of imaginative excuses and distractions the girls used to try to see Ben could have filled a book.

Kat was one of those lucky enough to see him before Jameela grew weary with their visits. Her heart went out to him when he opened his eyes and briefly drifted into consciousness. He had the same bewildered look as she must have done, and she stroked his forehead gently, reassuring him that everything would be all right. Eventually she left the chamber with a tear in her eyes.

The similarities between his arrival and hers brought back blurred and unwelcome memories.

Jameela didn't bother with her prisoner that day. She instructed her maid Alexandria to deal with him in any manner she saw fit. Punishing Mohammed wasn't her priority. Today her whole being was devoted to coaxing Ben back to health, and making his adjustment to his strange surroundings as painless as possible.

Despite obvious distress from her chest injuries, all the warriors noted the radiant glow about Jameela's face. She didn't need to tell them she was in love; it stood out in bright red letters a metre tall.

Prudr noted this too, and jealously conceded that perhaps love was what was missing in her life. She could have had this with Elijah, but that hadn't been their fate.

Until she found her soul mate, she could never travel joyously to Valhalla.

Bathing and supper were brief affairs that evening.

Socialising trailed off rapidly as the warriors coached their maids, and rivalries reared their ugly heads. It was a necessary evil, the girls needing to feel aggression to one another. If the tournament was to be a success, they had to fight with passion and desire.

Only then would Asgard find its next true Valkyrie.

"WAR–WAR–WAR–WAR–WAR–WAR–WAR!"

The chanting in the hall of Lyr grew louder and louder as a host of angry giants beat their chests and stamped their feet. Whipped into a lather by Thrym, the giants were foaming at the mouth.

Here at last was an opportunity to invade Asgard; a reason to destroy Odin and his deceitful band of treacherous gods.

Thrym watched and smiled contentedly. He felt satisfied that his speech had roused such passion in his noble clansmen; and his powerful words had stirred a rage in his heart as well.

He was angry that Thor hadn't responded to his challenge. This, he put down to Thor's arrogance, rather than Loki's failure as his messenger.

He was furious, too, that the earthquake that had devastated Nidavellir had caused so much destruction in his own mountain kingdom. Many giants now lay dead and buried amongst the rubble of collapsed caves and cottages. These had been destroyed by the force of the quake.

He hadn't received an apology from Odin for this disaster, nor any offer of compensation. To give neither was to dishonour Thrym, and that had cost him face amongst his brethren.

Finally, he still seethed at the humiliation of his mason, and the loss of so many slain friends. He would have his revenge, and the scarred and wizen old woman sitting by the fire held the key to his success.

Her name was Gullveig, and she was the last and greatest of the dark witches.

Thrym looked over at the sorceress and she returned his stare; black, beady eyes piercing his before she returned her hands to their toil.

Gullveig cackled softly as she stirred the contents of her cauldron. The tethered and gnarled skin around her lips stretched and split as she did this; and the cauldron steamed and hissed as it did every night.

She too had been humiliated by Odin, and her desire for revenge surpassed even that of Thrym's. The potion she was now brewing was but one of many she intended to unleash upon her hated foe.

There was still much work to be done before Thrym's giant host could take on the mighty gods and the strength of Odin's Valkyries. There were more enchanted potions to be brewed, foul curses to be cast, and magic spells to be woven.

Odin was a powerful lord and one not to be underestimated.

He too used dark magic, and she had to be certain of success before she dared march with Thrym's army and lay waste to his realm.

63

The Tournament

Kat was furious with herself. She couldn't believe she had butterflies in her stomach, and a horrible feeling she was going to be sick at any moment. It was stress, and she knew it. Of all the nine maids waiting outside Hlokk's former arena, she should have the least to worry about. According to most of the townsfolk and the gods, her chances of winning the tournament ranged from zero to non-existent.

Perhaps, the reason for her nerves was the fact that she alone believed she could actually win. Jess had been right at the funeral, she did have brains as well as brawn.

Over the weeks of training and sparring, Kat had made mental notes of all the other maids' strengths and their weaknesses. She had a battle plan for each girl, and more importantly, an unshakeable belief in her own abilities. It was this strength of character that had propelled her through medical school, and made her a state track and field champion. Still, nerves didn't help, so she tried relaxing by following the tufts of clouds as they scurried across the late August sky.

Inside the arena the atmosphere was like a powder keg, bursting with anticipation. It had been packed solid for hours, with a carnival atmosphere laced with friendly rivalries. Everybody had his or her favourite maid, and the excited roars from the crowd as each maid was announced bore testament to this.

It was considered disrespectful to admire the warriors, but the maids were legitimate targets for lustful desire. The biggest roar of approval came of course for Carmel, but Kat too was gaining admirers.

Many a drunken late night argument in Asgard was centred around the physical attributes of the maids.

Who was the fairest? Who the most buxom? And who the most lust worthy?

Often a composite 'Maid' would be agreed. One who had Carmel's shapely bottom, Kat's wasp like waist, Vicki's ample bust, and the smouldering eyes of Alexandria. Other combinations existed, but this was probably the most popular. Today was a chance for the men to show their admiration; and they intended to do just that.

One by one, as the maids were announced, they made their way over to the stand where Odin and Freyja were seated. There, they were given a silver tiara of oak leaves before being displayed before the ecstatic crowd.

Kat was the last to be presented, being the most recent maid to join the sisterhood.

With a huge roar rising from the crowd, Kat entered the arena. She had practiced here with Emile and Vicki many times, but today it seemed so much larger and intimidating. Part of her wanted to turn and run, the fear of a humiliating defeat before so many people was hard to face.

Cursing herself for being so pathetic, she forced herself to walk confidently across the sand, waving at the cheering crowds. "Relax and enjoy the show," she muttered to herself as she accepted her tiara. Then, she joined the other girls standing at the edge of the arena.

The tournament to choose the next Valkyrie followed a time honoured tradition.

There were nine warriors and nine maids. The first round would therefore be an elimination contest. Nine prisoners, one from each Valkyries arena, would fight with the maids. The first eight maids to defeat their prisoners would go through to the knock out stage of the competition; the unlucky ninth would be eliminated.

Fighting the prisoners was a race against the clock, but that didn't stop the girls from show boating and laying on displays of their skills. The tournament was as much about spectacle as it was substance. All the girls wore white leather tunics for the occasion, each being individually tailored and finished with trims of silver, gold, and jewelled studs. Their clothes sparkled in the sunshine, proudly enhancing each maid's beauty.

To win was one thing, but to do so with style was equally important.

Freyja raised her hand, and the crowd rapidly fell silent. An iron gate opened beneath the section where she, Odin, the warriors, and the other gods were standing. The nine prisoners for the elimination round entered, clustered in a small huddle beneath the stand. The maids picked up their shields and swords, and prepared to do battle.

"HAIL WAR! HAIL VALOUR! HAIL ODIN!"

Freyja exhorted the crowd with the customary tributes, and then as the cheering settled, she spoke once more.

"LET THE TOURNAMENT BEGIN!"

She announced loudly, dropping her hand as she did so. With one final mighty roar from the crowd and a blast of horn being blown; battle commenced.

Kat charged forward quickly. Her eyes darting around the motley selection of scum. Choice was everything, and she settled for a balding, grey-haired prisoner with hunched shoulders and skin that sagged from his arms and waist in great folds. He had layers of whip marks on his back. These were the hallmarks of one of Ruby's slaves. He didn't make eye contact, and looked broken in spirit.

He was an ideal opponent to gain a swift victory over.

Kat set to work immediately, wielding her sword without pause. Her blows rained down on his shield and he fell to his knees. With one final mighty blow she knocked the sword from his hands. Slamming her foot down hard upon it, she pressed the blunted tip of her blade against his neck. He yielded, and she looked around to check on the progress of the other maids.

To her immense surprise, she was the third to finish.

Jumping up and down with joy, she shared her jubilation with the crowd. She would go through to the next round, and was swept away by a wave of relief. She blew a thank you kiss to the stand where Jess was standing, and Jess returned the gesture. The outcome of the tournament reflected the training skills of the warriors, and Kat had already enhanced her status.

One by one the maids dispatched their opponents, and to everyone's surprise, Vicki was the last to finish. Perhaps it was the grief at the loss of her mentor Emile, or problems dispatching a troublesome prisoner. One way or another, the tournament had had its first upset.

Kat was through and she wasn't.

The rankings of the maids had to be hastily rearranged.

The prisoners were rounded up and lead away, and the remaining eight maids lined up on the side of the arena facing Odin. Carmel, the number one ranked maid, would fight first. Her opponent was Yuko, a slight but resilient girl of Vietnamese origin.

Each bout followed a similar pattern.

The maids would place their three spears, axe, sword and shield at opposite ends of the arena. No one wore helmets as blows to the head were banned. Other safety measures were also evident. Swords had their tips broken and their blades covered with twine, and axes were wrapped in leather. Spears too had their tips filed down, and then covered with a delicate gut pouch filled with pigs' blood. This would burst on impact, a bit like a paint ball, marking where it had struck.

The aim today was victory, not slaying.

Once their weapons had been placed, the two girls would walk to the centre of the arena, embrace, and then a horn would blow. This signalled the start of the contest. The two would return to their weapons, make their selection and then join together in combat. This could often take some time, as the girls enjoyed showing off and playing to the crowd before getting down to the serious business of fighting.

Carmel's fight followed the expected program.

It was heavily one sided, with Carmel eager to demonstrate her prowess. She relished the opportunity to defeat her opponent, and once she was assured of victory, she took her time and milked the crowd for applause. Eventually she forced a submission. Carmel was through, and the maids Alex and Priya followed suit; both winning their contests with equal comfort.

Finally it was Kat's turn. She was up against Lara, the second highest rated maid.

Lara was a loud, precocious girl with long blond hair, a strong chin, and somewhat coarse features. Extremely confident, it was evident from their embrace that she expected an easy win. Kat was an unworthy opponent for a maid of her experience, so she sauntered slowly back to pick up her weapons, waving happily to the cheering crowds. Everybody knew she would win, and they hoped her victory over Kat wouldn't be too humiliating.

Unfortunately, no one had read Kat the script.

In contrast to Lara's leisurely stroll, she hared back to her weapons and selected a spear. Turning instantly, she dashed back toward Lara and unleashed it. The spear flew through the air like an arrow, striking Lara on the side of her chest. Its blunted tip rupturing the delicate pouch of pigs' blood, and this exploded over her body. The blow was judged to be fatal.

Kat had won.

The crowd went crazy.

They cheered, screamed and stamped their feet. Never in their history had a maid won a contest so quickly, nor shattered the rankings so completely. Suddenly the hopeless outsider was a contender, and odds shortened dramatically.

Kat was a dark horse and the crowd bayed to see more.

Four maids now remained Carmel, Alex, Priya, and Kat.

Carmel was first up against Priya, and even her mood had changed. There was no show boating and dawdling this time. Kat had rewritten the rule book, and all the girls were on their guard from the moment they finished their embrace. The contest was close, but in the end Carmel battered Priya into submission. Her sword arm was simply too strong, and an exhausted Priya finally yielded to her will.

It was Kat's turn again.

The crowd roared with feverish expectation. Surely she couldn't cause an upset this time? Alex was a master with the sword, and in a different league to Kat. Reluctantly, they accepted that their new found darling must surely be defeated.

Nervously the two maids hugged, and then backed cautiously away from each other. Alex didn't take her eyes off Kat, aware of her skill with the spear. She was taking no risks of being caught unawares. The shock defeat of Lara had sent ripples of panic through the other girls.

Kat was no longer an opponent to be taken lightly.

To Alex's amazement, instead of choosing a spear, Kat picked up her sword and shield instead. Striding purposefully toward her, Alex found this tactic unnerving; exactly what Kat was hoping for.

Don't be predictable; keep your opponent off guard.

Kat attacked hard, and then retreated quickly. This was her simple game plan. The long hot summer had left the arena parched and dusty. After striking a few blows, Kat would retreat, deliberately scuffing her feet and kicking up dust and sand to irritate her opponent.

The strategy worked.

Harder and harder Alex attacked, and faster and faster Kat retreated. Each time, a cloud of dust temporarily blinded Alex, angering her and tempting her to strike out more rashly. Carefully Kat watched her body language. Some of the crowd started to boo her endless retreats, but she didn't care. She was waiting for the instant to strike, the time when Alex was least prepared.

Abruptly, sensing the moment was right, Kat pretended to stumble. Blinking profusely and partially blinded by yet another cloud of dust, Alex pressed forward with her attack. She lunged blindly toward Kat but in her haste, she hadn't seen her dart sideways, nor seen her outstretched leg across her path. Alex tripped and fell to the ground. Before she could rise, Kat's blade was digging into her left loin. It was over, Kat was victorious again.

Boo's turned to cheers, and flowers cascaded into the ring.

Kat was the champion of the crowd, and they were willing her on for one more victory. The Aesir loved Carmel, but they loved an underdog even more.

With great difficulty, Freyja attempted to calm the arena for the final contest.

It would be Carmel against Kat.

The victor would be crowned the next Valkyrie warrior.

Tensions were mounting, bets were finalised, and eventually the contest got under way.

Carmel and Kat embraced.

They were friends as well as sisters, and as they finished hugging they wished each other luck. Carmel felt confident of victory, but Kat was a surprise. Long ago she had had an inkling that Kat might be a contender, and she prayed to Odin that she wouldn't now be her undoing. She desperately wanted to become a warrior, and anything less than victory was unimaginable.

The horn blew and they returned to their weapons.

Kat checked the position of the sun. *Good.* It was just after midday and shining fiercely from behind her.

Her plan to defeat Carmel was part skill and part luck. It was based on a trick she had taught herself many years ago as a child in Midgard. She had used it to win snowball fights, and now something infinitely more important was at stake. She looked toward the stand and prayed to Odin for success. She had one chance, a single toss of the coin to win. It would all boil down to one simple gamble.

Left or right?

Reaching their weapons, both girls turned and eyed each other.

To Carmel's surprise, Kat picked up not one, but two spears. She held one in each hand. Carmel responded by picking up her shield and a single spear. She watched carefully as Kat began a run forward, then with a long, arcing movement, Kat launched a spear high into the air. It twisted and vibrated as it soared gracefully upwards; spinning with the force of her throw and the rifling she had given it. Higher and higher it climbed and then, after reaching its zenith, it began to descend; picking up speed as it hurtled toward the ground.

The throw was on target, and dropping like a stone toward Carmel.

Carmel followed its leisurely progress.

Its slow arc was easy to avoid, but the sun was behind it, making it difficult to see. Screwing her eyes up, she concentrated hard on its movement, preparing to raise her shield and dodge its impending impact.

Kat tossed the other spear from her left hand to her throwing hand, and then paused.

This was it.

This was where luck came into play.

Would Carmel move to the left or to the right to avoid her first spear?

Choose correctly and she would win, choose incorrectly and victory belonged to Carmel.

Kat made her decision, and while Carmel and the crowd watched the falling spear, she hurled her second missile. She aimed this one slightly to Carmel's right. This was the plan; both spears arriving at the same time, but in two slightly different places.

The first spear was a distraction, the decoy. The second was the killer missile. It was a knock out blow, and one that was now hurtling horizontally across the arena toward an empty space.

Carmel moved.

Dodging to the right, she stepped into the path of the second lethal spear.

Raising her shield, the first spear glanced harmlessly off it, burying itself into the sand beside her. The second arrived dead on target, exploding angrily on her chest.

Carmel fell to the floor winded.

The contest was over.

Kat was victorious.

The crowd were on their feet, rapturous applause erupting from every corner of the arena. Never had they witnessed so great an upset and they screamed their admiration until their lungs felt fit to burst.

Odin presented her with the silver crown of a warrior and still dazed by her victory, Kat turned and faced the ecstatic throng. Jess pushed her way through the jubilant revellers. She didn't care about protocol or etiquette. Arriving beside Kat she hugged and kissed her triumphantly. Flush with success, she couldn't have asked for a better end.

Kat was no longer her maid; she was now her sister warrior.

Kat was the next Valkyrie.

64

Consequences

As the celebrating came slowly and reluctantly to its end, Loki watched the crowds as they drifted noisily from the arena. It had been a remarkable tournament, and he was anxious now to comfort Carmel.

Kat's victory had been extraordinary, and he saluted her for her courage and her tenacity. Brains had once again triumphed over brawn. He turned and made his way toward the castle, desperately searching ahead for Carmel. Arriving in the courtyard, he finally spotted her, and hurrying over, he put his arm around her shoulders.

She shrugged him away.

Angry and humiliated, she couldn't face anyone just yet.

Without saying a word, Carmel made her way to the stables and saddled her horse. She needed to get away, to be alone with her thoughts.

Loki watched her departure, and felt her pain in his heart. He couldn't begrudge Kat her victory, but he had sworn to avenge defeat if Carmel lost.

That had been a promise, and Loki didn't break his word.

With a determined look on his face, he stormed irritably inside the castle.

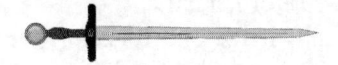

The evening after the tournament passed quickly for Kat. It was a confused blur of well wishers, all hugging and squeezing her at once.

One surprise well wisher however, was especially welcome. It was Freyr, and he eagerly congratulated her on her success. Handsome as ever, as he reached forward with his embrace, Kat whispered impulsively in his ear.

She couldn't help herself.

Freyr smiled, and then nodded with a mischievous twinkle in his eye.

It would have taken a keen observer to see the slight movement of his hand over his ring, or to notice Kat's ruffled hair and contented look an instant later. Freyr was an irresistible friend, an object of desire, and she had requested a much more intimate and exclusive congratulation from him. She enjoyed this once again in the privacy of Odin's timeless garden.

Only her satisfied smile now betrayed how pleasurable this had been.

To everyone's great delight, Jameela's hero, Ben, had improved sufficiently to join them at the celebrations. He sat with Odin, Thor, Freyja, Jameela, Jess, and Kat at the head table. Kat was grateful for his presence, she wasn't used to being the centre of attention and she welcomed his share of her limelight. Ben still looked bewildered, but she knew this would soon pass. It was a shame that he had to leave for Valhalla, but that was his destiny. Someday it would be hers, too.

After praising her victory, and offering his heartfelt congratulations, Odin invited Kat to join him in his citadel tomorrow at noon. She would receive her Valkyrie name there, and afterward she would become a true warrior. This would take place in a secret ceremony in the Chamber of the Valkyries. For this to happen, he explained, she must bathe in Mimir's Well.

This prospect filled Kat with dread.

She wasn't a great swimmer, and the thought of being thrown down a well didn't sound exactly pleasant. She asked the other girls what exactly Odin had meant by this, but none would give her a straight answer. In true Valkyrie fashion, they reassured her that it was painless and no one had ever drowned. Other than that, she would just have to wait and find out for herself.

Relieved by this knowledge and relaxed by Freyr's love making, she gradually submerged into the heady atmosphere of the raucous celebrations.

Hod wasn't sitting at the table with Odin, and he left the celebrations early. He felt ignored and frustrated. Having congratulated Kat, he had intended to spend some time with her on his own. Unfortunately, this hadn't happened. Kat wasn't being unkind or deliberately cold, she just hadn't understood his need to play a bigger part in her celebrations. He was proud of her success and had been eager to share in her triumph.

Feeling ignored and deflated, he headed dejectedly to his bed.

For her part, Kat could see that Hod was upset, but there was little she could do. Everyone wanted to be with her and all at the same time. Snubbing Hod wasn't her intention, but he did take things too personally. Still, she decided; if she didn't get too drunk, she would pop into his room later and see if she could make it up to him.

Kat hated to see him sulk, but tonight was her night, and she was determined to enjoy it.

Ruby left the celebrations early, too.

Putting on her leather tunic and taking her whip in her hand she rounded up six slaves and made her way down to her arena. She told them it was time to give Cole his first whipping and that this would be a private affair. Her decision caught the slaves off guard. They too had been enjoying the festivities, and resented being asked to work at such a late hour. They looked perplexed, but no one dared question the mighty Prudr.

Hurrying to do as she bid, they dragged Cole up from the dungeons beneath the arena and tied him tightly between the whipping posts. To their surprise, after securing Cole in place, Ruby dismissed them all.

Private meant private, and she wanted to be alone with him tonight.

Just her, Cole, and her whip.

Ruby left the celebrations early, too.

Putting on her leather tunic, and taking her whip in her hand she headed down toward her arena. As she walked, she noticed the startled expressions on the faces of the group of slaves as they made their way toward her. They looked terrified, like they had seen a ghost, so she demanded an explanation. Not daring to speak, they fell to their knees blubbering incoherently, shielding their faces from her angry glare.

Growing impatient with their delay, Ruby grabbed one by the scruff of his neck and forced an explanation. As he told to her about the whipping, her eyes widened with horror. She guessed at once who her bogus twin was. Demanding two slaves hurry after her, Ruby raced down to her arena.

She was too late—but only by seconds.

The ropes that had bound Cole were still swinging, and there was still some hope yet. Rushing into the dungeon below, they searched frantically in the catacombs. Cole's cell was empty; there wasn't trace of him anywhere.

Cole was gone.

Furiously, she threw her whip down on a wooden table. Loki had taken Cole, she was certain of that. Only he would have the nerve to shape shift and make such mischief.

Ruby was baffled.

Why had he done it? What was the point?

Looking around she spotted Slim cowering in his cell. He had been pathetically useless in the arena earlier today, and she dearly longed to flog the wretch. This would release her pent up anger quite nicely.

"Did you see where they went?" she shouted tersely.

Slim looked up nervously. He expected the worst; Ruby had no time for failure. He had seen Cole earlier, but they hadn't spoken, and Cole hadn't returned after being taken from his cell. Slim shook his head, not daring to speak up.

Prisoners were forbidden to look at the warriors, let alone talk to them.

"Hmmm, I thought not," Ruby retorted crossly. She was sick of the sight of Slim; his face reminded her of Cole. He was a broken, useless prisoner and had been an embarrassment in the arena today. She had a reputation and standards to maintain, and he had tarnished both of these. It was time for him to go, but unfortunately she was too busy to attend to this herself tonight. She had to inform Odin of the disappearance of Cole, and he definitely wouldn't be pleased.

Snapping her fingers at two attendant slaves, she issued her instructions.

"You take him outside and whip him hard." Pointing in Slim's direction, she hurled her whip at one of the slaves.

"And you," she picked up a long curved knife from the table and tossed it toward the second slave. Jumping nervously sideways, he let it fall clattering to the floor.

"When he's finished, I'm sure you'll remember what to do with this." She gestured with a slicing motion toward his groin, reminding him of his loss.

The two slaves looked at each other; both shocked with this sudden responsibility.

Ruby strode toward the exit, and then paused. She had a final, stern warning for Slim.

"I don't want you giving my slaves any trouble, do you hear?" her voice echoed with a chilling menace as she glared angrily at him.

This was a demand, not a request.

Slim nodded meekly; his fate had been sealed long ago. Slavery at least would bring an end to her ruthless whippings, and he prayed the two slaves would make his misfortune as quick and painless as possible.

It was in the early hours of the morning when Kat finally left the celebrations and made her way dizzily upstairs. She desperately wanted to share the rest of her victory night with Jess, but she knew she had to see Hod. She felt more than a little pickled, but she remembered enough about the evening to know that he was upset, and she had to make things up.

Entering the room, he confirmed her worst suspicions.

"Hod?" she whispered coarsely but there was no reply.

He was pretending to be asleep.

"Are you all right?" she drew closer.

"Yes of course, I'm just tired so go away." He snapped grumpily.

"Oh come on Hod, don't be like that, please." Stumbling tipsily out of her clothes, she climbed noisily between the sheets and cuddled up next to him; giggling inanely.

She was hammered, and she knew it.

"Look I'm tired so go away. Why don't you go and fool around with some other doting fan," he added crossly as he tried to wriggle from her grasp.

"I'm sorry. I wasn't deliberately ignoring you," Kat tried to apologise as she followed him across the bed. Pulling him close to her once more, she let her hand slide down his chest, massaging him as it moved. Drunkenly, she slid it further, teasing provocatively at his manhood.

"You don't have to do that you know," he pulled her hand away crossly, and turned his back to her once more.

"Look!" Kat exclaimed loudly, turning him roughly over. Trying to take aim, she slapped him clumsily across his face. It wasn't a hard blow, but it was hard enough to shock some sense into him. "Stop being such a silly, little boy. I'm here because I want to. So come on, just relax and be nice."

Hod sighed before propped himself up on his elbows. Stretching out with a hand, he found and then lovingly stroked Kat's face.

She was right, he was being stupid.

"I'm sorry; I guess I'm just being a selfish idiot," he apologised.

Gingerly removing her hand from between his legs, he gently held it in his. He wanted her so badly and yet he still feared her wrath. Kat was teasing his desire. Her hand promised so much, but he didn't dare judge it wrong.

He'd been down that road before and the bitter memory seared his soul.

"I'm so proud of your success," he began. "I just wanted to spend more time with you tonight. Please, allow me to honour you, my way of saying sorry and to celebrate your victory."

Kissing her tenderly, he let his caresses roam seductively down her neck. He was going to play it safe, let Kat's actions decide his fate. He loved her with all his heart and he begged her silently for this chance.

Cautiously, Hod let his lips nibble further down her body.

Kat felt the warmth of his kisses, and gasped eagerly at their gentle touch. Clasping his head with her hand, she tried to slow their stealthy progress. Urgently she tried to rein in her addled senses.

She mustn't hurt Hod, but how could she stop this tender advance?

Kat struggled desperately with her dilemma.

There was a triangle in her life now; Jess, Freyr—and Hod.

Kat recalled making love with Freyr. He was a wonderful temptation, his strength bursting inside her, filling her so wonderfully with his warmth. He was an itch she couldn't refuse to scratch. They would continue to share moments together, but that was all they could ever be—just moments.

Freyr was perfection, but he could never truly be hers.

His was the blood lust, not love from her heart.

Her thoughts then turned to Jess. She really did love Jess. She was her best friend, her true friend, and now she was her sister. Theirs was a love so different from that between a woman and a man that it was simply beyond compare.

So where did that leave Hod?
To be truthful, she didn't know.

She wasn't in love, but she had feelings and cared deeply for him. Their friendship was a gentle warmness and she wanted this to continue and maybe grow. She wasn't ready to take his strength yet, but equally she wasn't prepared to cause him more pain. He had suffered so much and for this she felt largely to blame.

Feeling Hod's eagerness rising, she could deny him no more. She would let him honour her with his lips, but that would be all. Perhaps even that kindness might be foolish, but alcohol had sautéed her brain and her resistance was ebbing fast.

Kat's emotions were a mess, but she couldn't destroy his fragile confidence, not after her hand's fickle tease. Hod yearned for her love and to reject him now would be unconscionable.

She had given him false hope—and that had been her drunken mistake.

Gently releasing her grip, Kat allowed Hod's sweet caresses to satisfy their desire.

65

Little Green Men

"Dr. Unadkat this is Detective Finch, Finch, this is Dr. Unadkat."

Finished with his introductions, Woods let the two men shake hands and then they all sat down. Nyran was the first speak.

"Do please call me Dr. Nyran, most of my friends do."

Marcus sat back and took stock of their surreal situation. You could not have found a more extreme antithesis of your Taliban fighter than the man who was sitting opposite him.

Dr. Nyran.

Here they all were, sitting in Agent Woods office in FBI headquarters, barely a stone's throw from the White House; but was this 'Dangerous' terrorist wearing an orange boiler suit? Could you hear the clank of manacles and chains securely binding him hand and foot?

No sir, you could not.

The relaxed, Indian gentleman was casually dressed in a blue and white-striped shirt, with jeans and a navy blazer. He was clean shaven, and spoke with a manicured English accent. He looked completely normal, and the only things that made this meeting look anything out of the ordinary were the American citizenship papers and a carefully wrapped bundle on the table. Marcus was desperate for this latter item to be opened, but he was too polite to ask Woods to do that now.

He knew it contained the Valkyrie knife, but he didn't want to sound like an excited four-year-old on Christmas Day.

"So, Dr. Unadkat, what exactly is it that you wish to tell me that makes you think I'll grant you citizenship?"

True to form, Woods spoke formally to Nyran, and cut straight to the chase.

Nyran looked around him in a conspiratorial manner, and Marcus chuckled. Of course the room was bugged and others could be listening. However, if Dr. Nyran thought the microphones would be visible, or have little placards announcing their locations, he would be disappointed.

"I assume you want to tell me about the American hostage. Jameela Masood?"

It was Woods again, encouraging Nyran to get on with his story.

"Yes, of course. But that isn't her real name."

"If you're going to tell me that she calls herself the Valkyrie Herja, then I already know this and you're wasting my valuable time." Woods interrupted Dr. Nyran. He was as eager as Marcus to hear what he had to say, and wanted the doctor to get to the point.

"Well," Nyran cleared his throat, and leant forward lowering his voice. "Do you know if your government has a Cyborg program?"

Woods looked blankly at the man, confused by this bizarre question.

"Because if they haven't, then you're all in trouble. Jameela Masood, the Valkyrie Herja, she's a CYBORG!" he stressed the last word as he sat back triumphantly.

This was his bombshell; a revelation so outrageous that not only would he get his citizenship, it would bring him fortune beyond his wildest dreams.

Woods looked at Marcus, then at Dr. Nyran, and began to laugh.

"I have always thought of doctors as sensible people, but if you're trying to tell me that the girl was some kind of a robot, then you are a complete and utter lunatic!"

Nyran began to fidget nervously in his seat. He hadn't expected this response.

"Okay, okay. So tell me, how else can you explain why she didn't have a pulse, and carried on fighting after being shot six times in the chest?"

These were Nyran's aces and he decided to come out fighting. He exaggerated a little on the number of bullets, but that didn't really matter. He wasn't a fool, and he expected them to treat what he said with a little respect.

He was a friggin' doctor for God's sake!

Woods laughed louder.

"My dear doctor, I can explain those things so easily it is hardly worth wasting my breath on them." Abruptly Woods mood changed, and he banged both fists down hard on the table before leaning forward on them. "Body armour and the fact that you are one seriously fucked up and useless doctor!"

Woods spat the last words angrily, defying Nyran to challenge his accusation.

"I do not believe in ghosts, fairies, elves, hob-goblins, vampires, zombies, aliens or, or—" Woods stalled, he was running out of ideas now, "or little green men from Mars for that matter."

This time it was Marcus's turn to laugh.

The situation was a bit farcical really.

Dr. Nyran couldn't seriously expect them to believe that the girl was some sort of superhuman robot that couldn't be killed, surely? That might be fine if Nyran wanted to make a movie, but not if he was serious about gaining his freedom from the FBI. He would have to come up with something a lot more credible than that.

"I don't care what you say, I saw what I saw. The girl wasn't wearing any sort of body armour, and she was walking around without a pulse. I don't care if you don't believe me. Others will." Nyran was on his feet now and shouting defiantly.

How dare this Agent question his integrity?

"All right, all right, Jeez, just settle down." Woods motioned for Nyran to sit as he pressed a buzzer on the table. He requested a guard to take him back to a holding room. They would talk again later, but for now he wanted to discuss more sensible things with Marcus; important things like the bundle on the table.

As Nyran was escorted from the room, Woods sighed with resignation. He knew that he would have to take his threat seriously, the little promise that others might believe his story. This was a very stupid thing for him to have said, given the extraordinary circumstances around this affair. Woods couldn't afford to have some loose cannon wandering the streets, spilling the Valkyrie story to the gutter press. They would lap it up, and the warriors might disappear.

Poor Dr. Nyran.

The fool had just booked himself a ticket to Guantanamo bay, or wherever the authorities rendered undesirables these days. His fate was sealed as surely as though he were dead. He would be buried in a timeless tomb, one that was covered in reams of paperwork and with endless, covert transfers as its headstone.

"Would you like to see the knife?"

Woods snapped out of his deliberations and began to undo the bundle on the table. He indicated for Marcus to pick it up.

Shit!

Marcus marvelled at the blade as he clasped it in his hands. It felt so light and so well balanced, and had the same exquisite swan-shaped handle as Jess's had. Squinting hard, he stared at its hilt. He was searching for the spot; the one Jess had shown him so many weeks ago.

Sure enough, there it was—the name 'Herja.'

"It's definitely a Valkyrie blade, no doubt about that."

Reluctantly he handed the beautiful knife back to Woods, who promptly wrapped it up once more.

"What do you really think about what Dr. Nyran said?" Marcus enquired curiously. The doctor had seemed so upset when they scoffed at his revelation. He sounded sincere, and obviously had acquired a good education to speak such perfect English. He must be a competent doctor, so why make up such a crazy tale?

"I don't know. Terrorists say the strangest of things if it means they'll go free." Woods paused, reflectively. "Surely you don't believe the rubbish he was saying, do you, hey Finch?"

"No, no, of course not." Marcus spluttered awkwardly.

He couldn't have Woods thinking he was a nutter and besides; who on earth would believe such crazy talk?

"Good. For a moment there you had me worried."

Woods sat back and stared intently at Marcus.

His spot of theatre had worked; the detective had bought his angry outburst.

Finch was a pragmatist, just as Woods had once been. All this talk of pulseless zombies and robo-warriors was bullshit to the man. The detective was a realist, a down-to-earth sceptic, and that suited Woods fine.

For the moment, the shocking truth behind the Valkyries was safe—and that would please the Contessa. Too much knowledge, or suspicious probing could put Marcus's life at risk, and Woods didn't need that inconvenience right now. The detective might be useful; an unwitting and ignorant ally in their quest.

Woods decided to put this to the test; keep Finch in the loop, close by, where he could keep a watchful eye on him.

"There's one good thing we have to remember," Woods began, breaking into a broad grin.

"We have one of their knives."

Marcus nodded, thoughtfully.

"Now the Valkyries will have to come to us," Woods paused dramatically as he pressed a finger pointedly into the table.

"And this time we'll be waiting."

66

What's in a Name?

*I*t wasn't long after noon and Kat found herself standing outside the black door at the bottom of Odin's citadel. She was nursing a king-sized hangover and feeling somewhat worse for wear.

What had she been thinking of?

Kat shook her head in disbelief. Thoughts of Freyr—and Hod—swam crazily in her head. The blood lust, guilt, and too much alcohol last night had played havoc with her mind. She cursed herself angrily for her stupidity. Her relationship with Hod was now sullied by this madness.

She wanted friendship while he yearned for love.

Sweet Odin! What a mess.

It was going to be a pig to sort out, and she really didn't want to hurt Odin's son yet again.

Nervously, she glanced at the two wolves beside her.

As usual, one of them was awake and he was eyeing her lazily as he panted in the hot midday sun. Although Kat knew them now both quite well, she wasn't sure if it was Freki or Geri who was up. Either way it didn't matter, she still felt uneasy. Being so close to such powerful and unpredictable beasts unsettled her. She thanked Odin that she was his guest and hoped he would open the door soon.

Odin knew Kat was waiting, and he was almost as eager as she was to find out her Valkyrie name. He just needed a moment to collect his thoughts.

It had been a busy morning.

Herja had been the first warrior he had seen and he had congratulated her warmly on her success. She had brought an excellent hero back from Midgard and his appreciation was sincere. Ben would make a great addition to his army.

Finding true heroes was getting so much harder these days.

Wars in Midgard were now technology-led, with less opportunity for soldiers to showcase their bravery. "Lowering the body count" was the buzz phrase, with generals taking fewer risks with soldiers' lives. This might be great for them, but not so good when you were cherry picking a fearless host.

Herja had come to the citadel with a heartfelt request for Odin, but unfortunately, he had had to turn this down. She was desperate to go to Valhalla with Ben, but he needed her for one last mission.

She had to recover her knife.

This had been left behind and although he understood the reasons for this faux pas, she would still have to go back and get it.

That could be a challenge.

He already knew of its whereabouts, but he didn't relish coming up against Midgard intelligence officers again so soon. They already knew too much, and were getting cleverer by the minute. Prudr and Brynhildr had had a lucky escape, and Herja might not be so fortunate.

Still, she would have to try—it was her duty to retrieve it.

After Herja had left, Odin invited Prudr to his chamber.

When she arrived, he could see that she was nervous, terrified as to his reaction about Cole. To his great surprise—and her greater relief—he was a lot calmer than anticipated.

They both knew that Loki had taken Cole and that a search party was a waste of time. This would only get tongues wagging and damage confidence in his Valkyries. Besides; they knew it would find nothing. Both of them were certain as to where Loki had taken Cole, and Odin was equally certain that he'd be back.

Unlike Prudr, Odin had a shrewd idea as to why Cole had been kidnapped.

Loki was curious about Cole's role in Ragnarok; but that was probably a secondary issue. The most important reason behind Cole's theft was Loki's notion to use him as a bargaining chip.

Loki would offer him a swap.

Cole for Fenrir.

The opportunity to make such a trade would be just too tempting to resist.

Odin smiled wickedly at this thought.

Loki might be a clever trickster, but he'd miscalculated badly on this stunt. Getting Cole away from Midgard had been Odin's sole goal. This was where he expected Ragnarok to begin. As Loki couldn't get Cole there, Cole couldn't make trouble which was exactly what Odin wanted. In a decidedly quirky sort of way, Loki had actually helped him in this matter.

Perhaps he should thank him when they met?

Feeling smug with this jest, Odin turned his attention to fair Kat.

She really was a surprise package, and her victory at the tournament had caused quite a stir. She was clever, resourceful, and resilient, and he had watched her gaining in strength and confidence with some admiration. He had a feeling that she would make a great Valkyrie, possibly one of his finest—thanks to the mead.

This was working its customary ghoulish nightmare; strengthening her body while wreaking havoc with her mind.

The mead gave his Valkyries their powerful blood lust, and numbed memories of their former lives. Its formulation was a secret, known only to a few; and its addictive power was extreme. This bound his warriors tightly while remaining oblivious of his control.

With this thought in mind, Odin waved his hand over his ring and summoned Kat up.

Shooting up to the Citadel, Kat very nearly threw up. The intense roller coaster effect as she whooshed up to the chamber was truly unpleasant, and one she would struggle to get used to.

As her bilious heaving subsided, she made her way gingerly over to the semi-circle of chairs before his throne.

Odin's citadel really was a wonderful room, bright and cheery with long, arched, sunlit windows. She had already spotted the two bodns in a corner, the ones filled with Kvasir's blood; but it was a cluster of telescopes that caught her serious attention.

As a child she had loved astronomy, and her greatest dream was to get a telescope as a present. Eventually she got her wish, but nothing as grand as the ones she now saw. They were all different shapes and sizes, collected by Odin over the centuries. Her favourite was a shiny new Schmidt-Cassegrain model, probably two hundred millimetres in diameter. *Wow!* What she wouldn't give for a little play with that.

"Do you like them?"

Odin interrupted her daydream. He had followed her eyes as they wandered around the room and he was delighted with her interest.

"This one is a beauty. There have always been incredible craftsmen on Midgard. Come on, come and have a look."

Kat hurried over, and for the next fifteen minutes they discussed the various merits of catadioptric telescopes, Barlow lenses, and other highly technical details. It was only with some reluctance that the pair dragged themselves back to the task in hand. They had a lot in common, and like so many others in Asgard, Odin found himself drawn to Kat's enthusiasm and seductive personality.

She was a true diamond, of that there was no doubt.

"Would you like to meet Mimir?" he asked abruptly and unexpectedly.

"I thought you had said he was dead?" Kat replied with another question. She was certain Odin had said he was dead. That was why he didn't know the full details of the prophesies.

"No what I said was he was in a very sorry state, not that he was dead. Anyway, as he's going to tell us your Valkyrie name, you really ought to say hello."

"Yes of course, that would be lovely. Um, by the way, where is he?"

Kat looked around.

Apart from Odin and herself, the room appeared empty and there weren't any doors.

Maybe they were going to disappear to his garden or somewhere equally exotic?

During breakfast that morning, Kat had asked the other warriors how her name would be chosen. It was a mystery and as usual, they hadn't spoilt its surprise. Without giving the game away, their cryptic clues had been "Don't be scared," and "He won't bite."

As far as she could tell, looking around her there was nothing remotely scary or vicious in the room.

"Ah, now, well, that's the thing."

Odin stepped forward and whispered quietly in her ear.

"Before I introduce you, you must promise me two things. Don't scream and don't be afraid. It really does upset him when people make loud noises; he has very sensitive hearing."

Kat nodded that she would do as he had suggested as he led her back toward his throne. For the first time she noticed the beautifully crafted casket that lay beside it. She was surprised she hadn't spotted this sooner. Apart from its generous size and beauty, a sickly sweet smell wafted from it. This was an odour that reminded her a bit of roast pork, honey, and rotting fruit. The scent was quite pungent, not particularly unpleasant, but definitely most unusual.

Odin indicated for her to open the cask, and she did so without really thinking. Maybe that was a good thing, because the sight that greeted her caused her to jump out of her skin.

There, sitting on a bed of soothing herbs and spices—was a head.

It was Mimir, or all that was left of him.

A thick, greasy mane of long, matted hair flowed down around his face, which had a horrible, grey waxy mask of death. The eyes were shut and sunken, and the lips cracked and faded to a ghastly bluish-black colour.

Mimir was dead all right, practically mummified.

What on earth was Odin doing with his head?

Odin saw her shock and put his finger to his lips. Luckily she hadn't screamed; but quite how she didn't know.

Odin pulled her forward and whispered once more in her ear. "Please, put your hand on Mimir's forehead and introduce yourself. This really is very important; we don't want him to think you're rude."

After giving Odin the funniest of looks, Kat gulped, and then nervously extended her hand. It was sweating and shaking, and she tried to calm herself as she dabbed her fingertips briefly on the skull.

It was cold and dry.

Kat felt like being sick.

"Um, greetings, er, Mimir. I, I, I'm Kat," she looked at Odin, and gratefully saw he was pretending to clap while mouthing "Bravo" for her to continue.

Relaxing just a little, Kat turned and smiled at the skull.

SWEET ODIN!

To her horror and amazement, she thought the eyelids fluttered.

Oh dear god of gods have mercy!

There they went again!

Mimir had opened his eyes and was trying to say something. His head was alive—and was trying to talk to her.

"He's telling you your Valkyrie name, go on, listen closer." Odin hissed instructions as he urged her to move closer. He could see that she was shocked, but they had to learn her name. He motioned frantically with his hands, she really had to get much closer.

Luckily Kat did so, although she now felt somewhat faint.

"Sss, Sssan, Ssang…"

Mimir's voice was quiet and rasping, hissing like a wounded snake. She couldn't make her name out.

"I'm so sorry, please could you repeat that?"

Curiosity was getting the better of her and she leant nearer to Mimir.

"Sss, Ssan, SANGRID!"

The effort of forcing the word from his mouth clearly exhausted Mimir, and his eyes and mouth closed.

He wouldn't speak to her again.

"Sangrid. I think that's what he said," Kat turned round smiling, relieved that the ordeal was now over.

"But that's impossible!" Odin exclaimed loudly as he began to turn pale. Pushing Kat hurriedly to one side, he asked Mimir the same question.

Kat heard his reply.

Her Valkyrie name was definitely Sangrid, and to be honest, she quite liked it.

Odin closed the cask and then slumped dismally into his throne. He couldn't look at Kat, he didn't dare. He was too overcome by shock to risk showing her his distress.

"Sangrid sounds like a pretty name, don't you think?"

Kat tried to chivvy him. She was growing alarmed by his look and knew something wasn't right.

"Look, if you don't like it, perhaps Mimir could choose another one?"

She tried to crack a joke, but it came out forced and rather nervous. Her attempt at a bit of humour hadn't help, nor did it lighten the deadly mood that had descended upon the citadel.

Finally, after several minutes of silence, Odin stood up and took her hand in his. He had to say something and he really had no alternative.

He had to tell her the truth.

"My dearest Kat, we cannot choose another name because this name is your destiny. It cannot be undone and it certainly isn't your fault. You cannot blame yourself for deeds that are yet to come."

Kat stared at Odin, eyes opened wide with alarm.

She didn't like what she was hearing.

"I'm afraid my fair Kat; you are now the Valkyrie Sangrid. Your name foretells great cruelty and warns of treachery for your friends. Your destiny is to destroy worlds," he paused, before choosing his final words carefully.

"You will take arms with your cursed sister and defy me at Ragnarok."

67
Niflheim

"**N**o problem."

These words had been drifting in and out of Cole's head ever since he had lost consciousness in his Miami suite.

He knew his throat had been cut, and he knew that he was dying. That was life—or death—as the case may be, and it sucked—but such was his lot.

Cole was an atheist. He didn't believe in heaven or the other more unpleasant place. When you were dead, you were dead—lights out, no more tomorrows and, of course, goodbye to Cole.

This thought gave him solace as he struggled to cope with his constantly changing hallucinations. Lying in a freshly harvested field of corn, being chased by rabid dogs, a dank prison cell, seeing Slim's ghost, and now this. All were figments of his imagination, vivid dreams spun by his dying brain; oxygen-starved nerves, desperately screaming "SOS" in a frantic and chaotic struggle to stay alive. Admittedly, this had been going on for quite some time now, but as in any dream, minutes can feel like hours. What was going on around him was a meaningless, jumbled mess; and one that would eventually fade. Soon he would see that wonderful white light, the one at the end of the tunnel, the one that would take him to oblivion.

All this craziness en route to his annihilation really was—"No problem."

Still, looking around him, he liked his current hallucination better than the others. At least he wasn't about to be whipped.

He decided to take his time and study this place in greater detail. After all, it might be his final thoughts before the white light snuffed out his existence.

Having been 'rescued' by Loki, the man who was anxiously pacing the floor opposite him, he was now sitting in a quiet room. Although this was well lit, the room felt extremely dark.

He put this down to its décor.

The panelled walls, ornately carved ceiling, and the overly large furniture were all made from oak. This had been deeply stained to a darkest shade of black. The ceiling was low and the room was too hot, with a stuffy atmosphere that was densely fragranced with a heavy and aromatic aroma.

The room was quite large—but it felt claustrophic and small.

Cole didn't have to look far to discover where the fragrant odour was coming from. He was sitting on a well upholstered chair at a dining table in the centre of the room. On this sat two ornate golden candelabras festooned with scarlet candles that burned brightly. Between these, and dominating the whole area, was an elaborate floural display.

This was literally breath-taking, not only from its heavy scent but also by its extraordinary appearance.

The bouquet was the strangest Cole had ever seen.

The flowers looked like poppies but had shiny black petals; and the centre of each flower was a brilliant scarlet in colour. This contrasted nicely with the black petals, stems, and leaves; and complimented the burgundy of the lush carpet, leather upholstery, and crushed velvet drapes that hung around a single, small, leaded window at the other end of the room.

Overall the effect was most unusual. The garish palette of bright reds, polished gold and richly stained blacks gave the room a Gothic feel that an aesthete might find pleasing.

Unfortunately, its oppressive elegance was wasted on Cole, but the room seemed like a decent enough place for his final delusion to run its course.

"Hello father, how lovely to see you."

Loki strode purposefully over toward a low door that had suddenly opened. Through this stepped a woman, one of the most beautiful Cole had ever seen. She floated effortlessly into the room, air-kissing the man as he hugged her tightly against him.

"Is this a present for me?" she pointed, smiling excitedly in his direction.

Loki motioned for Cole to stand up and for some strange reason he did so, grateful now that he'd been given a linen cloth to wrap around his groin.

Cole had been growing tired of his constant nudity in these hallucinations.

The gorgeous, white cutie strode briskly round the table. She was one fine looking woman, a girl actually, in her late teens or early twenties. Pert arsed and fresh-faced; she was dressed in a black, figure-hugging, sleeveless cat suit, her luxuriant black hair cascading down to below her shapely bosom. Her face reminded him of a rising starlet, the one in some film about robots changing into cars—or was that the other way round? Either way it didn't matter, she was one serious hottie; large, bright green eyes, lush, ruby lips and thick, long fluttering eyelashes.

Fuck! What a babe.

The girl started to examine him, walking slowly around his body and squeezing his strong biceps. She drew her long red nails down his back, and he jerked involuntary at the tingles these sent rippling down his spine. Standing before him once more, she ran her hand temptingly down his stomach before placing it firmly on his groin.

Squeezing hard, she took his masculinity viciously in her grip.

"Oh my!" The girl exclaimed with a little pur of satisfaction. "You really are spoiling me father. He'll make a BIG addition to my collection."

Cole groaned and began to double up. A mixture of pain and ecstasy swirling deliciously in his head.

Shit!

He hoped this part of his delusion would last long enough for him to nail the fucking bitch.

Moving closer, she released her grasp on his testicles before squeezed his cheeks between her fingers. Loki's daughter looked closely into his eyes.

"Does he speak?" She enquired irritably, glancing in annoyance at her father.

SMACK!

Cole didn't get a chance to reply.

He'd been hit by a hammer, his whole face smashed sideways by the force of her blow. The girl had struck him so fast he hadn't seen the slap coming and trickles of blood now dripped down his face.

The bitch had scrammed him—the fucking ho!

Cole shook his head; he was getting pissed off and seeing stars.

"Daddy, is he some kind of a retard?" the girl enquired crossly.

"No darling of course he isn't. Just be patient, he's still in a bit of a daze. I'm afraid he's taking time adjusting to his new surroundings."

"Yeah doll, just go easy on me," Cole moaned, shocked into speaking by the force of her hand. Ruby had punched him hard in their fight, but this girl was in a different league.

The bitch hit like a man—only harder.

"Oh, I'm so sorry," she mocked. "Here, let me make it all better."

Pressing her body against his, the girl ran the back of her hand up his cheek, collecting the blood that was now flowing more freely from her scratches. She licked it provocatively from her fingers, and instinctively Cole grabbed her behind, pulling her groin toward him and grinding it salaciously against his own.

He was going to fuck her right now.

"Hey, go easy tiger! Now, let me clean this up for you."

The girl reached over to the table and plucked a flower from the display. She held it under his nose.

"Go on breath in, nice and deep," she purred enticingly.

Cole did as she said and the pain subsided. His cheek was healing almost as fast as he was breathing in.

The girl laughed.

"You see Daddy, anything Odin's mead can do, I can do sooo much better." She paused, before tracing her finger along the line of the gash in his neck.

"Ouch! Did that nasty Prudr do this to you?" she enquired teasingly as she looked toward her father.

Loki nodded.

"Oooh, how vicious! I'll make that better too if you like."

Instinctively, Cole inhaled more of the fragrant poppy and the line of blood on his slit throat shrank a little further. Whatever was in that flower, it made one mother of a tonic.

"This is Cole," Loki began with a smile; deciding to introduce his daughter to her shiny new toy.

"According to Mimir's prophesies, he's the man from Midgard who'll bring his fire to Asgard. This is the one who's going to start Ragnarok."

Loki's daughter's eyes widened dramatically, and squealing loudly with delight, she ran across the room and flung herself into her father's arms. She held him tightly. To have Odin's nemesis, here, with her in Niflheim, was a present beyond compare.

Releasing her father, the girl scurried back toward Cole. She ran her hands across his body with renewed interest and vigour.

Cole chuckled.

His brain was playing weird tricks—but they were fun.

Whatever the man had said had had the desired effect. He was a celebrity now—and at least that should get him laid.

"So," The girl began, moving seductively away from Cole as she offered her hand for him to follow.

"Would you like to see your new home?"

Swinging her hips provocatively, she sashayed toward the window pulling Cole along behind.

"Oh yes, you're going to like this," Loki enthused as he followed them over to the opening.

"The realm of Niflheim is really quite spectacular."

Cole rubbed his eyes carefully before pressed his face against the window and looking out. The small, leaded panes of glass felt hot, almost unbearably so, against his cheek.

"Oh daddy, you're so old fashioned. Why don't you call it by its proper name?" the girl teased. "This is my realm and Niflheim sounds so yesterday. Besides, my name suits this kingdom so much better, don't you think?"

Loki didn't reply as he smiled knowingly to himself. Arrogant and pushy, she was every bit his daughter.

Trust 'The Black Valkyrie' to rename Niflheim after herself.

Loki's daughter linked her arm around Cole's, before pressing her face eagerly next to his.

"Do you like it? I hope you do, because this is your new home. This is where you'll be staying for all eternity."

She stood back, choosing to finish her little speech with a triumphant flourish.

"Welcome to my Kingdom."

She paused.

"Welcome to Hel."

68

The Chamber of the Valkyries

It was the maid Kat who entered Odin's citadel, but it was the Valkyrie Sangrid who left. In spite of the shocking portent of her name, Kat was at first too excited to notice the change in attitude from those around her.

As was the custom when first greeting a new warrior, all the people she met bowed or curtsied. Those of high enough rank also kissed her hand and congratulated her. Even her sister warriors and the gods did this, in recognition of her elevated status.

Next to Odin, Thor, Freyja, and Balder; the Valkyrie warriors held the highest rank in the realm. They were treated like royalty and they commanded the greatest respect. Over the centuries they had earned this right; bringing the finest heroes to Valhalla and protecting Asgard from countless invasions.

Being a Valkyrie warrior was the greatest privilege a woman could achieve, and they took their responsibilities seriously.

They were the defenders of the good and the destroyers of evil.

Among the first to greet Kat was Hod.

Helped by Jess, he bowed deeply before kissing her hand. He gave her two cards. One was from him and had the simple words 'I love you' written on it. The other was from Frigg, inviting "the esteemed Valkyrie Sangrid" to afternoon tea with her tomorrow. She was throwing a party in her honour and had invited all the other goddesses from Valhalla. Her reception would take place in Fensalir—which thrilled Kat. Her residence was a lovely place.

The terrible meaning of the name Sangrid was well known to Hod, but he cared little for its notoriety. He was in love, and whatever fate was implied, he knew Kat wouldn't dishonour her Valkyrie blood. Kat nearly cried when he told her this, and she hugged him tightly. She loved him dearly as a friend and prayed silently that her madness from last night could be undone.

She couldn't break his heart.

As more and more people greeted Kat and congratulated her on her success, the incredible joy at becoming a warrior soon faded as she measured the reactions on their faces.

People weren't being rude and they weren't even being impolite. They were just a little cold and standoffish and that didn't feel right.

Kat wasn't used to this attitude—and it stung.

Yesterday she'd been their darling—today she felt like a leper.

"I thought that name had been banned!"

The final straw came from Silk, with a terse back handed quip that was at best tactless, and at worst a searing insult.

With tears in her eyes, Kat pulled Jess into her bedroom and demanded to know what was going on. She knew her name meant 'Cruel and treacherous' but there had to be something more, something else to explain peoples' shock.

Taking Kat's hands gently in hers, Jess carefully explained the history of Valkyrie names.

Only about thirty had ever been used, and each had a different meaning. Some were very soft and gentle. Names like Mist and Skogul, which meant "Clouds" and "Tall stature." Others, such as Gunnr and Prudr were more violent. These names meant "War" and "Strength" respectively.

The harshest name of all was Sangrid—her Valkyrie name.

The name had only ever been used once before, and that had been many centuries ago. The first Valkyrie called Sangrid had a fearsome reputation, and eventually walked a path of evil. She was "The Black Valkyrie," a nickname that was well deserved. People could still recount many of her terrible deeds. She became so powerful, so treacherous, that eventually—as Hod had told her—she was banished from Asgard.

What Hod hadn't told her, was that Sangrid—The Black Valkyrie—had vowed to return one day and take revenge on Odin and the Aesir.

This was why people were so fearful of Kat.

They thought she was Sangrid's second coming.

Kat's shock victory at the tournament had helped to reinforce this belief. No novice maid had ever won at their first attempt, and the Aesir and Vanir were superstitious folk. They saw her victory coupled with her name as an omen; and a very bad one at that.

Kat felt a chill when Jess finished her explanation.

Things were falling rather unpleasantly into place.

Loki's daughter was The Black Valkyrie and she was the Queen of Niflheim. Kat now shared her Valkyrie name.

The association was odious.

Sangrid was her cursed namesake, and although this fact scared her, it strengthened her as well. Kat resolved that the second Valkyrie Sangrid would be remembered for noble reasons, like kindness and loyalty; and she vowed as such to Jess.

Hearing this, Jess cuddled her warmly. She was her sister now, and would soon bathe in Mimir's Well, receiving the gifts of the sisterhood.

Several hours passed busily by, as the warriors put on their finest tunics and polished their helmets, swords, and spears. Cloaks of swans' feathers were dusted down, and the one that had belonged to Emile was passed on to Kat.

To Kat's sorrow, Carmel remained absent. Her whereabouts were shrouded in mystery. Loki too was gone, and most people suspected that they were together, probably somewhere private and alone. Kat hoped this was so. Over the months she had become firm friends with Carmel, and she dearly wanted this to continue.

Perhaps Loki could restore her shattered pride?

Eventually horns blew from the hall below and forming up in pairs; the warriors followed Freyja down the winding staircase to the Chamber of the Valkyries.

Turning the first corner, the Valkyrie Sangrid didn't end up where the maid Kat had once done—back where she had started. This time a heavy, iron door was revealed. Guarded by two chained panthers, it opened slowly before her.

At last, the Secret Chamber would be revealed.

Stepping inside, Kat gazed slowly around her.

Here lay the source of Valkyrie power.

The room was large and circular, with a well lit central area. There were few obvious candles in the room, and the illumination faded rapidly as you walked away from its centre. The surrounding outer walls weren't visible, and it felt as if the room stretched out to infinity in all directions, a chamber outside the usual boundaries of time and space.

In the centre of the room stood Mimir's Well; and Kat had a bad feeling about this from the start.

The well was large and egg shaped, standing about two metres tall with the lower third buried in the stone slabs of the floor. The top of the oval structure had fine circular grooves etched in it, these radiated out in a spiral manner. They looked like the leaves of the iris in an old fashioned camera, ready to twist open and reveal a pupil in the middle.

Around the waist of the structure was a narrow band of fluorescent lights. None of these were lit up at the moment, and the top to the well—the iris—was also closed. On closer inspection, the egg appeared to be made of the same dwarf gold as their helmets, and it looked very solid and extremely heavy.

To Kat's inexperienced eye, it was the strangest well she'd ever seen—if it really was a well at all.

Above its oval form, and suspended about one meter away, was a matching metal sphere. This was about the size of a football and dangled freely in mid air. This too stood silent, devoid of noise and movement.

Moving away from these structures, and standing about two metres back, ten thick pillars formed a circle around the well. Kat reasoned that there was one for each Valkyrie—and one for their Queen. The columns were made from solid metal and each was cross linked to six adjacent pillars at the top. The whole arrangement formed a ring, a decahedron centred upon the well. The presence of the cross links suggested that they were bracing the columns in place. The whole structure looked immensely strong.

Beyond the pillars lay countless stone statues. These spiralled outward in all directions. Each one had the name of a Valkyrie warrior inscribed on its base, and each was life sized.

Kat could see the latest addition to these. It bore the inscription: Hlokk.

The head of Emile's statue was covered in a silken, black veil. She noticed that about one in ten of the statues were shrouded in this manner. Intuitively, she guessed that these were fallen Valkyries, the ones who had been denied the right to go to Valhalla.

Kat said a quick prayer. She prayed to Odin that that wouldn't be her fate one day.

As she gazed around the room, one figure stood out from the rest. It lay about six rows back and on the boundary where the more distant sculptures blurred into one. The statue was unique, not only because it had had its head struck off, but because red paint had been daubed over the body.

Kat gulped—and feared the worst.

Her Valkyrie name had only one evil predecessor.

After brief congratulations, and the chanting of verse in a language totally unknown to Kat, the warriors called out their salutes.

"HAIL WAR! HAIL VALOUR! HAIL ODIN!"

When these were finished, Freyja added the final and loudest tribute.

"HAIL SANGRID!"

The warriors whooped and shouted excitedly, hugging and kissing her wildly. The sinister significance of her name was briefly forgotten in the joy of welcoming a new warrior to the sisterhood.

Freyja bade Kat to come forward and kneel before her. She then gave her the gifts of a Valkyrie.

These items were secret and had to be guarded with her life.

The first gift was a flask of mead.

She had already been given one as a maid but this one was much larger, and her name was inscribed on the leather case. She must drink this when on a mission, taking a sip of mead every day. Failure to do so would result in ill health and possibly even her death. She must only offer the mead to fallen heroes, and they would also benefit from its miraculous powers.

The second gift was a small purse.

This was made from leather and fashioned in the shape of semicircle, folding open in its middle. Inside the purse were a shiny gold coin and a credit card. Kat noted briefly that the name on the card was 'O Dragza.' She felt she ought to know the name, but for the moment she couldn't place it. If ever she needed money on a mission, all she had to do was say the amount over the purse as she opened it. The exact amount would be inside, or if the sum was too large then it would be available with the credit card. A Valkyrie could also use the purse to order plane tickets, passports, and other essential documents.

The gold coin was her third gift and extremely important.

This was her passport back to the chamber. The coin had the head of a swan embossed on one side and the shape of the egg and the surrounding pillars and cross braces on the other. When she needed to return from a mission, all she had to do was hold the coin in her hand, and chant the sacred couplet that she would shortly learn.

Lastly, and most importantly, Freyja gave Kat her Valkyrie knife.

This was identical to those of her warrior sisters, except it had her name 'Sangrid' inscribed on its hilt.

This was the moment in the ceremony when Kat had to repeat a solemn vow.

She swore this out loud and before her fellow sisters.

She vowed that she would only use the knife to save the souls of fallen heroes, or to capture those who were truly evil. She swore this upon Mimir's Well and upon the fellowship of the sisterhood.

The oath was a poignant moment and was followed by a long silence as each warrior reflected on their duty.

"Now dearest Sangrid, it's time to bathe in Mimir's Well."

Freyja broke the silence with a warm smile and taking Kat by the hand, she led her to her pillar. The other warriors did likewise, standing silent and still before theirs.

This was it, the moment when she became a true Valkyrie. Once bathed, there could be no turning back.

Her fate would be sealed.

Standing in front of her pillar, Kat felt a cold pang of fear.

What about her cursed name?

"Remember," Freyja called over to her, trying to calm her nerves. "Look into the eye, not the well. Look only at Odin's eye."

Invisible straps slid silently from the column behind her and bound her tightly to it. These wrapped around her arms, legs, waist, neck, and head. She felt a sudden rush of panic; she hated this claustrophobic sensation.

Looking anxiously around her, she noticed to her relief that all the other warriors and Freyja had been bound in a similar fashion.

Freyja called out a short rhyming couplet and the well began to stir.

Kat stared hard at the well—forgetting Freyja's warning.

A tiny pin prick opened at its top, and she immediately felt her whole body being sucked toward this. The sensation was like looping the loop in an aeroplane, a colossal tug of gravity tearing her body toward the small hole. The chamber shook violently, the same sensation she had felt upstairs when a warrior travelled to Midgard.

Shock waves rippled through the castle.

Kat stared at the orifice, and tried to see inside the well.

She couldn't.

The colour of the hole was jet black. No; it was even deeper than that; the tiny orifice had no colour at all, an empty darkness, a complete absence of light.

Oh sweet Odin, you mad, crazy fools!

In an blinding moment of inspiration, Kat knew what the well was. This thought filled her with a horror more terrible than any she had ever known.

Odin, Vili, Ve, Mimir, and all those other insane gods had harnessed the incredible power of a black hole.

That was what was sitting inside the egg shaped structure; a massive black hole, swirling and clawing at everything that surrounded it. No wonder the world shook as it opened, and no wonder the gods and the Valkyries could wield so much power. The pent up energy squashed inside the structure was beyond her imagination. The well was a dangerous, unstable monster; a ticking time bomb that could explode at any moment.

Perhaps this was the true meaning behind Ragnarok?
Perhaps Mimir's Well spelt their doom?

"Look at the eye Sangrid, look at Odin's eye!'" Freyja was urging Kat to look up and away from the well.

She did so, before wishing that she hadn't.

The sphere above the well had opened, and a living eye, suspended in a bath of nutrients, was looking directly at her. This was Odin's missing eye, and it was staring deep inside her soul.

As she looked into its pupil, she understood why Odin had made this sacrifice. She could see everything; her whole life was there, laid open in her mind. It was spread out under her gaze, like a roll of living film. She could not only see it, she could feel it and live it; every moment of her life all breathed in the same instant.

There was her birth, her first day at school, her first bike, and her graduation; and there was also the moment of her death. It was all there, her biopic, her life in miniature captured in a microsecond.

The eye was reading her—and showing her the life that she'd lived.

There could be only one explanation for this bizarre phenomenon, one as incredible and as brilliant as the black hole itself.

Odin had used his eye to read the event horizon that surrounded it. This was the invisible barrier gravity created around a black hole, the layer beneath which light couldn't escape, and the area where space and time came crashing to a halt. The four dimensions of the universe, compressed by gravities incredible force, buckled and collapsed into one. All of time and space were captured here, smeared like wet paint around this barrier. Odin and the gods had learnt how to read this store of knowledge, images of everything that had ever been, or could ever be.

This was how the prophesy foretold what was to come; snatching merest glimpses of moments past, present—and in the future.

All were incomplete, but all would come to pass.

As her mind overflowed with these incredible thoughts, she noticed a pencil of light slithering slowly up her body.

The well was scanning her—but for what?

The last thing Kat remembered was a feeling of warmth and lightness—and then there was nothing.

For a matter of moments, Kat's body evaporated into a glowing ball of brilliant white light, which was instantly sucked deep into the well.

Then, and with equal suddenness, a stream of light returned from the well, and reassembled itself into Kat's form.

She had bathed in Mimir's Well—and the well had learned her pattern.

In that brief moment of nothingness, Kat's life had been rewritten by the famous line of Einstein's equation:

$$E = MC^2$$

All the matter (M) of her body had been turned into energy (E), and as a mass less bundle of countless photons travelling at the speed of light (C), she had passed safely through the centre of the black hole; a wormhole leading to Midgard.

She hadn't stayed.

The purpose of her journey had been for the well to get to know her and to return her safely back to Asgard.

Einstein's equation worked both ways.

Just as life and matter could be converted into pure energy, so energy could be converted back into life and matter.

This was the true meaning of the well; the very heart of the Valkyrie Chamber.

Mimir's Well was a machine, a device by which the gods, and their chosen few, could travel between worlds and between universes.

It took a while for Kat to recover from her journey. She felt nauseous and dizzy, disorientated by the sudden transition from life to light, and then back again.

Once the well had been closed, and their harnesses removed, the other girls crowded round her and congratulated her on her trip. Journeys through the well were unpleasant, and the first was always the worst.

Slowly, with their encouragement, Kat forced a weak smile. She was a true Valkyrie now; one blessed with their gifts—and armed with their power.

She felt exhalted and joined in their cheer. There would be another feast tonight, a celebration to welcome the warrior Sangrid to the sisterhood.

At the mention of her name, Kat suddenly remembered its bloody past. Tugging at Jess's arm, she pointed to the decapitated statue.

"Is that who I think it is?"

"Yes. That's the first Sangrid, The Black Valkyrie."

"Who exactly is she?" Kat asked, before hastily clarifying her question. "I mean, I know she's Loki's daughter, but did she have a name like mine before she became a warrior?"

Jess paused and looked Kat quizzically in the eye.

"Are you really sure you want to know?"

Kat wasn't going to like the answer, she could tell.

"Yes, please tell me, I must know who she is."

"I'm afraid that her maid's name was even more unpleasant than Sangrid."

Jess took both of Kat's hands in hers as she broke the bad news.

"The first Valkyrie Sangrid—her name is Hel."

69

Idun's Apples

Odin lay peacefully in his garden under the shade of Yggdrasill. The sun was beating down fiercely and as usual he was grateful for the tree's shade.

The Norn were softly singing their sweet song of love. They went gracefully about their business, tended and nurtured the massive roots beneath the great tree. Insects buzzed lazily around him, birds sang cheerily in the sky, and a great eagle high above him, let out a mighty squawk before settling back once more upon its perch.

The garden, and its inhabitants, felt safe and secure. Everything was as it should be, for now and all eternity.

Lying beside Odin was Freyja, snuggled up cosily under his arm. Her eyes were closed and she was fast asleep. Together, they were enjoying a moment of peace and solitude, one they needed after such a hectic and notable day.

At some point, they would have to return to the castle and throw themselves headlong into the festivities ahead. The evening promised to be a boisterous affair, the celebration of their new Valkyrie warrior.

The party would be fun, but it would also be tiring.

For now, Odin felt grateful that they could enjoy a moments rest in the timeless peace the garden had to offer. This was why he loved it here so much. The garden was a place he, and the other gods, could relax and get away from it all. It was a haven, a place free from the burden of their godly duties.

As he lay dozing, Odin reflected on recent events.

Only two days ago his life had seemed perfect.

A new hero had arrived in Asgard, another mighty warrior for his army. Cole—his number one suspect for Ragnarok—was captive and behind bars, Fenrir was bound, and one of the most popular maids he could ever recall, the fair and lovely Kat, she had won the tournament to become the next Valkyrie.

He couldn't have asked for more.

Everything was going as planned, Asgard ticking along nicely as he prepared for the storm ahead.

He had felt so confident and full of pride, but perhaps that had been his downfall. Pride always comes before a fall; and now it was his turn to fall.

The last couple of days had been disastrous.

He had dared to defy fate—so destiny had kicked him hard up the arse.

First there was Cole. The starter of Ragnarok kidnapped and taken to his cursed foe. What a time the three of them must be having, whooping it up down in Niflheim. Hel's jubilation as she fingered him in her evil grasp.

Odin chuckled.

At least he could turn this situation to his advantage.

Now what about fair Kat; his latest Valkyrie and already a firm favourite. How could such a dear child become like her namesake?

This thought confounded Odin as he struggled to come to turns with her foul destiny. Mimir never lied—or at least that was the truth Odin sold.

It was going to take some ingenuity to fit the new Sangrid into their future.

How could she be part of Ragnarok?

This was a baffling thought and a course still uncharted. Still, at least for now, he had time to figure it out.

He patted his pocket knowingly, resisting the urge to sneak a look.

Odin glanced over at Freyja and smiled as her sleeping chest gently rose and then fell. He wouldn't wake her yet and tell her of other disturbing news; the darkening spectre of clouds that were now rolled across the horizon.

Balder's dreams hadn't ended with Kvasir's funeral and this struck a fear in his heart. He was his favourite son and—after Freyja—the god he cherished most. It seemed impossible that he should die, and yet die he surely must.

Fate could be so unyielding and Odin had to stay on his guard. He would protect Balder with his life and swore to Yggdrasill as such. No harm must come his way; otherwise all his planning and scheming would be for nought.

Odin settled back down and lay with his hands clasped behind his head. Plucking a blade of grass, he toyed with it between his lips.

There was still one more piece of bad news to mull over—and it was a biggie.

Groups of giants were gathering on the other side of the Bifrost Bridge. They were setting up a camp, and this had been growing larger by the day. At first it had looked like a small gathering of hunters, but the number of giants had now grown to well over one hundred. Cheering, feasting and the banging of drums could be heard throughout the night, and Heimdall had seen them sparring during the day. It looked like a war party, and that could only mean one thing— an invasion of Asgard.

Ragnarok was coming, could this be where it all starts?

A cool breeze rippled through the garden, and a flurry of yellow and brown leaves fluttered down from the branches overhead. Odin watched them fall with a heaviness in his heart.

Yggdrasill was dying; the surest sign yet that Ragnarok was in the air.

"Would you like an apple?" he nudged Freyja, and then got up and strolled over to the wicker basket beside the bubbling stream.

The basket was empty.

"Idun?" Odin called and waited.

There was no reply.

"Idun, Idun?" he called louder and more urgently this time.

There was still no reply.

This was impossible.

Idun was always there, picking apples from her orchard and leaving them in her basket for the gods.

"Is there a problem dear?" Freyja enquired sleepily as she propped herself up on her elbows. Blinking repeatedly in the strong sunlight, she screwed her eyes up and looked enquiringly at Odin.

Odin paused, trying hard not to panic.

Idun's disappearance was unexpected and the worst news of all.

Without Idun there could be no apples, and without apples—the gods would die.

Unless Odin could do something and quickly–

He and the other gods were doomed.

TO BE CONTINUED…

The Valkyrie Sagas ~ Glossary of Norse names

Asgard Characters

Aesir. Inhabitants of Asgard

Einherjar. Heroes in Valhalla

Faurbauti. Giant father of Loki

Fenrir. Large wolf and Loki's pet

Fjalar. Dwarf merchant

Freki. Odin's wolf

Galar. Dwarf merchant

Geri. Odin's wolf

Gjall. Heimdall's horn

Gullveig. Dark witch

Gungnir. Odin's spear

Hel. Loki's daughter

Honir. Asgard leader

Hrungnir. Champion of the giants

Huginn. One of Odin's two ravens

Jormungard. Giant serpent

Mjollnir. Thor's hammer

Modsognir. Dwarf king

Muninn. One of Odin's ravens

Norn. Three fair maidens in Odin's garden

Ragnarok. Major war

Ratatosk. Squirrel on trunk of Yggdrasill

Sleipnir. Odin's horse

Surt. Giant dragon ruler of realm of Muspellheim

Svadilfari. Strong horse of the giants

Talwaar. Kat's sword

Tanngnost. One of Thor's goats

Tanngrisni. One of Thor's goats

Thrud. Daughter of Thor

Thrym. King of the giants. Great grandson of Ymir the first frost giant

Vanir. Inhabitants of Vanaheim

Yggdrasill. Ash tree in Odin's garden

Ymir. First frost giant

GODS

Balder. Second son of Odin and Frigg

Freyr. Brother of Freyja

Freyja. Queen of the Valkyries

Frigg. Odin's wife

Heimdall. Keeper of the watchtower at the bifrost bridge

Hod. Son of Odin

Kvasir. Boyish harpist and poet

Loki. Odin's main rival

Mimir. Friend of Odin

Nanna. Wife of Balder

Odin. Main god

Sif. Wife of Thor

Sigyn. Wife of Loki

Thor. First born son of Odin

Tyr. Strongest warrior god

Ve. Brother of Odin

Vili. Brother of Odin

PLACES

Asgard. Realm of the Aesir

Fensalir. Hall of Frigg in Asgard

Gladsheim. Main judgement hall in Asgard

Jotunheim. Realm of the giants

Lyngvi. Island in middle sea

Lyr. Hall in Utgard

Midgard. Name for planet earth

Mimir's well. Lies in chamber of the Valkyries

Muspellheim. Realm of fire and serpents

Nidavellir. Realm of the dwarves

Niflheim. Realm of the dead

River Iving. Flows through town of Asgard

Great Sea. Encircles all realms of Asgard

Utgard. Capital of Jotunheim

Valhalla. Odin's hall for heroes

Vanaheim. Realm of the Vanir

VALKYRIES

Brynhildr. Jessica. Name means bright battle

Goll. Mika. Name means tumult

Gunnr. Silk. Name means war

Herja. Jameela. Name means the devastator

Hlokk. Emile. Name means battle noise

Mist. Eve. Name means cloud or hidden

Prima. Juliet. Name means fight

Prudr. Ruby. Name means war

Skogul. Zara. Name means tall